AMERICAN RED CROSS
CLUBMOBILE

Good Night, Irene

Also by Luis Alberto Urrea

The House of Broken Angels

The Water Museum

The Tijuana Book of the Dead

Queen of America

Into the Beautiful North

Mr. Mendoza's Paintbrush

The Devil's Highway

The Hummingbird's Daughter

Nobody's Son: Notes from an American Life

Six Kinds of Sky

Vatos

In Search of Snow

Wandering Time: Western Notebooks

Ghost Sickness: A Book of Poems

By the Lake of Sleeping Children

The Fever of Being

Across the Wire: Life and Hard Times on the Mexican Border

Good Night, Irene

LUIS ALBERTO URREA

Little, Brown and Company
New York Boston London

The characters and events in this book are fictitious. Any similarity to real persons, living or dead, is coincidental and not intended by the author.

Little, Brown and Company
Hachette Book Group
1290 Avenue of the Americas, New York, NY 10104
littlebrown.com

First Edition: May 2023

Little, Brown and Company is a division of Hachette Book Group, Inc. The Little, Brown name and logo are trademarks of Hachette Book Group, Inc.

Book interior designed by Marie Mundaca

ISBN 9780316571913 (B&N Exclusive Edition)
LCCN 2023931174

Printing 1, 2023

LSC-C

Printed in the United States of America

I dedicate this book to my mother,
Phyllis de Urrea (1916–1990).

She was known in the Second World War
as Phyllis McLaughlin.

She served with Jill Pitts Knappenberger and Helen Anderson, crew of the ARC Clubmobile Cheyenne, *traveling the roads and locations visited in this novel.*

RIP, heroes.

* * *

And this one is especially for Cinderella, who traveled thousands of miles and visited many museums and warehouses and ruins and archives and countries and crematoria with me. And who helped me interview survivors and experts. And who read a hundred drafts.

Everything, always.

Some think we're so brave, but we really don't know enough to be scared. Some people think we're brats...some of us are. Some think we'd be better off at home, where a woman's place used to be...about 200 years ago. Some stare, shake their heads in disbelief. Some cheer, some scream and wave—everybody greets us. Some wolf, some worship, some think you're human and some don't....You're a Red Cross girl. You're on the chow-and-charm circuit. You're a griping, kidding GI. You're personality on legs.

—Anonymous World War II letter
quoted in Marjorie Lee Morgan's
The Clubmobile—The ARC in the Storm

I don't understand how you can
pass by and not see her

—"Irene," Joan Manuel Serrat

AMERICAN

PART ONE

This Is How We Remember

1

THEN IRENE WOODWARD escaped New York and went to war.

It was the beginning of October 1943. Irene was twenty-five. She tucked her official letter of acceptance in her pocketbook. She had never volunteered for anything in her life. Along with her letter, her bag held directions on reporting for duty once she got to Washington, her hotel reservation, and her appointment for a physical examination and inoculations at the Pentagon. The War Department had not paid for her train ticket. Nor had the Red Cross. Some of her papers were stamped SECRET. They were hidden at the bottom of her shoulder bag, which rode atop her suitcase, secured by buckled straps. She felt dangerous and at large. No one knew she had signed up, and she had left when nobody was looking. The empress of getaways.

Such intrigue: there had been many interviews. She had snuck to the Atlantic Region offices to be inspected. Her recommendation letters were gathered surreptitiously so nobody in her family would know what she was doing. She had signed on as a recreation worker with the American Red Cross, volunteering for overseas duty. For the duration of the war plus six months, however long that might be—barring injury or review. She was accepted and ordered to attend two weeks of training at American University in Washington, DC.

The air was crisp enough the morning she left New York for her to wear a long-sleeved white blouse under a pale red sweater. That was good, since she didn't want anyone staring at her arms. She was glad she didn't need a scarf. She had made up her eyes with great care—she was quite adept with concealers. She was sure nobody would notice. It might just look like she had been a little weepy over leaving. Still, for good measure, tucked into her hair, she wore sunglasses, which her friends called *cheaters*. Very dark. Very Bette Davis. Ready if needed.

Her engagement ring was down the storm drain on East Twenty-Eighth Street, halfway between Lexington and Park. The cab had collected her there in the dark. Her ring was probably rolling along the sewer pipe on its way to the river.

—

Before Irene was a fiancée, she had set out from Staten Island for Washington, DC, the story went, "to find herself." In a family whose eldest aunt was famous for being the first white woman up the Amazon, there was room for such things.

Irene had fruitlessly pursued several different careers in DC, but she was incurably restless and never quite satisfied. She first took a position as a secretary to a congressman. She then scurried to a job selling jewelry at a high-end boutique. Too proud to ask the Woodwards for money, she even tried working as a governess for a prominent family. When she found herself selling tickets in the evening at a burlesque theater and contemplating becoming a waitress in a café, she knew it was time to concede defeat and go back home.

For the last three years, she had toiled away in Mother's antique shop, ultimately managing it for her when she went on acquisition trips. Woodward's Antiques was Mother's crowning achievement and Irene dutifully took up the cause. For the family, the name blazoned across the storefront was almost more important than the goods within. It anchored the women in particular to a certain status in local society, not dependent on whom they married. They were always Woodwards first, New York matriarchs.

But it was in the antique shop where Irene met her notorious beau, the son of a prominent political family. After a few exquisite dates of champagne, lovely dinners, and flowers for her mother, Irene's family decided he was exactly what she needed. Mother began her campaign, reminding Irene that she wasn't getting any younger, though she was only twenty-three when he proposed.

Irene was fond of him, but she had no plans to marry anyone. She had seen her mother's marriages and wasn't interested. She was living in Mother's pied-à-terre, a tidy second-floor apartment in a brownstone, where Mother stayed only for special occasions or when she was on an antique-buying expedition for her shop on upper Broadway. Irene understood that no one in her family would have approved of her moving in with her beau. It would have been a scandal for the ages. So she didn't. Which, of course, stiffened her resolve to sneak him into the apartment whenever she could.

She had accepted the proposal only because the Woodwards had pressured her. It wasn't about the money—money was gauche, after all. Though nobody minded his money, of course. It was merely left out of the conversation. The point was the social register. The consequence of his connections. The father who was high in the ranks of naval officers advising FDR. And this one, the son, was destined to be a politician of profound merit. The family itself wanted to be his bride, she thought. As for her fiancé, he had his own family to contend with—they expected a good wife, from their kind of people. She had managed to put off the actual wedding for two whole years, and now this.

They would not approve of her escape, and that made her grin just a little in the cab's shadows. They would be appalled yet not overly surprised. She was infamous for her exits—once by leaping out her second-story window to escape the worst of those stepfathers, landing in the Staten Island snow and tromping downhill to her secret grove in the woods. But most infamous, after the shouting battle with Mother that followed this event, was the next Saturday, when Irene emptied Mother's cashbox in the pantry and went to the city to catch a Ford Trimotor to West Virginia to visit her aunt Sarah, whom she called from the Charleston airport after landing. She was thirteen years old. No one noticed she was gone until Aunt Sarah phoned Mother to ask how long the child intended to visit.

Irene laughed softly.

The nuns on Staten Island had once told her to step outside herself. What was that supposed to mean? Step where, exactly? She'd ignored them. Just as she'd ignored their recommendation that she write *Jesus* on a piece of paper and tuck it into one of her shoes so that every step was an automatic prayer. She wasn't even Catholic. But here she was, stepping out.

The cab carried her away in the dark as the edges of night caught fire in the east and smoldered red in between the buildings.

She rode in silence.

The cabbie dropped her off at Seventh Avenue. She strolled toward Penn Station, trying to look elegant wrangling her bags. She was greeted along the street by eighty-four columns made of slightly pink granite. Already this morning the vast interior, designed along the lines of the Caracalla Roman baths, rang with a silver thunder of feet and voices and announcements and slamming doors. She was going to miss New York.

The sun had sped into the sky behind her. Light poured down from the ceiling portals onto the echoing floors. It seemed ancient in there, a strange cathedral. She was forever seven years old when she entered. It was haunted by old men and by young boys hawking newspapers. The parade passed: many hats and many accents and odd languages she hadn't yet heard. Soldiers and sailors slumped on the benches and smoked. The wagons of luggage being pushed by Negro gents in uniforms could have been military caissons. She stared at her beloved labyrinth. What Minotaur awaited her? *Oh Irene, stop being so goddamned precious.* Those were the words he had spoken to her with composed disdain the night it all broke.

She surrendered her suitcases to a uniformed porter inside the main hall and carried her leather shoulder bag and purse slung from the same shoulder, one over the other.

She had in her bag the latest copies of *Vogue* and *The New Yorker*—the one with the newest John Cheever story. She didn't always understand the stories, but they filled her with a delicious melancholy. Also in the bag were her notebooks, pencils and pens, a tin of raspberry pastilles, lipstick and powder, combs, and Papa Hemingway's novel about war. The bag was heavy. Beneath all of these items, buried safely deep, lay her official papers. All around her now were the smells of roasted nuts and popcorn and coffee and cigars and pipes and cologne and Chesterfields.

The porter led her outside to the boarding area between trains. What could have been the voice of Zeus, if he'd come from Queens, bellowed from the speakers above: "Train 107, now boarding on track three." The porter muscled her suitcases into the baggage car.

"Thank you ever so," she said, and tipped him fifty cents.

His skin was the color of night. She noticed how careful he was not to touch her hand when she dropped the coins in his palm. "Bless you, miss," he said. "And God bless America."

On a propaganda poster attached to a nearby column, a GI straddled a rough peak, waving the American flag. WAR BONDS.

"We're going to win this," she said.

"You know we are."

"No matter what."

"It's how we do," the porter said.

The conductor at train-side stepped to her in his jaunty cap and took her elbow, looking like her uncle Will, gold specs and all. He helped her up the steps into the car. She hurried to a bright window seat on the left side, the best side if one wanted to see the woods and glimpse water heading south down the line. She wanted to see the small continent of Staten Island to bid it adieu. Her village of Richmond, with its haunted Revolutionary War–era houses. The island's scruffy hulk shrugging its shoulder below New York always seemed friendly, like an old man having a cup of coffee on his stoop.

She savored the chaos she'd left behind at the apartment. Key under the mat, as ever. Not even a note. All her photographs removed from their albums. What clothes and shoes she hadn't packed gone down the trash chute.

He'd walk in, sense something amiss. Open a drawer. Sit down at the table and have a glass of scotch. Now she saw how ridiculous he was, how predictable. He would grow rageful, realizing he'd been bested.

There would be a silent period, a few days, followed by a concerned yet reasonable-sounding telephone call to the Woodwards. He'd ask Mother if she'd seen Irene. And if Mother wasn't there, he'd try their country home up in Mattituck, on Long Island. He wouldn't relent. His suspicions would begin with the family itself—he'd be certain there was a plot to embarrass him. She smirked. She hadn't told them, either.

She placed her shoulder bag on the seat beside her to dissuade overly friendly gentlemen from sitting. Pulled her cheaters from the nest of her dark hair. It was curly today. She hadn't torn at it with her brush for once. Dropped the glasses in her bag.

Outside her window, sparrows and pigeons patrolled the platform, pecking at crumbs. Skirmishes broke out over peanuts. A rat swiped a peanut and dived off the platform. Irene loved her city. Her heart might tear away like paper when the locomotive chuffed. She knew there would be a stone-walled tunnel, she knew that suddenly they would break out into full daylight, and there would be trees flickering with sunbeams.

Bells clanged and she checked her face in the window. "You'll do," she said aloud to her reflection. She had hazel eyes and was tired of explaining what color they were.

A small thrill when the conductor called "All aboard!" and slammed the door of the car and the whistle sounded and the great train heaved like a beast and groaned away from the gate.

—

All the Woodward men had gone to war. Why not one of the women? Besides, it was the Red Cross. Not even guns. She put death right out of her daydreams. She prided herself on her ability to do this—unpleasant ideas flew away as if she were tossing cats out the back door. One does not wallow.

Staten Island soon appeared as they rocked down the line—she never spotted Old Richmond Town before it was all behind her.

By the time they crossed the state line, she understood that she was really doing this. She imagined women from all over the country leaving home and heading for DC, drawing inexorably toward her, bringing their stories and excitement and joys. She had mostly lived among difficult Woodward matrons and a few men. No childhood playmates, really, save for her terrible boy cousins from up on Long Island. What hilarious savages! It had delighted her that they all stormed around in cutoff dungarees and climbed atop old railcars in the field and drove the bodiless chassis of Jack Dashiell's Model T they called *The Platform,* with chairs and an old sofa tied to it. Jack was a suitor who'd pursued her a bit the summer after high school. He'd bought the jalopy for a sawbuck. They all got drunk off the bottles of bourbon that Uncle Will hid in the barn, and they smoked his stogies. They taught her to spit. She never once wore lipstick or a skirt in that gang. They had won a baby alligator for a dime at a ring toss on Coney Island, and had gallantly given her the heavy little box. Irene could feel the creature scratching inside all the way home. She kept the monster in her bathtub until Mother flushed it away. Forever after, the boys' code name for her was *Gator.*

Boys were still her favorite people, notwithstanding the fiancé.

She had meant to return to Richmond, to their elegantly shabby Victorian with its unsteady reading porch. It was halfway down the street from St. Patrick's. Her childhood bedroom was still there, above the porch—the Irene Museum, with her worn encyclopedias and books on the shelves, her stuffed animals slumbering on her bed. She had sought shelter there several times over the years. And why not—down on the shore, the island had a view of the Grand Citadel across the water. She walked the shoreline and looked at her favorite buildings: the Empire State, the Chrysler. The ferries were the friendliest boats she'd ever seen. There was enough child in her yet to hope Kong would be atop the skyscrapers, swatting biplanes out of the sky. The thrill of seeing the Statue of Liberty out there—especially in rain. But there was nothing dearer to her than the woods below their house.

Irene idly picked at her fingernail polish. Every time she had come back home, she remembered, she had snuck away to the woods. Just like the days of her childhood, when daily she defied Mother, or whoever Father was at the moment—the latest in a series, this one Hungarian—

and marched away with a favorite book. She had a routine, stopping to peer into the haunted rooms and basements of the abandoned old houses as she walked downhill in her shorts and sandals. She imagined war might be like this. Ambling. Filling notebooks with her own great thoughts. Perhaps some smoke drifting through the trees.

A man behind her sneezed like an air-raid siren. His seatmate said, "Christ, Benny!"

She tuned them out.

A convoy of trucks waited for them to pass at a crossroads; tanks rode upon flat trailers as far as she could see. It was all war, all the time. She wondered what her uniform would look like.

—

The whistle shrieked and she opened her eyes. They slowed, clacketing mightily and squealing. A Podunk Jersey town swung toward them on the right and the conductor rocked down the aisle clicking tickets. The rustling of newspapers intensified as men in brown suits spread out to set a bulwark against invasion, saving their islands of space against other men. Fedoras all around.

"Going good?" the conductor said to her. His walrus whiskers were white.

"Staying elegant," she replied.

He punched her ticket and tucked it into the back of the seat. "Well, hot dog," he said, ambling away with his knees braced against the seats along the aisle.

Out the window, the usual klatch of irritated-looking fellows stood on the platform. Irene had been hoping for a sister-in-arms who might be taking the train to DC. Someone who might offer some conversation. No one remotely like her was out there.

But then there was a soldier. He was taller than the men around him, his hair skull-short and topped by a jaunty garrison cap set at an angle over his left eye. She thought he was forty, though he could have been twenty-seven. Some colorful ribbons were pinned to his chest. When the herd climbed the steps into the car, she pulled up her full charge of power and aimed it at the doorway. One of her cousins used to say she could land the boys easier than catching a catfish with baloney bait. She was a glorious flirt and had a hypnotic gift for making men feel important even when she was secretly laughing at them. It was her power and her protection.

What was more difficult was how to make a man move past her, preferably in silence. Some of the gents from the platform now paused at her seat, casting their eyes at her shoulder bag expectantly as they waited for her to clear space, then huffing or rattling their briefcases as they shuffled away. Worse than rebuffed: ignored.

You are an insufferable brat, she scolded herself. *I am not,* she retorted.

The soldier came on board and she locked eyes with him. She raised a finger, then dipped her chin toward the seat beside her. He nodded once and pulled off his cap, tucked it into his uniform belt. He had a limp and walked with a cane, which she hadn't noticed on the platform. His uniform bore a Purple Heart medal. All down the aisle, people patted him or mumbled pleasantries to which he nodded without a smile. He shook their offered hands without looking at them.

Irene cleared her bag out of his way and he lowered himself into the seat. He kept his leg extended into the aisle, leaning the cane between his thighs against the front edge of the seat.

"'Preciate it," he said and closed his eyes, laid his head back.

She caught herself staring at him. He had the stillness of a statue. There was a scar at the corner of his eye. A glitter of tiny whiskers on his Adam's apple.

Then the conductor appeared and nudged the soldier and handed over a newspaper. "There you go, Sarge," he said. "Today's *Herald*."

"Thank you, sir."

"No—thank *you,* son."

The soldier opened the paper.

"How was it?" the conductor said.

"Hot, sir."

The conductor looked down as if expecting more. "Pacific?" he said.

The soldier nodded. Once. "Palm trees," he said.

The conductor patted his shoulder and moved on down the car.

The soldier studied the paper.

"So," Irene said. "You're a sergeant."

Another nod. She smelled bay rum and tobacco.

"All aboard!" and the conductor leaned out of the car, hung on with one hand, waved at the engineer, and swung back up and slammed the door. They rolled on.

Irene stared at the soldier until he looked over.

"I don't want to talk about it," he said.

"Does everyone want you to?"

"Don't you?"

She turned away. "Is that what happened to your leg?" she asked, looking out the window.

"What leg?" He laughed through his nose, a bitter puff, then leaned over to knock on his leg, which made a hollow sound. "Metal," he said.

Choosing audacity, she said: "Show me." Audacity always worked.

He was surprised but pulled up his pant leg. "Shiny, huh?" he said.

She put her hand on his forearm. "I'm sorry." She glanced at his leg and gave him the full-color gaze.

Apparently he was color-blind. He went back to the paper. "It's okay, lady. I had an extra one."

"Did it hurt terribly?" She hated herself for asking.

"Morphine. Breakfast of champions." He opened to the sports page.

Irene saw Spud Chandler and Stan Musial in the sports headlines. She wasn't sure why she kept coming at him. It was like a compulsion. "Baseball fan?" she said.

He raised the paper closer to his face.

"I need your advice," she said.

He grunted.

"I'm on my way to the war. There. I said it."

He put the paper down. "Jesus."

"That's what I wanted to tell you."

Now he couldn't help himself. "What branch? WAC? WAVES?"

"Red Cross."

He seemed to relax. "Bedpan commando. Still, nursing's tough duty."

"Not nursing."

"Oh yeah? What, then?"

"Clubmobiles."

He frowned. "The hell is that?"

"Mobile service. Comfort, moral support. As I understand it, we'll be backing the troops in the field. We make coffee and donuts. In trucks."

"You what?"

"Coffee. And donuts."

He laughed.

"Clubmobiles," she explained. "A Red Cross club . . . on wheels."

"Donuts." He shook his head. "I heard it all now."

She didn't appreciate his tone.

Again, he raised the barrier of the paper between them. "Good luck, sister."

Irene turned away. *Fine, be rude.* Outside her window, backyards and junkyards and loading docks and small scraggly forests and narrow roads and smokestacks. Slouching hills. Factories behind sagging fences. A barbershop with its pole rotating on an empty street. Great parts of the world seemed to consist of water towers and cars waiting at flashing crossing lights.

"Have you any advice?"

"Sure," he said. "Don't do it."

"Thank you for your insight." She crossed her arms.

"Cover your ass, how about that?"

"Sorry to bother you."

"Look, it's no place—"

"For a girl?"

He gave up and crumpled the paper in frustration.

She turned toward him. "I intend to serve my country," she said, "and this is what they'll let me do. I have never made a donut in my life. I don't know how to drive a truck. And the coffee I've made has been known to incapacitate its victims. So tell me, Sarge—you're an expert. How will I do?"

His head dipped slightly. "Swell," he said. "You'll do swell." He took a deep breath and let it out. "Look, you won't hear the shot that gets you. So stay un-gettable."

The train was slowing now. The whistle and the bells sounded and the conductor came through shouting out the name of the town. She knew she'd never remember it.

The soldier grabbed his cane and shifted around on the seat, trying to pull his metal leg out of the way. "This is my stop," he said. "Going home to see Mom."

She suddenly loved him. "Good luck," she said. "Any words for me?"

"Listen," he replied. "If you get to come home, you will be so grateful you won't realize at first that you survived. But once you know you survived, you'll only be starting to understand."

He braced himself against the back of the seat in front of him and wrestled himself into the aisle.

"Understand what?" she said.

He just stared at her and walked off the train.

2

The Blackstone Hotel, Seventeenth Street NW, Washington, DC.

Irene was there in the midst of other Clubmobilers; after presenting her papers, she was checked into a double on the fourth floor with a bedside view of the street below. Someone was in the shower. The marks on her arms were still purple, but fading to yellow and green in places. "You look like a chameleon," she said aloud.

She knew where this habit of voicing her thoughts came from: Grannie Effie. In Mattituck. Effie was her model pioneer woman. Irene was anything but bucolic, yet she bore a great shadow of the nineteenth century within her. Who didn't? She was born in 1918—to the family, she was some newfangled missy with scandalous ways. She was happy in this shiny new world. The rest of the Woodward clan in New York City were musty late Victorians and the Woodwards in Mattituck were descendants of Pilgrims who still used hand pumps to summon cold, iron-flavored water.

Irene rolled onto her back and kicked off her shoes.

Then the bathroom door burst open, unleashing clouds of perfumed steam. A redhead emerged in a white robe, her feet bare, rubbing energetically at her head with a towel. "Hey, toots!" she said.

"Hello, bunkie."

"I'm Ellie. Baranski. From Chi-town."

"Irene. Woodward. Big Apple."

"I hate the Yankees, though," Ellie said.

"But I love the Cubs," Irene countered, as if she knew anything about baseball.

"Okay, doll—we can be friends."

They shook hands. Thereafter Ellie irritated Irene for a few minutes, trying on various clothes, before storming out the door and calling, "See ya downstairs!"

Irene grabbed some hotel stationery and an envelope and began writing.

Dearest Mother—

She wadded up the page and tossed it in the wastebasket. Surprised that her hand shook, she took up another sheet that would be impossible to fill.

Hello Mother, I suspect you're wondering

She tore it apart and dropped it like snow into the basket.

—

Her other fellow volunteers were busy making their way across the country, equally full of doubts and excitement and resolve and dread. In a Greyhound bus fleeing Indianapolis, third row from the back, smelling of unwashed hair and sweat and cheap Woolworth's perfume, rode Dorothy Dunford, who slept sitting up with a jacket tossed over her shoulder and her shoes tucked under the seat, her feet swollen from sitting too long and her rear end flattened by the stiff springs. Kids in middle school had called her *Dung-Ford. The Human Flagpole.* Or *Paula,* after Paul Bunyan. They liked to ask where her blue ox was. Thanks to those yokel sons of bitches she never wore heels.

She came from Viking stock. The family members were Evangelical Lutheran Danes who carried in them a taciturn stillness, who had driven oxen-pulled wagons from the East Coast to the Indiana woods and prairies. That's when they'd run out of steam, near a feeder creek that led to the river, in sight of hills lit by a vast yellow expanse, close to bosques alive with squirrels and deer. The family spoke the old language and carried salted cod. They dreamed of Copenhagen and planted three apple trees and a hickory and put parts of the wagon into their first cabin.

Slaughtered an ox and collected the dung of the other to dry in the sun and fertilize their small crops. Great-grandfather made a smoke hut from cottonwood branches and jerked ox meat that they ate with wild onions and chokecherries. Their descendants had no concept of Copenhagen beyond a mythic watercolor that Father kept on the mantel.

Homemade clothes. Homegrown vegetables. Outhouses with broken doors, mail-catalog pages for toilet paper. A hundred years of that kind of family scrabble made Dorothy think she was dull, worn down. She thought she lacked mystery.

Well, she was an orphan now. Dorothy had been a year shy of graduating college in Bloomington when Pop was diagnosed with throat cancer. She came home to help nurse him through. But his death the following year unleashed a torrent of tragedy. Before she could decide about returning to school, her big brother, Donny, a midshipman with the navy stationed in the Pacific, was among those killed at Pearl Harbor. After that, her mother was broken. There was little she and Dorothy could do to save their ailing farm in the Maumee River watershed. When Momma herself had died last spring, Dorothy finally had to admit the farm was a bust. She boarded up the house, swinging the hammer herself. She sold the old barn for scrap, let the chickens go free, said goodbye to the terns and sandhill cranes and hawks and eagles and pelicans come south from the Great Lakes, and left the corn for the deer to steal. Sold the cows. Sold the land for pennies on the dollar.

She was so filled with rage. Her father. The farm. Her mother. Donny. She needed an escape, a valve to release her helpless anger. She needed to take some action. She decided to go to war. Yet no female military path was good enough for her. They all hunkered down in the rear. On bases, in liberated cities. She was no secretary. She wanted combat. When she saw a Red Cross recruitment ad for a new service that would support the troops on the front line, which was where she needed to go, she was quick to volunteer. If she had to feed the boys, fine. Yes, she would feed the boys. Donuts.

She'd seen a pamphlet about these Clubmobile jalopies they were supposed to pilot. They were 2½ ton GMCs that looked like a swollen version of her family's '36 International Harvester farm truck. The

Dunfords called it *Terrible Tilly*. She had learned to drive in old *Tilly*. She could drive the army truck in her sleep. But she knew she'd make a terrible waitress.

Before she left, she visited the family graveyard where her folks slept and her brother had a small memorial. She told herself it might be the last time. Her grandparents lay there, too, under a gnarled wild apple tree. The great-grands were under splintered nameless wooden crosses. She picked an apple and told herself she was eating some of the soul of her grandmother. She had planted tulips and daylilies furiously. She cried just a little before she left, alone on the land of her birth, vowing those would be the last tears she would shed.

In some almost unacknowledged place inside herself, Dorothy hoped she would be taken in the war, a clean shot, and then find peace beside them. Here where deer ate the grass and flowers and there were bluebirds. Where fireflies turned the whole landscape into a constellation on summer nights. She could think of no way to rid herself of her rage other than for it to lie here and fade away into the good soil. But first she was going to honor Donny by finishing his tour of duty.

Dorothy slept fitfully on the bus through Pennsylvania. Her head felt like it was clanging with random images of her old life. She was tired of having bright blond hair. And she was tired of being six feet two inches tall and making five-foot-seven men feel uncomfortable. Her shoulders and neck and lower back ached from always crouching a little, or hanging her head, to seem shorter. She was ready for a new life.

—

Furious, Irene sat barefoot on the hotel bedroom floor, playing solitaire with a pack of cards she'd found in a desk drawer. The last thing she wanted was to think about her fiancé, and she was enraged that she couldn't stop. She didn't need another father. She'd had a few of those already, thank you. Some snippy bastard telling her what to do. Marry that? Please. She slammed the cards on the floor, one after the other, blind to her own game. She could always feel the delight under his rage when he "corrected" her. The jokers in the deck reminded her of him and she sailed each one toward a corner.

So far, war was boring as hell. She hoped things would be more exciting when she got away from this hotel to wherever she was headed. Nobody would say where that was. It was all a mystery—some silly intrigue, like the Doc Savage stories her cousins had read. They'd all been warned when they checked in that G-men would be lurking about, trying to coax details out of the women. Seeing who could keep a secret and who couldn't. Of course, if you don't know where you're going, there's no secret to keep.

"I hope it's terrible there," she said aloud. For a moment, she was thirteen again, and whispered, "I hope I die." The floor hurt. She threw the whole deck, making a small blizzard. "Poor little Irene, pitying herself," she said.

She slipped her shoes back on and took the elevator to the lobby to see if she could scare up some ladies to talk to. The elevator operator raked her with his eyes on the way down. She exited in silence. No sign of Baranski of Chicago. Just as well.

A sign behind the concierge station read: CARELESS WAR TALK COSTS LIVES. Under which, in smaller type, as if whispered: *GUARD YOUR CONVERSATION*. Nearby, a friendlier banner read: WELCOME RED CROSS!

At a table behind potted palms she found three women playing dominoes. "Ah, here's some action!" she said.

"Welcome to the henhouse," replied one of the players.

"Ain't you dishy," said another.

"I do my best. Might I get an invitation?"

"Dive in," said the first.

Irene introduced herself. Her new companions—Jill, Phyllis, and Helen—had already finished their Clubmobile training and were awaiting orders. The three of them hoped to be assigned to the same truck and were delighted to welcome Irene into their circle.

When she sat, a waiter landed a gin fizz at her elbow. She wasn't about to reject that.

Everybody was très bohemian. Irene felt like she'd escaped into a Jean

Harlow movie. Ashtrays overflowing. Gun-moll banter. Stiff drinks. Pin curls. God's name in vain. One of the gals had a red bandanna tied around her big hair. There were no guys apart from the waiters.

—

Across town, Union Station was alive with women stepping off trains. The flood of volunteers flowed through the city until three in the morning. Yellow cabs circled the block like bees outside a hive. Fewer cabs found their way to the bus station—cabbies already knew those tips would be small—but the waiting lines were shorter. When Dorothy staggered out carrying her own bags, she had three cabs to choose from. The cabbie who jumped out and took her bags got her business.

"Where ya from, Stretch?" he said when she got in back.

Stretch. Didn't they have any better nicknames? "Indiana," she said.

"No kiddin'. I was raised in Indianapolis."

"We were out in the sticks. East of Fort Wayne. Closer to Ohio, really. State line was pert near our spread." Oh, good heavens: *pert near*? Her mother had just spoken through her mouth. She lit a Lucky and cracked the window.

"Nice over there?" he asked.

"Too many kangaroos," she drawled.

He stared at her in the rearview mirror.

"It's a joke."

"Right," he said. "I knew that." He faked a guffaw.

She looked out the window, hoping she would get to see the sights in DC. She wanted to see Lincoln. And the Washington Monument. She was so-so about Congress. "Give you an extra buck to swing by the monuments," she offered.

"You don't have to ask me twice."

She wondered what kind of training they were going to have. Making donuts? How did this business work—did she drive the truck and then jump in back to make the coffee and so forth? Hell no. There must be other gals on the crew for that happy horseshit. Uncle Sam had better not put some GI at the wheel. She wasn't going to the war only for men to tell her what to do.

—

An army of women had descended on the hotel. They sounded, from the street, like a madwomen's convention. Irene finished her cigarette and went back inside, a bit tipsy from the mere sound of so many women belly-laughing, though the gin didn't hurt.

Dorothy's cab pulled up at the glass doors of the Blackstone; the windows were bright yellow with light. Women had overflowed onto the steps to smoke and get acquainted.

A pair of uniformed soldiers stood at the doors. "Papers," they said over and over to newcomers, sounding very manly.

Dorothy hopped out, retrieved her own bags rather than waiting for the cabbie, and trotted up the steps. She blew past the guards and called over her shoulder, "Reporting for duty, boys. Hands are full. You wanna see papers, you'll have to dig in my purse."

She dropped her bags near the front desk and stood with her hands on her hips. Wall-to-wall women. She didn't feel the need to scrunch down even an inch. She threw back her shoulders and presented herself. (She remembered Pop always saying, "Gut in, shoulders back, chest out, chin high.")

"Dunford," she said to the clerk.

The little fellow slid a key across the counter and she jammed it in her trouser pocket without looking at it. The narrow wooden paddle it was attached to hung out like her own personal fob.

Meanwhile, Irene had made herself the mistress of ceremonies. She had organized the ladies into welcome squads and coffee ministries and domino and gin-rummy patrols. Of course, she had also browbeaten the deskman into getting carts with snacks and soft drinks and coffee urns into the lobby. No doubt the Red Cross representatives with their clipboards, taking names and jotting notes, approved of her activities.

She looked over from her seat at the domino table and beheld Dorothy there at the front desk. "What a monument," she said.

Her tablemates laughed. The tall woman seemed lost.

Irene sprang to her feet and traversed the space with one hand out. "Welcome to the Red Cross," she said.

Dorothy grabbed the offered hand and shook. Her palm was dry. Both women had firm grips, which seemed to please the other.

Dorothy saw the bruises peeking out from under Irene's right cuff. She turned Irene's hand and studied them. An eyebrow rose, but she said nothing.

Irene took her hand back. "Long story," she said.

Dorothy put her own hands in her pockets. "Hope you stabbed him," she said.

Irene's eyes brightened and they both laughed. She introduced Dorothy to Phyllis, Jill, and Helen. Handshakes and smiles all around.

They had already been there a while, Phyllis said—they were in the first group of recruits and were just waiting to see where they'd be posted. Like the other recruits, they'd been told to be ready for anything. A suggested packing list had advised the women to bring clothing and supplies for cold temperatures in the European theater, but also for possible tropical conditions in the Pacific.

"Just like the boys," Jill said. "We go where they tell us and we're always the last to know the details."

"Speaking of which, I thought there'd be more boys around here," Dorothy said.

"Guess we'll have to go it alone," Irene said.

Dorothy half-grinned. "Darn." She looked around, as if trying to get a grasp of the situation. "Tell me what I need to know," she said.

"The bar's in the basement," Irene said. "That's a good start."

"First things first," Dorothy said. "Lead the way."

—

Soon, all was revealed.

Irene and Dorothy had barely finished their drinks when they were summoned to the ballroom by serious women in starched uniforms and strange-looking caps pinned to their hair. Few of the fresh Clubmobilers had much experience with institutional garb except for those who'd been school lunch ladies or meter maids. The nurses among them had already found their own cadres. They felt superior to these would-be coffee makers.

One hundred fifty potential Clubmobilers sat in curved rows of hard-backed chairs facing a small stage and a podium flanked by two American flags. Irene sat in the front row, mostly to see better. She hated being behind people bigger than she was. And she was too vain to wear spectacles, so she sat in front so she wouldn't have to squint her bad eye too much. Dorothy sat in the back and stretched her legs into the aisle. Nurses appeared and handed out spiral notebooks and pencils. Two soldiers came in with electrical box fans and diffused the body heat in the room. Women wolf-whistled the boys, and their faces were beet red as they hurried back out. Irene spotted Ellie waving at her and nodded back. Winks, thumbs-ups, women on the gad all around.

A trim, redheaded soldier stepped briskly into the room and hopped onstage, and everyone took their seats. The soldier had freckles. "It's Andy Hardy!" somebody shouted.

He cleared his throat. "Ladies," he said, reading from a scrap of paper. "I am Corporal Russell Penney. Tennessee's finest. After Jack Daniel's, that is." He grinned and paused for the polite titters from the audience that were perhaps fewer than he'd hoped for. "Joke," he noted, and reached a finger underneath his collar.

His accent was endearing. The loudspeakers squealed with feedback.

"I am your U.S. Army liaison. I want to welcome you and thank y'all in advance for your service."

Whispers and smiles spread at his *y'all.*

"I am here to assist you in all things military. Weapons, gear, the trucks. Like that." He stared at his notes. "And, um, so. If you have any questions or concerns, be sure to find me. Thank you." He threw himself offstage like a suicide jumper and scrambled out to overenthusiastic applause.

Then a nurse captain came into the ballroom. White uniform with bars and medals, white shoes, and a white nurse's cap pinned to her graying hair. Irene thought she might be a thousand years old. It took her a couple of bounces to get both feet up on the low dais. She tottered back and raised her arms, as if she might fall, then bent forward and charged the podium, which she grabbed firmly.

The nurse, who introduced herself as Captain Marjorie Miller, didn't waste time on niceties. She didn't refer to notes. She looked the recruits in the eye and launched without fanfare into her speech.

"As you were, ladies. Welcome to the Clubmobile Corps. The issue at hand is war. Without war, none of you would be here. You are here for one purpose. It is a simple calling. You are here to become America itself. You are hereby commissioned to represent the nation and all it means to a young soldier facing terror every day. A young soldier who may flirt with you on Tuesday and be reduced to a red stain on Wednesday.

"But where did you come from? What is your history? That no longer matters. Our history is now yours, and this is who you will be. We came into existence in 1917, during the Great War. Salvation Army volunteers entered the trenches with the boys and lived in that squalor and horror. And the boys in their suffering asked the ladies if they had anything sweet. Any cake, any pastries. You can imagine that there was no such thing.

"So some of these women snuck to farms and purchased eggs. They returned and used biscuit flour with the eggs to make a dough. They added sugar, and they filled those Brit helmets with oil and heated it all over a fire. And that's how our donuts were created.

"I was one of those women. This bad hip"—she gestured toward her leg—"is from an ambulance crash in that war."

Applause broke out and she waved it off.

"Eventually the operation moved into buses. Thus the Clubmobile Corps was born. People immediately started calling these women Donut Dollies. You are not a Donut Dolly. And you mustn't let them call you one."

She sniffed to show her disapproval of the modern age. It was stirring, really. Irene felt a thrill shoot up and down her back.

"You ladies are all older than the majority of the troops you'll attend. General Eisenhower is nobody's fool. You are hereby ordered to be big sister, girl next door, mom, or sweetheart to each one of these brave boys. You are nothing less than home." She removed her spectacles, wiped them, put them back on as if to glare at the audience more clearly. "These wonderful guys will be your best friends for five minutes. Make those five minutes count. Each of your Clubmobiles has a record player and a selection of records. Music and donuts and a cup of joe. You are going to go win this war for the USA. Each one of you people is just as heroic as GI Joe."

The women in the room chattered and regarded each other with smiles and winks.

"Shush," Captain Miller said.

They shushed.

"You'll be shocked. You'll think you're strong, you'll think you're tough. You'll think you can take it. You cannot take it. And then you will not be shocked anymore. That's what war does to you so you can keep on going. You will be in mortal danger beside our boys. You will do things, some of you, that should win medals. Remember Captain Miller and what she told you today."

She took a slow breath and seemed to hold it.

"We are the Red Cross. *Red* because every American, man or woman, bleeds the same color. You will see that even the enemy does the same. There are ladies present here that you might not deal with back in the world you came from. Colors, cultures, accents—all together now for this great cause. These are your sisters and the GIs are your brothers and we expect you to treat them as such. Win this war with your decency. Because we are Americans. And this is what Americans do."

She walked away from the mic, then came back.

"When you see me, or I address you, do not use my first name. Do not call me *Nurse Miller.* And don't you dare call me *ma'am.* You call me *Captain.* And when I ask you what Miller's Law is, I expect you to remember it: *Never Let Them See You Cry.* Get it? Got it? Good. That is all."

She dismounted the dais as the women stood to applaud, then walked out the door without looking back.

3

SOMEHOW, DONUT BOOT camp failed to be Irene's greatest triumph.

It should have been simple. The donut mix was prepackaged in twenty-pound cloth bags: flour, sugar, spices, baking powder, a pinch of salt. The motto they were ordered to remember and repeat was WE WEIGH OUR WATER.

Weighing water was apparently the ultimate Clubmobile wisdom. *But who is going to stop a battle and weigh water?* Irene wondered. This was ridiculous. *Any cook could eyeball it,* she told herself. So she did. But try as she might, she could not generate batter that would produce donuts. The infallible donut machine splurted globs and wads of misshapen, over-wet dough to splash into the hot grease, abominations that were then fried into donuts resembling golden underpants and topographical maps of ancient lands.

The cooks were expected to use two wooden dowels to flip over their creations to bask evenly in the grease, thus splattering small drops that burned the backs of their hands and wrists. Donuts reduced Irene to tears. She threw her ridiculous wooden donut flippers at the wall and cried, "This is stupid, stupid, stupid! We are going to waste our lives doing this..."

Captain Miller was suddenly in the kitchen. "Zip it, Your Highness," she said.

"But."

"Zip."

"It's just—"

"Zzz!" She handed Irene a pitcher. "The machine doesn't make mistakes. This is what happens when you aren't careful with the recipe. Pay attention. Weigh your water," she said and exited the kitchen like the pope, raising her hand in benediction to the gathered flock.

That entire first day of classes was an absurdity. They were taught how to pack—two girdles and two sets of garters. Dorothy threw hers out. They were given workshops on playing board games: easy and quick so that the guys might win and get back to soldiering. No long poker or gin-rummy games. Irene drew the board games in her notebooks. They sat through ridiculously detailed instructions on how to make up their faces, with men explaining to them in bureaucratic terms how to do what they had been doing all their lives, but in proper fashion.

Their secret weapon, they learned, was that they would have an officer's rank. If any grunt over there got too frisky, they could pull rank. If any of them were captured by the enemy, they might be accorded certain considerations. Irene didn't want to think about that.

They were also being trained relentlessly to "remember to forget." Dates, places, details were not to be written down or even noted. They were expected to operate on the military "need to know" basis. On a practical level, that meant they were to focus their energies on service, the men before them, the sinkers and coffee. But it was also safer for everyone involved if the women possessed no information that could be accidentally revealed or compromised.

That night, Baranski of Chicago snored. But Irene lay awake, her mind churning through her worries: capture, torture, the donut machine, the presence of spies everywhere, and the question of whether she would have grace under fire.

Suddenly it was morning again. This one was worse. They were rousted at 6:00 a.m. and fed coffee and biscuits, then hustled onto trucks—the same model GMC trucks that would later carry their kitchens, though they didn't know this yet. They were seated across from one another on hard wooden benches under canvas roofs, pressed knee to knee, facing their partners for the entirety of the convoy to some Maryland military base. Or was it Delaware? Dorothy sat across from Irene. They couldn't see anything outside. Women drowsed around them.

After their lurching drive, they were unloaded like cattle onto a void of tarmac half-encircled by dull tan military buildings and anemic evergreens. Flags were greatly in evidence. Green vehicles lurked in the background, and recruits trotted along being hollered at by apoplectic drill instructors. The lone army tank seemed depressed—its barrel hung at a melancholy angle.

Before them, about fifty yards away, was a huge Quonset hut, cavernous and painted a flat tan. Rust coursed down the indentations in the sheet metal of its curved roof. Twin sliding doors revealed a black interior. Deep within the gloom, small rectangles of light glowed. Back doors.

A bullhorn squealed and a man's voice announced: "Welcome to Hell Day."

Men in full white bodysuits exited the Quonset hive like insects and stood at parade rest beside the doors.

"That don't look good," Dorothy noted.

A group of lanky bastards wearing jaunty caps and leather jackets sauntered out of one of the military buildings.

Ellie appeared and whispered, "Flyboys."

The tallest one winked at Irene, a slight nod and grin.

Ellie sighed. "He looks like Gary Cooper."

One of the various GIs charged with keeping them in a group said, "Fighter pilots. Army Air Force. About to go back to England."

"They been already?"

"Oh yeah. Big heroes. Look at 'em. Struttin'."

"Who's the yummy one?" Ellie asked.

"I don't see nothin' yummy, ma'am." He moved away. "Probably Handyman," he called back. "He thinks he's famous. Gals can't get enough of him."

"Neither can he," said a DI the size and shape of a small boiler who came charging at them. "No time for bullsquat like that! Form up!" His flat-brimmed hat clamped his bristly head, cinched by a strap to the back of his skull. "Goldammut!" he shouted. "What kinda ragtag slack-ass lines is this!" He tore through the meandering files of women, shoving and elbowing them and even kicking their boots. "Laze! Form up!"

He apparently could not pronounce *ladies.*

"You will get yourselves in straight lines, laze, and you'll do that immediately!"

They tried.

"Straighten your foot, girl. Is your leg broke?" He went on howling with rage at every evidence of slackness.

"Sarge needs a hobby," Irene said.

His face instantly manifested itself before hers, red and sweating. "You got a complaint, Snow White?"

She shook her head. "No, sir."

"Don't call me *sir*! I *ain't* an officer. I *work* for a living!"

He was clearly delighted to shout this old army cliché at her. The mist of his saliva did not cool her face. He sped away, arms working in mad spasms, his voice echoing off the Quonset. It worked—the horrified women fell into four semi-straight lines.

Behind her, Dorothy whispered, "If you're Snow White, I must be Grumpy."

From the next line, Ellie gawked at them.

"Who are you, Dopey?" Dorothy snapped.

Ellie already found Stretch insufferable—Indiana hick. *Try that talk in Chi, you snotty Hoosier shit ball,* she thought. She looked away, flush of crimson on each cheek.

The DI blew three blasts on a whistle hanging from a lanyard around his neck. Seemingly out of nowhere, carts rolled forward loaded with gas masks.

"Take one," the soldiers pushing these carts said. "One mask each."

The men arrayed before the Quonset seemed to be enjoying this show and stood there laughing and nudging each other.

"Laze!" the DI announced. "You will put on your masks. When I give the order, you will run through the gas chamber."

"Gas chamber?" Irene said.

"These gennermen in front of you will be masked up, and they will be inside. You got to get through them and out the back door. Like football practice."

Football? What beastly event was this?

Sergeant Charm signaled the gents in the white suits and they dragged their goggles and hoods and aerators over their faces and stepped into the darkness. There followed popping sounds accompanied by plumes of tear gas. Even from this distance, Irene's eyes stung and began to water.

"Get them masks on!" the DI called. He himself was evidently immune to the gas.

Irene wasn't the only one who was shaking, confused, and fighting back tears. The entire day had turned to craziness. She pulled the mask on and thought she would suffocate. It stank. Her straps covered her ears. The DI's diatribes were slightly muffled now, but she could still hear him. She had been screamed at before. Many of them had. It was old news. They weren't as impressed as he seemed to think they would be.

"Tighten up them lines! Ain't got all day. You ain't gettin' your nails done!" He shoved a few more women around. "One here. One here. One here. You're moving like pond water." He slapped his hands together. "Dollies, I don't care if you're laze or not. I will bury my size-eleven boot in your behinds if you don't get these lines in order. Think I'm funnin'? Nice and tight. Nuts to butts."

"We don't have nuts," Dorothy yelled back. "And don't call me *Dolly*!"

He looked at her once, then blew his whistle.

They ran. Irene could hear her own breath inside the mask. Hollow and frightening. The mask was loose and it bounced and she had trouble seeing.

"Don't stop! Don't stop! Don't stop!" men shouted from the dark, gas-clouded maw of the Quonset.

And they were in. Blackness slapped her. She ran into a man and bounced off him and almost fell but was so panicked by the stinging gas seeping into her mask that she focused on the far open door and ran faster than she'd ever run. Her eyes burned. Tears blinded her. The doorway was now just a watery oblong of light. She was aware of women falling to their knees, crying out in distress. Dorothy passed her on the right—a soldier tried to block her and she sent him flying. Irene followed her friend's back all the way through and out the door. Sunlight hit her hard. She ripped off the mask. Soldiers with canteens came around and splashed water in the eyes of women who hadn't tightened their masks enough. Dorothy was over by a truck, splayed out on her back, breathing hard. But laughing. Ellie was bent over, blowing snot out of her nose. The guys in jumpsuits were dragging the fallen out of the gas chamber and sending them away in a sad line to the left, where they coughed and gagged.

The DI came toward the survivors and blew his whistle. "Get up!"

They groaned to their feet.

The DI stepped over to Dorothy and looked up at her. "Did you grow a pair yet?" he said. "Masks on! Round Two!"

"Can do, Sarge!" Dorothy hollered back at him. She grabbed Irene's mask strap from behind and pulled it painfully tight.

Again, the whistle. "Move! Move! Move!"

They moved, running back the way they came.

Afterward, on the other side, as they leaned against their transports and gulped fresh air, the DI walked up to Irene and Dorothy. He lit two cigarettes and handed them over. "You two," he said. "You passed."

They took the smokes and nodded.

"Hate me now," he said. "When you're over there, you're going to thank me."

They got back on their truck, under the canvas roof, and went out the gate and all that was left outside the Quonset was the sound of the engine.

—

They were starting to feel powerful.

Slowly, both the vaguely ironic and the deeply sincere among them came to see how seriously the Red Cross and the army took this service. And they started to take it seriously, too. They didn't feel like cooks, didn't feel like waitresses. Ellie said they were *ass-kicking bitches,* and they knew that they were. Though Irene said: "I was thinking of Amazons." Ellie and Dorothy stared at her—she made a soft little muscle—and laughed.

They were desperately trying to figure out how to pack their supplies.

The women had armloads of extra clothing and impracticalities piled on their beds and on the floor around them. The trick was to fit the essentials but save room for the fun stuff. Except for the pin-curled debutante from Texas who had hauled a week's worth of evening dresses to training. Try as she might, she could not figure out how to stuff even one ball gown into her footlocker. Captain Miller left her in tears when she mocked her and made her throw the ball gowns in the trash bin. "If you have any tiaras," she said, "make sure you throw those away, too."

Ellie leaned over to Irene and Dorothy and whispered, "I don't think she's gonna make the cut."

The Clubmobilers were drilled on transport, on recreation, on crafts and their psychological value to the fighting men, on the importance of observing all national holidays, on the American Red Cross (ARC) Code of Professional Ethics, all the way down to awareness of individual soldiers' backgrounds and a sense for their regions of origin—hometowns, climate, topography, even population. They were shown how to do crafts: stencils, block prints, spatter painting, finger painting. How to organize and direct games. They were to come out of this time with a wizard's power to summon comfort in the face of suffering and chaos.

Then they were thrown into trucks and shuttled to the Pentagon for physical exams and various inoculations that gave Irene painful red wens on her upper arms and right buttock.

Captain Miller posted the crew assignments on a great board in the lobby of the Blackstone Hotel. It was like high school awards season. Cheerleaders and actresses and marching-band veterans knew a cast list when they saw it.

A forlorn short list of culled names hung in the corner, with REJECTED stamped in red across the page. The longer list of the chosen took up center space: sixty-five women who would join others already there on the forty trucks that they would take charge of in Europe. Each truck had a name attached to it, like the name of a navy ship. These were all American place-names, part of Eisenhower's plan—continuing his belief that these rolling bits of the homeland would bring comfort to the boys.

Irene grabbed Dorothy by the arm and dragged her over to see the list.

The two of them, together with Ellie, were assigned to ARC *Rapid City*. Destination, England.

"I can live with that," Dorothy said.

—

Dinner appeared amid a storm of laughter and shouting and debate. Great embraces and sullen silence from those eliminated and a long buffet laden with sandwiches and cold chicken and potato salad and olives and cheeses and raw vegetables and cookies and brownies and lemonade and bottles of white wine.

Dorothy and Ellie followed Irene, stacking meat on their plates. There were full wine bottles in ice buckets, and Dorothy requisitioned one and tucked it under her arm, then snagged three glasses. Irene filled a cloth napkin with desserts. Ellie was smuggling most of the raw vegetables and olives.

"Grab another bottle," Dorothy ordered Ellie.

They clomped down the hall in their boots.

"These boots are awful," Irene said. "I have blisters on my blisters."

"I grew up in boots," Dorothy countered. "Don't bother me none."

"I grew up in heels, dahling."

"I'd break my ankles in heels."

"I can't work in heels," Ellie said. "Can you picture me selling red hots in them at my dad's dog stand outside Wrigley?"

The elevator doors opened and there appeared a little fellow who looked like an albino monkey in a spangled suit with a cap on his head, ready to accompany an organ grinder. "Going up," he said. His tiny white mustache twitched like a caterpillar.

"I'm gonna catch me a husband in this war," Ellie said. "I love a man in uniform."

The elevator doors closed behind them.

"I'm available," the decorated monkey said.

4

AND THEY AWOKE on a ship plowing white furrows in the dark sea.

The day after their training ended, the Clubmobile Corps was dispersed, some directly to their assignments, others still awaiting theirs. The largest contingent was bound for the European theater and would travel as part of different convoys heading across the Atlantic. Irene, Dorothy, and Ellie were part of a group that had taken a train from Washington to Brooklyn, where they stayed at an old brown hotel that allowed them out only to serve food at Red Cross service centers. They were not to call home. They could only wait and wait.

By now it had been weeks since Irene fled and she felt she had come full circle. Back in New York. It was time to make amends to Mother for disappearing.

November 1943

Dear Mother,

I have so much to tell you but so much I can't say. I am sorry that I won't be home for the holidays and it might be a while before I see you again. As soon as I am free to explain, I believe you will be proud of me. I have joined the Red Cross and I'm going to do my part.

I had to make a change. I will explain more when I can.

Love, Irene

When no one was paying attention, Irene slipped the letter into the mail slot.

—

It was the week before Thanksgiving when they boarded a ship at the navy yard, accompanied by about a million young soldiers. They were the only Clubmobilers on this particular ship. Irene swooned when she saw the Brooklyn Bridge, and teared up when they left it behind. Dorothy had never seen anything like New York. Ellie wasn't about to admit it impressed her, since that would have betrayed Chicago.

Their ship was running silent, lights out, to avoid detection. Up the coast in Portsmouth they would pick up more convoy ships. Then on to Newfoundland, there to gather with more destroyers for a speed run to Ireland and a loop down to Liverpool. They'd zigzag the whole way to thwart U-boats. Nine days. Superfast ships like the *Queen Mary* went direct and could be there in five days.

The sea was coming hard. Waves from the starboard side rocked the ship and knocked passengers off their feet. Everything churned. When night fell, the bow waves almost glowed. The sound was of endless breakers foaming to their deaths. The engines were a persistent throb they felt more than heard. Smokestack clouds stretched like vague chalk marks across the black water behind them.

They traveled in convoy with ocean liners and destroyers and a submarine and three small aircraft carriers crowded with F4U Corsairs, their wings folded up like resting pelicans. Most of these ships could be seen only in daylight. Their portholes were covered and taped down at night. Radios had to be whisper-quiet, not that they could pick up much at sea anyway. Between ships, most communication was via Morse code on the lamps or, during the day, by semaphore flag signals. Everybody feared U-boats. Irene thought she saw them everywhere, moving like huge evil sharks through the cold water.

The three-woman crew of the *Rapid City* was on a modest passenger liner, the *Monarch of Bermuda*. It had a British crew and during peacetime it made the tourist circuit from New York harbor to Bermuda's pink sands. The crew wore starched white uniforms, and the holds were jammed full of GIs sleeping in their bags—Irene was amused to hear them call their bedding *fart sacks.* Women and officers got upper-class cabins, and the grunts grabbed any spot they could. Steerage and even hallways.

Dorothy had discovered that the third smokestack of the *Monarch* was fake, a hollow radio-antenna cover that crew members climbed to enjoy cigarette breaks. She was eager to tell Irene all about it, but Irene was seasick and busy vomiting operatically in their cabin. Ellie was apparently her nurse.

"Earl's knockin'," Dorothy said when she saw Irene kneeling before the bucket.

Perfectly timed, a brisk knock sounded on their cabin door. Ellie opened it.

A steward stepped in bearing a silver platter holding a cup of mint tea. "Ma'ams," he said. (It sounded like *Mums.*) "This should help calm the innards."

Irene erupted once more. "So sorry."

"Is miss feeding the fishes?" he asked mildly.

Irene did not laugh.

—

The convoy rushed relentlessly northward into the next day. They had strict orders: no ship was to stop or even slow its pace. In case of U-boat attacks or, worse, a sinking, each ship was to continue at speed to lessen the possibility of further strikes. No one on the civilian ships paid much attention to these orders except for the captains.

Irene was a bit better that morning. The three friends had been ordered to sleep in their clothes and leave the cabin door ajar in case a torpedo struck.

"One wouldn't care to drown in the bunk, would one?" the steward had said.

They now stripped to their underwear and laid out their handsome new uniforms on their bunks. Light summer duds and heavier winter outfits. Uncle Sam had hired Brit haberdashers to create bespoke blue-gray jackets and trousers. White blouses. They must have cost a bundle. The three of them dressed for breakfast.

Along with the new uniforms, the army had provided each woman with a metal footlocker, green, with reinforced corners and a hasp on the front. The owner's name was stenciled across the top: WOODWARD, IRENE. The Red Cross had allocated to each of them a bag packed with white cotton underwear, socks, matches, a small first-aid kit, Kotex, toothbrushes, nail kits, aspirin, sewing kits, Sen-Sen breath fresheners, and other toiletries and potions. Condoms. Chocolates.

"Oh look," Irene said. "Silk stockings."

Dorothy tossed Irene her pair. "Not going to start now," she said.

They headed for the dining room for breakfast. Strictly for women and officers. The non-coms and enlisted men were eating C rations and K rations and sometimes hitting a chow line deep in the bowels of the ship. The women ran into the soldiers on the way, excusing themselves and squeezing through.

Irene called, "Good morning," to each group of boys as she went.

"How you, ma'am?"

"Feeling a little green, boys." She made a face and rubbed her belly.

"Jimbo, too, ma'am. He yakked all night."

"Your mother!" Jimbo said.

"Meet you over there, gents," Irene said. "I'll be in the Clubmobile *Rapid City*."

"Will you give us a dance?" a kid holding a sock with holes in it said.

"Might do," she replied as if she were really considering such a thing.

The women passed through the hatch and scrambled up the stairs.

"You'll be darning their socks next," Dorothy complained.

"After the war," Ellie said, "you should come work the hot dog stand. You'd make a million in tips."

Irene and Dorothy glanced at each other and rolled their eyes.

"That would be dreamy, Ski," Irene said. "Truly."

They came out on deck. The wind hit them, forcing their eyes closed, and when their eyes opened again, the sight of the massed ships made their mouths fall open. American flags on each gray warship, each blue-and-white liner. Long white tails of smoke merged behind the warships as they hurried themselves northward. Irene could see crewmen on the decks of nearby ships. She waved. They waved back. Seabirds glided along on stiff wings, looking like white kites on strings, keeping pace.

"God Almighty," Ellie said.

They hung on to the rails and stared.

—

The dining room was crowded with tanned, salt-and-pepper-haired men in uniform. Cigar smoke made Irene feel a little rough.

The steward from the previous night seated them at a central table. "Is miss still feeling bilious this morning?" he asked.

Irene waved her hand to show how gamely she had recovered. "A new day," she pronounced.

"Lovely," he said, placing menu cards before them. "I shall bring tea and lemon water."

Furness Lines
MONARCH OF BERMUDA

Breakfast

Orange Juice
Chilled Grapefruit
Stewed Fruits
Boiled Hominy Grits with Milk
Assorted Dry Cereals with Milk
Tongues and Sounds in Creole Sauce
Boiled, Fried, or Scrambled Eggs

Broiled Beechnut Ham
Sautéed Potatoes
Hot Rolls, Toast, Assorted Coffee Rings
Jam, Assorted Marmalades
Tea, Coffee, Cocoa

For reasons of her own, Dorothy decided, as she studied her menu card, that the steward was named Willie. "Willie," she said, when he came back with their cups of tea, "what are *sounds*?"

"Phenomena experienced with the ear, if I'm not mistaken."

Oh, Irene liked Willie.

"Cute," Dorothy said. "You're a regular laugh riot."

"Must be the rum, the dancing, and the late hours," he said. "All this excitement, miss. Got me off my game, I'm afraid." He made great theater out of mopping his brow.

"Cheeky boy," Irene said.

"*Sounds,* madam," he continued, turning back to Dorothy, "are delicacies like gizzards, I imagine. Tripe, awful things like that. Lungs? D'you think? Surely not. Though kidneys would be all right, wouldn't they? I like kidneys in a pie."

"Gack," Dorothy said.

"I'll just have toast and butter and marmalade, please," said Irene.

"Ma'am. And—?" He looked at Dorothy.

"Eggs, Willie. Pastries. Coffee."

"Bangers?"

"Might as well live large."

"My philosophy in a nutshell," he crooned.

"Extra bacon."

"Certainly. A meat lover's repast. Madam is a woman with a firm grasp on what she likes, if I might say so. And you?" He ravished Ellie with his eyes.

"Hell, you only live once, Willie," she said. "Pile on the sounds."

He tipped his head. "No tongues, miss?"

"Not on the first date."

"I shall make a note of that." He hurried away.

"Cripes, Ski," muttered Dorothy.

Irene's head had a rock in it—she hated everyone in the room. "I expected more of you," she said in her finest motherly tone.

"You're so fake," Ellie said with a sniff, as she dumped cubes of sugar into her tea.

They all studied the tabletop and didn't even look up when Willie delivered their platters.

Dorothy and Irene were already getting tired of Ellie. And Ellie knew it.

—

Late that night, Ellie was snoring again and Irene was making little peeps in her sleep when Dorothy crept back into the cabin from her nocturnal rambles.

Dorothy grabbed Irene's foot to awaken her. "Come on," she whispered. "And grab your coat."

Irene got a strong whiff of whiskey.

Out in the hallway, Dorothy said, "Me and Willie are drinking joy juice in the smokestack."

"Show me the way," Irene said, rubbing the sleep from her eyes.

They put their Mae Wests on over their coats and pulled them tight against the icy northern sea air and the needle spray that reached them all the way up on deck. They admired the gargantuan bustlines these life vests gave them. The ships made mile-wide Vs of the pummeling waves. The faintly luminescent foam coming off their bows folded and refolded itself and vanished under multitudes of lace, constant on the black face of the sea.

Dorothy led Irene to an open hatch in the side of the first stack. Up a narrow ladder they went, rocked back and forth by the ship, slamming their hips into the curved metal of the stack.

"Get your hands off my bottom," Irene said.

"Well, get movin', then."

"Dorothy!"

"Just checkin' to see if you padded it."

Up top, Willie was disheveled and jolly. He held an empty whiskey bottle in the air. Its open mouth hooted softly in the wind. Willie studied the moon through the brown glass. "Demon rum," he said and pitched it overboard, then pulled another from his back pocket. "I'm no twillip," he boasted.

Neither Irene nor Dorothy knew what this meant but they let it pass unremarked.

Irene stared toward the invisible horizon. She took a pull from the flat bottle, choked on the burn in her throat. She handed it over. It changed hands from Dorothy to Willie back to Irene. She took another snort and coughed. She squinted ahead, her bad eye watering. There was a glimmer. A spark of orange. It was far off, but their pace would bring them abreast of it soon. The light seemed to go out, then flare up. Dorothy and Willie were jabbering and laughing. Irene wished they'd be quiet, as if that might allow her to see better. What was it? A beacon? Lightning?

"What is that?" she finally asked.

Willie glanced up and she pointed out ahead. He leaned out as if that would bring the flashes closer. He was suddenly sober.

"In that locker," he said to Dorothy. "Binoculars. Get them."

She did.

He surveilled the scene before them. "Shite." He handed the binoculars over to Dorothy and scrambled down the ladder.

Dorothy looked through them as well and whistled softly. A low boom rolled at them across the water. Irene took the binoculars from Dorothy but already knew what she would see.

When they tumbled out of the open portal at the bottom of the smokestack, the deck was already crowded. Irene lost Dorothy in the crush. She pushed through the men and grabbed the rail on portside. The smell of burning oil was already reaching them. Flames a sickly orange and red and green doubled and shattered on the black oiled water. The ship ahead of theirs had been hit by a torpedo. It had ruptured, breaking in half, both ends tipping at sharp angles as the center sagged into the waves. The munitions aboard it caught fire and went off like fireworks, shrieking through the air, trailing sparks, then exploding and sending myriad smaller comets into the sea.

The captain rang the bells, and the *Monarch* surged like some grand whale as the propellers churned harder. In spite of their increased velocity, heat from the burning ship reached them all, reddening their cheeks and stinging their eyes, making them avert their faces. Its bow was sliding backward into the ocean and sailors leaped from it only to disappear as it sucked them down. The ship looked at once small and vast. Underwater, it blew again, and the light was horrid green as the sea boiled up and turned white.

Ellie jammed in beside Irene and grabbed her hand. "I ain't doing this," she said. "This is too much."

Irene shushed her. They laced their fingers like schoolgirls and wept as bodies appeared in the water, facedown and vanishing as the *Monarch* sped away.

"I can't, Irene."

"You've got to."

Then living men appeared. Held up by their life jackets, waving their arms over their heads. They screamed for help, their voices echoing between the juggernauts, as if heard in a terrible dream. Muted by the immensity of all the world passing over them but close enough that Irene saw their eyes.

"Lady! Lady!" they cried, reaching up as if she could lift them to safety.

"For Christ's sake!"

"Over here! Help!"

Then so quickly past, she wondered if she'd imagined it.

The men were already freezing to death in the icy northern sea. It didn't take long for them to become very distant. Tossed in the wake of the ship, they were as seabirds resting on the water, their voices growing ever smaller and quieter as if they were a radio show being turned down at bedtime. Then they were lost in the foam and the darkness.

"Screw this," said Baranski of Chicago.

5

LIVERPOOL HID BEHIND a wall of morning fog. It was days later, though none could quite remember how many. Once the world ended before their eyes, they had slipped into a form of time they did not know how to measure. Ellie had become a ghost. She seemed to be able to pass through walls—she'd be there with them, and they'd turn around and find her gone. She was gone again now.

Irene and Dorothy stood at the starboard rail, squinting into the gray. They could smell the land. It smelled of salt and oil, smoke and dirty water. Engines, fish, creosote, and cooking. Soil. Metal banged and men's voices were flattened by the mist. They could hear whistles and laughter and lorry engines.

They knew the city had been ravaged by German planes for a year and a half. They dreaded what the gray curtains might be hiding. The dinosaur roars of the ships' horns seemed to echo one another all around. The American armada lurked near them, and the huge dark shadows of docked ships loomed vaguely in the fogbanks as well. Invisible gulls called and hollered as they dived past the *Monarch*'s deck line and splashed into water Irene could not see. Dorothy stood smoking.

"I never saw anything like that in my life," Irene said.

"Back there?" Dorothy said, as if Irene could be talking about anything else. When her friend made no reply, she said, "Same for me."

"Those poor sailors," Irene said. "I'm sick at heart."

"We all are. Doesn't make you special. And it doesn't fix a thing. We just keep doing our jobs. That's it."

"Right," Irene said.

Dorothy tossed her cigarette into the fog. "Friggin' harbor stinks." She was picking up the language of the soldiers.

Irene had not slept well since the sinking. The wounded ship's sundered body had towered over her dreams. On each of the remaining nights of the crossing she'd had a recurring nightmare. Black sky, black sea. The moon cast a bright wedge of sparkles on the water, as if there were a long bridge of silver coins floating on the tide. And standing alone on the coins, a drowned sailor. Just staring at her. Whispering, *Irene*. Falling farther and farther behind.

"You don't get extra pay for feeling bad," Dorothy said.

"We get paid?"

"Hundred and fifty a month and all the donuts you can eat, lady."

"Oh, right. I forgot. We're going to be rich."

Bells clanged alongside the tumult beyond the fog: cranes and tractors, a metallic cacophony. Squinting brought nothing into sight. Right now it was a world composed solely of sonic reverberation and smell.

"I can't eat anything, Dot."

Dorothy looked away and smiled to herself at this new level of familiarity. She had come all this way and escaped from all the goobers in Indiana who called her *Dot,* and now here she was again. *Dot*. "Know what I think, Gator?" she said. "I think it'll get worse before it gets better."

A tugboat materialized below them where the sea fog was separating into wisps. It snuggled its nose to the stern of their ship and churned the water. The ship slowly swung around. Dorothy was intensely interested in seafaring things, having never been near such exotic creatures as tugboats.

"I'm tough," Irene said.

"I know you are."

"I'm worried about Baranski."

"Let her do what she's got to do," Dorothy said.

A voice came over the loudspeakers: "Prepare for docking. Disembarkation begins at oh eight hundred hours. Officers first, then enlisted men, followed by volunteers and ladies. Thank you."

There was a sense of the interior of the ship surging to life, of bodies rising and moving.

—

The sun had broken through by the time most of the troops were stumbling down the gangplanks. The thinning fog raised like a curtain to reveal the vastness of the harbor, the ships scattered in its waters and those waiting off the coast. Battalions of cranes worked against a smoky sky. GIs piled into truck after truck and rattled away. Irene glanced at the clock tower visible above the docks. Dorothy and Ellie rambled along the railing, waving at the boys departing down one of the gangplanks. Irene stayed in place. She could not imagine what it would take to walk down that gangplank. If she didn't disembark, they'd have to take her home. But then how would she explain herself? Another failure.

She was rooted in that position for a long while.

An hour and a half later, the *Rapid City* crew was finally free to lug their heavy footlockers down to the docks. Now that the storm of American troops had passed, the docks seemed hollow and silent, in spite of the endless noise of the machinery. To Irene, the air itself felt British, though she could not have said what she meant by that. England didn't smell like New York.

Their extra bags hung off their shoulders. There was no soldier left to assist them and the British crew of the *Monarch* was nowhere to be seen. Beyond the wharves lay streets with businesses and row houses standing among ruins. Not all the streets were wrecked, however. The randomness of the destruction shook them. None of them had ever seen a bombed city before.

There would be a block of tidy yellow and pale blue houses, redbrick buildings—and the next street would have gaps and rubble and raw holes still gaping, toppled trees, wood everywhere charred black. Workmen leaned on shovels or swung picks. Beside the bomb craters rose ivied buildings with smoke curling from chimneys. Pigeons and seagulls scattered in the air like confetti. Was that a thatched roof? In the distance? The sight made a tangible pain in Irene's chest.

Ellie stood above her footlocker and pushed it with her combat boot. It squealed against the tarmac. "It ain't movin'," she complained. "And I'm not, either."

Long warehouses formed a barrier between the city and the docks. Several of them also stood broken and burned hollow. Cranes lifted fat nets loaded with cases and boxes, while others ferried trucks and jeeps and cannons out of the seemingly bottomless holds in the middles of the ships. It was like a magic trick. One of the cranes sported a bedraggled wreath with a fluttering red bow. Christmas was coming, after all.

Irene had never seen a half-track except in movies, and now three of them rumbled by, the blue stench of exhaust in their wake, as if in a military parade. Their .50 caliber Browning guns pointed at the sky. Painted on the tailgates were various GI graffiti messages: Go Get 'Em! and SPECIAL DELIVERY! and two arrows, one to the right, one to the left, with the instructions Men This Way Ladies This Way.

A jeep roared up and a familiar voice called, "How y'all doin'?"

They spun around and dropped their bags atop their recalcitrant footlockers.

"Russell Penney!" Ellie shouted.

"I got jump-stepped to lieutenant!" he said. He seemed not to know if he could hug them, mumbling something about ranks and protocol, but they hugged him, so he went with it. "Howdy, howdy, howdy," he said. "I've been assigned to your unit, so you'll be seeing a lot of me. I'm going to be handling the logistics for you gals and the other trucks in Group F."

Ellie made a kitty-cat sound in his ear. "I'm going home," she said.

"No she isn't," Irene said.

Russell grunted, a sound perhaps meant to indicate support all around, and said brightly, "Let's get you squared away." He whistled for a few soldiers sneaking a smoke beside the warehouse nearest them. They double-timed it over to carry the footlockers to the Willys jeep attached to a two-wheeled trailer. The lockers seemed light in their hands.

Back at the ship Willie stood forlornly at the rail. The three women waved at him. He turned and went inside.

Dorothy took the front seat, beside Russell—she needed legroom. Irene and Ellie tucked themselves into the back, which was about as small as a footbath. Russell had the windshield down and latched to the hood.

"Over here," he said, "they call a hood a *bonnet*. And the windshield is a *windscreen*."

"How elegant," Irene said.

"How stuck-up, you mean," Ellie said.

"What's your frickin' problem?" Dorothy snapped.

"Car trunk's called a *boot*," Russell enthused.

"Not every place is Chi-town," Dorothy said. "They have their own way of talking over here."

"I like Berwyn better," Ellie said. "Lincoln Park. People speak American."

"It's English, dear. Who do you think gave you English?" Irene demanded.

"The English." Ellie was sick of the whole bit. "Bitches."

"Now, ladies." Russell glanced around but motored along the port without further comment. He resumed whistling Bob Wills songs. He swung over to an old London city bus repainted olive green and parked. "This here's a Brit Clubmobile. You'll be doing duty in one of these for a spell, then you'll be going down to London to set up a Donut Dugout and then do some officers' mess duty."

"Donut Dugout," Dorothy repeated, trying it out. "Everything is so damn cute with you people."

Russell's ears burned. "By the way," he said, "regulations state you can't call them *Brits*. Or *Limeys*. Lord, don't ever do that. So forget I said it."

"What do they call us?" Ellie demanded.

"*Yanks!*"

"I been called worse."

"Ain't that the truth," Dorothy said.

The three women nodded to one another. They got out of the jeep and looked inside the modified bus. When they crammed themselves aboard, they realized right away how tight it would be. The donut machine squatted in a corner, looking like a Flash Gordon apparatus, and the grease cooker stood beside it on the counter. Coffee urns in each rear corner. Same basic equipment as the USA version, only older.

"Our American trucks have a little more room," he said, his pride seeming to add a few inches as he straightened up. "GM deuce and a half. That's two and a half tons of American iron I'm talkin' 'bout. Ain't no buses for Ike, I'll tell you for sure."

The women raised their eyebrows at his bluster and examined the shelves and the cabinets. They'd heard this truck propaganda a hundred times, but Irene played along by sighing, "Ooh."

"Coffee cups," Dorothy reported.

"Teacups," Russell corrected. "But we'll fix that. Inside our trucks, it ain't England. It's the US of A."

Irene patted him condescendingly.

"I like you, Russell," Ellie confided.

"Do I drive this rig?" Dorothy asked.

"Well, an English soldier will drive the bus when it needs to move. I guess they might not trust you ladies to drive just yet."

"Oh really," Dorothy said.

None of the women were impressed. They stepped outside and Dorothy turned her back on the bus. As they walked to the jeep, Russell mentioned that Command had heard there was a ship sunk in transit. When none of them answered him, he cleared his throat and piled into the vehicle. The women did likewise. Russell ground the jeep into gear and lurched away. The women rode it like rodeo gals—the trailer bounced and so did they. Russell was a real aficionado of heavy military ordnance. He zipped around the port complex so they could behold clanking behemoths lumbering by.

His running commentary had the enthusiasm of a boy listening to the World Series on the radio: "That right there is a howitzer M8! Motorized!" He swerved between the cranes. "Sherman tanks here," he confided. "And look at that sumbitch over there. M7 Priest. Kinda like a tank, kinda not."

"Do tell," Irene cooed.

"M26 Pershing!" he cried. "It's a monster, ain't it?"

"Where can I get one of those?" Dorothy asked. "I'm not even kidding."

They drove to a barracks at the farthest end of the docks; their bivouac lay nestled in the shadow of a water tank. They could leave the docks and walk across the road and into town. Irene was thrilled when a pair of red double-decker buses rolled past. She held down the urge to point and yelp. *We are not seven years old, Irene.*

In the barracks they had their choice of twelve empty bunk beds. They were the first of the Clubmobile Corps to arrive.

"Head's at the end down there," Russell said. "About twenty commodes." He looked at the floor, blushing. "Ten shower stalls. Plenty of towels, soap bars."

Irene was touched by his innocent embarrassment in mentioning toilets to ladies.

"I'll be back for y'all at seventeen hundred hours for chow."

"Seriously, though," Dorothy said. "How do I get on that M26 crew out there? I want to shoot stuff."

"You do not," Irene said.

"Just watch me, honey."

Russell laughed, clearly thinking she was joking. "Ladies," he said. He didn't exactly salute them, though he tapped a finger to his forehead. "By the way," he said, "you can call me Rusty if you want."

As he walked to his jeep, Irene cried: "Wait! Wait! Your name is *Rusty Penney*?"

He hurried away as the women collapsed in laughter.

—

Irene had found a black-and-white postcard of Liverpool.

Mother Dear,
Guess where your errant child has gotten to now?

With love, Irene

For supper they dined on bangers and mash, the sausages fat and oily, the grease congealed on the metal plates. The potatoes were soaked in butter, butter biscuits continued the theme, and Earl Grey tea tried to cut the fats. Each of them had a pint of heavy brown beer. It was warm.

They crawled into their bunks feeling forty pounds heavier. After being stuck in a cabin for their sea crossing, the three women enjoyed the luxury of spreading out and using every bit of the space available to them. Ellie climbed up on a top bunk near the doorway while Dorothy and Irene each claimed a bottom bunk in the far opposite corners.

Dorothy belched like a lumberjack.

"How ladylike," Irene noted.

"Thank you," Dorothy belched out.

"You burp-talked," Ellie narrated.

"The cook called dinner *airships and clouds,*" Irene said.

"What a poet," Dorothy said.

"Has a ring, don't it?" Ellie said. "I can see a shop in Lincoln Park. 'Ski's Airships and Clouds.' Right by the Biograph Theater. You know it? That alley where the G-men drilled Dillinger?"

"They gave him lead poisoning," Irene said, being up on gangster-movie dialogue.

Lights-out.

Dorothy boasted, "I can sing an entire song in one super-belch."

"Please don't," Irene said.

"Do it," Ellie said.

"Absolutely not," Irene insisted.

"Go! Go!" Ellie was hopping around in her bunk. *What a colossal stick Irene hads up her butt,* she thought.

"OH GIVE ME A HOME!" Dorothy roared.

"Stop," Irene said.

"WHERE THE BUFFALO ROOOOAAAAM!"

"Stop it!"

"Jeepers," Ellie said. "I can't stop laughin'. I'm about to tinkle."

"Where the DEER and the ANTELOPE PLAAAYYY!"

This was Team *Rapid City,* Irene thought.

But then Dorothy cut the burp song short. "Hey," she said. "Nobody dies. Nobody friggin' dies."

"Good plan," Irene said.

"Deal," Ellie said.

"Three girls loose in the world," Dorothy said.

They lay in the dark, trying to sleep.

—

Rusty was outside their barracks at 5:30 a.m., grinding the gears of their donut bus. His musical accompaniment was screaming gulls and roaring diesels and rattling cranes and ship horns backed up by the percussion of crashing metal surfaces. Dorothy was the first out the door, tucking her shirttails into her trousers. Ellie sleepwalked to the bus. Irene came last.

A P-51 screamed overhead and cut a sharp curve over the harbor and beelined back across the city.

"There goes Handyman," Ellie said, nudging Irene. "He's lookin' for ya."

"Who?" said Irene, feigning ignorance.

At the open door of the bus, Dorothy was already arguing with Rusty. "Don't you know how to work a clutch, son?"

"I do just fine."

"Sure, if you call stripping the gears fine. You're grinding it like a sixth grader in his daddy's truck. Scoot over."

"I do not *scoot over* for nobody. I am your driver."

"No you're not. Not today, by God."

Rusty gripped the wheel fiercely and stared straight through the windshield as if sailing his ship into a maelstrom.

Dorothy put her foot inside the bus. "Scoot."

"I won't. That there ain't my orders."

"Get on out of there, and stop embarrassing yourself."

"I'll catch hell."

"You're catching hell right now. Un-ass that seat."

He stepped down, shamefaced, and Ellie hooked her arm through his.

Dorothy fiddled with the shifter knob and the clutch, both on the wrong side, and said, "This rust heap's built backward." The engine coughed and roared. "Let's roll."

Irene felt constricted in the tight galley. It was dirty, too. Flour on every surface. Scent of sugar and donut mix, spent tea bags, and burned grease. And old bus—that was the secret ingredient. Was that a spider in a web in the corner?

Dorothy docked the donut bus alongside an administrative hut on the main quay. In a few hours, more GIs would be storming down gangplanks. The women jumped to their work. They tied on full white cotton aprons that covered them from chest to knees, bandannas around their heads. Broom, mop, rag in hand.

"Join the Red Cross and see the world," Irene said.

"I give this one more day," Ellie warned.

Coffee duty fell to her, and the donut cooker and making the mix were Irene's duty. Dorothy busied herself investigating the tires and radiator and checking the oil before ambling down the docks and along the warehouses. She called back, "I'm going on a little recon. Irene—weigh your water!"

"Go screw," Irene said under her breath.

Ellie snickered. "I never took Stretch for lazy," she said.

"She has her own schedule," Irene said in her first mediation of the war. "I've learned that much."

Before they'd had the chance to lift the side shutter of the bus to reveal the serving counter to the world, Englishmen had already queued up, knocking on the metal. Dockworkers. The men peeked under the lip of the shutter.

"Are you available?" a fellow called.

"Me personally?" Irene deadpanned. It was time to put on the charm jacket, all sparkles.

They opened the serving window.

"We don't quite know what we're doing," Irene warned. "But we'll do our best."

"Right," said a chap with a red face and whiskers. "I'll take a cuppa."

"Eh?" Irene said.

"Tea, innit? Cuppa tea."

"Oh dear." Irene whispered to Ellie, "Do we have tea?"

The man reached in and took the lid off a small urn on the serving counter, then fished out a bag of tea and dropped in it a mug, which he held out to her. "I'm here every day, aren't I?"

Irene didn't understand every accent that came to the window; she was smitten, nonetheless. Their first service was spotty. They ran out of hot water. But the boys didn't seem to care. They stood around smoking and flirting.

"I ain't a bolshie, don't you fret. Besides, bullshit baffles brains."

"Aye," agreed an older man with a pipe, sounding weary with wisdom.

"What are they saying?" Ellie whispered.

"Love your accent," one man said to her.

"I thought *you* had the accent," she replied.

When Dorothy reappeared, annoyingly fresh, she climbed aboard, pushed her friends aside, and hollered at the gathered men: "You blokes in the mood for some fine American baking and brewing?"

"I'm in the mood for love," said the one who was not a bolshie.

"Saucy lad," Dorothy said.

He grinned beatifically.

"I'll dip my finger in your cup, then, and give you a thrill," she said. "I'm sweet as honey and twice as potent as rum."

They gave her a wee cheer.

"Where'd she learn that?" Ellie whispered.

"One of you boys say *blimey,*" Dorothy called out. "I always wanted to hear that come out of somebody's mouth."

"Blimey!" they shouted in unison.

She looked at them a good long while. "Disappointing, really," she said.

They roared at her as if she had just scored a goal.

"The men," Dorothy said, turning to Irene, "adore me." She winked.

They all jumped when a foghorn roared and a ship seemed to break open as American GIs poured onto the dock.

"Time to get to work now," hollered one of the Englishmen as they scattered to their tractors and lorries and began the long task of unloading the ship that had just pulled in.

The realization of the work about to befall them stunned Irene for the briefest of moments. "Where are the rest of our ladies?" she said.

"I think that ship went to Edinburgh," Dorothy said. She hopped out of the bus in search of more water.

—

The women enacted the donut service for the more than two hundred American soldiers hooting and shoving and spitting and cussing. Here came Idaho. Here came Louisiana. Here came Nebraska. Here came Alaska. Here came New Mexico. Here came the Navajo. Here came the Sioux. Here came the Yankees. Here came the Poles. Here came the Negroes. Here came the ol' boys. Here came the cowboys. Here came the Italians. Here came the Portuguese. Here came Hawaii. Here came Samoa. Here came Puerto Rico. Here came Brooklyn. Here came Salt Lake City. Here came Houston. Here came Cicero and Cody and Helena and Butte and Bakersfield and Bucksnort. Petoskey and Chula Vista and Kankakee. Here came Southie and the North End and Concord. Here came the Mexicans. Here came Frisco and Deadwood and Wetumpka. Here came El Paso. The human wave rolled in and foamed around the Clubmobile as Irene spun records and the coffee ran out. They grew alarmed at how quickly every soldier's face became every other soldier's face.

It seemed to go on for thirty hours. Fortunately, Russell Penney pulled up in the afternoon.

"Coffee, Rusty?"

They were astounded at how exhausted they were.

He put on his cap and stood before their window, looking up at them. "Time to shut her down," he said.

"So soon?" Irene tried to hide her delight.

"We were just getting the hang of it," Ellie lied.

"You have orders," he reported. "Just came through. London. It's going to be like that for a while. Go where y'all are needed. Trouble-shooters. Train pulls out in"—he studied his wristwatch—"ninety minutes. Y'all gotta pack fast."

They hustled out of the bus, tossing their aprons behind them.

"Everything hurts," Irene said.

6

THE TRAIN COULD have rolled out of the pages of a Dickens novel. It awaited at the Lime Street Station, seeming a bit weary, sighing steam. The gold-leaf trim on the carriages had flaked and the paint was faded and the stout black-and-copper steam engine was grimy. Shrapnel wounds had been puttied over, leaving awful blemishes on the skins of the carriages. Twin Union Jacks were affixed to the top of the cowcatcher up front. The engine puffed as the train awaited its passengers.

Rusty organized a few roustabouts to shove the women's footlockers into the baggage car. Each passenger carriage had an outside door with a tidy set of steps like an entry into the porch of a summer cottage. Inside were eight compartments for passengers, cabins with two facing benches and glass doors that opened onto a central corridor. At the far end of the train, in place of a caboose, stood a guardian's car packed with soldiers whose heads periodically hung out the windows as if they were dogs in an automobile.

"Ladies," said Rusty, and helped them board.

Their uniforms were lovely, though the jackets itched. As soon as they were aboard, all three of them peeled the jackets off.

Ellie was tired. She needed a nap, she said. They were learning that Ellie slept more than any human being they'd ever known. She was stifling yawns and ignoring poor Rusty, who seemed eager for a farewell embrace. Irene threw him a kiss instead, but they all knew it was a consolation prize.

"How come you're so tired all the time?" Dorothy asked.

"War's exhausting," Ellie said, yawning.

Rusty stuck his head in the doorway. "Now, remember. Euston Station in London. They'll know where to send you when y'all get there. Cars'll take you to your billet." He slammed the door and waved once.

Dorothy, feeling hilarious, waved a hankie like some dame in a movie. "Was that funny?" she asked Irene.

"Devastatingly."

"Are you being snide?"

"Devastatingly."

Ellie curled up on the backward-facing bench and fell asleep.

"She's already snoring," noted Dorothy, who let Irene take the window seat, and opened a book.

Irene asked what she was reading.

"*Yellow River* by I. P. Freely."

After a moment, Irene said, "Very funny."

"Oh, sorry. Boy Scout humor. Learned it from my brother." Dorothy glanced at the cover. "I meant to say I'm reading *Run to the Outhouse* by Willy Make It and Betty Don't."

"Honestly. What are you? Twelve?" Irene let it go for a moment, as they listened to Ellie's soft snoring. Then: "What are you really reading?"

"*Under the Grandstand* by Seymour Butts."

"I could just strangle you."

The whistle blew and the steam engine chuffed and threw out curtains of white clouds and a drizzle of cinders and ash and they rolled out of Liverpool, past the craters and burned wrack and the many cranes and ships and vehicles swarming like the ant farm of the Titans.

"I'm going to get sick of acting like wacky broads all day every day," Dorothy said.

"It seems to be the Red Cross position," Irene said.

"I didn't see it in no rule book," said Ellie, suddenly awake. "But we're here to be spry. Right?"

"We serve fresh hope with a cup of joy," Irene said.

Dorothy folded her arms. "I only got one letter from my brother before he was killed. He called war *being in the shit*. He was pretty spry, I guess." She stared out the window.

The names of train stations and towns they passed were painted over in case the enemy happened upon them.

"We never know where we are," Ellie said and closed her eyes.

"We're no place," Dorothy said.

They rode along looking out at unknown villages and military emplacements and cows.

"I like cows," Dorothy finally said. "I grew up with them."

"Did you have a farm?" Irene said.

"Yup. All I wanted was to get away from there."

"Chicago was burned down by a cow," Ellie offered, feeling like she'd failed again to enter their conversation.

They just stared at her.

"We have a farm," Irene said to Dorothy. "Well, my aunt and my grannie. My uncle, too. He's gone now, but I still see him sometimes."

Dorothy nodded. Every farm had a ghost.

The train clacked on.

Irene hooked her arm through Dorothy's. "After the war, let's go," she said. "There's a cabin there. We can move in there for as long as we like. It's not far from the ocean. We can drive to the shore."

"Not me," Ellie said, to save face. "I'm a city gal."

After an hour of this pastoral calm, air-raid sirens began to howl. It was early dusk. The land was graying, nearly purple, and the sirens went off in a series, forming a vast chord as the news spread north that havoc was drawing near.

One of the soldiers clanked down the center aisle, his rifle at port arms, knocking on each compartment's door. "Middle of the carriage, please," he said, and went on repeating the instruction at each compartment. "Stay clear of the windows. Lie flat. Cover your heads." He was gone as abruptly as he'd appeared, not quite running.

Irene froze in her seat. She stared out the window, thinking she would spot formations of German aircraft. She imagined flocks of huge iron crows with swastikas on their wings.

Dorothy shook Ellie awake and said, "Air raid, El. Get out of the room."

Ellie was gone as fast as a startled cat.

"Come on, Shorty," Dorothy urged Irene.

"I will be so damned mad if I die today," Irene said.

Dorothy yanked her off the seat. They fell into the center aisle, where they huddled with Ellie. Civilians piled onto one another. Some of the smokers still puffed their malodorous cigarettes, dropping ash on everybody. They smelled of onions and wool, cake and tea. Strangers clutched other strangers, and men stretched out their arms to cover the women as best they could.

Thunder. Was it going to rain? Irene wondered. She'd never heard bombs explode. In a picture at the movie house, sure. But the heroes in war pictures never died from bombs. Bombs just kicked up great gouts of dirt. Blew up a building or two. *Bombs can't hit a moving train,* she told herself.

Now the noise was louder. It didn't sound anything like the bombs in the movie house. It didn't even sound like the bombs on the Fourth of July, not really.

Louder still. The train shuddered, as if the noise itself could topple the locomotive. Clods and rocks hammered the roof. She broke free of the man holding her down and poked her head up to stare outside. Trees flew into the air on geysers of flame.

"They're heading for Liverpool!" someone shouted.

The train accelerated and unleashed a bestial cry.

Irene couldn't see the bombers, and this invisibility hurling down destruction terrified her all the more. She could feel more than hear the heavy drone of them, the wasp buzz of those monstrous engines, followed by the shriek of falling bombs. And the darkening plain was again rent by black eruptions and the blast wave hit the train and almost knocked it off the track and Dorothy pulled Irene back to the floor before the outside window shattered.

Everyone there on the floor all crowded tighter. Then came the dive bombers, swooping out of the flock of larger planes and screaming toward the ground, their sound rising in pitch and their bombs seeming to blow them back into the sky as their engines changed tone and dropped octaves. In the carriage ahead of theirs, one side of the train was now aflame. The blaze licked back and smoke came through their broken window. The man covering Irene used his foot to hold the cabin's door shut so they didn't choke. Bullets struck the roof.

"No!"

Irene didn't know who had shouted it. Was she the one? Had someone been hit? Was she wounded? She clamped her hands over her ears. She could not quite comprehend that she was actually there.

She wanted to tell Dorothy that the Woodward farm was in Mattituck. And that trains ran nearby. And that she hated the pig slaughter more than anything in her life, because the pigs knew they were going to die, and the men cut their throats and the pigs screamed like women, like children, and Irene hid in the cabinet under the sink with her ears covered, just like now. She still had nightmares about those screams. And Uncle Will kept bottles of bourbon hidden from Auntie in the barn. And her terrible cousins took Gator out there for a snort because Uncle Will could never report them to Aunt Eva, so they got away with their pilfering. She wanted to say that.

Now in scattered emplacements along the tracks antiaircraft gunners fired into the sky. Tracer rounds like flaming arrows vanished into the smoke and clouds eating the sky. Royal Air Force fighters swarmed from some nearby hive to counterattack.

"Oh Jaysus," a voice cried. "Oh Jaysus."

7

IT WAS FULL dark when they disembarked at London's Euston Station. Irene's mind was numb from tornadoes of fire. Trees lifting into the clouds. She shook shards of glass out of her hair. Dorothy, Ellie, and Irene were all covered in dust, as if a field had blown through the train car. The passengers grimly patted one another's shoulders and backs and unleashed small gray clouds from their neighbors' clothes. They shuffled away, fading from sight.

The Luftwaffe had hit the outskirts of London, too. Flickering orange flames in the distance launched dense smoke columns into the sky. The glow of fires showed through the ruins of buildings. Churches that had already been reduced to shells by the Blitz were now transformed into enormous candles.

Men in railway uniforms studied the fresh holes that pocked the sides of the locomotive's engine. The smell of charcoal came from the burned train car. Flashlights bobbed all around. A few searchlights dragged their beams like fingers through high clouds. Klaxon howls sped away into the darkness. The smoke billows in that direction glowed pink.

Fat fish seemed to drift above the dark buildings. Irene stared up at the fish and thought for the tenth time that she might be dreaming. Dust fell out of her ear.

A soldier in a British frying-pan helmet peeled away from the crew that was hustling to retrieve the bags from the smoking baggage carriage. Noting her look of confusion, he said, "Barrage balloons, love. Tangles up Jerry when he flies over."

Nearby, a group of American MPs shoved a disheveled bunch of manacled American GIs toward a truck. Some of the drunker soldiers were singing and cursing, and one unfortunate was vomiting into the street.

"Shame, really," her British soldier commented. "Your boys tend to get into dustups here in Old Blighty."

"Whyever so?"

"I'm not one to criticize," he criticized, "but some of the Yanks don't know how to behave. They seem to think they're on holiday." He turned away from the arrest and made a show of looking at the sky. "You know what they say."

"I don't."

"They say the American GI is overpaid and oversexed. And over here." He nodded politely and moved on.

Ellie nudged Irene in the back. "I'm done," she said.

"Me, too."

"No. I mean done. This stuff ain't for me, sister. Bombs? Are you kidding?"

With that, Ellie melted into the dark.

The truckload of miscreant American soldiers rumbled away. Irene felt as though her body had been stuffed with cotton and sawdust. She was a badly stitched taxidermy, mobile somehow, exhausted and languid. Dorothy had wandered off to inspect the damage to the train. Irene could only stand in the middle of the confusion, staring. Dorothy came back and found her exactly where she'd left her, in exactly the same position, her mouth still open in exactly the same way.

She bumped Irene with one shoulder. "Easy there, Gator. It's too early for shell shock."

"Is that what I have?"

"Snap out of it, short stack. Look, Ellie's over there blubbering and getting patted by a bunch of Limeys. That's her. Not us."

"She says she's quitting."

"We'll see."

Irene looked into Dorothy's face. "Doesn't anything upset you?" she asked.

"I don't have time to be upset."

"Never let them see you cry, huh?"

"There you go." She smacked Irene's bottom. "Let's roll."

They collected Ellie from her cadre of comforting males and climbed into a staff car that maneuvered through bombed streets and fallen buildings and small fires. They were followed by a truck that held their footlockers. In the blackout, the drivers seemed to feel their way through the murk like cats, their headlights taped down to yellow squints. The smell was of smoke and rubbish and urine and more smoke, punctuated by sudden wafts of cooking, like a tiny respite.

Irene sat as if alone, not talking. London Town. She leaned her head against the cool window glass. All she saw was gray and black.

"The Blitz, ladies," their driver said. "Now, that was quite a rough go. This's not so bad, if you compare."

As they made their way over toward Oxford Street, the narrow headlight beams briefly illuminated a building that had lost its outer wall. The rooms within were laid bare, open as a dollhouse. Irene caught the briefest glimpse of furniture and beds sitting as if on a stage. Stuffed bears still reclined on a small bed, staring out at the night. It was immeasurably sorrowful. Instantly gone as the car thumped over random fallen bricks.

"London," the driver said, "prevails. Don't you worry."

Some shadowy people perched on what looked like a fountain.

"Piccadilly Circus," the driver said. "Quite a jolly spot when Jerry buggers off and the bombs stop droppin'."

The two-vehicle caravan turned into a small maze of buildings and a ruined church, then onto a narrow street that seemed unscathed. There were row houses here with postage-stamp lawns and miniature gardens behind low iron fences interrupted by stoops. Above them, in shadows, a fire escape or two clung to the walls.

"It's just like New York," Irene said, crushed by homesickness as the words escaped her lips.

"Gosfield Street, miss," the driver said. "Your billet."

He stopped the car and got out and held the door open for them.

Dorothy and Ellie were instantly out on the sidewalk, looking up at their new home. It was narrow, with four stories, and the lower windows glowed very faintly with yellow tallow candlelight peeking through the gaps at the bottom of the siege curtains.

Irene, still drifty, was slow to emerge. She was sure she just needed a little rest. A little sleep—and zingo, she'd be all set.

"Mrs. Bridger will house you," the driver told them.

The soldiers wrestled the women's footlockers out of the truck. The men seemed to be steeling themselves for the haul up to the stoop and then the staircase to the bedrooms upstairs.

Normally, the army would have them in the Grosvenor House Hotel, their driver told them, but it was full with officers. "It's a landslide of Yanks. God bless 'em all, eh, lads? But not to worry, ladies. You'll be working the officers' club there, tasting the high life soon enough."

Irene was about to reply when a head hung over the roofline and said, "Oi!"

"Evening," their driver called up.

A second head appeared.

"Hi, boys," Ellie said.

They whistled.

"You'll have to biff up if you want to impress these lasses," their driver said. "Gunners," he explained to Irene. "Got a nest up there. Shooting down Jerry."

"Everybody's so jolly," Ellie said.

"What's the point in being gloomy?"

Mrs. Bridger stepped out on her porch. She wore her gray hair in a bun and had spectacles. "What is all this bobbery?" she said. "We need to get these girls settled." She gestured at the ladies. "In you come, then."

The two drivers took a footlocker between them and trudged. The three women followed.

"Welcome to Old Blighty!" one of the gunners called.

"Happy to be here," Irene replied.

And, even with her head a-spin, she was.

After three trips upstairs bearing the footlockers, the two drivers said they'd be back at 7:00 a.m. sharp. Uniforms required. As soon as they were gone, the door was bolted and the war vanished. Mrs. Bridger cranked up her phonograph and dropped some Noel Coward.

She reminded Irene of Grannie so much that she had to stop herself from calling the woman Effie. Mrs. Bridger tied on an apron. She laid a serving of chamomile tea out for each of them, along with a small pitcher of cream, a little bowl of sugar cubes, and a few cookies, which she called *biscuits.*

"Rations," she said, sighing. "They do hamper one's style."

Her sitting room was yellow and cozy, full of old-lady things like porcelain dolls and sachets. One wall was crowded with pictures of a dashing British officer in uniform. Shadow boxes held his medals.

"Father never did come back," Mrs. Bridger said sadly. Then she sat down to a piano and tinkled a few old songs for the girls.

They did their best to stifle yawns.

"Right, then," Mrs. Bridger said. "Beddy-bye, ladies. Your flats are upstairs. You'll find a kitchen and a loo and a sitting room on the second floor, and three bedrooms on the third. I'm afraid your drivers selected the rooms for you. Luck of the draw."

She was not interested in hugs, so they each bid her good night with nods and awkward pats and ascended to their rooms.

"Those aren't ghosts you hear," Mrs. Bridger called up. "Just the gunners walking around on the roof. And, if you don't mind, no smoking up there. And no men."

"Yes, ma'am," Ellie said.

"Men!" Dorothy shouted. "What's that?"

Irene's room was in the front, her window looking down on Gosfield Street.

Dorothy lingered at Irene's door. "I slept with Willie on the ship."

Irene turned from the window and raised her eyebrows. "You slept with the steward?"

"It's a war," Dorothy said. "We can have men."

"Honey," Irene confessed, "men are the furthest thing from my mind."

Dorothy started to exit, but stopped and said, "It wasn't that great. The top of his head kept knocking into my chin. But what else is new."

Laughing, Irene waved her off.

Down the hallway, Dorothy called from her bedroom: "That little Limey got tipsy and tried to measure me from head to feet. He said, 'If we're nose to nose, my toes are in it. If we're toe to toe, my nose is in it.' "

"Stop!" Ellie shouted.

They all laughed for a while. Once they quieted down, it wasn't long till Ellie's snores started up.

Irene sat at her window. A shadowy cat patrolled the fences down below. A firefly swirled up the dark street, then revealed itself to be the end of a cigarette being smoked by a tall shadow sauntering into the night. Later, though she didn't know why, she would be sure that it was the fighter pilot— Handyman—from that gas-attack training a hundred years ago, on the other side of the ocean. *But even if it was him,* she insisted to herself, just as she had to Dorothy, *that was not important in the least.*

8

Dear Mother,

I watched a torpedoed ship sink into the North Sea. It was aflame, standing erect like a sounding whale, its fuel and munitions exploding, soaring like fireworks across the face of the moon. And men, Mother. Men were calling to us for help, yet we

She crushed the page and threw it in the wastebasket, where it joined the other drafts that had been started and abandoned.

Dearest Mother,

She crossed the greeting out and set the page aside.

Mother Dear—

We were bombed today. Hardly what one expects on a train ride from Liverpool to London. I must admit, though I strove to maintain my inherent Woodward aplomb, it scared the daylights out of me. To see trees exp

Too dramatic by half. She crumpled the page and added it to the small snowdrift of failed drafts filling the wastebasket. She leaned her forehead on the cold glass of the bedroom window. Dawn had to break soon. The dream of the burning sailor standing on the waves and staring had jerked her awake. Again.

—

Finally, daylight. Irene threw open her bedroom window and heard budgies fussing in their cages across the street. A single dog was barking. A car horn sounded. The gunners on the roof coughed. She could smell their Navy Cut cigarettes. Normal life. It was everything.

Mrs. Bridger was chortling with Dorothy as Irene and Ellie came down to scones and tea.

"This tall one's called Dorothy," she said. "And I'm Dorothea! Isn't that something."

"Two Dots," said Dorothy.

"Polka dots."

"What's this BS about you quitting?" Dorothy asked Ellie.

"Weighing my options," Ellie replied. She was pale, with dark rings under her eyes. She smelled a little sweaty.

The driver came on time—7:00 a.m.—and the ladies went to him in their Red Cross outfits. Irene couldn't shake the sense that she was going to a costume ball. She felt fake and kept fretting over the idea of everyone else seeing through her in this military garb.

"Good morning, beautiful people!" called a gunner from the roof.

They waved from the truck before getting in, then slammed the doors.

They rattled away and Irene brightened. This was more like it. Although daylight revealed the wounds of London, the Grosvenor House Hotel, in Mayfair, stood undaunted. The driver seemed to be calling it *The Gruvna*. Irene leaped out of the car before it had stopped and walked into the hotel as if she were home.

Dorothy and Ellie, however, hung back.

"This is awful ritzy," Ellie complained.

"It ain't Indiana," Dorothy said, "that's for sure."

They shuffled around and shared a smoke and made believe the doorman wasn't staring at them.

The Blitz had not destroyed the greenery of Park Lane. The outside of the hotel was protected by a few thousand sandbags.

Irene reappeared in the doorway. "This was the home of the Duke of

Westminster!" she called. She flung an extravagant wave at them, nodded to the liveried doorman in his red, black, and gold Beefeater suit, and vanished back into the shadows within.

"How's she know this stuff?" Ellie said.

"I think these New York types have it in their blood."

At last they walked up the steps together.

"Ladies," the doorman said, holding the door for them.

"Officers' mess, please," Dorothy said.

"Straight in, then to your right. In the Grand Ballroom."

"Nice coat, Bubba," she said as they blew through.

—

Their new boss never stopped scanning the busy dining hall, his head rotating like an antiaircraft gun.

"This isn't KP duty," he said. "Want you gals to know that right off the bat. So don't get all down in the mouth. Yeah, you're wearing aprons. Yeah, you're serving the fellas. Okay, I got that. But you're more than bread sergeants. All right?"

Sergeant Milburn was the King of Chow. They were servants in his realm. Before them, hundreds of officers sat at long tables eating roast beef and potatoes and turkey and chicken and biscuits and peas.

"We serve big American portions," he continued. "That's what my guys like. Six thousand meals a day, all right? Top-notch. I run the house, Sergeant Chipps runs the bakery. Funny for a baker, right? Chipps. Of course, over here they call French fries *chips* and they call chips *crisps* and they call cookies *biscuits*." He shook his head as though disappointed in the United Kingdom.

"Mennnnn," Dorothy whispered.

"Dot, please," Irene said.

"Shrimp! We fly in shrimp from the USA," the sarge boasted. "Best eats in London right here. Fifty cents a plate. Every plate is a corner of home, all right? Yessir, we build these gents up to go win this daggone war. That plate on that table is a baseball field in Nebraska, by golly. You catchin' my drift? It's like, uh..."

"A nice pâté de foie gras and champagne at L'Aiglon on Fifty-Fifth?" Irene said.

He stared at her as if she had spoken Mandarin.

"Right off Fifth Avenue?" Irene said. "Manhattan?"

"Okay, then," he replied.

The hall was vast. No columns, which they learned was one of the famous details of the ballroom. A long row of serving tables stood at one end, and swinging doors behind them led to the maze of kitchens where American cooks and hired Brits toiled away.

Sergeant Milburn pointed to a balcony that circled the second story. "Bar's up there, for any gent that requires a snort or two."

English girls hustled between the tables, carrying pitchers of coffee.

"Got twenty ladies in back doin' nothin' but peelin' taters full-time." He was so thrilled with this revelation that he was moved to clap his hands as if knocking dust off them. "I'm putting you on desserts and bread, down on this end. A simple job so you can pick up the p's and q's. Then we'll move you up to beef." He watched the men eat as if he hadn't seen such a display in his life.

"He'll move us up to beef," Ellie enthused.

"Patton himself came in here once," he continued. "He liked a good joke. Hemingway ate here. Big fella. Wanted to box somebody if I remember right. Sat over there. Ate fish. And Ernie Pyle. You know Ernie Pyle? Heckuva writer, not much of an eater. I never knew a guy like that. What are you supposed to do with a fella that don't like to eat? We have watchers, all right? If you don't clean your plate, you get bitched out by these lieutenants. Ernie just wanted some soup. He caught hell."

Ellie, amid the cupcakes and crullers, couldn't keep her eyes off a table directly in front of them. Right side of the room. She simply stood and stared. Dorothy nudged her with an elbow, pointing out the empty bowl that needed new butter balls and fresh ice underneath. But Ellie was as one hypnotized.

"Coloreds," she said.

Dorothy glanced up. Yeah. Four Negro men laughed and worked on meat and potatoes and cups of coffee. One of them glanced up at her, waved once. Dorothy waved back.

"And?" she said.

"What are they doing in here?" Ellie said.

"They're officers," Milburn said. "It's an officers' mess."

"But how'd they become officers?"

"Young lady. Belay that talk."

"Was that dumb?" she said. "I'm just asking."

The sergeant ignored her.

"Do they stay here?"

"No, they do not," he said, his irritation plain. "They stay in segregated hotels. If Ike ever comes in here, I'm going to take it up with him. You bet." The situation seemed to cause the sarge pain. He clutched his hands behind his back and walked off without another word, giving the stink eye to the other servers as he went.

"I was just askin'," Ellie said.

Irene's gaze went to something else. The double doors of the ballroom had swung open, and two flyboys stood there posing arrogantly in their leather jackets and their insouciant crusher caps set at angles on their heads. One was short, the other tall and slender, and she could see the silver wings on his collar from where she was.

I knew it. I just knew it.

"Who let Gary Cooper in?" said Dorothy, already bored out of her mind by the endless process of doling out slices of white bread or yellow cake as if they were cards. She glanced at Irene with appalling and unabashed pleasure on her face.

"It must be fate," Irene said.

The flyboys stopped at various tables to slouch and josh as other men jumped from their seats to greet them.

"Ain't he pretty, though," Dorothy said. "I like the short one, too. Looks Eye-talian. But the tall one. Handy Dandy? Was that his name?"

Irene refused to play. "You like that short boy because you can push him around," she said.

"If you're nose to nose…Hey, pull up your girdle, Irene. Here they come."

"Stop it."

"Look busy."

The two flyboys made their way down the room and stood grinning as the women at the end of the table loaded their plates with meat and gravy and veg. Dorothy nudged Irene as they came down the table. Irene batted her away. The short one parked himself in front of Dorothy and stared up at her.

"What," she said.

"I died and seen an angel," he replied.

"We don't serve dead men."

"I get excited when you're mean to me."

"Keep yappin' and you'll get some treatment that will leave you delighted."

"You make me delirious and I'm being serious."

She laughed. "Have a butter ball," she said. "Poet."

"I'll be back."

"O pleasant hope."

He scooted off with his plate.

"He's a ball-turret gunner," Gary Cooper said from the other side of Irene. "They're a little goofy."

Irene stood there feeling invisible. Dorothy nudged her and moved down by Ellie.

"Bread?" Irene offered.

"Better not," he said. "Minding my waist. Smitty has to be short for his job, and I have to be thin for mine." He took a cup of black coffee.

"Oh? Are you a fashion model?"

"Just a fighter pilot. But pretty soon I won't be able to fit into the cockpit." He patted his flat belly.

"Why do you do that?" she asked.

"Do what?"

She pointed to her head. "That irritating thing with your cap. All bent down to your ears like some thug."

"We call 'em *crusher caps*. Earphones." He grinned. "Sometimes, when you're up there all alone, you need to hear a voice. It helps." He toasted her with his cup. "Merry Christmas, by the way," he added, and was gone.

He never even saw her, she thought.

"Nicely done," Dorothy said.

"I ignored him."

"If you say so."

"I wasn't interested."

He sauntered over to the table of Black officers. "Where's my Buffalo Soldiers at!" he cried.

"Red Ball Express, present and accounted for," replied their captain. "We keep the war effort rolling."

"Captain Walker, sir!" Irene's pilot sprang to attention and saluted.

The men at the table shook their heads and chuckled at their food.

"Sit down, cracker," Captain Walker said.

They all laughed, and one of the officers slapped the pilot's proffered palm. "What you know good, youngblood?" the man said.

"I know enough to find the best saxophone player in this damn room," the pilot said, shoving in beside the officers.

"Handyman," the captain said. "We told you, stop playing guitar like Jimmie Rodgers and learn to play some real music and we might allow you to jam with us."

"Huddie Ledbetter," said Handyman. "That's what I'm going for."

"Shoot."

"I ain't worthy."

"No, you ain't."

They laughed again. Handyman removed his cap and looked up at Irene under his brows and winked. It made her angry for some reason, this awareness of his that she'd been watching him all along.

—

After their daily duty, the women were taken to a base for driving lessons. The 2½ ton GMCs were not exactly Buick sedans. The women were also trained in "first echelon" maintenance—they had to be mechanics as well. Changing a fifty-five-pound truck tire was a new one for Irene and Ellie, though Dorothy had changed more than a few tires in her day. The three of them were issued Zone 5 patches for the left shoulders of their uniforms. Proof that they were going across the Channel to the Continent if there was an Allied invasion.

That night, though she was exhausted, Irene could not sleep. She wrote by candlelight:

London, December 21, 1943

Gosfield Street, Number 27½

Dear Mother,
If you were wondering what I'm doing here…
He hit me.
Merry Christmas, Mother.

Good night, Irene

9

IT ALL CHANGED at dawn.

Mrs. Bridger handed them a note on blue paper. It was from Ellie.

> *So sorry. I just can't do this no more. You were mostly nice to me. But I can't die over here. I'm bad homesick I guess. Sorry to let you down. Come see me in Chicago when it's over.*
>
> *Best Wishes,*
> *Ski*

Irene and Dorothy read it together, without comment, and when they were done, Dorothy wadded the note and shoved it in her back pocket.

Mrs. Bridger wrung her hands as if she had betrayed them. "She summoned a cab and left without breakfast."

They thanked her and went out to the waiting car.

"Where's—?" the driver started to say.

"Shhh," Irene answered.

They rode to the hotel mostly in silence.

"Just like that," Dorothy finally said.

Irene simply looked out at London, hoping to memorize as many details of it as she could. "I always wanted to come here," she said.

"Never thought about it. Used to want to visit Chicago. Not doing it now. Damned quitter."

Irene patted Dorothy's knee.

"She's dead now and buried," Dorothy said. "Don't bring her up again."

Irene nudged her as the car slowed to a stop. "Here we are," she said.

Though she didn't want to admit it, Irene was disappointed when Handyman and Smitty didn't return that day, or the next, and soon she and Dorothy were reassigned.

—

They went wherever they were ordered. Weeks and weeks of rushing from duty to duty—back to Liverpool, greeting pilot crews arriving for deployment to air bases; from there to the London docks at the mouth of the Thames; and back to the officers' club, with an afternoon's duty at an American enlisted men's Donut Dugout club not far from Gosfield Street. In their spare time, they often delivered mail from the back of a truck.

Wherever they went, they were stars. Every GI wanted the Donut Dolly treatment. Just a flirt. A baseball score. Some jokes. A wink. They all dreamed of a dance. They drank the women's American accents like beer. They were all homesick, even the ones who didn't know they were. They were awkward and had Adam's apples and jug ears and ill-fitting uniforms and lots of big American teeth. The Brits were amazed by their teeth. No matter what the women did, the guys called them *sweetheart* or *honey* or *babe* or, worse, *sweet cheeks.* Those were the guys who stared at the women's chests or brushed too close or sneered at anything they said.

When they weren't on duty, Irene and Dorothy were delighted to spend time with their pals Phyl and Jill and Helen (now called *Hellcat* by the boys). Together, they joined forces with any other available gals from the fresh crews invading the city. It was their delight to roam the streets of London Town and Liverpool, snapping pictures and visiting those arcane chapels known as pubs. They'd been warned that some American soldiers lost their minds in London and dog-packed together in dark alleys. There had been some terrible scenes with English women that had been hinted at but never completely revealed. The women made sure to stay together. Jill and Dorothy each carried a roll of coins clutched in their fist. Hellcat had brass knuckles. Irene kept a steak knife tucked in the back of her belt.

The ruins and constant reconstruction of London were like movie sets to them. Not entirely real. Incomprehensible, really. As were the vehicles always driving on the wrong side of the street. But mostly they saw the boys. The endless precious tides of the boys. Our boys. Irene searched their faces, hoping for some sign of who would survive and who would be lost. But there was no sign. She refused to believe any of them could be evil. There was no way anybody could ever know what would befall any single one of them. No shadow. No light. Just smiles and laughter and no hint of what they knew had to come.

—

Their fresh orders came at night and Rusty Penney reappeared with a pair of jeeps on Gosfield Street at dawn. As the women came down the steps, he greeted them like a scratched record: "Good to see ya, good to see ya, good to see ya."

They were heading to their new home, he told them. The 457th Bombardment Group at the army air base, Glatton, in Cambridgeshire, two hours north of London. Home of B-17s. Their housing would be in the nearby town of Conington. By now they were accustomed to being moved. Already, nothing surprised them.

Mrs. Bridger came out to bid them a tearful goodbye and good luck. They hugged and pressed their remaining ration cards into her hands.

Rusty handed over the official papers. "Sorry about Big Red. Going home and all."

In the jeep Irene mouthed *Big Red* at Dorothy, who snickered.

It was a lovely day. They had their hair tied in scarves. If they didn't know there was a war going on, they would have thought they were on holiday. Irene was far from that stifling New York apartment. That was all that mattered.

Irene asked what Glatton was like, and over the road noise Rusty shouted that it was brand-new, the newest base in the UK. It had a village in its midst, and a farm. Behind the military gates. The village was actually called Conington, he said, but the Brits were worried the Yanks wouldn't understand their accents over the radio. Or some such flapdoodle. So they'd named Glatton after a town up the road. That's where Irene and Dorothy would be living.

"Scintillating, Russell," said Irene, slipping her cheaters over her eyes.

The Americans had apparently revamped and expanded an existing Royal Air Force base. There was a club with music and dances, a bar. And of course a lot of big-ass planes.

He swerved around a lorry. "It's like these bases come up overnight," he said. "None of these Brits can believe what a bunch of ol' boys with some tractors can do."

"That's how we win!" Dorothy shouted.

"Roger," he said, nodding. "Roger that."

American hilarity carried them along.

"There's a pub in Glatton, too," Rusty shouted. "Just in case you run out of booze between the base and your quarters."

"I'm flippin' my lid over here!" Dorothy lied.

"We'll get you a new crew member," Rusty promised.

"Actually, I'm bored," Dorothy said. "Let's play a game. Russell, name me some of the war machines we have over here. In alphabetical order."

"Ten-four, Dunford. You got your Alligator. Your Amblance. APC for sure. Got your Beachmaster."

Much more of this would lull Irene to sleep, she thought.

"Let's see," Rusty continued. "Got your Chaffee. That's a light tank, small gun. I already know you ain't partial to that. You like that big armament!"

"You are responsible for this," Irene whispered to Dorothy.

"Crab—that's a weird one, I tell no lies. Greyhound. Half-track.... And hell, can't forget the LST!"

Dorothy donned her sunglasses and smiled serenely.

"'Course," Rusty enthused, "that daggone Duck can't be ignored!"

"Duck," Irene reminded Dorothy.

—

"Welcome to the Midlands," Rusty the tour guide announced as they neared Glatton, seventy-odd miles later. Along the way he had thrilled Irene by pointing out the route of an ancient Roman road that was now partially covered by a country lane. They were driving through time.

They heard airplanes before they saw the base. Two guards at a booth waved them through. American flags and 457th standards flapped in the wind. The complex stood in an expanse of fields, former farmland given over to runways and hangars and the stink of fuel. It seemed as though a military invasion from the future had landed in the seventeenth century. Airplane hangars had gaping black mouths. The huge water tower, along with the Conington church tower in Glatton town, served as a guidepost to pilots. Off to their right lay the Aero Club. The first of the butterflies bounced drunkenly above the emerging wildflowers. Massive B-17s lurked all around, along with falcon-like Hurricanes and Mustangs and an evil-looking twin-tailed P-38. Lethal, every one of them. Except for the C-47 Gooney Birds, earnest and fat along the far side of the complex. "Them's taildraggers," Rusty informed them.

Farther off, in an enclave of its own, stood a mysterious bunker with a C-47, unmarked. "*OSS,*" he confided. "Office of Strategic Services. The top secret boys. They never come out. If you're cleared by the FBI, then you'll go in and serve them."

"We're making donuts for spies," Irene gushed.

"Just don't call 'em *spies* when the FBI gets here," Rusty said.

Nothing else held their attention as much as the bombers, which were so large that they dwarfed the coverall-clad men scurrying about the aircraft. Blocks of the big planes stood together in the yellow fields to the west and east and north of the bunker and hangar complexes.

"See our tail insignia? The circle with a *U* in it," Rusty said. "That's our wild bunch."

A green military tractor came toward them pulling a series of trailers laden with bombs. Laughing ground-crew boys and soldiers in khaki sat astraddle the bombs, riding them like little boys on a fairground ride. One of them saw the women and shouted, "Hey, hon—hop aboard! Take a ride!" General hooting from the others.

Dorothy stuck two fingers in her mouth and unleashed the world's loudest whistle. "I love a parade!" she hollered. She galloped over and jumped aboard to high fives and cheers, and vanished into a hangar.

"She's the real McCoy, that one," Irene said.

Rusty assiduously deployed message discipline and lit a cigarette rather than comment.

But the bombers. The bombers were the thing. Irene was both thrilled by them and afraid of them. They seemed alive. Deep within, her response was to the unmistakable power arrayed before her. The gorgeous danger of these machines. The B-17 cockpits had dark windshields that reminded her of eyes regarding her coolly, as a dragon might. She was small as a sparrow standing there.

Dorothy strolled up to them, whistling. "That was fun," she announced. "Riding around with those bowleggers."

Beyond the resting line of bombers, a second string of monsters, preparing for a mission, was coughing smoke from those huge engines, propellers starting to rotate. Carts and service trucks hustled out of the way as the flaps on the big wings lifted and dropped, and the tail rudders wagged. Those tails! Tall as apartment buildings. Men in coveralls with heavy sound baffles on their ears signaled the pilots with colored batons held high. Forward, left, right. Slow.

Backfires made Irene jump until they didn't. Belches of smoke bounded away in the breeze like flying black sheep. Wind socks stood firm off their stanchions. Men appeared in the windows and the open machine-gun ports in the sides of the planes. Easy to see why they were called *Flying Fortresses*. These machines were castles; they had open battlements in their sides filled with archers who manned machine guns rather than bows and arrows. Twin guns sticking out of the rear ends like stingers. A ball turret beneath each, rotating. Was Smitty in one of them?

It seemed impossible that one of these contraptions could lift into the sky. A side gunner waved at Irene. She waved back, calling out to him, though not even Dorothy beside her could hear her voice now. The ground crew yanked wooden chocks away from their great tires, and one after another they moved away from their angled parking spaces. Each bomber's four propellers were metal blurs.

The planes were not castles after all, she thought, but dragons—some of them painted the green and khaki of the military, but others bright silver, reflecting the blue of the sky and the yellow and green of the fields, the silver ones blinding her with fluid reflections of the sun that wobbled and seemed to flow like mercury down their flanks. Surely the crews should be sitting atop these creatures. Then each plane with men and bombs and bullets in its belly paused at the mouth of the runway and turned, like some living creature looking around itself, until its engines changed in pitch and volume—oh the volume!—and it bore down the runway, with Irene plugging her ears, and claimed the sky.

The fighter planes came to life as well in this roaring and followed the line of waiting bombers to the runway. One after the other the lumbering behemoths in front of them ran down the long tarmac, gathered themselves, and leaped. A leap that became a glide, straight over the far trees. The drone of the engines settled into a musical tone, as of a cataclysmic flight of iron bees far above. All these engines harmonizing, creating a sky-wide chord. Each new bomber joined the flight as the others circled high above, staging, awaiting their fighter consort with its crazy speed and its own steel stingers.

It was the most spectacular thing Irene had ever seen. The shock of the ship sinking, the train bombing...no. This was almost religious. Even Dorothy had a slack-jawed expression. They were going to save the world.

The long note of the engines played inside Irene's belly, making every part of her tingle. The high armada seemed to fill the entire sky, then rotated east and drifted away, both dark and brilliantly silver, until nothing was left in its wake but empty blue etched with contrails and filled with the racket of crows.

Irene staggered, drunk on the immeasurable height of the air. She steadied herself by leaning on Dorothy, then had to go sit in the jeep. "Oh my God," she said to herself.

The shushing of wind returned, like the sound of a faraway seashore. She ran her hands through her hair and pulled it back. In the distance, a runway connected two long landing strips. She was startled to see a small white house and barn in the triangular patch of land between them. Two cows ruminated behind a fence. And out in the field, a farmer rode an ancient red tractor.

Russell appeared by the jeep. "He didn't want to sell his land."

This struck her as unbearably funny.

"He's kind of a grouch, but he makes a tasty cheese."

Russell, you dolt.

"This wonderful, wonderful world," she said.

—

Their Clubmobile was another old Lend-Lease London bus negotiated for by the U.S. It was painted dark gray and parked in yellow weeds by the Aero Club, stationed close to the briefing buildings where the crews got their orders and classified maps and flight plans. Smoke came from the windows of the Aero Club. The women could smell cooking meat. Male voices and gruff bursts of laughter rolled out the open doors. An incense of fuel and exhaust, along with mown hay and clover, also drifted in the air.

"You'll be reporting for duty tomorrow," Rusty said, all business again. "First thing in the morning. *Before* first thing. We'll be waiting for that mission that just left."

"Do I smell hamburgers?" Dorothy said.

"All day," he replied.

"Hoopty-doo!" Before she headed into the chow hall, she grabbed Rusty's arm. "What's with the old bus? Where's my truck?" she asked. "I want my truck."

"Don't worry, the Twenty-Ninth will bring y'all's Clubmobile. Fresh off the boat."

He was gone into the club before she could respond. Dorothy shook her head and went inside after him.

Irene had barely heard her. She was looking out beyond the huge base—this desert of concrete and blacktop, all runways scored with black rubber smears from a thousand landings—at this green. These stone fences. Those far villages. These stands of flouncing trees. That heather. Those low rolling hills. This vast meadow. She tied her scarf back over her hair and donned her dark cheaters and breathed it in. Nearby, bicycles leaned against several walls. She climbed aboard one and took off down the runway. Nobody raised an alarm.

The English air fluttered her clothes. She pumped hard and flew all the way down to the end where the first turn was. She skidded around the turn and stood as she pedaled to pick up speed. Imagined her liftoff. She could hear the motor of the tractor and the farmer's dog barking as it ran along the fence. She waved at the farmer but he ignored her. Smoke rose from the farmhouse chimney.

Rusty had come back out to check on her and stood by the Aero Club with his hands on his hips and a smoke in his mouth, watching her, no doubt thinking she'd gone daffy.

She rattled up, winded, her face bright pink, and leaped off the saddle. "I'm famished, Russell!" She dropped the bike and rushed inside.

Rusty just rubbed his eyes and took a puff. "Dames," he said with a sigh, picking up the bike and leaning it against the wall.

—

After dinner, Rusty drove them off the base and through trees for a couple of miles.

"Welcome to Glatton town," he said.

They came upon narrow streets and the pub he'd mentioned, which was white, with more bikes leaning against its wall. Lazy dogs wagged their tails and wandered along beside the vehicles. They passed another stone church: another guidepost for the pilots. The churchyard below the bell tower was filled with mossy gravestones. The houses, white like the pub, had thatched roofs and hedges, with roses crawling up trellises.

"How delightful," Irene said.

They parked beside a long house with its shoulder turned to the street. Rusty set the ratchet hand brake. In the silence came the sounds of distant wood chopping, and dogs, and a chicken fussing. Somebody seemed to be practicing a French horn. And farther away, the basso profundo growl of massed engines. From the pub flowed the happy wheeze of a squeeze-box. The thatch on the roofs looked like wigs.

"Welcome home," Rusty said.

They went into the back courtyard, where a little black-and-white spaniel charged out and fell at their feet, wagging and kicking at their ankles with her back feet. All three of them were instantly slain by the dog.

"I've never lived under a thatched roof," Irene said, as sparrows pulled small bits from the thatch and flew into the trees.

Trellises formed arches at the edges of the flagstones, and they were vined with spent roses, once fat as cabbages, now wilted and giving way to the tight buds of the early spring. The house stood beside small woods, then a meadow.

"Uncle Sam has leased it for you," Rusty noted.

"I love it," Irene said.

"The owner left a note to not tamper with the canvas in the ceilings. Keeps rats and squirrels from falling on you if they get in the thatch."

Irene found this provision hilarious.

"No electric," Rusty added. "Oil lamps and candles."

"I'm going to steal a generator and change that," Dorothy vowed.

The windows were narrow and covered with white curtains. Irene was delighted by the rounded dormers above, peeking from the thatch like eyes with their brows raised in surprise.

"That's mine," she said, pointing to one small balcony above the front door on the left.

Dorothy didn't care—she could tell her room had a better balcony.

A single American fighter screamed over them, banked around the bell tower, and slid down toward the air base.

"Get used to that," Rusty said.

Irene loved the Glatton house and wished she could stay there forever. It had started life, they were told, as two thatched huts that grew together over the centuries until they were fancied and harried into a grand T-shaped country house. When she wasn't at the air base, she haunted the churchyard across the road. That spring, she wandered the small woods, where she found hedgehogs and rabbits, as if she were ten years old again. The small stream behind the property had minnows and salamanders and piping frogs and dragonflies. Wasps made mud balls on its banks and bees hung fat and voluble in the lavender. A pair of ducks ignored her until she brought them her breakfast rolls. Then they were loyal, if temporary, friends. Crows flew their circuits and seemed to insult her. They were too shy to land. This amused her. An errant cow wandered along the stream—it had a bell under its chin. Irene was so happy hearing that rusty music. She never knew if it had wandered away from the grim farmer's mid-runway kingdom. It ate grass and flowers from her hand.

In the house she had found an old collection of John Clare's poems. The troubled nineteenth-century poet had walked miles in these same kinds of places. And then was locked away in a madhouse. She loved him. He touched her heart as though he were the brother she'd never had. She carried the book on her own careless rambles. It was a way, she thought, to set him free again.

She read verses among the trees. To the trees. And to the birds, to the rabbits, to the deer she believed must be hiding nearby.

Dorothy watched her from her bedroom window one day. *Irene's gone crazy*, she thought, as her friend declaimed to the birds:

> *I long for scenes where man hath never trod*
> *A place where woman never smiled or wept*
> *There to abide with my Creator, God,*
> *And sleep as I in childhood sweetly slept,*
> *Untroubling and untroubled where I lie*
> *The grass below—above the vaulted sky.*

Dorothy threw open her window. "Hey, Lady Shakespeare!" she hollered. "Lookin' for Romeo?"

Irene glanced back at her, then leaped over the tiny stream and vanished among the white trunks of birch trees. Dorothy slammed her window.

Irene's secret notebooks hid austere sketches of stone walls, gravestones, a meadowlark that had commandeered the low railing of her balcony, with small bursts of text in and around the drawings. Pencil sketches of soldiers looking up at her in her serving window, rakish children in the streets of London. Later, she added this title to the first page of the first volume of her notebooks: *Footloose Woman and Free—My Careless Rambles.*

10

MAIL FOUND THEM, even at Glatton. Soldiers simply addressed their letters to the crew of the *Rapid City* and wrote "c/o ARC" or "c/o U.S. Army" on the envelopes, and the letters managed to make their way to the women.

"I used to think our service was foolish," Dorothy confessed. "Until you showed me this."

"What did you think we were going to do?" said Irene, who held the letter she'd just shared with Dorothy.

"Kill Nazis."

Well, they were not doing that, but the letter encouraged them that they were making a difference.

> *Dear Irene, Ellie and Dorothy:*
> *You won't remember me, but I will never forget you. I came off the troop ship in Liverpool more frightened than I had ever been in my life. I did not think I had the wherewithal to disembark, much less march into war. I was trying to hide my terror from the other guys, but all I could think of was home. My hands were shaking. And then I saw you. I saw friendly faces. And you were kind to me, welcoming me. I know I was just a face among hundreds of faces, but you looked in my eye and gave me some coffee and made me laugh. I just wanted you to know, I have carried you in my mind every day since. Every time I see a Clubmobile, I hope it's yours.*
>
> *In gratitude,*
> *A Soldier (Bradley)*

They started their work every morning at eight o'clock. Russell brought a jeep or they rode bikes. It was joyous to coast down the gentle slope toward the base. Once there, they opened up the bus, hooked it to power to get the coffee started, fired up the cooker, and got to weighing that damned water.

They did their duty while maintaining strict hilarity. The flight crews and pilots and gunners and ground-crew members were the happiest men they had ever met. Officers were distracted and too busy to banter, and most of them avoided donuts to keep their trim physiques, but they were hell-bent on coffee. Ball-turret gunners were smaller men big on chewing gum. They ate more donuts than the pilots. Irene started to believe some of them were hoping to get too fat to fit inside those deathtrap metal blisters dangling off the bellies of the bombers.

"How do you fellas pee up there?" Dorothy asked one of them.

"Carry a bottle."

"Sorry I asked."

Rose, a British Red Cross lass from the lunch club, joined them to assist with things like fetching water, translating any odd UK accents, and hauling the bags of sugar and flour and baking soda and jugs of water to the mixers. Irene was greatly relieved that the bus had futuristic automatic donut-cooking machines rather than the frustrating manual dough-crankers of her training days.

They slowly adopted the vocabulary of the ARC Corps. Of course, donuts were *sinkers.* Cans of Carnation milk were *steel cows* or *tin cows.* The serving windows had shutters that seasoned Dollies who were hip to the jive called *flaps.* The layout of the galley was tight—Irene and Dorothy learned the steps of the dance quickly. The flaps were on the starboard side of the bus, where the counter was. Coffee makers fore and aft. A working sink behind them. Shelves and racks in every available corner and under every counter. They were hooked to a generator so they didn't burn petrol running the machines.

Ninety-nine percent of their clients were American boys, with a few Brit mechanics and drivers thrown in. Dorothy dictated that the crews line up aft of the counter to keep the flow moving. She couldn't abide the chaos of a human traffic jam.

The bomber crews were the stars. Even the grungiest gunner from Canarsie or Sheboygan was a hero. And they all knew the Clubmobile ladies might be the last women they ever saw, which made them pause for long chats that the ladies didn't have time for.

The bomber crews called themselves the Fire Ball Squadron—not, as Dorothy and Irene first assumed, due to their combat prowess, but because the unofficial base cocktail was a fireball, that weirdly delicious mixture of low-octane whiskey and cinnamon oil. The mechanics had them, the Aero Club sold them, and the runway managers hid bottles of fireball in their desks. Irene and Dorothy both accepted shot after shot until they were bouncing off each other and cursing like the mechanics and cooking oblong mutant batter crustations rather than pastries. But after enough toasts, nobody seemed to notice or care.

The hours went quickly because there was never a moment without work. And when that moment did roll around, hijinks broke out. The base had a camera crew that snapped promotional shots constantly. These were for *Stars and Stripes,* the military newspaper, and for the newspapers back home. Scores of them went to parents and grandparents and buddies and wives. The camera crew was abetted by Hollywood film crews that shot miles of film for the newsreels in the Stateside movie houses. More often than not, when a camera was in sight, the boys wanted to pose with the ladies because they were such an unusual treat. Irene sat on a hundred laps in the Aero Club's makeshift portrait studio. Dorothy grumbled, "They are like kids wanting to pose with Santa Claus at the department store." So many boys snuck a kiss. She never kissed them back, no matter how they begged.

With more than fifty air bases scattered around the UK, the handful of Clubmobile crews were stretched thin. There was no more than one crew at any base and the women were often reassigned at a moment's notice when a jeep showed up to collect them. It was the *Rapid City*'s fate to be the only crew associated with the officers' club in London, and regularly at least one of them was sent back to serve a heady helping of high spirits.

The *Cheyenne* was assigned to neighboring airfield Polebrook. When Jill told Irene that Clark Gable was stationed there, Irene coerced Dorothy into volunteering for a regular Monday shift at Polebrook. Every Monday, after the breakfast service was done at Glatton, Dorothy would requisition a jeep and they would speed to the Polebrook gates, reapplying their lipstick on the way. Once there, they would try to look casual and charming while helping the *Cheyenne* crew, eagerly scanning the faces of every GI in line, hoping to spot the movie star.

After a few weeks of this double duty, Phyl sidled up to Irene one afternoon and said, "Girl, he never comes."

From the other end of the truck, Jill laughed. "He's a movie star, he has to watch his weight!"

"That's what we get for trying to help out," Irene said, stung, and the women all laughed.

—

Shortly after first arriving at the Glatton air base, Dorothy was ordered to report to London and begin two weeks of training in the fine points of piloting a Clubmobile. While she was gone, their pals in the *Cheyenne* rolled in and lined up with them like circus elephants, nose to tail. Irene was so jealous that they had a handsome GMC with a dark gray galley on the back that she could just spit. But it made life better in two ways: the *Cheyenne* had a record player, and Phyllis would play swingin' records over their loudspeaker, and Jill came over to help Irene in her bus, which meant she did not have to work it alone. There were days when winter did not want to loosen its grip. Outside, unexpected snow fell on the fields and everything seemed gray. But inside the Clubmobiles, it was warm and bright. Though the others grumbled, Irene actually enjoyed the wintry respite—something about needing an overcoat and gloves reminded her of New York.

As the missions picked up, a typical service day started before dawn, with a clean bus and brewing java. The fryers had to be connected to power right away to have time to melt the congealed grease before frying donuts for the first sortie. It was a production line and they hoped to have several dozen donuts done and racked up before the flight crews arrived. They didn't need that many donuts because the morning boys had already wolfed down their scrambled eggs and sausage. It was more about the coffee. The most important part of the service was their blessing, their flirtation, their "Be careful! We'll be here when you get back!"

The time the flight crews left depended on logistics that Irene and Jill had no knowledge of. But it took just a couple of weeks before they began to understand the patterns on the base and could surmise what kind of mission it might be. They had heard enough stories from the pilots and crews to be able to read the situation. A sudden influx of fighters meant an especially dangerous mission. A dawn liftoff suggested a very distant target. Midday takeoff meant either a shorter run or a very long journey that required the cover of darkness. The Clubmobile crew had to adjust their days and nights accordingly.

They were usually done with the first wave by nine or ten in the morning. They scrubbed the galley clean, dumped the old coffee, greeted the water truck that refilled their tanks, then hoofed it over to the club for a leisurely sandwich or steak-and-kidney pie. Dorothy was pleased that they served Moxie, her favorite soda, which Irene thought tasted like cough syrup. On the days they were tired of each other, they sat in opposite corners of the room. Then they'd take a rolling cart to the officers' command center and deliver coffee and sinkers. The mechanics hit the serving flaps around noon, when some fighter pilots or Gooney Bird delivery flights came through. One of the women could nap while the other passed out what she had on hand.

The difficult job began in the afternoons, when everyone watched for returning missions. The base became tense, silent, with all eyes on the sky as they waited to see who didn't come home. They searched for smoke trailing across the sky, which signaled B-17s missing engines. These planes were uncanny. They could fly with huge holes blown through their fuselages. They could fly with half a tail. They could fly with pieces of their wings missing. Everyone had heard the legend about the Fortress that flew back across the English Channel with no cockpit—no front end at all. A ghost ship. And the story was that it had landed itself.

They all waited deep into the night. More than once, Irene and Dorothy never got back to their billet. They waited until sunrise and began the morning service all over again. On those days, in spite of their efforts to buck each other up, they burned their hands and scalded themselves and cursed, but still called each guy *honey,* or *brother,* or *babe.* By noon they would be asleep on the floor.

It had not taken them long after arriving at Glatton to understand that their service was not truly about the donuts and coffee. They had seen enough boys fail to return from a morning flight. The real service was that their faces, their voices, their send-off might be the final blessing from home for some of these young pilots. The enormity of this trivial-seeming job became clearer every day.

—

The movie director John Ford, already famous for *Stagecoach* and *The Grapes of Wrath,* had sent a small camera crew to be embedded at Glatton—they lived on the ground floor of Irene and Dorothy's house. The women imagined the day John Ford himself might appear, but he never did.

The camera crew had converted the downstairs into a smoking lounge and whiskey bar. They weren't interested in ducks or trees. They were there to film the war. Socks and boots and abandoned bottles littered the floor. Neither Irene nor Dorothy intended to clean up after them. Fellow cameramen ambled through town to grab some footage of the big planes and the dashing crews. The house became an unofficial party center with officers, visitors, neighbors, and even celebrity author John Beverley Nichols, who lived down the street. It was a welcoming respite for anyone who could ride a bike up the hill from the air base.

One of the party boys was Gilbert B. Peek, a photographer from the *Los Angeles Times* who arrived in the spring. He snapped pictures of

Irene and himself and the roses and the church tower. While Dorothy found Irene's fascination with the old Norman graves morbid, he found it quite enchanting. Irene felt that the stones, faded by time so that the names were almost lost to centuries of rain and wind, were some kind of contact with the beyond. She could whisper to the forgotten in their quiet garden. She was certain she dreamed in their language. Gilbert caught a strangely romantic shot of her with her hand upon an eighteenth-century date and her head bowed, her dark hair just long enough to hide her profile. Just a slight hint of her pale cheek visible. She might have been a ghost herself, or a maiden in an old poem. He later published it in an American magazine and for a brief moment it was a celebrated shot.

—

At their end of day, Irene and Dorothy usually biked the nearly three miles home. Crows drifted above them. The women chatted and scattered chickens and accrued honor guards of barking dogs. There wasn't a night they didn't pull up outside the pub for a game of darts and a session of gossip and sometimes some kidney pie or toad-in-the-hole. On a good day, they ate fish-and-chips. Dorothy had scrounged up air-base coveralls and wore them day and night with a rag tied around her hair or a scarf at her neck. Irene opted for dark trousers and white blouses, with the official ARC dark wool sweater vest on brisk afternoons.

Whenever a preflight check-in was taking place, someone came for them in a jeep. Call time then was four in the morning, and it was out of the question to ride bicycles in the dark. Hungover or not, the ladies had to be aboard the Clubmobile and working fast to attend to the crews being briefed for their secret missions. Coffee had to be hot by 5:00. Sinkers right behind.

Dorothy took to calling these mornings *church,* and they did feel like religious services, with the men heading into peril, to do deadly work, and everyone knowing but not acknowledging that they might never return. On these mornings, the hilarity ceased. Everyone was serious, though a few of the boys still threw a wink or two.

The men went in the briefing room with steaming cups, and they came back out somber and quiet. The pilots and copilots and bombardiers were often preoccupied and almost sullen. The ladies didn't hold it against them. In fact, on these mornings Irene and Dorothy often fought through the sting of tears to get the service out to them. Irene wrote in her notebook, *Knowing we might never see their faces again,* but had to cease mid-sentence and didn't dare look at that page again.

Gunners were a bit more cheerful. They never failed to bring the big laughs. The ground crews came along raising quiet hell and irritating Irene and Dorothy, who were frantic to get the next round ready for the flight crews, while those sleepy sack rats were always running late and looking for a chance to goldbrick. Dorothy called them *the gazoonies.*

Then came the somber ritual of everyone going to the edge of the runway to bear witness to the liftoff. This never failed to make Irene and Dorothy cry. It was something about the roar of the planes. The drama of the leaving. But it was also the unbearably touching sight of those young men climbing aboard. Doing chin-ups through the underbelly hatches of the planes. How they'd curl up and into the fuselage like athletes. How they would sometimes hug one another briskly. How they'd take a knee like a football squad for a flash picture, all pilot's caps and knit hats, leather jackets and gloves, oxygen masks and bright smiles in the gloom. And the fighter pilots walking to their planes alone, slapping the ground-crew men on the back or shoulder and climbing into their cockpits after scrambling onto a wing. How many of those men winked at them or nodded at them or even blew them a kiss. Every single one of them giving it his all to look undaunted.

After the missions, the broken and the dead were tenderly lowered from the open hatches, dark blood dripping into the gravel.

Dear Rapid City Ladies!
I'm home now. Got that million dollar wound they talk about. I guess I got my foot knocked off, but I don't remember it. Isn't that eccentric? I was with the Devil Doll on a sortie to Bremen, and right before that flight you ladies took good care of me. I dream

about you all, and I pray for you every Sunday though I'm not that good about the God business. Just wanted you to know I'm OK and thinking about you with gratitude.

All Love—Just a Gunner

PS Esp. you, Stretch.

These days were hellishly long. Perhaps it was the worry. They at least had seen the faces of every man in every plane. They had seen the chewed-up bombers limping back across the sky. They had watched the wounded peeled out and laid in ambulances. They had seen the plane come in on fire and explode in the grass. Nobody had to tell them what it was like up there. And nobody would. There was a silence they all shared, and the Dollies, like the nurses, didn't feel it was their place to try to pierce it.

Once the planes were gone, the women had quiet hours of waiting. Imagining the worst. Keeping the gazoonies and officers in coffee and sinkers. Interpreting the faces of the flight-control team to see if the news was good or bad. Most of these runs lasted well into the night. They pitched in at the Aero Club, and at the infirmary, helping to clean up, prepare bandages. They washed their bus. They were free to bicycle back to the village—there was never a lack of bikes. They'd know when the bombers were returning because they could be heard for miles. But their free time was fretful, and they didn't often head back to their rooms. A pall lay over the entire base. If the planes didn't come back by midnight, everyone was on duty, to wait out the hours, watching the sky and straining their ears, afraid their fortresses might have been shot to pieces.

The *Rapid City* duo set up in the debriefing shed. They had a table ready there with sinkers and hot-coffee urns and often a hug or a smooch as the airmen dropped off their parachutes and went into the big room to report to the OSS officers.

It was finally time for Irene and Dorothy to receive their clearance. The FBI agents found them there in the debriefing shed. One at a time, the agents took them into a small office and grilled them. Contacts, political beliefs, family, voting record, affiliations, religious beliefs. Piles of trivia jotted onto forms on clipboards. Lots of cigarettes. When the pair were cleared, they were allowed access to the secret compound. After that, they wheeled a hot urn and a few dozen donuts down there every morning, in addition to their other duties. They neither confirmed nor denied whether anyone was actually in the compound, nor if they interacted in any way with said possible occupants.

—

By late spring, the scuttlebutt was that something major was coming. Nobody talked to the women about it. Least of all the flyboys. Spring was knocking at the door. The U.S. had been in the war for more than two years. Churchill droned and cajoled on the radio. The skies above the base were crowded. The docks were bustling with fresh shipments of GIs. News came daily from Africa and Italy. Everyone in England was thinking about what lay across the Channel.

There were several calls for donut duty at the ports. Dorothy and Irene sensed a kind of vibration in the great web of war stretched over them all. Their sister crews based around the isles sensed it, too, and the two of them heard things here and there. Irene didn't know what was gossip and what wasn't anymore. Pilots told her about foo-fighter ghost lights that chased them around and sat on their wings.

To help break the tension they all were feeling, Irene decided they needed a talent show. She suddenly became the Queen of Organization, a person Dorothy hadn't generally witnessed inside the truck. Having figured out the workings of the military, Irene first went to the ground-crew chiefs, then to the club and mess-hall managers, then to the nurses and the medics. Once that wave of excitement had swelled, she went to the gunners and the navigators. And finally, the pilots and the base commander. It was a question of morale, she said; it would be therapeutic care for the wounded, she argued. Her project was okayed and went into the base bulletin the following morning.

"Voilà!" Irene announced, thumping the bulletin advert with her finger before hopping out of the galley and rushing off on her show-biz rounds.

"Shorty beats all," Dorothy said to Rose, who they were glad to still have assisting them on the *Rapid City,* because it was all too much work for two. Together they swept and scrubbed the bus.

"I find her quite delightful," Rose said.

"I could listen to you talk all day."

Rose laughed. "You sound like a cowboy talking picture to me. I quite like it."

"You going to do it?"

"Sorry?"

"The talent show."

"I can shake a leg for the boys, I reckon."

Dorothy had no interest whatsoever, but kept her critique to a low mumble.

"I'm the third girl on the bus, aren't I?" Rose said. "Got to be a team player."

That day the category was born: Third Girl on the Bus.

—

Back at Glatton that afternoon, a silver streak roared overhead. They peeked out to watch it. A P-51 Mustang—from London, given the direction it had been flying.

"Listen to that music," Dorothy said, hopping out of the back and craning her neck as the fighter banked and burned a curve toward Conington. "Rolls-Royce, twelve cylinders!" she cried.

Irene was amused that of all the things Dorothy could have celebrated, a motor made her yell.

The plane buzzed the church tower and came back, did a low pass and banked again, then screamed into a climb.

"Hotdogger," said Rose. "Isn't that what you Americans say?"

"Well," boasted Irene, "*I* do not."

Up, up, bank to the right, and drop. His landing gear came out of his wings. He waggled twice and settled in for a delicate landing, his wheels chirping twice and small puffs of smoke behind him. The ladies applauded.

The plane rolled in from the landing strip and spun into a parking space past the hangars. Crew guys trotted out to it and chocked the wheels. The blades of the plane's four propellers blurred and feathered and slowly went still. The canopy popped. They rolled a ladder to him, but he climbed out and hopped off the wing.

"It's your boyfriend," Dorothy said. "Better put some Sen-Sen in your mouth."

Irene ignored her but then the pilot smiled at her from across the tarmac. Even from that distance, his teeth were unfairly bright. He had dead aim.

"Incoming," Dorothy said and strolled off, whistling. She and Rose resumed their positions in the Clubmobile.

Irene looked after them, and when she turned back, the pilot was looming over her.

"Hey, stranger," he said.

"Do I know you?"

He rubbed his chin. Squinted at her. "You're the one that gave me food poisoning in London, right?" He tipped her a small one-fingered salute, then stepped past her but paused and spoke over his shoulder: "Say, word is you're throwin' a talent show up here. I'm going to give it a shot." He didn't look back as he sauntered into the mess hall.

Dorothy and Rose were busy inside the bus. When Irene climbed aboard, she said, "Oh be quiet."

—

The *Cheyenne* crew arrived with their bus. Phyl, Jill, and Hellcat would be joining Irene and Dorothy at their thatched-roof house, where they would have to share some tight accommodations in the attic room, but they were beyond delighted to be living with Hollywood royalty.

The camera crew made them endless rounds of improvised cocktails and regaled them with tales of movie stars and starlets and their bad behavior. ("Clark Gable? You kiddin' me? Don't even start with Clark Gable.") Laughter overtook the courtyard, even when the women rehearsed their dance moves. Rose rode over on her bike. They were five, since Dorothy would have nothing to do with it. Her concession was to watch the routine, but she muttered constantly. "Flashing gams at horny sonsabitches," she noted while sipping an improvised Manhattan in a GI mess-kit cup.

One evening, after rehearsal, Irene tossed her notebook in a satchel and nabbed a bike and wobbled on down to the pub. She wanted to gather her thoughts for the big show. When she pulled up to the door, she could tell which bicycles had been ridden from the base because their front tires pointed at the town, while the local population left their steeds with handlebars aimed toward the base. One learned to read the language of every place day by day, an observation she paused to jot in her notebook.

She stepped inside and took a glass of white wine to a small table in the corner and continued jotting: *Any place on earth speaks its own language. A language of accents and shadows, of birds and the various barkings of dogs in the night. Every alley, I have found, speaks in the discordant cries of its cats. In the colors of the walls and the vines upon the gravestones. Our lives are written in laughter and bicycles.* It had nothing to do with her talent show, but that was okay.

Then the door flew open and her fighter pilot appeared, backlit by a sunset, as if on some tawdry movie lot. He was accompanied by his Negro friends from the Grosvenor, in London.

"Make way for the Red Ball Express!" they cried.

"Ignore these truck drivers," the pilot said. "You got a killer-diller American ace right here."

American soldiers threw him salutes. The Brits kept on talking and throwing darts.

"Boys," the hotshot continued, "I'd like you to meet Captain 'Honeyman' Walker, the best sax player in the war."

Well, hell, Irene said to herself. She put her pen away and closed the notebook.

"Just came back from Belgium, boys!" the pilot cried. "Flew in on fumes. Had to crawl out on the wing over the Channel and pour whiskey in the tank!"

Captain Walker guffawed, shook his head. "If you believe that," he said, "you're dumber than you look."

"More bollocks," the barkeep said.

The Brits paused their dart games and in a jocular tone hollered, "Go home, ya bastard!"

Irene sipped her wine, trying to hide behind the glass just a little.

"You look like you need a pint," the barkeep said to the pilot.

"Draw me a stout," he said. "I'll be at the table over there with that young lady."

Oh no. So she had not avoided detection.

The flyboy pulled a chair over and sat down across from her, spreading his legs halfway across the floor. He dropped his cap on the table. "Did you miss me?" he said.

"I don't believe we've met," she lied.

"Met you twice. After that magical moment on the runway, I think we've got some history."

The barkeep dropped off the stout and slapped the pilot's shoulder.

The pilot said, as he leaned forward, "I've missed you so much."

She laughed through her nose, hoping it showed the right level of derision. "Pish tosh," she said, followed by a strategic sip of wine. "Is that the best you've got?"

He scratched his cheek, squinted at her, then took a nice bite of the stout. "You know you missed me, lady. Don't tease a war hero."

Was this his line of BS that went around the world? She dramatically stifled a yawn with the back of her hand. He watched her over the rim of his pint.

She tapped her upper lip. "Foam," she murmured.

He actually blushed as he wiped it off.

"You've got a speck of lipstick on your front tooth," he said. "Want me to get it?"

She grimaced and swiped at her mouth with her napkin. She saw him smiling into his beer. *Damn it.* She'd surrendered a point without his even having to try.

"I heard you donut girls are the life of the party around here."

She sipped her wine with profound ennui. "I'm hardly a girl, dear boy. I am a Red Cross warrior queen."

"Boy howdy!" he said, fake hick now. "Hey, I didn't catch your name in London."

"I didn't pitch it."

He made a small sound in his throat that she took for approval and fished a slim silver cigarette case out of his jacket. He let a chuckle slip and gestured toward her with the case, raising his eyebrows.

"Oh no, thank you ever so," she said and hid behind another sip of wine.

"These are somethin' you haven't tried, I'll bet you ten dollars. From Europe, all sweet with rum and lavender. I feel like a girl every time I light one."

"Well, you do have luxuriant lashes. Do you have a particular salon you favor?"

"Oh stop." He offered her the open case and she took one and he took one and then he popped open a Zippo and lit her up first. "What a gentleman, right?"

"Only a cad would make a point of it. But I can forgive you this once. You're learning."

He savored the candy-awful cigarette. His Adam's apple bounced slightly. "I'm Hans, by the way."

"What kind of name is that for an American pilot?"

He stretched, blew a ring above her head. "Mine."

"Irene. Irene Woodward." She tipped her head his way.

"Hans Michael Henricus Vanderwey." He shrugged. "I come from pioneers. Settlers. They call me Hands. And Handyman."

"Is that a pilot thing?" she said. The conversation was not exactly scintillating. But the way he looked at her—straight in her eyes.

"I guess I'm good with my hands. You can call on me anytime and I'll get the job done."

"That sounds faintly naughty."

He actually smirked in a by-golly fashion.

"*Handyman,*" she said. "So... so masculine." She smiled very slightly, almost dismissively, a move that she knew drove some men crazy. Then she made a little muscle and growled.

He stared at his hands.

"How many kills?" she said, floating a little on the wine.

"Thirteen," he said to the tabletop. He seemed interested in his knuckles.

"I'm sorry," she said. "I didn't mean to embarrass you."

"I'm just a guy driving around in the sky killing other poor guys who are trying to kill me."

It set her back a tiny bit. "Don't tell me you feel sorry for them."

"We're all the same up there, Irene. It's hard to explain." He sat back a bit and took a drink. Let the foam slither down the glass and enter his mouth. Wiped his lips with the back of his hand. "You're all alone up there," he said quietly, seeming to wish he was anywhere else for a moment. "And you know that they are, too. And there is nothing friendly anywhere." He stared at his hands on the table.

Irene noticed he was intentionally not making eye contact with her.

"Y'know, whenever I fly to this base, I watch for that church tower. It tells me I'm safe, I'm home. I can land and walk away from the sky."

It had turned somber awfully fast. Irene instinctively switched into Clubmobile mode. "But you're an ace up there, Handyman. Just like in the movies, right?"

"Miss Irene, I do my job the best I can. I'm just a cowboy from Oregon."

Their duet seemed to be satisfying both of them.

"You really are a cowboy?" she asked.

"Born and bred."

"You don't sound like a cowboy."

"Only when I want to, ma'am. And you're a fancy city lady, and you do sound like one of those."

"I don't know if *lady*'s the word."

He seemed to like that. "Where from?" he said.

"New York. Can't you tell?"

He shook his head. "Never been. I knew it had to be someplace fancy, though."

She finished her wine.

"But if I'd known that's where you were," he said, "I woulda gone to look for you before we ever got over here."

She crossed her ankles. "I'm going to have trouble with you," she said, stubbing out her awful cigarette.

He seemed to be trying to figure out the color of her eyes. He raised a finger to the barkeep, then pointed at Irene and waggled his finger between them. She tried to demur, but Handyman just smiled some more. When he smiled, he looked about sixteen.

"Miss Irene?" he said. "London? That morning? Honestly, I never did forget you."

"Handyman," she said, sighing, "you really must do better than that."

He nodded and stared at the table. "I'll work on it," he said.

It had happened quite suddenly, but the sun that had been setting behind him when he came in was now gone. He was heading back to a bunk at the base, he told Irene. He handed over some British bills to the barman.

"Give 'em hell, mate," the man said.

"You know I will," he said, and waved at Honeyman Walker, who was destroying the locals at darts.

Then he and Irene walked outside together and embraced. It wasn't a romantic crescendo. He was all muscle and ribs. When he pulled her to her toes and tried for a kiss, she quickly turned to the side so he caught only the right edge of her mouth.

"Sorry," he said, and kicked a dirt clod. "I really wanted that kiss, though."

She nodded sympathetically and pulled a tragic face. "So sad. But here's what I'll do for you—I'll let you know if *I* ever want one."

He worked his cap onto his head and said, “Ma’am,” mounted a random bike, and wobbled away. She was certain he was going to fall.

“I don’t need a hero,” she called after him.

He steadied himself and glanced back at her. “But *I* might,” he said. He raised a hand to wave but almost toppled.

She got on her own bike and pedaled back to the house, dogs heralding her passage, her heart drumming in her ears.

11

So much smoke, you could hardly breathe.

Dorothy sat in the back of the Aero Club. She enjoyed a cup of tea because she had vowed never to touch coffee after serving however many thousand gallons she had doled out by now. A tail gunner tipped a shot of Irish whiskey into her teacup from his flask. That improved the taste immensely.

On an easel sat a gaudy cardboard sign painted with the proclamation IT'S SHOW TIIIIME! Where'd they get the glitter? Dorothy wanted to know.

The "talent" was shuffling around in front of the stage and sitting on folding chairs like restless schoolkids. The Aero Club combo sat before the stage and squawked through a couple of spry standards. Good ol' Gary Cooper was down there carousing with his jazz combo from the Red Ball Express. She enjoyed seeing the ace roughhouse with the Negro fellows, just as he had at the Grosvenor. They had apparently brought him a guitar. And—oh God, a cowboy hat.

The lights blinked out and the stage, what there was of it, lit up and the band honked away and here came Irene with her Donut Darlings. Dorothy did not approve of this name. But Gator was cute, no question. "Cute is as cute does," Dorothy announced to the airmen sitting near her. They ignored her, rapt as they were already by the show.

Somehow, Irene had gotten all of her Darlings into short pants and fishnets. Irene, then Rose—ecstatic with being tarted up—then Phyllis and Hellcat from the *Cheyenne*. Oh no—here came Jill. Dorothy could not believe it. The driver shouldn't be out there bare-assed. They step-danced sideways like Rockettes. Their bright red lipstick matched. They were all smiling insanely, like mannequins, moving into some little two-step, each carrying a blank white placard up against her chest. At the perfect moment they stopped jiggling and spun their signs around. They read: H E L L O.

Whistles and shouts and bellows of joy erupted. The four backup Donut Darlings stormed offstage and Irene took the microphone in hand and cried, "Hello, you heroes!" with her arm flung out and her fingers wiggling. The guys came out of their chairs. Dorothy stuck her fingers in her mouth and whistled. She couldn't help grinning. The whiskey in her cup helped. Her face was hot. To hell with it—she raised her eyebrows at Flask Man and he delivered another dollop. She wouldn't remember the show.

"And for our first act," Irene belted, "the comedy stylings of Biff and Ralphie!"

Two guys in ill-fitting coveralls and little caps shambled out and reenacted Abbott and Costello's "Who's on First?" It went down gangbusters, as the soldiers and pilots roared and whistled and yelled the lines back at the duo.

Irene retook the stage and introduced the tap-dancing artistry of Flight Surgeon Bob Something, and he did his bit to a scratchy record (and to whistles and a few jeers). They liked it when he ran in place, though, with a demented-looking tooth-baring grin.

The show rolled on like this for about forty minutes. A panel of judges sat along the west wall looking less sober as the night wore on. A local girl from the village—a barmaid at the pub, wearing her headscarf and a bell-shaped white skirt and apron—performed a tremulous "Ave Maria." The boys were torn between staring at her legs and weeping over her singing, which even Dorothy would admit was angelic.

The wildest uproar was reserved for a ball-turret gunner who had billed himself as "Der Führer of Furor." Smitty! She had served him in London. Why, that li'l bug! She could carry him home in her pocket.

He stormed onstage dressed as Hitler with blackened oily hair and a tiny shoe-polish mustache. The guys booed, shouted insults. Smitty screamed, "Schvine!" and goose-stepped around the stage screaming gibberish and holding his right hand in the air. And they started to laugh. They convulsed. They were jumping out of their seats. It was stupid but nobody cared. They almost threw chairs at one another. They were crawling on the floor, clutching their ribs. They laughed so hard they couldn't breathe. They threw trash at Smitty in their appreciation. The base commander seemed uncomfortable when the boys began chanting, "Shitler! Shitler! Shitler!" When Smitty finally surrendered the stage, it took fifteen minutes for the riot to die down.

Irene came into the spotlight and stood as the boys calmed themselves. "What a monkey house," she said. They started back up. She covered the mic and laughed at someone offstage, then turned back to the crowd and put her fists on her hips and scowled. "Now, boys," she scolded, "am I going to have to put you in the corner?" Whistles. "Or do I have to spank you?"

Some yahoo shouted, "Please, baby, please!"

That ignited another half minute of uproar. Dorothy was slumping a bit by now. Listing to port.

"Clam up, you apple-knockers," Irene ordered. When they seemed to be calming down, she leaned into the microphone. "Our last act is a swinging musical combo. A fighter ace and some heroic supply truckers. They promise to steal the show." She pulled a card out of her waistband and stared at it. "They are called... Oh my." She laughed and shook her head. "I can't." The band was already onstage. "Give a warm Glatton welcome to... Handyman and His Red Balls!" She ran off the stage.

It took a minute for the band to set up. One guy with a snare and a stool and a pair of brushes. A stand-up bass player. Captain Walker on sax. And Handyman with guitar, strumming away at the mic.

"Hello," he said. "My name is Bob Wills and these are my Playboys. I been out shooting down Krauts and these here fellas been delivering everything you need on time and in perfect condition. Give 'em a hand!"

They launched to a great roar of approval.

The Red Balls suffered through two cowboy tunes, then Honeyman Walker took the mic and said, "This is a song no white man could sing. Wrote it myself. It's called 'The Chicken Pot Blues.'" He puffed out his chest and vaulted himself into a low growl:

Went into the kitchen to make somethin' to eat
Said went in the kitchen to make somethin' to eat
Said hey there darlin'
Fetch me a noodle and bring me them chicken feet.

It got filthy after that.

As predicted, Handyman and His Red Balls won the prize money.

At the end of the show, the base band sqwonked back to life, and the Donut Darlings danced back out with their signs, but when it was time to reveal their message, they had changed a letter. Now the signs read: O H E L L.

12

Two days later, before dawn, their truck arrived. It was so loud the whole village heard it: the rumbling of the engine, the gears shifting as the driver maneuvered through the narrow lanes, the bicycles toppling, the dogs going insane. The camera crew was too hungover to rise. But Irene and Dorothy stumbled downstairs, Irene barefoot and still in her dressing gown. The truck was huge. Hideously beautiful. Its cab was gray-green, the galley on the back tall and darker gray, almost black.

"By golly," Dorothy said, as if she'd just turned into her Indiana father for a moment.

The driver shut the truck down and hopped to the cobbles. He brandished a clipboard with documents to be signed and offered a pencil. "ARC *Rapid City,*" he said. "Sign here."

Dorothy signed.

He gestured at the back steps of the vehicle. "Let's have the grand tour. Ladies first." They clambered into the tidy galley and he creaked up behind them. "Fourteen feet long," he said. "To the starboard is your serving window. The counter here has two coffee urns on either side of the window. Room for two ladies side by side. Up top, racks. Beside the urns, donut racks. One on each end." He pointed up to the right-hand corner, then forward: "Water tank. Below that, boiler and burner. Under your counter, cabinets and drawers. And two more urns."

They opened and closed the doors.

"Room for contraband," Irene joked.

The driver ignored her and continued his monologue. "Port side.

Fore: sink with cabinets. Above: Water tank. Cabinets. Next to that bad boy, your stores of sugar and flour. Aft: the business end. Donut machine. Electric. Donut shelf and bin beside that. Burner by the back door. Primus stove, access through a portal outside the galley. Up above, your slider window to let out the cooking smoke and steam. In the back door area, by your burner, your record player. It connects to your loud-speaker on the roof of the cab. Above it the record racks. There's some blue straps to keep your records from falling out and breaking on the road. In the ceiling, them cranks? Three of them? They open up vents in the roof."

They oohed over it all.

"Got it?" the driver said.

"Roger," Dorothy said.

"Have a jumpin' time, ladies." He tossed them a loose salute and hopped out, clambered into the jeep trailing behind, and disappeared.

Irene and Dorothy stepped down the metal steps and slammed the door. They walked around like shoppers at a car dealer's showroom.

Dorothy pointed to clips beside the doors. "Rifle clips," she said. "Just where you can reach 'em. In case we need to kill Krauts."

They surveyed their beast: a GMC 2½ ton with double axles in back. The nose was emblazoned with a white U.S. Army star in a white circle. The doors had the star as well in a bright red circle. And numbers. The sides of the engine compartment bore shovels painted army green, the fenders had extra lights to augment the big headlights up front, and the fat iron bumper had a winch wound with metal cable, its hook attached to the base. Four gas cans bracketed the winch in receptacles sunk into the bumper.

"You ain't gonna run dry, I see," Dorothy told the truck.

The top of the galley hung over the truck's cab, extra space. "I could sleep up there," Dorothy told herself and the truck. She climbed onto the running board and peered in: that good smell of a no-nonsense work machine, oil and exhaust and the seats. Immaculate. There was a stiff, split-bench seat, a split windshield with a vertical bar, a great steering wheel, and five frigging stick shifts. "Hell, Irene—I could live in this truck." Visions of restless roaming flooded her mind. Mornings at the Grand Canyon. Parking on some prairie surrounded by buffalo. The Secret Dorothy.

Irene jumped when Dorothy yanked the chain on the air horn and blasted the town with a bellowing yawp. The beast straddled most of the lane, from their garden wall to about two feet from the gates of the churchyard directly across.

"I never had a new truck," Dorothy said, sighing. "No keys for this bad boy. You just push a button and pump the gas until it wakes up."

"It's like a little yacht," Irene said, getting into the spirit of things.

—

Quick note to say thanks. I never been scared and lonesome like I been over here. I always counted on you Angels tho to pull me out of it. And I don't have no good words, but I had to let you know. I'd marry any one of ya just write me back and I'm yer daddy.

A Gentleman from Hell,
Smiley

—

The Good Ship *Rapid City* was greeted with uproar at the air base. It was banged on and petted. Boys climbed on the running boards as it rolled by, and when it stopped, they opened its maw to inspect that big Detroit motor. Dorothy was telling everybody stories about how the truck cracked cobbles in town and scared sheep. They figured out the wires to hook up the record player to the battery and then to the public-address speaker on the roof. Benny Goodman made the morning very good indeed.

Somebody shouted, "It's a donut bomber!"

A water-buffalo tanker truck trundled up to them and pumped water into the truck's various portals, filling the tanks and making the shocks squeak almost inaudibly. Inside, the cups and saucers chimed quietly in their racks like silver bells.

"Our own mobile bedsit," Rose enthused.

Their first service went as smoothly as if they'd been raised in the galley. Hip bumps and wild flirting, boys giving them cigarettes and candy bars in exchange for their own cigarettes and candy bars. Accidental elbow crashes. Blown kisses and daring come-ons and one improvised bouquet of small yellow and blue flowers from the hardy plants between the runways. After a while, brass descended from the tower to "inspect" the truck. They begged off the coffee and donuts, patting their trim middles, their hats tipped at a rakish Hollywood angle.

"Those guys are seeing themselves in an imaginary mirror," Dorothy whispered.

At the end of their day, they were invited to join a caravan to Cambridge. The guys were driving down to a watering hole that aircrews from all around claimed as home base. Of course the warning "It gets pretty wild and you might not want to go" made them certain it was exactly where they wanted to go. Pilots and crews back from battle went to the bar to dance and howl and talk and fight.

The *Rapid* was jammed with partyers in the back as Dorothy followed the jeeps to town. Rose sat on a pilot's lap. Irene sat up front in the copilot seat, hanging on as they banged over bumps. The club in Cambridge was smoky and loud as advertised, replete with much dancing. Irene kept an eye open for the cowboy, but he was not there. She hadn't seen him since the talent show. Rose danced herself dizzy. Irene was observed sitting on a bombardier's lap. Dorothy spent a lot of time leaning over tables explaining over and over: "We drive that big sumbitch right into combat and make coffee and donuts." And schnockered soldiers wagged their heads and said, "No kiddin'?"

The white ceiling was famously etched with graffiti. Pilots and crew members had been burning their initials and names into the white plaster with lighters for a couple of years. Anyone not too drunk to balance on a tabletop used a Zippo to scorch the letters up there. A fresh burst of glee made Dorothy look over. There was Irene, atop the bar, with helpful males clutching her legs to hold her up as she teetered on tiptoes. She was branding them into history, using a tube of Clubmobile lipstick. The red letters formed a wobbly couple of lines, looking like the red stripes of the flag in a breeze: *ARC Rapid City! Dot, Irene, and The Third Girl!*

"There it is," Dorothy said. "It's official."

The next morning, guys who painted nose art on the bombers hit the *Rapid* with handsome two-tone logos. But they already knew better than to call Dorothy *Dot*. Only Irene got away with that.

AMERICAN RED CROSS
CLUBMOBILE RAPID CITY

Starring
DOROTHY! IRENE!
Featuring
THE THIRD GIRL IN THE TRUCK!

By the time the ladies dragged to work, hungover and sore, some idiot had already added a sketch of Kilroy right behind the cab. Even Dorothy smiled a little at that.

13

By the end of May, the tumult at Glatton had intensified. Fighter planes flew in and out like hornets, buzzing the tower. Extra ground crews were brought in to help tend to these planes. There were also more jeeploads of officers. Even four new OSS men in their black suits who locked themselves in the compound with the other spies. The *Cheyenne* trundled over from Polebrook to help handle the surplus and it already looked a little battered next to the brand-new, shiny *Rapid City*.

When the Red Ball Express came in and backed their supply truck up to the Clubmobiles, Captain Walker stepped over to Irene. "Have you seen Handyman about?" he asked.

Irene was confused. "No," she replied. "He's not stationed here."

Walker looked at her for a moment, then deadpanned, "Well, you never know." He winked, climbed back in the truck, and headed to the gates.

The boys who recognized Walker from the talent show hollered out and applauded as he passed and he raised his arm at them.

Clubmobile service was basically running around the clock for more than a week and the women were exhausted. Whenever Irene and Dorothy could go home, they often collapsed on their beds without taking off their uniforms, immediately asleep.

One warm late night in early June, Irene came in, kicked off her shoes, and threw open the doors of her balcony. She lay on her quilt listening to the sounds of crickets and frogs and the last planes coming in for the night. Then there came a rustling and banging from outside the window. The strangest sounds. And then a loud crack.

She went to the balcony and peeked over the edge. Handyman, with his guitar, had a handful of pebbles he was tossing at her window. "Handyman?" she said. "What in the world?"

He dropped the rest of the pebbles and smiled up at her with an insouciant grin. "Oh, hi, Miss Irene. I got somewhere to go. But before I leave, I wanted to bring you a serenade."

Two of the film-crew guys, drawn by the ruckus, wandered out the front door, drinks in hand. They stared at Handyman and then looked up to see Irene on the balcony. Recognizing a moment when they saw one, they toasted the couple, went back inside, and closed the door.

Handyman made a show of tuning his guitar.

"Are you going to sing me another one of those filthy songs?" she asked.

He laughed. "No, my call time is oh three hundred and I won't see you tomorrow," he said. "So I rode the bike out here because I sorta wrote a song for you. I don't have any words yet, but I needed for you to hear it. Something's coming and you just never know. I wanted to leave this with you."

Irene leaned on the balcony rail, watching the way the moon stretched out Handyman's shadow on the yard. He began to play something vaguely Spanish, vaguely classical, nothing Irene had heard before—a lyrical piece that rose and fell in her mind like butterflies. It felt like flying and she let her heart soar. When he finished, she had tears in her eyes. Something this beautiful and he wrote it for her. For once in her life, Irene was speechless.

Handyman slung the guitar around to his back. He gazed up at Irene and nodded. "I hope you liked that," he said, as he fetched the bike from the yard.

"Wait!" Irene called. "What are you gonna call that?"

Handyman straddled the bike and smiled up at her. "I call it 'The Pearl of Great Price,'" he said.

Irene stood staring long after he rode off into the darkness.

—

Soon enough, the reason for all the recent hubbub was manifested. The D-Day invasion. The day before, Glatton was transformed into an exploding whirlwind. No one knew any details or exactly what was coming. Sorties came and went with little relief. Strange groups of men appeared and disappeared. All the radios were on all the time. Scuttlebutt was rampant and officers had nothing to report.

Well before dawn on June 6, the women were on duty serving coffee and donuts to strung-tight flight crews and pilots. By 4:30 a.m., most of the bombers were in the air. A few hours later, all returned unscathed with nothing much to tell the anxious Dollies. They said it was overcast when they arrived at their targets and they could see nothing when they released their payloads. They had no idea what was happening on the ground.

But the influx of combat soldiers, whose mission had been top secret, put pressure on Red Cross operations in London. They needed someone from the *Rapid City* to head back and support the Dollies on duty there. The call to Glatton was for one of the crew to report for breakfast duty in the officers' mess at the Grosvenor. The two who remained would attend to the massive augmentation of flight crews and fresh planes. It would be for a few days until new Red Cross volunteers were able to follow the troops across the Pond.

Rose in recent weeks had discovered Rusty Penney, his Tennessee drawl an unlikely but intoxicating pairing with her English lilt. Dorothy, meanwhile, had unexpectedly started to visit with Handyman's short friend they'd met in London, Smitty, the ball-turret gunner who had brought down the house with his Hitler impersonation. In truth Dorothy was more interested in mastering the new Clubmobile than in Smitty. But she was intrigued to have a man she could pick up and carry around.

Neither she nor Rose wanted to return to duty at the officers' mess in London. Dorothy was eager to reach France, not head back to the dining hall. "I need to get this show on the road," she had taken to saying. As for Rose, despite having taken a shine to Rusty, she also hoped to make it back to her British Red Cross unit.

Irene knew right away that she was the one who'd go to London. It irritated her to leave her woods, though. Rumor had it that they'd be shipping out soon. She wondered if she'd ever see Glatton or Conington again. But the grand hotel in London had opened a room for her. That was a consolation. Perhaps it was what she needed, after all—luxury. A touch of glamour. Cocktails served by waiters. Porcelain bathtubs and luxurious linens. Room service. She bucked up. One did occasionally have to sacrifice when called upon.

In London, a black cab picked her up at St. Pancras train station and deposited her before the Grosvenor House Hotel. She hadn't worn her uniform, just slacks and a white blouse, a silk scarf, and the beloved cheaters hiding her eyes. The June day was bright. The trees on the street looked soft, as if they were covered in green feathers. Soldiers and military trucks crowded the streets. Airplanes droned above. The streets seemed frantic with activity.

The liveried gentleman guarding the door greeted her by saying, "Wonderful to have you back, miss."

She breezed by, hearing some theme music in the back of her mind, perhaps Count Basie and his orchestra. Something swingy. There was no trace of war in the lobby, aside from the uniforms. She kept her face averted from the double doors of the great hall. She was simply not disposed to serve dinner. Tomorrow morning would have to be good enough.

She closed her eyes in the lift and breathed in the perfumed air. The hallway was muffled, flowers burst from vases on low tables. Her room was all she wanted out of life. The walls were pearl white, the wallpaper satiny. The drapes were a restful mauve. Her bed was extra wide and generously pillowed. The tub was commodious. She ran hot water immediately. It looked deep enough that she might float.

After her soak, wrapped in her snowy robe, Irene collapsed on the bed and read more of her purloined John Clare volume. It was already late afternoon. She called down for a *Times* of London and a supper of rare steak and veg, a cup of tomato bisque, a baked potato, a bottle of red wine, and a small flask of brandy. And apple tart with French vanilla ice cream. *Might as well be fat and tipsy,* she told herself. Possibly out loud.

On the wireless, Churchill offered triumph and accolades for the successful invasion of Normandy.

—

It was June 13 now. The Allies had been on the mainland for a week. Everyone was on alert. All of London watched the skies for reprisals.

The first buzz bomb came over the roof of the hotel while Irene was lying in the bathtub amid clouds of steam, her glass of wine on the rim of the tub, staring out the small high window. The flying torpedo that crossed the sky was so bizarre she didn't know what it was. The very sight of it filled her with terror. It could have come from another planet, or from the future. It could have been a flying shark.

She'd heard it before she saw it. There came an odd sound, like some old car backfiring and sputtering. But roaring, too. It grew louder. Then a flurry of pigeons burst over the roof, and the buzz bomb appeared as if chasing them. Irene cried out and kicked water from the tub and across the floor. The bomb was a dull gray shark shape, with some kind of structure above its rear end, like a fat bazooka, and it was burping out black puffs of smoke and spraying a long cone of orange flame; she could swear that sparks rained out of its vents. A swastika was emblazoned on the craft's tail.

Irene rose naked from the tub, soap bubbles running down her back and legs. She continued watching out the high window. She was deeply aware of the tenderness of her flesh as this iron monster roared in the sky. And then its engine sputtered to silence. A final puff of smoke burst out of the tail, and the missile sailed on for a few feet, then dropped. Blocks away. It fell. Not fast, just down, as a stone might drop, or a tree trunk dislodged and tumbling from a cliff.

It vanished behind the rows of houses beyond the hotel. When the explosion came and the window cracked and the thunder came, Irene hurled herself back into the bathwater, which splashed over the lip of the tub and onto the floor. A woman in another room screamed and the air-raid sirens groaned to life and began to wail.

"I am completely alone," Irene's voice said.

Boiling smoke blotted out the small slice of sky in her window. Then greasy flame roiled up through the smoke. She did not know what to do. Were more coming? Had they a target? Would they hit the royal palace? The hotel?

Pounding on the door of her room. It was Sergeant Milburn. "Bombs! Come on, Woodward! They got the enlisted men's club! We got to hurry!" He charged on down the hall, yelling as he went.

The spell broke: Irene didn't think at all. She flew out of the water and barely dried herself, flinging towels as she ripped into her closet for her uniform. She threw on her trousers and scrabbled out a white blouse. She thought to wrestle into a brassiere first and grabbed her jacket but forgot her cap. Shoved her bare feet into shoes and stormed down the hall, running with all the other running people, everyone heading for the stairs. Then into the street, where some Brit soldiers scooped her into their lorry and sped through the chaos.

"Grove Road!" they yelled to the driver. "Mile end! Center of the city!"

Fire trucks stalled in the madness. Smoke stank all around as they got closer to the bomb site. The column of darkness and fire was a block beyond them. Then the lorry stopped. The soldiers leaped out. She followed, elbowing through the crowd. The sirens were deafening now. People streamed into the Underground in case more bombs were coming. It felt as though the entire world was helpless before the fall of metal. She saw for the first time that her body was made of gossamer. Her hair was still dripping rivulets down her back as she ran toward the fire.

Destruction smelled filthy. Within it, the stink of burning meat. Distant Klaxons sounded as fire teams rushed to the scene. She rounded a corner to an array of overturned cars, their tires aflame. Glass covered the cobbles of a wide alley, and there was an upended wagon on fire and a dead horse spilling its insides onto the street. Horse blood in the gutters.

Irene saw it all in flashes. She couldn't catch her breath. What appeared at first to be a red bundle of rags under the wagon was the deliveryman, dismantled. He was both under the wagon and all over the street. How odd, she thought, that he could be two places at once. Smoke enveloped her and she was choking and blinded and remembered suddenly the gas-mask training that seemed to have happened years ago, but she had no mask.

"Who do I help?" she shouted. "Where are you?"

Noise battered her. Firemen slammed past her and vanished into the smoke. Part of a building fell. She danced away sideways as the bricks crashed at her feet, coughing up red dust and cutting her ankles with flying chips. She heard a terrible yowling and wiped her eyes. A small shadow coalesced in the gray black white brown smoke. A cat, burned, dragged itself toward her screaming for help. She put her hands over her ears and ran on.

She didn't have time to worry about it. A wounded soldier stood before her. He was catching the blood from his forehead in his hands as if he were in prayer, sweating blood. He knelt. She dropped down beside him and ripped a swatch from the tail of her blouse and held it to his head. His ruined uniform smoked. His face was a mosaic of glass shards in a field of red. His hair had been singed down to little ashy quills, which were also smoking. He was horribly fascinating to look at.

"What do I do?" she kept asking. "What do I do?"

"Thank you, miss," the soldier said. But he was somewhere else. He sat on the curb.

"Don't you die, big boy."

"I'm doing fine," he murmured. "Just need to stretch... out..."

This was too much. Simply too much. Irene stood and backed away a step or two. Her hands shook violently.

The soldier gulped air like a fish laid out on a dock. "The girl with the flowers," he said.

"What?"

"The girl. We flirted. She walked that way. Prettiest girl I ever saw. That way."

"What way?"

"That way. Flowers in her arms. Said she was taking them. Sell. Walked. Blew up. Help her." He closed his eyes. A red bubble formed at his lips and expanded until it burst. Another began to inflate, then popped. "She walked into it." Opening his eyes, he leaned back against a lamppost, put his hands in his pockets, and crossed his ankles. "Like waitin' for the bus," he said, and his eyes closed again.

When he said nothing more, Irene didn't know if he was dead or unconscious. The noise around her was so loud now—so many Brit and Yank soldiers and police and bystanders and firemen and voices and the fire roaring—that she felt deaf. But she walked toward the smoking wreckage.

"Girl?" she called. What was she supposed to say? "Girl with the flowers!"

Her eyes stung and she coughed rough clots in the smell of burning. A broken water main gushed geysers into the air, festive and refreshing. The water soaked her, blinded her. Her blouse stuck to her skin. She realized she was thirsty and opened her mouth to take a gulp. The water tasted of ashes. When she stepped away from the geyser her feet sank into soft objects she would not look at.

She made it beyond the ruined block of stores calling, "Flower girl! Flower girl! Come to my voice!" and then a shadow wavered before her.

At that moment, a man's voice shouted behind her. An American voice. Had he called her name? For a moment it seemed as though her uncle Will had come for her. Then the voice was overwhelmed by the din.

She did not feel brave, despite having run into a flaming bombing. She was simply there. And the wraith before her moving strangely in the smoke frightened her. But she stepped toward it anyway. "Here," she said loudly. "Come to me."

Irene felt drunk, confused by everything. The shadow before her in the smoke, for example. It had to be a ghost. Absolutely some shade from *A Christmas Carol*. After all, snow was falling. Gray snow. No, not snow—ash. Half-blinding her.

The ghost came forward dragging her feet, and the man behind Irene came rushing and both were yelling. No, the ghost was wailing, not yelling. As a gust blew apart the smoke, Irene stopped breathing or moving and tried to stop seeing: a woman in tatters, her eyes empty, her mouth black-lipped and open, sending tendrils of horror into the air. In one hand, she held her other hand, as if she were walking herself to the museum; the rest of that arm hung down, its stump dragging on the bricks, leaving a long line of red behind her. Flowers were stuck to her legs with blood.

"Help me," the woman said and fell facedown.

The back of her head was caved in, and she was instantly dead, as if her body needed only a moment's rest to abandon its weary struggle.

Irene dropped to her knees and touched the flower girl. Her stillness was horribly, densely solid. Bits of flowers stuck in her hair. She had petals inside her skull. Her arm lay abandoned. Irene imagined someone would want it. Someone would surely collect the parts. There must be a service to reattach limbs, she thought. A registry. She clutched the woman's arm to her chest and rose. Limbs were too important to simply toss into a rubbish bin somewhere. The flower girl's hand bore a small golden ring with a green stone on one finger. Her hand was warm. Pliant. As if it could feel the world independent of the flower girl's body. Irene became afraid it would close on her own fingers and squeeze.

Now she heard pounding on the bricks of the alley, the boots of the man who'd been yelling from behind her. He caught her and put his arms around her. Two arms. Complete arms.

"Miss Irene," he said.

She tried to move away from his grip.

"It's me," he said.

She turned and looked up into her pilot's face. "Hans?"

"It's me."

"How?"

"I've got you," he said. "You're all right. Let's put that down here. It'll be safe here. Come on. I'm going to help you." He took the limb from her gently, laid it on the cobbles. "Don't worry about anything." He kept one arm around her waist and steered her out of the blast area. "D-Day's past. This is just mop-up. You'll see."

"You," she said.

"Me, that's right. Let me help you, Miss Irene. I've been through a lot of these things. Let's just get out of the way and let the rescue crews handle it." He walked her back down the street.

—

She couldn't recall how they got back to the hotel lobby. He kept his arm clamped around her as they walked. It was quite embarrassing. The hotel staff stood silently and watched them enter.

"A bottle of gin and tonic and limes," Hans called as he steered her to the lift. "What floor? Irene. What floor?"

"Five."

"Give me the key. The key. Thank you."

When they reached the fifth floor, he maneuvered her into the room and got her to the bed.

"I am fine," she protested. "Really, I am."

"Of course you are," he said. He never raised his voice, talking to her as if she were a skittish horse.

He sat at the foot of her bed and worked off her filthy shoes, tossed them in the corner. She had blood on her bare ankles. Cinders were smeared on her flesh. Her feet stank of wet leather and smoke. He brought a wet cloth from the bathroom and cleaned her legs. She watched dispassionately. He covered her legs with the little knee blanket from the settee by the window.

"You've seen things like that before?" she asked.

"'Fraid so."

"Don't they upset you?"

He looked at the floor and shrugged, which made her angry. Everything was making her angry now.

"Damn you," she said. "Have an opinion!"

Fortunately, there came a soft knock on the door. He went to it, took the liquor cart, and wheeled it into the room.

"I—" she said and began to tremble uncontrollably. "I'm so sorry. I don't know what's the matter with me."

He didn't rush to her side. She appreciated him not trying to embrace or comfort her.

"It's normal," he said. "I promise." He stepped up to the bed and looked down at her. "Don't worry."

"I must get up," she said, shuddering. "I need to wash this off."

"Do you trust me?"

"I don't even know you."

"But do you trust me?"

She shook as if infected with some grave disease. "Should I?"

"Right now, yes." He held out his hand to help her up, then steered her to the bathroom, holding her up as she walked. He sat her on the toilet seat and bent to the twin levers of the half-filled tub and started the water.

"Surely you don't think," she said.

"I ain't joining you," he said. He poured bubble solution from a lavender decanter into the water. "Nobody will see a thing," he promised. "I have three sisters." He put his hand in the water to test its temperature. "Can you get yourself in?"

"I'm not an invalid."

"I don't mind settin' you in the water."

"Don't you just wish."

He closed the door almost all the way but left a crack so he could hear if she needed anything. He mixed the drinks and carried the sweating cold glasses to the door and leaned against the wall, not looking into the open gap. Well, not past her feet, up by the faucet.

"Do you need me to soap your back?" he asked.

"Absolutely not."

She was bent forward now into the bubbles so that only her shining back was visible. And her shoulders. And her dark hair. She had folded her hands around her body, her fingers resting on each shoulder as she clutched herself.

"I brought liquor," he said.

"Leave it by the door."

"Done," he said, then sat cross-legged on the floor.

"Thank you," she said.

"It gets better," he said.

"Does it."

"Irene, I'm not all that smart, so I won't give you advice. But I've been in a few jackpots. And what I tell myself is, *You walked out of there. You get one more day. So you win.*"

She sank into the bubbles.

"I won't lie," he said. "It's the quiet times that'll get you. I stay busy. But you gals, you have something going for you that we don't. You can always go home."

"I'm not quitting."

"I know you're not."

"It was so..."

"Yes it was." He rose. "Will you be okay for a minute?"

He heard her turn the spigot, water running. The tap squeaked as she turned it back off. The water moved. He heard a bit splash on the floor.

"Just a minute," he said. "I need to fetch something." He closed the door and hurried out of her room.

—

When Hans came back, darkness had fully settled against the windows. It was silent in the room except for the gentle slosh of the water against the side of the tub when she moved. He settled himself cross-legged outside the bathroom door. It was still cracked open enough to let a narrow wedge of light and some steam escape, the scents of the perfumed water.

He had brought his guitar from his room. It was a Gibson J-45, top of the line, with inlaid roses on the neck. He strummed an open chord and heard her sit up in the tub.

"Cowboy?" she said.

"I brought you a serenade, city girl."

He started to play quietly in 3/4 time. "A song by Huddie Ledbetter," he said. "I kinda rewrote it just now." And he began to sing—

Irene, good night
Irene, good night
Good night, Irene, good night, Irene,
I'll see you in my dreams

This last line almost a whisper.

She had never heard the song quite this way. His voice was soothing. Her eyes closed. When he finished, she said, "Again."

And he sang.

As he vamped a few chords to drag out the tune, he heard her rise from the bath. The door opened. She stood there, wrapped in a towel. Water dripped from her hair and from her knees. She stood there, staring down at him. Shivering, but this time from the air, not terror.

She came forward, moved the guitar out of the way, and sat in his lap, sideways. She pulled her knees up.

He was instantly wet, but didn't mind. Her cold slick hair rested beneath his chin.

"I've got you," he said.

"Just hold me for a moment."

They must have slept like that, leaning back against the side of the bed, still entwined. They awoke together and looked at each other for a long time in the half-light.

—

Back at Glatton, Irene told Dorothy and Rose every detail of the bombing she could remember, including the rescue by Hans, but she drove them crazy by refusing to tell more. That serenade was only hers. Forever.

There was hardly time for stories, anyway. Everything was happening so fast and so constantly, they didn't have time to recognize that a week, then two had passed. They didn't have time even to say farewell to dear Rose, who got the reunion with her British Red Cross unit that she'd been hoping for.

Within a few weeks of Irene's return to Glatton, the *Rapid City* and its crew were sent to Southampton to be shipped out to Utah Beach.

As Dorothy drove the truck through the air-base gate, the mechanics and ground crew stood as an honor guard and called out to them, "Good luck, Dollies!"

In unison, the women yelled back, "Don't call us *Dollies*!" Dorothy pulled the air horn to the cheers of the men.

Upon arrival in Southampton, the *Rapid City* was loaded onto an LST, an awkward-looking craft known as a Landing Ship-Tank, and her crew was hustled up the ramp of a crowded troop carrier. Once near the French shore, the sailors dropped nets of heavy rope over the side of the ship. The women strapped on army helmets and clambered over the railing, struggling to climb down the cargo net. Irene was swung out by the rocking of the ship and slammed back into the hull. Below them, the huge LST carried trucks and the Clubmobiles. (Everybody knew that *LST* really meant *Large Slow Target*.) Though the shore was no longer a combat zone, Normandy still sported crowns of smoke across the water. Planes like crows swarmed the sky. Great military machines roved the sand.

Irene was sure they were all going to die. She fervently prayed: "Bless me, Father, for I have sinned." But her mind clamped down on that part of the prayer and refused to let any more loose—either to God or to Dorothy—merely repeating those seven words over and over.

Fighter planes shrieked above them. Handyman might have been looking down at that moment. There was no way to know. But she wasn't going to waste time worrying about that now. Even after the night in London she wasn't going to admit it mattered to her. She had ten feet to go to the deck of the rocking transport. The trucks shuddered and creaked, and the coffee cups and saucers rattled inside the Clubmobiles.

"Jump!" Dorothy shouted.

They kicked off and thumped to the landing craft's deck. They held to the sides of the *Rapid City* as they made their way to its cab and climbed aboard. The LST's huge diesel engines engaged and the craft peeled away toward the shore and began to surge. It felt as though they were driving on the water. The *Rapid City* bounced and jerked, its springs groaning. Irene's lips jiggled double time.

A whistle blew and all the truck motors around them came to life. Dorothy started theirs up as well. The truck shuddered. Waves were crashing and then the great front of the craft dropped and formed a ramp and men with whistles were shrieking and waving their hands and shouting, "Get your asses off-loaded!"

Dorothy wrestled the *Rapid* into gear and the truck mule-kicked once and they hit the ramp and went into water that reached above their fenders. For some reason, rotting oranges were bobbing in the water. Before them lay the ruined sweep of Utah Beach.

PART TWO

Personality on Legs

14

THE OLD LIFE was over.

A month had passed since D-Day, and Command had finally cleared the beach and authorized the landing of relief vehicles. When the *Rapid City* got ashore at Utah Beach, its crew was ordered to drive five miles to the transit area where they were to bed down for the night. It was their first experience driving the truck through a literal war zone. Impatient soldiers waved them forward, yelling, "Go, go, go!" and they felt impossibly exposed as Dorothy struggled to get the truck through the sand and up onto the dirt road that climbed through the cliffs. Scattered gunfire echoed from the hills.

When they topped the cliffs, they were flanked by two sandbagged machine-gun nests, one on each side of the road. Soldiers watching for snipers waved and called out to them, but the women were too nervous to wave back and hoped their gritted teeth would pass for a smile. The noise, the chaos, the constant overflight of planes—all of their senses under assault. They weren't sure if their sweat was from fear or from the heat.

A sarge flagged them down near a sandbagged radio command post camouflaged by netting. "Follow those supply trucks," he said, pointing them in the right direction. "They're waiting for you. And hey, put your fuckin' helmets on!"

For the first time, Irene and Dorothy understood what it meant to be under fire. They both reached under their seats for their helmets and cinched them on tightly. The road was damaged, with craters in the fields alongside. They saw demolished trucks, exploded buildings, burned trees, and farmland in the distance still smoldering. Two fighter planes screamed overhead, banking toward low hills to the north, and unleashed a torrent of machine-gun fire into the trees before pulling away.

Following the slow-moving trucks was torture for Dorothy, who more than anything wanted to floor it and speed past all of this. They were going at a snail's pace, utterly vulnerable to whatever danger might be targeting them.

"This is what we asked for, Dottie," Irene said in a small voice.

"Yep," Dorothy said. "This is where we show 'em what we're made of. We can do this." That five-mile drive felt like fifty to them both.

—

At dawn the following day, they joined VIII Corps at Montmartin-sur-Mer, a small town in Brittany, the peninsula to the southwest of Normandy. The *Rapid City* was in a cadre of eight Clubmobiles—the *Cheyenne*, the *Annapolis*, the *Albany*, the *Boise*, the *Atlanta*, the *Empire State*, and the *Wolverine*—from Group F. The trucks and crews went back and forth among the divisions attached to the 8th—the 5th Rangers, the 27th, and the 29th—as well as the field hospital and the replacement forces in Brittany.

The crews organized a round-the-clock schedule to make sure they always had supplies, they always had coffee and donuts at the ready, they always had banter and small talk and a smile for whoever needed it. Exhausted as they might be, they each knew their job was to be there whenever a soldier ached for a taste of home.

"No matter what, you don't want to be the bitch that breaks his spirit," Dorothy said when they gathered late one night with a bottle of purloined gin.

There was no time to notice a sunburned field, a stone church, a cobbled alley—it was all the same to them. Irene didn't even take the time to work on her sketchbook. The boys were so grateful for their attention and care that it was heartbreaking and gratifying. It made the women single-minded in their rush to duty.

They often slept under the trucks, or in them, or sometimes on top of them. Occasionally, they would be bivouacked in an abandoned home or a hotel where they could sleep in real beds and sometimes even luxuriate in a bath. But wherever the Clubmobiles pulled in, the soldiers were always happy to assist in lugging water or digging a latrine ditch. Sometimes the soldiers offered to let the women sleep in their sandbag bunkers. The nights they would gather with a group of soldiers at an impromptu bonfire—singing songs, telling stories, passing around a bottle or two—were precious.

The rest of July passed that way, and in August they were moved to the town of Morlaix, the Red Cross's staging area for service to the troops liberating the port city of Brest, at the far edge of Brittany. Headquarters was an old building the Germans had fled. German graffiti covered the walls, but nobody could read it. A wobbly swastika took up the whole of one rough wall.

Irene and Dorothy were ordered to camp the *Rapid City* atop a hill along some hedgerows. It made them feel like clay pigeons. Irene played records for the soldiers through the truck's PA system. Bombers droned overhead day and night, fighters among them like wasps.

Morlaix was an ancient town with cobbled streets and a tidal bay fed by a river. Even now, the bay was crowded with old fishing boats. But Irene's favorite feature was the tall viaduct that crossed the entire valley in which Morlaix was tucked.

The Dollies wore fatigues and helmets just like the men. If they remembered, they donned the white aprons that covered them to the knees and kept off the flour dust. They were allowed one canteen of water a day to wash their clothes. It was used for underwear. They bathed in what was left in their helmets.

"Pits and cracks," Dorothy said.

"I'll get the hang of this," Irene said, "but I'm still having trouble getting my knees in the helmet."

Dorothy slapped her back. They kept laughing. Why not.

The *Cheyenne* was parked next door, and Jill spotted a clear stream at the bottom of the hill and suggested they bathe down there.

Irene pointed to a pickup baseball game in the nearby field, crowded with GIs. "I don't want to cause a riot," she said.

"Honey," Jill said, "you're not that hot."

"To those yahoos," Dorothy said, "my granny would be hot."

Soon, Dorothy got wind of a plan to drive the Clubmobiles to the 102nd Evac Hospital. It sounded so noble—pull out of the usual duty to go cheer up those wounded boys about to go back to England or even home. But their real attraction to the assignment was the rumor that the nurses there would allow them to take hot showers. They hadn't had a real bath in eight days and smelled as bad as the men around them. They decided to leave before the caravan, with dreams of enough hot water for a satisfying shower.

"We'll make up a reason later if anybody asks," Dorothy said. "I mean, we are running low on *something*, right?"

They pulled into the hospital to be greeted by seriously excited ambulatory GIs who howled and shrieked like monkeys when the trucks appeared. The crew members paid for their sin of coveting a shower with hectic service first, then dangerous night-driving afterward. But in between, soap and hot water and shampoo were their rewards, and it felt like the best moment of their lives. Irene marveled at the dirty water cascading off her body and swirling down the drain. Could have been hot chocolate. When she stepped out of the stall dripping water, Dorothy was standing outside her own stall, naked.

"Look at you," Irene said.

"Look at you!"

"I guess we've got no secrets now."

"Oh, I still have a couple," Dorothy said.

Irene grabbed a towel. "So do I."

"I won't ask if you don't ask."

"Deal."

They rubbed themselves pink, then tore at their hair with huge combs in happy silence.

In September, they were ordered to roll out. Patton's 3rd Army was on the move to capitalize on de Gaulle's liberation of Paris. From there, Patton intended to chase the Germans all the way to Belgium. The Clubmobiles in Brittany would accompany the convoy, moving from servicing the rear to being available to the frontline troops. This was exactly what the Clubmobile Corps—or at least Dorothy—had hoped for: finally, they were about to be part of the action.

Once the women had arrived on the European continent—that ancient, bloodied soil—everything had transformed. The first casualty was any vestige of civilized decorum. They were not easily offended, least of all by each other. They were not queasy. They judged themselves and each other by their level of panache amid the turmoil. They wondered if they'd get yet another Third Girl in the Truck, though they had become a perfect donut-coffee machine. It was extra work, sure, but one less person to deal with. They didn't cherish the thought of training some poor victim in the ways of their truck.

War stank. They stank. The GIs stank. The insides of tanks *really* stank. The civilians stank. The dead stank. The mystery meat in the C rations stank. The mud and the ruins and the shell craters and the trenches and the foxholes and the latrines and the garbage fires all stank. Even the smell of the donuts was unwelcome by now. But it beat the sewage that seemed to make up half of every bivouac.

Rolling, Irene wrote in her notebook, *like a herd of turtles.* Though sometimes they were hares, burning down those cracked roads in storms of dust or flung mud. In the past couple of months they'd seen firefights and refugees, conflagrations and broken churches, farm animals massacred. Women with shaved heads—collaborators—kneeling in a town square and being kicked and pelted with rotten cabbages. The wreckage of human bodies forgotten on the land, some of the old ones appearing like little more than rags and jerky stretched over broken wooden frames.

They had learned that the surprises war had in store came when you least expected them. The best thing they could do was to keep the water tanks full, though they sloshed endlessly, and sometimes their weight threatened to tip the truck over on tight turns. Water was the key but there were other imperatives: keep the galley stocked and the truck fueled; never walk into a field, because of land mines; keep your apron clean, because it added a touch of hope to the day.

On that first day, after they'd survived the wild road leading inland from Utah Beach and had arrived at the transit area, Patton himself stepped up to the *Rapid City* for a cup and a sinker. He winked at each of them and said, "You're tougher than every one of these sons of bitches." That day went into their dreams and thereafter seemed like a fantasy. Irene put the moment in her notebook, but was too shy to ask the general for his autograph. Otherwise, they never saw the big boys, just the grunts.

"Old Blood and Guts," she said to one of the soldiers, after Patton had left their truck.

"Our blood, his guts," a kid retorted. It was a standard GI complaint, they would learn.

Everything they'd held dear before they came ashore seemed naive and silly when it didn't choke them with emotion. To compensate, they compiled unwritten commandments:

Roll on down the road.
Nothing means a thing.
Don't look back.
Don't apologize.
Don't concede.
Don't let them see you cry.
The *Rapid City* comes first.
Never surrender.

—

With days on the road from Brittany already behind them, they were somewhere past Troyes, southeast of Paris. The men of V Corps, the heroes of Omaha Beach who had then helped de Gaulle liberate Paris, were on the move. It was America's own Blitz—payback against the Germans, pushing deep into France, leaving destruction. German tanks like enraged aurochs hid in the woods and hedgerows, waiting to burst out with a roar, while snipers concealed themselves in bell towers, in foxholes, behind walls of sandbags. The entire U.S. Army, it seemed, was running over the land to meet them.

"I don't know where we're going," Dorothy said.

"I thought you had a map," Irene said.

They'd gotten up that morning at 4:30 and climbed out from under their truck. It had rained. On good nights, the army requisitioned a country home or inn for them. But they had been too tired to bother last night and had just unrolled their bags under the big gray beast. They could always be confident that bullets would have trouble getting through their Jimmy.

Then they were on their way by 5:30. But a jeep had slid off the road into a flooded ditch, and as the others had tried to heave it back out, Dorothy had pulled around them and taken off. She didn't have time for this. She'd driven so fast that she pulled away from their cohort before she noticed.

Dorothy wrestled the wheel now. It seemed alive, some circular creature that resisted her grip. It was usually recalcitrant, but this road made the truck downright moody today. What a mule.

"Aren't you supposed to know?" Irene demanded.

"Said the lady that never drives." Dorothy's back and rear end hurt. Her left leg ached from working that savage clutch. Her stomach was sour. Her shoulders ached, too, and the endless bouncing had given her a headache that felt like she had a sharp stone lodged in her brain. She didn't need any crap. "I'm cross-eyed over here," she said.

Irene clutched her own gut and kept a hand over her mouth. "We're just tired," she said.

"Tired. Right."

They had been stopping to serve three times a day, these Sisters of the *City*, as they'd been nicknamed by some of the boys. The work had all faded into a long line of faces—faces and faces lined up at the window, staring at them. Faces that were all the same unless the Sisters really concentrated. Their muscles were always sore. It hurt even to sit down at the end of a shift because they knew how much it would strain their overtaxed thighs to get back up. Small trucks came and went laden with more damned donut mix and coffee beans and sugar and grease and bags of letters they had to distribute and candy and chewing gum and old magazines and stale cigarettes and cans of milk and, when they were lucky, new records for their Victrola. They sometimes enjoyed restocking the truck because it gave some order to their day and didn't involve the endless smiling that made their faces ache.

On their right hands both women sported aluminum rings fashioned by GIs out of the downed German airplanes scattered around the landscape. Small gestures of love. They each felt like war brides to a few thousand husbands.

One thing they loved was the soldiers' obsession with the ledger that each truck carried. In the heavy tome, beneath a heading for each state, was a list of names and the hometown and military division for each of those names. Even more than donuts, more than flirting, these men wanted to see who was listed in these huge volumes. And they entered their own names so the next guys might find them. Men cried as they studied the pages. It was strangely beautiful. But more beautiful still was when a lieutenant who didn't believe these ladies should be in the field unprotected slipped Dorothy a .45 automatic and holster, along with a full box of fat bullets. He didn't even ask for a kiss.

It was also becoming clear, the deeper they went into France, that their job had yet another feature nobody had trained them for. They were engaged on most nights in listening to confessions. After service was done for the night, the women sat out on the back steps of the truck, having a cigarette and whatever drink might be available. The boys would find them. They needed to talk and the women learned to be quiet and receptive and never criticize the nightmares and shame the boys had come to tell them in secret. It was the Great Unburdening. They vowed never to share these secrets with anyone else—though they did whisper about them to each other after midnight, and though they carried a shell of strangers' sorrows that grew ever thicker.

One boy had stomped a civilian to death and didn't know why. Another had hidden under a fallen barn wall during a firefight, crying in terror, without firing a single shot. And that one was going to shoot himself because his hands couldn't stop shaking and he couldn't stop throwing up and he couldn't sleep. Still another boy had kissed a fellow soldier and was afraid of him now. A captain had brought them his Dear John letter from a wife in San Francisco and wrung his hands as they read it. It smelled like Chanel No. 5, which Irene and Dorothy found especially cruel.

Some days back, they had gotten delayed leaving Caen, their most recent base, because of the amount of mail they had to deliver to the troops. They hollered names like announcing a prize raffle. Excited soldiers pushed forward to collect a treasured missive, and everyone dreaded the occasional silence when there was no answer to a shouted name. It had been a pleasure to deliver the letters, but it had taken so long that the division had left without them, and the *Rapid City* had been forced to catch up later.

As they'd cleaned and repacked the truck that last day in Caen, its citizens were still climbing out of the vast mines under the city, where they had waited out the bombs. Hundreds of them, blinking in the unexpected sunlight. Irene delivered leftover sinkers to them. Dorothy and Phyl, from the *Cheyenne*, passed out chocolates and cigarettes.

—

They'd been driving for a long while this morning with no sight of anyone.

"Wish I got more mail," Irene said, though she didn't acknowledge to Dorothy that she was thinking of Handyman. She'd snuck a letter to Hans into one of their mailbags, just telling him she was thinking of him, that she watched every fighter that went overhead imagining it might be him. She didn't risk much, except when she signed it *As ever, Good night, Irene*.

"I don't get any mail at all," Dorothy said, coming out of a trance at the wheel. "The hell are we?"

Though she had learned to drive even when her mind was elsewhere, it was a bad habit, she knew, almost like drunk driving. They were each in their own small universe. Irene stared into space, probably composing poems. One of the troubles with driving in a trance, Dorothy understood, was when you came out of it and didn't know what road you'd gone down and were caught looking around dumbfounded for the long caravan of U.S. Army ordnance that had been your constant companion but was now nowhere to be seen.

"We might be going the wrong way," Dorothy admitted.

The road had roughened, become increasingly broken and cratered. It was ragged with brambles, and branches in the narrower passages scraped against the truck as if trying to tear its sides open. Carrion crows were harried across fields by small brown birds spinning in their wake like leaves in a storm.

Irene tried not to slide off the seat onto the floor. "Our country drive," she said.

The wheel jerked left. Dirty bastard had a mind of its own. But Dorothy avoided showing either annoyance or weakness. Instead, she craned her neck and searched the brushwood along the road. She hadn't seen a GI for about twenty miles, she realized. "This day is bullsh," she said.

"You know what the Brits say," Irene told her. "Take the bull by the tail and face the situation."

"Who taught you that? I thought you were the classy one."

The dig brought only silence from Irene, who gazed out at the passing trees on the starboard side of the truck. "I feel so glamorous when nobody's shooting at me," she announced.

"I don't feel like battin' the breeze right now," Dorothy said. "I'm trying to drive."

"Witch."

Dorothy ground her teeth.

Irene struck a noble pose in the window. She always knew how she looked—as if a movie camera were perpetually coming in for a close-up. Her uniform was uncharacteristically unkempt, though. They were both in uniform, or much of their uniforms, anyway. The white blouses now stained and with yellow armpits, the royal blue wool trousers gray at the knees after their last few nights of sleeping under the truck. Dried mud flaked off and fell to the floor of the truck cab. Their boots were a ruin.

Irene lit up a smoke and curled a strand of hair around her finger and snapped her gum in the most irritating fashion. Smoke leaked out of her noisy mouth. Sometimes she blew chewing-gum bubbles full of smoke and burst them on her tongue like mortar rounds.

Dorothy coughed theatrically to express her displeasure. Lately, everything irritated her. She was always driving the *Rapid City*, a freedom whose initial pleasure had begun to dissipate, but if the fancy-pants nincompoop beside her ever tried to drive, odds were they'd end up in a ditch. She could hardly focus on anything except Irene's gum-popping, and now they were tootling down an old road completely alone in unknown territory.

"Where'd you learn to do that smoke trick?" she said. "The cathouse?"

Irene fumed. "Go screw," she finally replied.

Dorothy spread her personal road map over the wheel. It drooped down on either side. She studied it as she drove.

Irene couldn't watch this performance. They were surely both going to die.

The truck rolled over a small hill. The racks of coffee cups in back rattled musically and the mailbags slammed. Irene braced herself against the dash.

Son of a bitch, Dorothy prayed, her hands shaking.

In spite of the relentless bouncing, Irene hung partway out the window, her eyes closed, her dark brown hair tossing in the wind.

Ain't we a set, Dorothy thought. "Toots," she said, "you're always glamorous. Whether they're shooting or not. But if you don't get your head back in the truck, it's gonna get torn off, and you won't be so fancy then."

Their conversations often remained sporadic like this. A topic could be abandoned for ten miles, then suddenly flare up again as if they hadn't stopped talking about it. Once, Irene had startled Dorothy when she announced, "Anyway," and resumed a story she had been interrupted telling two days earlier—some whopper about her *Gator* nickname that Dorothy had already heard twenty times. It was all flapdoodle.

"Dear girl," Irene said, doing that arch New York thing her partner found intriguing and exasperating in equal measure. "I am hardly glamorous. I'm wearing army boots, after all." She pulled up her trouser leg to demonstrate.

Dorothy double-clutched grimly. The guys in the motor pool called it *double-ugly*. Dorothy thought this would be the title of her memoir if she ever wrote one.

Their bladders were screaming, a reality that Irene voiced first. "I have to wee," she said. When she got no response from Dorothy, she added, "I really do."

But Dorothy didn't stop and Irene suddenly hated her.

The odor of dead cows was in the air. At least, they hoped it was dead cows. And old smoke—the air had a charcoal bouquet. There were yellow flowers, too, and Irene's beloved sunflowers, dry and rattling, among them. And those angry little birds fussing at the sunflowers' wide, seed-filled faces as they plucked out food.

Irene was right about one important thing. Nobody had shot at them today. There wasn't even artillery in the distance, that sound of gods stumbling drunkenly over the hills. The road remained fraught, though. They occasionally forgot this, with their boredom giving them a devil-may-care insouciance, but everything was dangerous. It was just that no one wanted to be reminded every minute of every day that death was everywhere around them.

They rounded a curve and beheld a sad-sack Andy Gump shuffling along, his rifle down around his butt, hanging low. He was wailing on a harmonica.

"American grunt on the port side," Dorothy said.

She downshifted, and the soldier spun around, grabbing at his rifle. When he saw the red cross on the front of the galley he smiled. His teeth were long and yellow in the midst of the dirt and stubble on his face.

Dorothy braked and rolled down her window. "Hey, GI, which way to Hoboken?"

"Hot damn," he said.

"Yeah, it's a truckload o' dames. Can you handle it?"

"Why gosh."

"I know. It's a shock."

He was craning like a giraffe, and the Sisters waved their fingers at him.

"Hi, handsome," Irene cooed.

"Shit fire!"

Dorothy snapped her fingers, and Irene fished out the box of stale donuts she'd stashed under her seat beside the .45 the lieutenant had given them.

"Want a donut?" Dorothy asked.

"Don't have to ask me twice."

He stepped up on her running board. God did he reek.

"Got any smokes, doll?"

Dorothy handed him her pack of Luckies just to get him to step back down and told him not to call her that again.

"Are we going the right way?" Irene said.

"Not if you're going to Hoboken," he said.

Dorothy gave him a thumbs-up and kicked the truck back into gear.

"Don't leave!" he called.

"I'll see you in my dreams," she shouted and stepped on it. They drove in silence for a minute, until Dorothy, without looking over, sneered, "Hi, handsome."

"I am doing my duty, as we were trained to do, missy. So you can just sit on it." Irene folded her arms and spun away, studying the roadside, where signs warned of snipers.

The Sisters felt secure. Who would dare shoot them? The truck bore Red Cross insignia on its back and brow and flanks. The extended galley deck in the rear made the *Rapid City* look like a bloated ambulance. With chimneys. Who shot at ambulances? They might as well be driving a rolling billboard that read: HOLD YOUR FIRE.

A small gathering of civilians in raggedy clothes waved at them as they approached. It wasn't the first time weary people along the decimated route had come out to stare. Many of them were tattered and often looked like they were sleepwalking. Sometimes they waved little flags, and their kids ran alongside the trucks. The crew had stores of Hershey bars and Beeman gum, which they threw out the windows.

It was a miracle anyone was alive. Village after village looked like a volcano had erupted in its central square, and the land had been riven by its explosion. Whole neighborhoods were strewn bricks and dappled flows of slag. In some fields, bits and jags of walls rose like gargantuan headstones, some with doorways still void in their centers. They could have been a thousand years old. Every bomb crater collected foul brown water and often seemed to contain a dead dog or pig. Bodies like forgotten laundry hung from lampposts. The stench came through the closed windows. Crows everywhere you looked. Crows appreciated the war.

A jeep coming the opposite way flashed its lights at them, and a guy in a white-striped helmet stood on the passenger side, clutching the windshield and waving his free arm.

"I guess we're on the right road," Dorothy said. She yanked the truck over to the side.

The jeep rolled on. Ahead, a line of vehicles appeared around the bend whipping toward them. Ambulances. Irene and Dorothy jumped out to see them. Three big Red Cross ambulances followed by an army ambulance, making good time. The ambulances passed, sirens howling, with screams and groans coming from within the vehicles. Nurses hung halfway out the backs of a couple of the rigs.

"Run!" one of them shrieked. Her face was white, black shadows around her eyes. The wind held her hair off her head like some cursed crown. Her mouth stayed open. She was as one who had flown down from a terrible mountain crag, chased by thunder.

Once the ambulances were past, their sirens dropped in volume and pitch. Irene held her hands over her ears.

A trailing jeep appeared in their wake, rolled to a stop. It held a GI driver, and beside him a nurse whose white cap had blown loose and hung on by a few bobby pins.

"How's it going?" the driver said.

At first the Sisters could do nothing but nod. Then Irene confessed that they were lost.

"Just go straight," he said. "You'll know where the war is when you get there."

"Guess you're right about that," Irene said.

"Bad?" Dorothy asked the nurse.

She stared at them. "Tell me something that ain't," she said.

"There's some POWs coming down the road," the driver told them. "See if you can run 'em over."

Dorothy looked down the road and spit. "Krauts. I'll give it my best shot."

The nurse kept staring at them as if she'd never seen a human being before. "Donut Dollies," she said at last.

"Don't call me *Dolly,*" said Dorothy.

"Whelp," the GI said, "gotta scram. Keep your heads down."

"Keep your powder dry," Dorothy said.

"Au revoir." He jammed the jeep into gear and sped after the ambulances.

They'd driven not a mile down the road when a band of backlit men looking like X-rays crowded the lane. Dorothy braked. An MP stepped forward, pointed at the women, and waved them over to the side. Dorothy pulled over and shut down the motor. The *Rapid City* shuddered like a horse.

"Is that the POWs?" Dorothy called out the window.

"That's the dirty bastards," he said.

Irene craned her neck. GIs stood in a semicircle around four battered Germans in their ruined uniforms. The Americans kept their weapons aimed at the prisoners. The biggest German sneered.

"Most of them's just kids," the soldier said. "Just ground-poundin' grunts like us." He shook his head. "It's them SS shits, though. That big boy. That's the devil, pal."

"He don't care if they shoot him," Dorothy noted. "Can we get a look at the master race?"

"Knock yourselves out," the MP said, and walked away.

They climbed down and peered at these strange creatures. Like all men, the prisoners stood a little taller when the women appeared. The big one grinned at them, his eyes roving up and down.

Dorothy sniffed the air. "Smells like pig shit around here," she said.

The prisoner flushed, but his grin didn't falter. After that, it was silent—only a few crickets in the weeds, distant crows. The prisoners' boots made scraping sounds in the grit of the road, as they shifted their feet and kicked at loose stones. So these were the warriors of the Thousand-Year Reich. The Sisters walked around the tattered figures, keeping behind the GIs.

"They don't look so tough," Dorothy said.

"Except for that big monkey," Irene said.

The Germans were filthy. Their uniforms were torn. Only the tall one stood unbent and blond, arrogantly staring at the jumpy Americans waving rifles at him. When he stepped forward they moved back.

"Afraid?" he said, and laughed. "Heil Hitler." He smiled pleasantly when he said it, then lazily raised the salute.

"He's having a wonderful day," Irene whispered.

The other three prisoners were just boys, as the MP had said. They all made eye contact with the women. Flies had found their nostrils and tried to sip from them. The boys waved their hands before their faces, slowly, as if in a trance. One of them said, "*Bitte,*" to Irene.

"What's that mean?" Dorothy said.

"*Please,*" Irene replied.

"*Bitte,*" the kid said again, putting his hand up to his mouth.

"I should shoot you right now," a GI said.

The prisoner lifted both hands to his mouth. "*Wasser,*" he said. "*Bitte.*"

"He wants a drink," Irene said.

"Cry me a river," Dorothy said.

She marched back to the truck and climbed in. Irene stood her ground, unsure what she should do. Dorothy started the engine with a roar. Still, Irene didn't move. Dorothy put it in gear and kicked up gravel. Irene had to run to catch the door handle and pull herself up onto the running board. Dorothy hung her hand out the window and gave the finger to the pleading soldier.

In a minute, it was as if the scene had never happened.

—

They went around three bends and through a blackened field and came upon a family standing along the roadside with a goat on a leash.

"Those civilians are watching us," Dorothy said.

Irene reached across her and threw candy and packs of gum out the port-side window. The family stood their ground, merely glancing at the offerings and looking back up. The goat broke loose and ate the Beeman packs.

A truck full of GIs rumbled past in a cloud of cigarette smoke, and the boys whistled and cheered as Irene managed to transform a restorative stretch into the pose of a languid model, her hands raised beside her face, which she turned toward the mottled sun dropping through the leaves. She waved and called out to one monkey boy hanging out the back.

"Knock it off," Dorothy said. "They're gonna think you've gone khaki-wacky."

Irene just sniffed at her.

"Everybody loves Irene," Dorothy sighed, though she knew she was half in love with her, too.

It was four hours to combat, though the women could not have known that. They had no premonition. No angel offered them any portent. They had been lulled by their own boredom and by the early autumn itself. Who could imagine anything but peace in early autumn?

A lone soldier stood beside the road.

"Hey, soldier boy!" Irene yelled. "What's cookin'?"

"Chicken!" he called back. "Wanna neck?"

She waggled her finger at him like a schoolmarm. "Naughty boy," she called.

Autumn was Irene's favorite season—the word itself coated her memories in a sad light, the northern sun coming through the stained glass of the foliage. Flaming leaves, the colors echoed by the small ponds of her girlhood, those mirrors full of the borrowed illusion of fire, some giant's coins scattered among the maples and oaks between cattails and reeds. Oh, she ached for home.

Here, in the French countryside, burned-out vehicles lay on their sides in the ditches. A skeletal plane, its nose buried in the earth, was angled out of the soil of a field, encircled by a deep black ring of charred grass. Incurious cows tore at the yellow forage outside the burn. Far to the east, thin ropes of smoke rose from behind a stand of hemlocks. A ruined church stood alone, occasionally emitting pigeons from its shattered belfry.

Irene swam out of her reverie to hear Dorothy complaining.

"That damn donut cooker in back is shorting out, I'm telling you. I got a shock off that sumbitch day before yesterday. 'Bout blew my socks off."

They both looked up at a plane wasping its way across the sky. Not knowing whether it was a Stuka, Dorothy downshifted and stopped the truck under a thick overhang of oak branches.

Irene lit a smoke. When Dorothy snapped her fingers and held them open, Irene put her lit cigarette between Stretch's long fingers and lit herself another butt. "I'm going to quit," she said.

"Right." Dorothy blew a smoke ring. "Maybe that's your boyfriend up there," she said.

Irene feigned indifference, though she always looked to the sky whenever she heard a fighter, watching for his Mustang, and was even now wondering if the plane was his.

"Why do they call him Hands?"

"Well, Stretch," Irene shocked Dorothy by saying, "he's good with his joystick."

"I-*rene*!"

They were still laughing as they checked the plane above them. It was a Spitfire. Not his.

Dorothy shut down the engine, stretched, and said, "Break time!"

"Great idea," Irene said. "Let's have a picnic." She dug out a can of peaches from the rations stashed in the back of the truck.

Dorothy was already lying under the tree with her boots off and hands under her head, enjoying the sunlight coming through the leaves and a few moments of quiet peace. Irene sat down next to her and popped open the can. She slurped some of the syrup, sucking out a slice of peach, then passed the can to Dorothy, who finished it off.

"There is never enough," she said. After a moment, she added, "You think about your boy a lot, don't you? Your Handyman."

"Don't you think about Smitty?"

"Smitty?"

"I saw you two flirting. You took a shine to him. Admit it," Irene teased.

Dorothy sat up, locked eyes with Irene, and said, "No, I do not think about Smitty. I didn't come here for that and neither did you. For all I know, Smitty is dead somewhere."

Irene pondered this and, in a moment of clarity, said sadly, "For all I know, Handyman is married."

Dorothy snorted. "You've got a little too much sugar in your sinker recipe. We have a job to do. This isn't some romantic vacation. This isn't a movie, Gator."

A truck sped by on the road and the GIs within called and whistled as they passed and both women absent-mindedly waved without looking.

"Listen, we are both here trying to start all over again," Dorothy said. "You are barely recovered from that poisonous bastard who hurt you. Your mother still hasn't answered a single letter you've sent. God knows what else you're hiding."

Irene reddened and looked away. Her friend's honesty stung.

"I have lost my entire family," Dorothy continued. "I have lost my family home. My brother died in this war. So no, I don't think about Smitty. I think about my duty, I think about Donny." She turned to Irene and took her hands, looking closely into her eyes. "And I think about you. We are all we have right now. You and me. I think about us getting through this. What good does it do either one of us to get all moony over some guy who might end up getting blown out of the sky? What good will you be to me then? I will walk through fire for you. I need to know you will do the same for me."

Irene pulled Dorothy to her and bent her head over their clasped hands. Dorothy could feel tears falling on her fingers.

"Irene, you are my family now," Dorothy said softly. "I need you to understand what I'm saying. This is *our* story."

Irene reached up and embraced her friend. The two held each other, and though Irene wanted to speak, she could not. She trusted no words. But she trusted Dorothy to know what was true.

Two more trucks blasted down the road, kicking up pebbles and dirt, reminding both women that despite this moment, they needed to re-armor for the war still ahead of them.

Irene stood up and brushed off her pants, put her hand out to pull Dorothy to her feet.

"Thank you, Gator," said Dorothy, with mock seriousness.

Irene bowed to her. "Oh, it is my pleasure to serve you, madam."

They climbed into the truck and Dorothy restarted the engine.

"Back to work," Irene said, putting on her sunglasses.

Dorothy was especially careful not to grind the gears as she got the *Rapid City* rolling again. As they were pulling away, they saw the fake Burma-Shave signs that GIs had mounted onto tree trunks:

WHISTLE WHILE YOU WORK

HITLER IS A JERK

MUSSOLINI BROKE HIS WEENIE

NOW IT DOESNT WORK!

BURMA-SHAVE!

15

Early afternoon. Three and a half hours to combat.

The springs in the seat squealed incessantly, and Irene often had to press her hand against the roof of the cab to keep her head from hitting it as she bounced. *You're in the army now.* Scruffy foot soldiers stumbled along the road as the truck passed. More and more of them. They were feeling sorry for themselves. The whole army was. Sore feet. Aching backs. Heavy loads. Heavy rifles. Half of them had the squirts. Their helmets were loose on their heads, the rims banging their noses. Their postures were as sad-sack as beleaguered plow horses at the end of a hard day. It wasn't for nothing that people called them *blisterfoots.*

More than one of them stuck out a thumb when the *Rapid City* went by, and they all guffawed. When they saw Irene instead of some grunt, they stopped and hollered in surprise. Threw open their arms.

She opened her window and blew several kisses. "Let's pull over," Irene said. "Let's give the boys a treat."

Dorothy flatly refused.

"Give them the service," Irene said. "It's why we're here." Before Dorothy could stop her, Irene hung out the window again. "Gentlemen!" she cried. "How's about a visit from the Clubmobile! How's about a cuppa joe and some hot fresh donuts!" She laced her fingers beneath her chin and batted her eyelashes, basking in the soldiers' uproar.

The GIs immediately broke into double time and headed toward the women, their gear jangling and clanging all the way. Their boots on the road sounded like the hooves of dairy cows trotting home to the barn.

Their loose helmets slid around on their skulls. They formed a redolent honor guard, rifles held across their chests.

There goes the rest of the day, Dorothy thought. She maneuvered the truck into a grove of pines and oaks and yanked the brake. Branches covered their roof just enough to halfway hide them from German planes and give some shade to keep the truck cool. That kitchen warmed up fast, which felt good at first on a damp day but quickly became a sauna. They were lucky they had racks of surplus sinkers left over from yesterday. Dorothy had no intention of getting in the galley.

Outside the truck, the boys were already raising a fuss, churning mud.

"You asked for it," Dorothy told Irene. "Lift the shutters. Play some records."

Both women jumped out. Soldiers caught them and swung them down like dance partners, as if everyone was, for one moment, sixteen years old. Irene shoved aft through the crowd. Three pinches to the bottom as she maneuvered through, swatting them back like biting flies.

"All right, you stinkers!" Dorothy shouted at the GIs. "Help us put up the tarp. You want a roof, don't ya? Rain ain't gonna make this party fun, you know. And stop playin' grab-ass, boys. Momma's here to whip you into shape."

The soldiers hopped to.

"Are you a gentleman?" she asked one whose stubble was already gray.

He scratched his chin, pushed his helmet back on his head. "I could try it out," he said.

"Outstanding."

Irene muscled up the two shutters on the starboard side. She put out sugar, then punched open two cans of evaporated milk and set them beside the sugar dispensers. "Got a couple of armored cows over here," she called, "for you delicate types who need cream in your coffee. Sugar, too."

"Coffee with milk and sugar," a soldier said. "That ain't joe, that's dessert!"

Others were already leaning on the counter, asking for coffee, mail, chocolates, Chesterfields. And talk. Irene thought of her terrible boy cousins. All these dirty-faced, lonesome guys whose eager babble overlapped: "Where you from, honey? / You seen Dingus back there? / You married? / Seen action? / See any Krauts? / Got a boyfriend? / Any sports news? / Miss, you wouldn't have any books in there, would you?"

They did, in fact, have a couple of books and some *Life* magazines. Irene knelt in the back end of the galley to retrieve them. Boys started to crowd in the open door.

More overlapping questions: "Can we help? And are you single? / Got any chores for us? / Didn't I see you in Normandy? / Izzat a record player?"

"Not currently married, my dears," she said. "I will have chores for you in a minute. Normandy—probably. And this, indeed, is a record player. So let's dance."

The last statement provoked general uproar and elbowing in the ranks.

Dorothy, meanwhile, climbed into the galley and fired up the cooker and broke open the racks of day-olds. Filled the coffee urns and shoved in the ground-coffee baskets. Then she was back out on the ground, and Irene was still curating her library of swing records.

"Which one of you sad sacks can knock it out on the dance floor?" Dorothy called out.

They razzed a guy in back: "Schmidt can't dance!"

"Can too," Schmidt insisted, his face deep red. "Just watch me."

Irene plugged the Victrola into the electrical system. She twisted off the wing nuts. Swung it down and freed the tone arm from its clip. The truck was like a little B-17. Everything in its place. Bombloads of donuts in the racks, all arrayed vertically, waiting to be delivered.

"You boys like music?" she called.

"You bet!"

"Got any cowboy music, doll?"

"'Fraid not, lamb," she said.

"Play some love songs, lady."

"Aw," said another grunt, "you just gon' cry like a girl."

She was older than all of them. She loaded the spindle with records.

"I'll Be with You in Apple Blossom Time," "Cow-Cow Boogie," "It Had to Be You," "G.I. Jive."

"Schmidt," she said, hopping down and extending her hand.

He hurried away to great waves of laughter. Irene shrugged elaborately and wiped away an imaginary tear before squeezing by one soldier seated on the steps of the truck and climbing back aboard.

"Andrews Sisters," the soldier said, sighing with his back to her.

"That's right, soldier."

He had taken off his helmet. The back of his neck was red and scrawny. Lines of grime were etched in the wrinkles there. His hair stood straight up on his head, and sweat and grease had run down behind his ears. His shoulders were slumped, his elbows resting on his knees. A slash of dried blood stained his sleeve.

"Could you play that again, ma'am?"

"Sure, soldier." She put the needle down at the start of the record again and the muted brass vamp led into the languid harmonizing of the Andrews Sisters.

"I am dog-tired," he said, and dropped his head.

Her hand rose involuntarily, reaching toward his anonymous back. But she caught herself and turned away, then got to her feet and moved in behind the counter. Outside, Dorothy was barking orders at soldiers as they manfully wrestled with the segmented aluminum poles to hold up the green tarp.

Irene's fingers stung. They had thin red wounds like paper cuts around the knuckles. Both she and Dorothy had rough hands now. They kept bottles of lotion in the truck, but it didn't help. Their nail polish was chipped. They doused themselves with eau de toilette but still smelled like cooking grease. In a way she couldn't have explained, Irene was overwhelmed by love for everyone whenever she looked at her hands.

She went to the sinker racks and opened them, freeing the donuts. Sure, they were stale, but nobody cared. Soon enough, the fryer would be working and hot soft fresh greasy donuts would tumble out. The coffee urn was already starting to hiss. It was going to be a twenty-gallon afternoon, and all for this impromptu stop of hers. Their water tanks would be empty if they weren't careful.

After her grunts had put up the tarp, Dorothy hung back and used her old Kodak camera to shoot a few glamour shots of the *Rapid City.* There was Gator, waving from the window. Dorothy snapped six frames. Irene pouring coffee into a grunt's tin cup: two shots. *Better thee than me,* Dorothy thought. She had never been partial to cooking, no matter how much Momma had tried to get her in the kitchen. She would always rather have been fishing than peeling taters or buttermilk-frying a chicken she'd been forced to kill.

Trucks were rolling up the road, parking willy-nilly. A water-buffalo tanker truck pumped a few extra gallons into the *Rapid City*'s tanks and rolled away without fanfare. Some ferociously weird vehicle with what looked like sections of drawbridges atop it squeezed by and followed the tanker.

Irene had no idea where the convoy was heading. She just wanted to catch up to it and hoped it was heading to a town, where she could sleep in a real bed, eat some real food, sit on a real toilet. Bathe. Yes—a nice bath. Then drink a big bottle of something tasty, locked alone in her room. Open a window and let all these secret confessions she had collected from the soldiers fly away like sad butterflies.

In the galley, the new coffee was getting hot. Irene was on the second urn already. Unable to keep her hair out of her face, she tied a bandanna around her head. She swayed her hips to unkink her back and kept working. Guys held up their mess kits for donuts. Irene poured coffee into cups and slid them out the windows. Dorothy kept the line moving. "In the Mood" dropped on the spindle. Duke Ellington's "Rockin' in Rhythm" followed.

"That's an oldie," a soldier said.

"So am I," Irene said.

"Not so's you'd notice!"

"My achin' back says different."

"Move along, bub," Dorothy said. "This ain't the zoo. No gawkin'."

"Yous girls is pretty!"

"Pretty bored with your shenanigans," Dorothy said. "Keep the line moving."

"Slide to your left, boys," Irene said. "My right. Don't block the window."

"The *D* in *D-Day* stands for *Donuts*!" one happy idiot yelled.

Then a slender, dark GI with no helmet and a little black mustache and tiny chin beard stepped up. The other guys were calling him *Zoot,* and *Zoot Suit,* and *Bone Face,* and *Garsha.*

"Make way for Swede!" A burly chunk of florid roast beef announced himself and pushed his way to the front of the line. "Garcia," he said, towering over the smaller man. "You're a spic, huh?"

At first, Irene thought he was trying to be funny—one soldier ribbing another.

Swede pulled a cigarette out of his pocket, lit it, and squinted at her through the smoke. "Give me some goddamned coffee," he said, and snapped his fingers at her.

The other troops in back appeared to find this hilarious.

Without warning, Garcia knocked his rifle butt into the back of Swede's knee and toppled him. He stepped around the man and stood before the window, smiling up at Irene. He spoke over his shoulder to the fallen hulk: "Sorry, bud. I guess I swung that popgun a little wild."

Swede got up, red in the face, his jaw muscles rippling, his fists rising to his chest. The other GIs, smelling a fight, made room.

Garcia pivoted to face Swede. "*Spic?*" he said. "What is that? I heard that somewhere. Some dimwit one time. I shivved him just in case he was disrespecting me." He showed Swede his back and looked up at Irene. "May I have two donuts, please, miss?" He laid his tin cup on the counter.

Swede gave the impression of emitting actual steam from his ears, like some mad bull in a Tex Avery cartoon.

"I'm a private first class, motor pool," Garcia said to Swede, barely moving his head. "Lightweight boxer. Won twelve, lost one. What are you?"

Irene poured Garcia a coffee, and he took three donuts. Swede had backed up a few inches after the boxing mention.

"What's your problem?" Garcia said as he sauntered past. He threw a fake jab with his left and Swede flinched.

The next GI stepped up to the big man. "I'll take two donuts and coffee, cream and sugar," he called to Irene. "I'm a kike," he told Swede, then walked away.

Swede looked terrified when a Negro soldier stepped up. The other troops were now laughing at him.

"Guess what I am," the soldier said.

Dorothy stepped over to Swede. "Take it from Momma," she said. "It is time to get your fat ass out of here and let actual fighting men enjoy their sinkers while you go sulk in the latrine."

Swede charged away, knocking GIs aside as he went, and Dorothy winked at Irene. She could not recall ever being in any big gathering of men when at least one of them didn't have bad intentions. That kind of casual violence seemed to percolate up through gangs of men, and all the women she had been close to knew it. She wasn't going to allow any funny business with Irene, so she kept her eyes open and roving.

Some GIs hung back and smoked. They had that haunted look, the blank and sunken eyes. Irene and Dorothy called it *the thousand-yard stare*. They never laughed. Nothing could get them to flirt or step forward, least of all coffee. Dorothy kept watch on them. You could see in their faces that there was more than one Swede in any crowd.

—

A jeep skidded into the clearing, kicking up twigs and clods of mud and making troops dance out of the way. Dorothy swung her camera at the driver. He had lieutenant stripes. When he pulled off his helmet the hair underneath was redder than the turning leaves.

"Why, Russell Penney, as I live and breathe!" she called.

Rusty blushed immediately.

"What's buzzin', cousin?" Dorothy said.

"Ma'am," Russ said as he climbed out of his vehicle.

"Coffee, Russell?"

"In a minute, Miss Dorothy," he said. He looked over at the soldiers. "Who's drivin' those rigs in the road?"

A few hands rose.

"Y'all do know about Kraut planes, don't you?"

Abashed, the boys hung their heads.

"Let's get this situation repaired double time. Y'all fubared my road up."

The drivers rushed to their trucks.

"Sorry, Loot," one called back. "We was excited about the Dollies."

"Don't call me *Dolly,*" said Dorothy for the umpteenth time.

"Get those trucks snuggled up next to these trees," Rusty shouted.

Up and down the road the engines burped to life. Dorothy leaned on the *Rapid*'s fender. She shook out a smoke and extended the pack to Rusty, who stepped over to her and took it. She lit him up.

"Gonna quit," he said.

"Me, too."

"Pretty soon."

"But not today."

"Goldang soldiering," he said.

"Be glad you aren't us. Full-time KP."

"I never studied up on that," he said. "But hey, you get to see the world."

"Shee-it," she said, just like her brother used to do—head down, digging in the dirt with the toe of her boot.

They blew smoke away from each other.

"How's Miss Irene?"

"Swell," Dorothy said, and gestured with her chin toward the *Rapid City*.

"She looks busier'n a cat tryin' to bury crap on a marble floor."

"Funny," Dorothy said, not laughing. "I like that one."

They smoked on, philosophically. Behind them, the cups clattered and the GIs flirted and the donuts flew.

"Go say something sweet," Dorothy said.

—

Unbeknownst to the Americans, men in gray uniforms lying prone deep in the woods were watching their every move through large binoculars. It was a reconnaissance patrol, an outlier of a combat troop a few miles behind. Helmets lay on the ground near them. One black peaked cap had a silver skull above its bill. All their radios were silenced. No one spoke. They communicated via hand signals. Their rifles were wrapped in camouflage cloth. Wehrmacht troops behind them in the woods were moving west.

—

Russell took cuts in the line, not even bothering to excuse himself. The other soldiers hated it when an officer pulled rank, but they had to let him in. Shit flowed downhill in the army. They moved back a step and made faces behind his back.

"Lieutenant!" Irene said. "I am so happy to see you!"

"Howdy, Miss Irene."

"How are you, Russell?"

"I'm so hungry my stomach thinks my throat's been cut."

Irene loaded a plate with sinkers for him and produced a steaming mug of black coffee. She went to put more records on, then yanked a fresh apron free from its box and tied it on. Dorothy moseyed over and made wan gestures toward serving. All in all, it hadn't been too bad, really. Only about a hundred GIs. It had taken them two hours. They were setting speed records. Fortunately, yesterday's leftover sinkers had knocked out half of the orders.

Dorothy tinkered with the wiring of the donut cooker while Irene hauled the coffee urn down the back steps, where a few soldiers took it for her. There were about five inches of coffee left inside. They watered a tree with it. Irene sat on the back steps of the truck and daydreamed that she and Handyman were walking across the fields to the maples and the one great oak on the far side of the Woodward property in

Mattituck. Better yet, she imagined a different day when Handyman took her to his mountains in Oregon. In her mind, they looked like the snowy Himalayas.

Dorothy was checking the tires when Rusty came out of the woods zipping his trousers. "Ladies," he said, "are you partial to minor infractions?"

"Like?" Dorothy said.

"Like maybe assisting me in evading some orders."

"Russell Penney," Irene said. "What fresh hell is this?"

"Well, ain't no big deal. No crime at all. Just a little runaround on some orders I got. But since y'all are volunteers—not egg-zackly army, right?—my orders are not your orders, strictly speakin'. Get me?"

"Not really," Dorothy said.

"There's a town not forty-five minutes away," he said. "You just gotta haul it there."

"Haul what?" Irene said, growing exasperated.

Rusty looked around to make sure none of the men could hear him. "We got word yesterday to stop liberatin' things from houses and hotels. He led them over to his jeep, where, behind the front seats, sat a pair of crates covered in burlap. He pulled back the burlap and the lids of the crates to reveal dusty bottles. "Fruit brandy," he said. "I kepped it out of a kitchen at a li'l hotel back there that the Germans was using. Some rum, too."

The two women bent to the bottles as though shopping.

"Ain't like I'm smuggling gold, for gosh sakes," Rusty said.

"This serum heals what ails ya," Dorothy noted.

"I'd love a snort," Irene conceded.

"I'll drink anything but coffee," Dorothy said.

Rusty put his hands in his pockets and hung his head. "I know drinking is y'all's biggest diversion," he said, as if by way of persuading them. "Y'all got room to hide this hooch in your rig. Y'all could smuggle a cow in there if you wanted to. There's a million places to hide contraband in there. I'll find y'all later tonight and we'll have a party."

Why hadn't he said that from the outset? Instantly, the liquor was tucked in an unused cabinet beneath the counter and behind sacks of donut mix and a small sign that read: WE WEIGH OUR WATER.

Russell hopped into his jeep and took off down the road.

—

Already, the main body of the German combat group had curved like a scythe around the western and northern perimeter of the small French town up ahead. The Germans were only waiting for full dark to take the town back. And this time, they intended to strike with punishing severity.

16

One hour to combat.

Dorothy didn't feel like talking. Irene wasn't talking, either. They wanted to get drunk, take baths, go to bed. They didn't mind being silent.

A mile from town, they came across overturned German vehicles, burned. Charcoal effigies of men with bright white rictus grins lay about in strangely casual poses. Although most of the phone poles were still standing, their lines had all been cut. Wires lay across the road.

The truck parted a small flock of sheep, and they entered the town, nestled in a shallow valley surrounded at a distance by dark forest on three sides. Neither of them had the slightest idea what the town was called. Saint something. Steeples showed through the damage. In the afternoon sunlight, the central plaza seemed festive, completely at odds with the horrors they'd just witnessed. Church bells were ringing out six o'clock. The houses had faded yellow walls and red tile roofs, and there were small statues on pedestals, welcome flags hanging from upper windows. A few people waved American flags. The counterpoint was the bullet holes stitching the walls; the cracked and shattered windows; the bell tower split apart by a cannon fusillade. The familiar smell of smoke permeated the scene.

"I hope we're lucky enough to find a restaurant open," Irene said. "It would be nice to be spoiled."

Dorothy steered around a crater ringed with piles of bricks and soil the color of old blood. Some buildings were peeled open. American soldiers lounged in the shade, scratching hard-luck cats behind their ears. They waved, cool as movie stars. Dorothy maneuvered the *Rapid* between walls and phone poles. Dogs launched suicidal assaults on the tires.

The buildings themselves seemed exhausted and demoralized. The charred hulk of a German staff car lay like a dinosaur skeleton in a pool of cinders off the main drag. A U.S. jeep with a mounted .30 Browning sat ten feet away from it. Some of the citizens shuffled along, staring at the ground, as if lacking the energy to look up when their more joyous neighbors cheered.

Dorothy stopped the truck for a moment and hung her elbow out the window, closing her eyes and holding her face up to the lowering sun. "When women rule the world," she said, "we'll have smarter wars."

Irene leaned forward and viewed the world through the bug-encrusted windshield. A single tall ash tree peeking over a small church had not yet lost its leaves, though they were already red and yellow against the darkening China-blue sky. Sparrows fussed along the curbs and in the gardens. Above, swallows cut the air with their scissor tails.

In a four-way intersection, where the main street met three lanes, a statue of a gaunt Saint George thrust his crooked spear into a tragic dragon. The fountain upon which the two figures stood was empty.

"Those poor things need a donut," Irene said.

There were blue and red doors all around in the yellow walls. Black shutters pinned open to the fading light. Another European town, wondering what had had happened to the world. Bullet strikes as big as teacups pocked the walls. But the square featured tables in the street, spread with tablecloths and bearing small plates of white bread and sausage, as if warfare were a myth. Locals sipped wine and blinked at a sky suddenly free of danger. They nodded at the *Rapid* as it groaned past. Crabby waiters dragged chairs out of the way so the truck could rumble along.

"Cheer up!" Dorothy yelled. "We're liberating you."

The waiters didn't even look up.

"They've seen it all," Irene said.

Dorothy shifted gears, working that hard clutch with her left foot.

They rumbled past the last recalcitrant café and into the residential area. Dorothy smoked without touching her cigarette. Some streets were blocked by waving, tattered people. The civilians who saw the Red Cross design on the truck probably assumed they were nurses come to administer medicine. Dorothy and Irene paused to admire stone horse heads protruding mysteriously from third-story walls. The stonework seemed alive, as if the horses regarded them with curiosity. GIs smoked and cleaned their rifles, calling, "Hey, dolls." Dorothy made the Victory sign.

The very old houses—those small gray peasant dwellings made of stacked stones that had stood unchanged for hundreds of years—were everywhere reduced to small mountain ranges of rubble. The fresh smells of baking bread wrestled with the pervading stench of garbage. The disappearing sun busied itself with laying its final watercolor yellows and oranges across the walls. Everything was unbearable.

"A bath and a bed," Irene said.

"A good night's sleep," Dorothy said.

"A bottle of rum."

"Two bottles."

Dorothy ignored the tumult, still looking for some protected spot to park. She hadn't been raised to be a fool. There wasn't a secure village in all of Europe. Bloomington was safe. Indianapolis was safe. This burg? She spit out the window. It was pretty enough but all it would take was one dive-bomber to destroy the *Rapid City* and everything around it.

They were already on the outskirts, and she found a small barn standing at a slight angle, off plumb. It was empty, with copper shafts of slanted light cutting through its shadows. Dust and chaff drifted almost white in these narrow beams. Beyond the barn lay fields and a bog of some kind. No damn Germans were going to come rolling out of *that*. So they were safe on one side, at least. She piloted the truck into the barn with the steady hand of a sea captain.

"Atta girl," Irene said.

The truck shuddered as Dorothy shut it down, the engine knocking a few times, as if unwilling to stop. Once it quit, they could hear the faint notes of a brass band playing sourly back in the square. Before she opened her door, Irene reached under her seat for the .45 and holstered it. Small goats sniffed the truck's great tires and pressed themselves against the women's legs as they stepped down, butting their knees as they waded out of the barn and into what remained of the day. The little beasts leaped through the air, landed on the running boards of the truck, and dived back off.

"Let's go," Dorothy said, "I need to find some food."

They began to walk back toward the town.

"Only the dead have seen the end of war," Irene said.

After a few steps, Dorothy said, "What kind of bullshit is that?"

"George Santayana."

Dorothy fumed for just a moment, then said, "Jesus, Gator. Who the hell is that? And anyway, just be a little more morbid, why don't you?"

They came around a corner and were accosted by a bedraggled family. A skinny little girl, all eyes, all snot on her face, her filthy black hair a corona around her head. An older gentleman and a thin woman stood with her. At first, she took these people for beggars. The child's too-small dress made of her body an ashy red triangle with two scabby legs sticking out of the bottom. A shawl was wrapped around her shoulders. The adults wore black coats, the father's torn at the shoulder. A red-pink bandage was wound around his head, a ghastly wet patch taped over his eye. His hands were wrapped in soiled bandages.

Dorothy offered him a cigarette. He lipped it out of the pack and Irene lit him up. He closed his good eye and held the smoke for a moment.

"Sanks," he said.

"You're welcome," Dorothy said.

"I was mayor," he said, surprising the women with not only his English but also this fact.

They glanced at each other.

"I know, I know," he said, brushing off his hopeless jacket. "Before. Now I'm not so debonair."

"Good evening, Monsieur," Irene said. "I'm sorry but we're in a bit of a hurry. Can we help you?"

"Please," the man said.

"We don't have any money," Dorothy said. "Sorry."

"They ruin my hands, you see."

"Who?" Irene asked.

"The Germans. They take my eye," he said.

The older woman shuddered and turned her face away.

"With spoon," the man said.

The woman put her hands over the girl's ears.

"Jesus," Irene said.

"Please," the man said.

"What do you need?" Irene asked.

"They come back."

"No," Dorothy said.

"Oh no," Irene agreed. "We beat them." She smiled reassuringly.

The little girl suddenly wept and hid her face behind her mother's skirt.

"They come back," the man insisted.

"No," Dorothy repeated. "They won't." She went to pat him but he jerked his arm away.

"No! They come back. Finish me then. Finish all of family." He put his hands on his wife and daughter.

The last of the setting sun touched their faces. They could hear a trumpet somewhere. Crows raised an alarm in the trees.

"Finish all family. *Totenkopf*, yes?"

They didn't know that word.

He gestured at his family with his shattered hand. "Please, look at my Lily. Look at my Lina."

They didn't want to look.

"Is coming back for us. Look." He moved his arm as if to take in the whole of the beaten town. "Is kill us all."

"Don't worry," Irene said, knowing it was ridiculous as she said it.

"Don't be stupid," he said. "You save my Lily."

The girl looked up at them, her eyes scanning their faces. Very dark eyes.

"Sir," said Irene.

"You take Lily. Take her, please. Save our baby. Take to Belgium. Paris. America."

The mother covered her face with her hands.

Irene and Dorothy made their excuses. Regulations would never allow such a thing. They were neither trained nor prepared to save Lily, as lovely as Lily was. The family would have to trust the American soldiers. The U.S. Army would not abandon them. George S. Patton was their liberator and would protect them. In the morning there would be coffee and donuts. You know donuts?

They closed their ears to the man's further entreaties and handed Lily a Hershey bar and hurried away, as if they could escape their own consciences if only they moved fast enough.

Around the corner, they found hell.

17

DARKNESS HAD FALLEN, and as they turned the corner to the main square, a monstrous wave of sound crashed upon them. People were already stampeding, blind, their mouths open.

Instantaneously, all was eruption. All was fire. Without preamble, the earth seemed to shatter. A church spire exploded. Gray tanks spewing black clouds of exhaust ripped through the warehouses a hundred yards away, one of them vomiting gouts of fire from its muzzle. Orange flames spewed and dripped, cast lurching shadows of deepest darkness that were almost audible as they crashed across buildings and down streets, creating ink-black ghost houses and elongated wraiths jigging across the walls.

Irene ran across the burning square. She hung on to Dorothy with her gaze, as if vision itself were a rope that could pull her. Dorothy ran faster than she could, and she thought she would collapse long before Dorothy vanished into the night and abandoned her. She could not be alone. She forced her legs to pump harder. She could not breathe but she sucked air around the stone jammed down her throat.

She managed to let loose a primal shout.

"Don't talk—run!" Dorothy yelled.

They had only each other. There was no thought, just terror. Just eyes gone feral in their panic, their animal gazes searching for any escape.

Dorothy looked back to Irene and waved her forward. Irene ran faster than she knew she could. Nothing mattered aside from this: she wanted to live. More than anything she had ever wanted before, she wanted life. At any cost. She would be glad if the civilians around her fell, for it might mean she could live another minute.

"*Run!*" Dorothy shouted again.

How savagely the center of the town burned. How quickly it had ignited. Sparks already spiraled into the sky above them. More detonations. Irene felt a relentless pounding in her chest from the rifle fire. Every sound was an assault on the senses: the howl of conflagration; the immense crackling of the old buildings; the collapsing roof tiles going off like small bombs; the shattering windows; the popping of more rifle fire in the smoke. The engines roared louder than the many civilians chased into the avenues and alleys. The rumble of heavy boots charging into the streets, screaming male voices—it was all around them, without focus.

Other bodies slammed them and hands and elbows bashed them aside. They broke away from the crowd, aiming to throw themselves at any dark aperture ahead. Flames pursued them around the corner and set fire to small birches and maples already lit with Irene's beloved fall colors. All the dogs had run for the woods, where they barked and yowled in the shadows. Planks of burning wood flew from the shell strikes around them, trailing smoke like rockets.

They didn't believe anymore that they had years ahead of them. How easily that illusion had been shattered—all was survival now. This afternoon they had been joking with some scruffy GIs, sharing smokes and yukking about the Dodgers. Now, dragons that had screamed to life and ripped out of the forest were blowing up cafés and stores all along the main boulevard. Men themselves exploded like small houses hit by bombs. Irene took a spray of blood hot to her face and screamed because she thought she'd been shot.

A GI shouted, "Run!" and fired at the German tanks.

They had fallen out of the world they thought they knew and into a fragmentary place. A world where bricks flew. Where roofs suddenly came apart like leaves in an upward wind. Where noise was so assaultive that they could no longer hear it.

Only one thought: *Escape.*

"Irene—duck!"

Irene went to her knees. A storm of stone and powder flew over her head, and Dorothy was pulling her up by the back of her blouse.

"Go, go, go!" she yelled.

Gunfire looked like low lightning between the walls of old buildings, but it sounded nothing like thunder. The engines, though. The engines. The engines of the advancing tanks sounded as if living monsters were advancing on them. And the explosions kept echoing: every boom was immediately answered as it bounced off the walls of the town.

The sounds echoed in Irene's flesh as well. Her insides wobbled within her like painful jelly. She could hear the end of the world through her bones. The women's boots made them stumble, and no matter how hard they tried to run, they felt themselves going slower, as if in a dream that batters the heart until the dreamer chokes awake.

Dorothy got behind Irene and pushed.

"I'm doing my best!" Irene shouted.

"Do better."

GIs flanked them, spun around, and knelt to provide covering fire. Dorothy was yelling again, but Irene couldn't hear her and was afraid to turn her head, because the only way she could avoid falling on these cobblestones was to watch her feet.

Then she heard what Dorothy was yelling: "Haul ass!"

And on they ran. German bullets popped over their heads, loud sonic breaches in the air, vacuums formed and bursting invisibly in atmospheric space. *Crack! Crack!* Rounds speeding lower, past their ears, were wasps shrieking into the greater dark. *Zeeeee!* GIs fell to their right and to their left.

They relied on their training: they ran bent at the waist, they zig-zagged. They broke protocol by holding hands. Smoke choked them. They ran around another corner, and it was clear. Clean air here. As if they had flown to some new city. Even the noise was diminished.

They slowed to catch their breaths. Dorothy clutched her side and walked at an angle. Irene wanted to bend over and put her hands on her knees.

"Oh, Mother," Irene said. "Oh, Mother." She trudged on, choking for air.

The narrow alleys presented a gray maze. Any wrong turn could be their ultimate error. Cats like dark shadows scrambled over walls. *Bam! Bam! Bam!* The sound could be coming from anywhere. Rats swarmed out of sewer holes, and the Sisters of the *City* ran again.

They had no idea where they were in the town. They simply leaped over any barrier in their way. A ruined chair. A pile of brick that had once been a chimney. A pool of black water. Glass exploded out of auberge windows above them in a cutting rain.

Male voices shouted behind them, primordial, issuing guttural obscenities and commands in an unknown language.

"Run, Dorothy!" yelled Irene, who had pulled ahead.

"What do you think I'm doin'?" Dorothy said, and she grabbed Irene and threw her over a low, crumbled masonry wall and dived in behind her as enemy rounds stitched a diagonal line of dust blooms behind them.

Civilians shrieked like graveyard spirits as they ran past the wall. Boots and radios chased them.

"Will they find us?" Irene said, her face pressed to the sour black earth.

"Shh."

"Dot— "

"Shush now."

They kept their faces down between their hands.

Of all the sounds that night, the shrieking was the worst. Irene couldn't stand its high pitch. It put her back at the Woodward farm, at pig-slaughtering time, just as the terrible shrieks on that train to London had done. She knelt in that dirt and moved her fingers into her ears. Dirt was in her mouth. She put her forehead hard against the soil and moaned.

Dorothy, sprawled in the garden near her, whispered, "It's gonna be all right, Gator. I promise."

They reached out and took each other's hands. The low masonry wall was all that stood between them and the Panzer tanks, one of which was destroying a house half a block away. The noise was immense. The tank pivoted on its track and backed out through the far wall of the house and rumbled around the corner.

It had been less than twenty minutes since the tanks had torn open the forest and rolled into town, but it already seemed like hours. Splinters and brick rained down on the garden in cascades of dust. The stink of mulch and soil was almost an exotic flavor. Wan root vegetables were limp under the women's hands, and spoiled old leaves in vegetal compost leaked fluids between their knees. There was a trapezoidal shed down the yard from them, half-broken, and a terrified goose within voiced its endless alarms.

"Dot," Irene whispered. "Over there." She gestured with her chin at the house across the narrow yard, where the kitchen door hung loose.

"Let's go," Dorothy said.

"Roger," said Irene, and charged away on her hands and knees.

"Irene!" Dorothy whispered. "Keep your butt down!"

Irene hit the leaning door and shoulder-rolled into a dark kitchen.

Dorothy barreled in after her, flipped onto her back, and kicked the door shut behind them. It bounced back open. "Bastard!" she said and kicked it again.

The sky outside the windows flashed red and yellow. They lay on their backs, splayed in the crucifixion pose of the truly spent. They gasped, ripping breath out of the air. Dorothy had one knee up. Irene put her hands behind her head and crossed her ankles. Her chest heaved for a long time. They looked absurdly comfortable. Irene's body seemed to be acting on its own volition now. Shudders charged across her belly and arms and legs, and her feet kicked by themselves.

"Holy God," Dorothy said.

A grease of sweat smeared their faces. They breathed until the rasp had gone out of their throats.

Dorothy turned her head and spit out dirt. "I nearly pissed my britches," she said.

In the fathomless night, they were cut off, blind, several streets away from the heart of the destruction. They felt as though they had run five miles. Warehouses on the main road burst into flame, and now the buildings were already beginning their agonized collapse. The oily orange light splashed up and down the alleys in tidal surges. Houses all around them wobbled in the glare.

The gunfire momentarily abated. Dorothy was up on her knees, peeking over the window ledge, careful not to cut herself on the jagged daggers of glass protruding from its frame. Then she surveyed the dark room around them. Apparently, the people who lived here had thought to blow out the kitchen's lamps before they fled. Flickering light from the fires outside dimly illuminated everything with a dirty ocher glow. The room smelled of cabbages.

A shabby little table and three rough chairs were jammed into a corner beside some bare shelves. Irene, also rising to her knees, could make out some plates on the table in the murk. Supper, abandoned. She sank back to the floor. The iron stove was to her back, cold and dense. There was a pump beside the basin with a pail next to it on the floor. Well water. She wondered briefly if this was the mayor's house. The man with one eye. And what was the name of the girl, his daughter? Lily? Lina?

"Hey, Gator," Dorothy whispered. "I smell bread. Is there bread on that table?"

"All I smell is smoke."

"On the table."

Irene crawled over, reached up, and felt around. "Hey," she said, and grabbed a loaf of black bread missing a great bite on one end. Then she brought down a platter. "Cheese," she reported.

The cheese was limp and greasy, tart. Irene licked her fingers. Dorothy shuffled to her on her knees. They squatted like cavewomen and tore into the bread with their teeth.

Dorothy tried to say something, but her mouth was so stuffed that it sounded like "Marfle, marfle."

Irene laughed, and a piece of glass fell out of the window and broke on the floor. A metallic *click,* followed by the rasp of a sleeve on the sill, sounded behind them, and they responded instinctively. Dorothy hit the floor and covered her head. Irene clawed at her holster—but it was empty. A German soldier was staring at them, leaning in through the opening where the glass had been, his rifle pointed loosely into the room. He made eye contact with Irene. His helmet was gone. He smiled as his finger went to the trigger.

"*Nein! Nein! Nein!*" Dorothy hollered. "*Nein,* you bastard, *nein*!"

They slapped at their shoulder patches.

"Red Cross! Red Cross!" they both shouted, as if it were an incantation that held the power to save their lives. "Red Cross!"

He simply stared at them, closed one eye, and took theatrical aim.

"*Nein!*" Irene said. "*Nein! Nein!* Red Cross! *Bitte.*"

He glanced over his shoulder at the apocalypse consuming the town, then turned back to them.

"*Bitte!*" Irene repeated.

"*Français?*" he said.

She shook her head.

"*Belge?*"

"American, goddamn it," Dorothy said.

He smirked. "Jew?" he said, in English.

"Presbyterian, you ironic prick."

He stared at her.

"Dottie," Irene warned.

"*Rotes Kreuz?*" he said.

"*Ja! Ja!*" Irene was bilingual in her terror. She kept pointing at her patch. "*Rotes Kreuz.*" She held her hands up before her, as if they could stop a bullet.

He yawned. "*Jawohl,*" he murmured, finger still on the trigger.

She could never forget his face, Irene thought—how tired he seemed. How much he resembled someone's father. Some dad recently torn from his newspaper and cup of coffee after a long hard day at work. But he couldn't be older than twenty-five. Smirking in absolute boredom. She had seen his look many times already. Every GI lining up for coffee outside the truck had that same expression. A face full of disgusted amusement. If they'd seen him walking down the street in the States, they wouldn't have looked twice. And now he was going to kill them.

Dorothy, too, opened her hands to catch the bullets when they came. "Come on, man," she implored him.

He blinked slowly, as if sleepy.

They tapped their shoulder patches some more. "Yeah?" they said. "Okay?"

He stifled a yawn. In heavily accented English, he said, "Yes, but I don't really care."

Another shard dropped from the window and shattered musically when it hit the floor.

He glanced down as if mildly surprised. "I kill women," he noted as though apologizing, and gave a slight shrug. Another very long blink. He smiled as though he were shy about killing women. "It won't hurt," he said. He appeared to work at some morsel between his teeth with the tip of his tongue, the wide hole of the rifle barrel levitating before their faces all the while. "Nurses?" he said.

Irene shook her head. "No. *Nein*. No."

He took one hand from his weapon and rubbed his eyes. "Then what?" he said. *Zen vott?*

"Donuts!" they cried. "Coffee! We make coffee!"

He cocked his head. "*Was ist das?*" he said, swinging the rifle back and forth at each of them.

Dorothy pantomimed sipping coffee from a cup.

"Not nurse?"

"No."

Irene wrung out a little more of her Staten Island high school German: "*Kr*..." she started to say. Put her knuckles to her forehead. "*Krapfen!*"

"And coffee," Dorothy added.

Irene drank from her own phantom cup.

"Yeah," Dorothy said. He must think she was saying "*Ja*," she realized. She probably looked German to him.

"*Ihr machen Kaffee?*" he said.

"*Oui!*" Irene blurted.

He coughed out a laugh. "*Scheisse*," he said.

His expression suggested that he had seen it all now, as if the ridiculousness of life just reminded him how pointless it all was. Probably he had a sweetheart back in Bavaria who looked like Dorothy. Maybe he used to read Novalis and Rilke to her in the town square while they nibbled on marzipan stollen and sipped cups of *Kaffee*. Everything was absurd, his face said. There were no words for it.

"*Albern*," he said, and lowered the rifle. He gestured with his free hand: *down, down—stay down*. "I come for you later."

He ran off into the dark.

18

They breathed again.

The shooting was now distant. Someone else's neighborhood. The rifles and machine guns sounded flat, artificial. No boots ran down the alley. They couldn't hear the terrible engines anymore. They were both nauseated.

"I was ready to smack him," Dorothy boasted.

"She says after he's gone."

They were being extra-American for each other: nobody was going to break their can-do spirit! Around their hideout all was silence now, save for the crackling of the fires and the poor goose still fussing in its shed.

"Is it over?" Irene said.

"I wouldn't go out to find out if I was you."

"I'm sorry I lost the gun, darling."

"Don't call me *darling*. People will think we're in love."

They giggled, their eyes bright with adrenaline.

"I actually hate you," Irene said.

"Hate you, too," Dorothy said. She dug a crushed pack of smokes from her breast pocket, straightened one out, and hung it on her lip, then struck a match on the floorboards and cupped the flame with her free hand, lest some sniper outside should target her. "Gonna quit," she promised.

"I didn't mean to lose the gun," Irene said.

"Right," Dorothy said, floating the word away on a blue cloud of smoke.

"It's not like I wanted to lose it," Irene said.

"Right." Dorothy's hands were shaking, as they had earlier in the day when she was driving.

"Oh, I'm useless!" Irene cried.

Dorothy just stared at her.

Irene snapped her fingers. "Give me one of those."

Dorothy tossed her the pack.

"Darling Dot," Irene said. "You sleep. I'll stand watch."

Dorothy didn't even pretend to argue. She rolled onto her side and laid her head on her arm. It looked miserably uncomfortable to Irene. But soon utter exhaustion took Darling Dot down, and she started to snore.

Irene crawled under the table, in case the German came back. She ate the last of the bread and cheese. "Stay awake, Irene," she whispered to herself.

She was vigilant. The night was turning viscous, flowing slow as batter rolling out of a bowl. The air was humid, cloying. At the window she saw runners of fog creep through the yard. Time congealed. An hour felt like a day. The tired world was rusting all around her. She curled up under the table and lay with her head on her crossed hands like some child, watching Dorothy's widening sprawl, listening to her sleep. Irene herself was restless. She crawled to the window and peeked out again. Nothing but flickers and smoke in either direction. Heavy rumbles as weakened edifices collapsed from time to time. A dense lid of gray clamped down. The air had the ugly scent of battle. Gunpowder and burning. Rank biological stink. Meat. Through the clouds and smoke came the sound of throbbing engines.

She pulled her face away from the shattered glass, crawled to the open doorway that led to the rest of the house, and peered into the next space. She was startled to see shadowy stairs leading to an upper room. Neither of them had noticed a second story.

A kind of half dream fell upon her, such that she seemed to be dreaming right where she knelt. The room at the top of the stairs was bright—it was spring or summer. That room was the only refuge from war, she saw. There was some kind of magic in it, some spell. It was never dark or dangerous there. But when she dreamed herself running up the staircase and reaching the room, it was crowded with skeletons, all of them staring out the window with their black eyeholes.... She kicked awake, still at the bottom of the stairs.

The room before her, there on the ground floor, had been semi-demolished by machine-gun fire. The thin white curtains in the windows had burned from the heat of the bullets. Their charred tatters moved in what ambient light there was. Glass and wall fragments blanketed the floor. There was a heavy desk to the side of the room, its chair overturned, and the far wall held bookshelves.

She crawled forward into this library, careful not to slice her knees or hands on the shards. Books had been massacred. They lay scattered on the floor, their covers thrown wide like broken wings. Blossoms of paper stood up from perforated pages. She dragged a few volumes toward herself. Goethe. Voltaire. Each one assassinated. Shakespeare had been shot through the heart. There was no exit wound. She pried the heavy volume open and peeled the pages all the way back to the bullet itself, lodged in the middle of *Romeo and Juliet*. She extracted it like some spoiled tooth. Powerless and ugly, it lay in her palm, as unimpressive in death as a garden slug. She tucked it in her trouser pocket.

She went back to the kitchen, under the table, and listened again to Dorothy sleeping nearby. Her own eyes slowly closed. She jerked awake. Dorothy snored louder and snuffled and kicked her feet. Irene tossed a small throw rug over her.

Her eyes... closing... no!... again.

—

She dreamed. It was before the attack on the village. After Dorothy parked the truck, they shuffled along together through the French town as if they were in Jersey, strolling through Cape May on a summer's afternoon. War, in spite of the smoke still rising in the outskirts, in spite of the tumbled church tower, seemed far away. The GIs napped in the shade of walls, under little trees with whitewashed trunks. They handed these soldiers packs of gum. The dead ones didn't accept. "Ghosts can't chew," one spirit explained. The ladies made fluty sounds with their voices, as if they were shining blue-and-golden birds.

Then the dream shifted, quite suddenly. She found herself on the old family homestead in Mattituck. Goat's Neck Beach wasn't far away. Greenport to the north with its sunken little wooden docks, underwater rowboats waving with bright green seaweed, full of small fish. They had served as her own private tide pools every summer. She wandered alone among half-collapsed boatwrights' shops and weathered storehouses still carpeted with discarded documents, including old paychecks.

She looked out the door and coming through the trees under the brilliant fall colors of the leaves was Handyman. He carried his guitar in one hand and his crusher cap was jaunty on his head. As he raised his hand to wave to her, a burning B-17 fell out of the sky.

She woke and jumped up, smacking her head on the underside of the table. The noise of it terrified her. Dorothy was still snoring there on the floor. The Germans would hear that and burst in on them. What had awakened her from the dream? Irene wondered. She squinted, cocked her head, listening more than looking, for unless she was at the window she still could not see much in that darkness. Boots ran beyond their garden wall. Metal jangled, clanked. Men shouted, not in English.

Irene scrambled out from under the table to where Dorothy lay on the floor and clenched her hand over her friend's mouth. Dorothy jerked awake and Irene whispered, "Shhh, Dottie, shhh." Together they belly-crawled back to the shelter of the table. They covered each other's mouths with their hands. The noise, like a flood, rushed at them: motors, crashes, curses. Women screaming. *Oh my God. They have the women.*

A multi-engine airplane passed low overhead, and the figurines on the shelf beside the stove rattled. Irene and Dorothy both held their breath, expecting bombs to drop. Far above, against the deep gray and orange of the clouds visible through the window, random tracer rounds ripped bright red lines through the air. The sky was cracking, and beyond it there was no heaven—only hell itself burning eternal.

"I'll never bitch about Indiana again," Dorothy said.

Irene's eyes were wide with dream-panic. Laughter burst out of her.

"Shh, poodie. Jesus." Dorothy pulled Irene's head down. "Quiet," she said. "It's okay."

And again, outside, screaming.

19

In the kitchen, the Sisters clutched their bellies, their bowels cramping with fear. They were burping because their insides could not process more violence. Their insides wanted to vomit the bread and yellow cheese. They closed their eyes, as if this could somehow keep from them the understanding of what was happening outside. They covered their ears.

A drumroll of shots echoed.

"Shh," Dorothy said.

A woman's groan floated up from the cobblestones outside their wall. Irene and Dorothy dug their fingernails into their palms. The groan rose and fell. Broke to sobs. Grew terrible wings and flew into a scream. Then: one more shot.

"No," Irene said.

Dorothy turned Irene's face to her own with one hand. "Irene. Not. Us. Yes?"

Her face still cupped in Dorothy's hand, Irene nodded. "Okay," she said.

But when they heard children screaming, Dorothy finally broke. Her head dropped. She cried with no noise.

Irene dragged her partner farther under the table until they were crammed against the rough stone wall. "Why, Dottie—crying—" she whispered, fighting back her own tears. "Crying's for ninnies."

"I don't want to die," Dorothy said, shivering.

Irene had never imagined such a thing could be possible for her fearless friend. She smoothed Dorothy's hair back with shaking hands, comforting her like Aunt Eva and Grannie Effie had comforted her when she was a child. "Irene's here," she soothed. "Hang on to Irene."

Beyond their wall, German voices cursed. Bricks clanked dully on the cobblestones. Engines sputtered and strained. The steel plates of tank treads shrieked as they ground the bricks against the greasy stones, gnarling them to powder, breaking up the roughcast and mastic of the ruins in martial rhythm—mindless, percussive, vast.

In the distance, a child's wail was silenced. Irene begged: *God in Heaven, Heavenly Father, not children. Not the children.* She wanted to offer herself but she knew suddenly that she was a coward. For while she would have immediately offered herself instead of these children if she were sitting in her Episcopal church back home, she would not do it here. Not now. Instead, she damned herself forever by praying an abomination: *Oh, bless them, Lord. But let us live. Keep the men busy out there. Don't let them find me.*

Coming now across the darkness, from all directions, like an earthquake, the symphony of full battle resumed. They had thought the men satiated, but it was not so. The noise surged—from chaotic bass roar to treble shatter, from shatter to gunfire, from gunfire to thudding explosions. They didn't have time to move. There was no place to move even if they did. They tried to shrink.

The door burst open and a big male body somersaulted across the floor, all boots and helmet and gun belt and burp gun rolling at them, and he flipped to his knees and saw them and aimed his weapon and said, "Criminy!" All at once. He lowered his submachine gun. "Girls!"

"Red Cross!" Dorothy cried.

"Boy, are we glad to see you," Irene said.

He rubbed his face with one hand. "You all right?" He had deep shadows under his eyes.

They nodded.

"Eighth Army," he said. He aimed his weird-looking weapon away from them, at the ceiling, smoke threading from its barrel. He looked over his shoulder, back out the door at the fires, and reloaded. "Thirty-round clip," he boasted. "Hey, you two scared the crap out of me. I almost shot you."

"A German already tried that," Irene said.

He stared at them for a long moment.

The running boots came back up the alley. The three of them fell flat on the floor and covered their heads like children. They all started to shush one another at once.

"Yeah," the soldier finally said. "Germans don't love me, either." He rose to one knee. "Gotta go," he said. "You got a firearm?"

"Irene lost our gun."

"Well, hell, Irene!" he scolded.

"I am very sorry."

The soldier drew his .45 from his holster and handed it over, butt first. "Take mine," he said. "Don't worry, I got my grease gun." He brandished his ugly rifle.

Now they would have a .45 to replace the one the lieutenant had given them. Irene took the pistol, her arm immediately dropping from its weight.

"Hey, Red Cross," he said. "Don't ask questions. Shoot. Then run like hell."

"Roger," she said.

"Save some donuts for me." He turned to leave, still down on one knee. "Want my advice? You ought to melt some of those chocolate bars you've got on your truck. Make frosting for the donuts. Think about it." He stepped to the battered door. "I'm gonna draw them away. Stay put till it's clear, then scram, okay?" He pointed. "We're all hauling ass that way." He saluted them loosely and charged through the door.

They wanted to cry, *Wait! Come back!* But he was already gone.

Irene handed Dorothy the heavy pistol as they scuttled into the library and watched from the window as the soldier zigzagged down the sloping yard. He vanished into the open door of the wooden shed. The outraged white goose exited the shed with its wings spread. It leaped into the air as the gunfire resumed and suddenly exploded into a firework of feathers and blood. The shed was then dismantled by volley after volley.

Irene and Dorothy crawled into the snug kneehole of the heavy oak desk. It felt like a fort. They breathed the comforting smell of pipe tobacco.

"Do you think he made it?" Irene said.

"I hope so."

"I'm sure he made it."

"Yeah, he knew what he was doing."

The room was cold.

"There's an upstairs," Irene whispered.

"Go."

They commando-crawled across the floor and up the dark stairs. The bedroom they discovered smelled of lavender sachets. They lay across the slumping bed.

"Irene, I can't make it."

"Yes you can. Sure you can."

They held the .45 between them. It was an icon, full of religious power. It was their dearest friend. They loved it. They prayed to it. They had faith in their deliverer.

On the floor, dolls lay staring. They looked more helpless than anything Irene had ever seen. Worse than the wounded books. She snagged a porcelain girl in a blue dress and stuck her inside her own blouse. In case she saw the bedraggled daughter of the mayor again. In the morning. She couldn't remember her name, but she'd at least give the girl a doll.

"We are all right," she whispered. "Dot, I promise."

"Right? It's almost over, don't you think?"

"Of course I do. Of course. Don't worry."

From the murkiest corner of the hall came a clank, then a ratcheting. They got up from the bed as soundlessly as they could and leaned out the doorway and squinted into the dark. Dorothy swung the pistol at the shadows. Then another sound, like a spring. They held their breath to hear better. Dorothy aimed at the sound, clutching the .45 in both hands.

A cuckoo clock came to life. They could see it in the shadows now. Chains dangling beneath it began to cycle upward, lifting iron pine cones.

Then the doors on the face of the clock popped open and two stout figures came forth and bowed to each other. Irene and Dorothy gaped. A third door opened and the cuckoo sprang forward to begin its demented squawking. Midnight.

Dorothy lowered the pistol.

They looked at each other and collapsed in laughter. They clutched themselves and shook with it. Sobbed with hilarity. Then gasped for air when a Panzer tank burst through the outside garden wall and slammed into a corner of the house. The outer walls collapsed, and their screams could not be heard as the roof and the floors dropped and carried them down to the dark library and then through its floor to plunge into the black cellar.

20

When the upstairs bedroom had fallen, the bookshelves in the library beneath them had toppled, blowing a flock of books into the chaos like terrified pigeons that followed the women down as they screamed against their wills and the ground floor cracked and gave way, sending everything cratering into the cellar.

Irene and Dorothy lay on the mattress, pinned underneath the library desk, with the bookshelves jammed against the top of the desk. The bed had made a half rotation as it dropped, ending bedsprings up. Most of the rubble had tumbled atop the backs of the bookcases, cracking them. But they had held fast. All that wood and rubble now formed a small bunker. Around it, a minor avalanche. Dust filled the dark.

The Sisters lay atop each other in a narrow wedge of airless space, coughing and choking.

"You okay?" Irene said.

"I think so."

The Panzer above, now in the house itself, revved its engine. Fumes they could not see choked them. Then the Panzer clanked into another gear, and its tracks screamed deafeningly on the fence ruins and the cobblestones of the street as it backed from the wreckage and pivoted away.

They did not know if soldiers had rushed in. They did not know if any part of the house was still standing above them. All they could hear was the caterwaul of the machine. Neither of them could breathe. They turned their faces away from each other and bent to the cold cellar floor and gulped what little air there was. Everything stank of exhaust and rotting potatoes.

The tank rolled past, its ponderous movement shaking the foundation, spilling earth and more plaster into the pit. Dorothy was on her belly now, Irene riding her back.

"Get off me," Dorothy said.

"I can't."

"Woman, get off me right now."

Irene struggled to move forward. She reached out for something solid in the total dark but was blocked. "Sorry."

"You keep crawling around on me, you better buy me flowers."

Irene felt behind herself with the toe of her boot. There was a void. "I'm moving," she said. She struggled down Dorothy's back and managed to get her knees onto the floor, though she couldn't sit up straight. She worked her head down around Dorothy's boots.

Dorothy strained and grunted until she got turned over on her back. She kicked Irene in the head.

"Sorry."

"Least of my worries." Irene crossed her arms and rested them on Dorothy's ankles.

"Anything broken, Gator?"

"I think I'm all here. You?"

"I bet I have a shiner."

"I might have a little blood," Irene said. "A nail snagged me on the head."

"You dizzy?"

"No."

"You're probably all right, then."

The wreckage above them shifted. They clenched against the imagined collapse. Held their breath as if one careless exhalation could topple the ruins of the house even more. The broken wood settled—small groanings, a series of thumps and bangs, but no avalanche.

"Jeez," Dorothy said.

Irene eased onto her left side and wrapped herself around the lower part of Dorothy's legs. "Maybe this is the worst of it," she said.

"Don't lay odds on that."

At least the air was beginning to clear. They could breathe better. They dug plaster powder and grains of dirt out of their nostrils.

Dorothy struggled to get comfortable in her cramped space. "I vote we just lie here," she said. "Get some rest. Let those shitbirds roll out of town."

"It's not like we're going anywhere," Irene said.

They were wrung out. They had no idea how much time was passing. What if they were dead and didn't know it? What if they were never found? Their bodies like the ones at Pompeii. . . . Irene's head was busy with such ideas. Dorothy was thinking about her old farm in Indiana.

Inanely, the cuckoo clock went off again.

"I'll be dipped," Dorothy said.

They drowsed fitfully. After a while, Irene woke Dorothy by shaking her leg.

"Germans?" Dorothy blurted.

"Just me."

"What."

"There's one thing I cannot get used to."

"What's that?"

"This girdle. It's killing me."

Dorothy lay there for a moment, then erupted. "You're wearing a *girdle*?" she yelled.

It might have been ten minutes; it might have been an hour. But a new sound was building. It started as a ground thrum, a light tickle in the ears. It was different from the tanks and the trucks. And it grew. Was it an earthquake? If they hadn't been buried twelve feet underground, they might have recognized the dissonant harmony of engines in the sky.

When the German bombers dropped their payloads, the world was suddenly so loud they went deaf. Everything was bouncing. Fire flashed between the timbers and bricks above them. The crust of the earth bent. Everything rose, even the cellar. And the dust. If there had been light, they would have seen thick gray air. Smoke. Then, exhausted, the earth settled again and slumped. An unending rumble seemed to move away.

When the water pipes under the street erupted, black water overtook the ruined street, flooded the yard, and coursed over the lip of the small canyon where the Sisters lay trapped. They were pummeled, then submerged, beneath a black cataract.

In an instant they were drowning, the water having closed over their heads.

Dorothy kicked her feet so hard that her boots almost knocked Irene out. She flailed and rose in the water and bumped against the desk and the ceiling of bookcases and wood and bricks. She breathed in water and panicked, battered her arms against the wood.

Irene could hear her screaming underwater. But Irene was a water baby. Her ponds and beaches on Staten Island, the ponds and bogs of Mattituck, the Sound, and the bays. She would not let her friend die right beside her. She kicked straight up until she hit the broken roof and floor, then felt along the barrier until she found an open space above her. She crammed her face into one dry triangle of wood open above the waterline and gulped air, then upended herself and stroked back down to Dorothy.

Irene reached into the flooded darkness beneath those shelves, where books now drifted like fish, and snagged Dorothy's arms. Her body had already gone limp. Irene braced her feet against the floor and tugged, straining until she extracted her friend like some great molar from the jaw of the cellar. She shoved Dorothy up into the wedge of rubble above them and muscled her friend's face into that miraculous bit of air. She clutched Dorothy's chest from behind and gave her a vicious hug that made her retch and puke and kick.

Then Irene crept up beside her and stole another gulp of air for herself. "I've got you," she said, her voice raspy as if she'd been screaming for hours. "Brace your legs," she said. "Push."

The waterfall streaming into the cellar pounded onto their heads.

"Against the wood. I said *push.*"

They shoved, giving the wood all they had left. They pushed so hard their backs felt like they would break, and at last the weight above them budged.

Dorothy reached her hand up into the darkness. "A space," she said. "There's a space."

"Go!" Irene said.

Dorothy wiggled her way into the small void. There wasn't much room, but she reached back for Irene and dragged her up on top of the debris, tearing Irene's uniform as she pulled her onto the dribbling bricks and swollen books and rotten food. Irene's knee broke a plate. They were both shaking. Their breath wheezed in their throats. The influx of water was thinning now, the cataracts slowly shutting down. Dorothy felt for Irene and her hand fell on her friend's shoulder. They were both icy to the touch, as if dead and buried.

—

They had fallen asleep again when the rats poured in like the flood, bursting from the broken sewers, nearly invisible in the blackness, bringing the stench of centuries on their backs. Squealing, their feet scrabbling against every surface, against the bodies and faces of Dorothy and Irene.

The rodents had fled the smoke and destruction above, only to fall into the foul water below. They scrambled and leaped, climbing the walls, the wood. It was sheer animal panic. They climbed Irene and Dorothy, too. They savaged the women, clawing into their backs, biting them all over their bodies, biting their faces.

Dorothy dragged a rat off her throat and threw it against the wall. Others swarmed over Irene. They nuzzled the backs of her ears, dug into her hair. Tried to make their way up her trouser legs, clawed at her thighs.

"Go! Go!" Dorothy shouted. "Climb!"

She pushed harder than she had ever pushed, and the wood and remnants of flooring above them shifted and let in a thin gray light.

"Here!" Dorothy said.

"Out of my way," Irene said, and climbed her friend as though Dorothy were a tree and she one of the rats.

—

Outside, morning was announcing itself through the smoke, using the voices of songbirds and ravens to stake its daily claim. Dogs emerging from their hideouts added their barking. A single surviving rooster crowed unheeded.

From their would-be grave, Irene and Dorothy were driven upward by this dawning. Rats clung to their feet. Aboveground, for anyone watching, the first sign of their resurrection would have been Dorothy's boot kicking at a fallen slant of roof, which creaked open like a jaw, its nails like the great crooked teeth of a barracuda. Red roof tiles clanked off. Dorothy's leg extended, shoving the edge of the roof upward. She unleashed a roar, the defiant scream of some woodland creature. A second leg, dark in shadow, rose to join its mate and pushed even harder.

Then Irene's face appeared. It was white with powdered masonry, her eyes like small dark oases. A rivulet of dark brown blood crossed her forehead in the shape of a lightning bolt and gathered at her left ear. Rat bites leaked red down her cheeks.

Dorothy's muffled voice said something from within.

"I'm trying," Irene said. She clutched at the edge of the broken front step and shoved herself up. When the big boot gave her a boost, she flew out and belly-flopped on the ground. Her blouse had vanished—she was in her besmirched undershirt, no longer white. The slant of roof slammed shut behind her. She went to it and hooked her fingers under its edge and heaved. When that section lifted an inch, she yelled, "Push!"

The wedge of roof creaked up and fell backward in slow motion. A dark shape rose. The shadow that was Dorothy drove upward with unrelenting force, her back bent, her long legs braced on the wrack below. Irene leaned in, grabbed her hand, and wrenched her friend the rest of the way free.

They patted themselves off. Great clouds of dust rose from them. Crusts of black mud peeled from their legs. They had shiners and blood mustaches and cuts on their arms. Irene spit like a cowboy. They stared at the wreckage of the house, then at each other. All around was mostly smoke. A couple of trees down one way. Some ghost shadows of ruins over yonder. Miniature forest fires. They sat on the ground.

"Well, hell," Irene said.

They laughed, in spite of it all.

"Where'd everything go?" Dorothy asked.

21

THE SMOKE WAS blue. They could smell acres of fire. Dorothy found a cigarette in her blouse pocket, looked at it, put it back. They were beyond wonder, beyond awe, beyond even fear. The breeze parted the curtains of smoke before them. A chimney or two still stood, and it was as if the houses that had contained them were now invisible. Ragged dogs wandered like jackals, worrying pieces of clothing sticking out of the ruin.

"Huh," they said, more grunts than words, ancient sounds from the age before there was language.

They felt packed in cotton. They were gray and black and brown, devoid of brightness. Their heads rotated and their eyes saw but they had no opinion.

Far away, flattened by distance, pops and bangs barely moved the air enough to be heard. Ah, battle. Boys running around in the woods, hiding behind trees and shooting at other boys. *Pow, pow! Bang, bang!* One side was bad, Irene remembered, and the other side was good.

Dorothy used her chin to point right, then left, looking a question at Irene.

Irene tipped her head to the left. Back toward the square.

They rose and stepped through the demolished garden wall. The great artists of chaos had left them masterpieces. A comfortable chair in a shaft of sunlight held a dented copper pot full of rice. Two shoes lay before this tableau as if they had recently been kicked off by a middle-aged burgher. There was a bone. It could have been his, could have been a cow's. Best to step over it.

Irene wanted to tell Dottie about the paintings of Yves Tanguy. How she had spent hours at the Pierre Matisse Gallery, on East Fifty-Seventh, gazing into the deep melancholy of those canvases, the austere gray fogscapes before which stacks of abandoned forms and objects stood forever. For some reason she didn't, but she wanted to tell Dorothy all her secret memories.

The world around them was an ashen desert now. Rubbled, hilled, a slag of brick and river rock and lath and shingle. Geysers of sewer water jetted in the distance. Relentless tendrils of smoke curled into the filthy sky or spread laxly into the blue fog that hugged the ground and made them feel as if they were levitating. Bits of wall and shards of church. An armless Jesus with his amputated stone hands lying before him. All about, flies had already come, targeting the partially entombed soft ruins of flesh.

The mute Sisters headed in the direction of the square, or what they assumed was its direction. Buildings loomed down there through the smoke. The Germans seemed to have been pushed to the outskirts of town. There were echoes of distant rifle fire and the unmistakable faint rumble of tanks. They walked on empty clothes. Here and there an arm or a leg protruded from the rubble. Irene couldn't help being fascinated by a pair of dead feet shod in burning boots.

The silence was strangely meditative. They enjoyed the quiet. The spent rifles on the ground were nice and still. Only the squabbling of birds pierced the hush.

Four short blocks on, measurable as such only by the dips in the debris that denoted former streets, they were already exhausted. Movement in this desert required endless climbing and sliding. Smoke and black water had filled the streets completely. Their eyes burned. If either of them fell over, she would break apart and leak into the mud.

Dorothy dug her crumpled pack out of her befouled Red Cross blouse again. *Screw it,* she thought, and offered the pack to Irene, who demurred. She lit up two anyway and handed one to Irene. "Maybe we're dreaming," she said.

"Oh, hell."

They stared out of dark eyeholes, their faces expressionless.

Irene raised one shoulder—at least they were still here. She plucked some tobacco off the tip of her tongue.

Dorothy curled her upper lip. "They can't kill us."

Irene was looking at something behind them. "What's that?"

Dorothy turned to see.

"There," Irene said. "Right there."

It could have been a Great Dane, moving around. Or a small donkey. Something flailing, knocking down the burned planks of what once might have been a shed. Then it rose. A male body. It was two-thirds charred. The left shoulder and arm and half its face were white. The right eye was gone. Teeth burning bright. Left eye staring furiously at them.

Its unburned hand lifted a bayonet. "*Ihr seids!*" it shouted. "*Ihr seids! Krapfen!* Red Cross!"

You've got to be kidding. It was him!

They tossed down their cigarettes and ran. He chased after them, silent but for his chuffing breaths. Irene looked back. He was slowed by his terrible burns, but he came on regardless, swinging the blade in his left hand. He grunted like some heavy animal. Their boots ground through broken rubble as they all ran.

"I want *Kaffee*!" he screamed. "I want *Krapfen*!"

Jesus God. They tripped, fell to their knees, tore their trousers. Blood seeped into the stinging cuts. They scrambled up and fled again. But there was nowhere to hide. When they looked behind them, their tormentor was closer. It wasn't possible. But he was thumping the ground, his boots carrying his body automatically, like some machine run amok, picking up speed.

"*Krapfen*. I want *Krapfen*."

He was going to kill them. They had survived it all and now it would be him to do them in. The absurdity of it outraged them.

Ahead, a small bonfire blazed. Improbably, they heard music—right in the middle of a semi-cleared cul-de-sac. The sound was coming from an upright piano, burning merrily. It was playing the blues.

A black-haired man with a little black mustache and tiny chin beard stood up from behind the piano. He wore a sleeveless T-shirt. He stared at them, then at the German behind them. "Get down!" he yelled.

Irene and Dorothy dropped to their bellies and the pianist grabbed up an M1 rifle and fired one round. Irene looked back just as he fired. A puff, as of mortal dust, burst from the German's chest. He stopped and raised his arms a little and dropped his bayonet and sat down and died.

"Sorry, man," the pianist called. "Hope you like hell." He looked down at Irene and Dorothy. "U.S. Army," he said.

Irene rose to her knees. The GI nodded at her through the piano smoke, put his rifle down, and sat back on his stool. They gathered before him. Nobody felt anything about anything, it seemed. The soldier played a jaunty honky-tonk tune. The heat was rather pleasant, like a fireplace stocked with aromatic cedar and pine.

"My riffs are so hot I set this piano on fire," he said.

The piano was going out of tune as it smoldered, the strings audibly breaking and popping within. His dog tags clanked along in rhythm as he swayed. He looked like a wolf in one of those cartoons.

"Hey," Irene said.

"Qué te pasa, calabaza?" he said.

"You're Garcia," she said. "From yesterday."

"Am I?"

"I thought I'd seen it all, buddy," said Dorothy.

Garcia was focused on his hands. She saw that he had a small blue cross tattooed on the skin between his thumb and forefinger.

"Some night, huh?" he said.

"She's Irene," said Dorothy. "They call me Stretch. And thanks for saving us."

"They call me Zoot. As in *suit*. All reety all rooty."

"What?"

He looked oddly bored. He played a little jazzy riff until at last the piano collapsed on itself and the mechanism inside caved backward and spit up a galaxy of sparks. He lifted his hands and let it fall. "Watch yourselves, locas," he said.

They skipped away from the piano.

Zoot had small burns in the legs of his uniform trousers. He kicked the stool into the fire and took up his rifle. "Let's boogie," he said and landed his helmet on his head, straps swinging.

"Where to?" Dorothy said.

"I thought *you* knew."

Irene had fallen asleep standing up. Dorothy took her elbow and led her along behind Zoot, who swung his weapon back and forth in case some other pendejo attacked them. Mostly, they saw stray cats and dogs.

Eventually, Irene awoke, her body pointed toward the main square. She could tell they'd gone off course. They didn't know how she knew, but she was looking at the spot where the bell tower should have been. She realized she had lost her doll in all the excitement. The one she was going to give that silent girl, the mayor's daughter. Instead, she dug that Kraut bullet out of her pocket and rewarded Zoot with it.

"Firme," he said, dropping the slug into his own pocket.

The square was just black. Trees were bones. Some buildings stood between empty sockets where others had stood. A festive pension still had red-and-white-striped awnings over the door. Otherwise, all was war. Same old same old. Burning trees out there beyond. That distant little *pop-pop-pop*. Towers of smoke leaning to the east.

"I got sisters," Zoot said.

"Yeah," Dorothy said. "You got us now."

They walked on. They looked like tramps, all tattered and smudged.

There wasn't nothing left to see, Zoot said. *Except that*, *over there*.

He pointed and they turned around. The *Rapid City* sat before them in a gray and black expanse of ash.

"Somebody stole my truck!" Dorothy shouted.

22

BEYOND THEIR CLUBMOBILE, that end of town was more or less still standing. Little by little, people appeared between the buildings and shells of buildings that ran down the slope to the fields and to the road the Sisters of the *City* had driven in on.

Garcia still held his rifle across his body, down low, but he was relaxed.

"Where you from, Zoot?" Irene asked.

"Clifton, Arizona."

"Fabulous," she said.

Dorothy banged around the cab of the truck, pumped the gas pedal three times, and started it up. Belches of black smoke issued forth, and there was a loud roar of Detroit iron coming awake. People in the ruins ducked and scattered. Garcia waved at them: *Don't worry, all clear.*

Irene drifted forward and laid her forehead on the fat hood of the truck. There was a bullet hole near her eyes. It looked like a cave, like a tunnel. She stared into it and the vibrations of the engine made her fall deep into that tunnel. On the other side, she found her family farm through the woods near Mattituck and watched a heron lift off like a kite made of sticks and paper.

Dorothy hopped down, handed a bottle of hooch to Garcia, and went from tire to tire.

"Órale," he said, admiring the liquor. "Where'd you get this at?"

"Smuggled it."

"Chingona!"

"Why would they try to steal my truck, Zoot?"

"They're Nazis," he said.

He took a drink from the bottle, then nudged Irene, who was still leaning over the hood, and handed it to her. She slugged one down, coughed, wiped her mouth. Dorothy came over for a shot and passed it off to Garcia, who went back in for a long pull. The bottle continued its rounds until it was empty.

Garcia held it high and dribbled three final amber drops into his mouth and tossed the bottle aside. "Ah," he exhaled like some sybarite's prayer.

Dorothy's hand was shaking again. She stuffed it in her pocket.

"You all right?" Irene said.

Dorothy cut her eyes to the galley. "You want to make coffee?"

Irene nodded and they headed to the back of the Clubmobile.

"Would you like a donut?" Irene asked Garcia.

"You know it."

Dorothy called out, "Zoot, you're motor pool, right?"

"Claro que yes."

Dorothy could see he was already feeling the rum down to his feet. "Can you teach me to drive a tank?" she asked.

He sat on the back steps of the galley. "Sure." He wore a crucifix hanging with his dog tags. "I seen weirder things than that." The sounds in the galley reminded him of home. "It was jail or the army for me," he said. "I shoulda chose jail. And you?"

"I told you. I wanted to drive a tank."

"It ain't that hard. Shiiiit. You're used to shifters."

She handed him out a bottle of peach brandy.

"Don't mind if I do."

"You'll get a headache mixing liquor," Irene warned.

"Yeah, but I'll be knocked out so it don't matter."

Dorothy fired up the Jimmy again. It idled roughly, but the generator worked. They still had water in the tank beside the record player. Private First Class Garcia filled the coffee makers. Irene scooped Sanborn grounds into the tin percolator baskets. The sinkers left in the vertical racks were dry and dusty but nobody was going to care.

Dorothy flipped the switch on the donut maker, avoiding the spot on the door that shocked everybody. She had never thought she'd feel affection for this cramped kitchen. Was that what her feeling was? She wanted to weep. No she didn't. Maybe.

Irene brought the Victrola down on its swivels and knelt at the record bin. The records had melted together into something resembling a thick platter, with no grooves at all on the B side. That was okay—the top of the platter, an Edith Piaf tune called "*L'Accordéoniste*," would play. Dorothy squeezed past and touched her shoulder; Irene touched her knee as she went by.

Irene went around to the cab of the truck and flicked on the loudspeaker. It squealed and survivors fled once again. But soon the tones of Edith Piaf wafted out to them. And the smell of coffee. They began to climb over the bricks and busted walls. She gave them a thumbs-up and went back to work.

Garcia wandered over to a swirl of flies ten yards away.

Irene was afraid of the moment when the numbness dropped away and she felt the looming avalanche of the day and night she had just survived. She didn't want to have any more nights like she'd had after the buzz bomb. It was as if some terrible entity was stealing her sleep, sitting athwart her chest and eating it in greedy mouthfuls. She took hold of the handle of the donut maker and pumped furiously.

The donuts came out perfectly.

Garcia knelt beside a poncho in the road under the flies. He reached for a hand whose fingers were arrayed on the brick as if the dead man were hitting a C chord on the keyboard. The hand was icy but still pliant, sticking out of a U.S. Army uniform cuff.

Garcia took the hand in both of his own and bent to him. "Hey, GI," he whispered. It took a good while to say what he had to say to the dead man.

When he was done, he made the sign of the cross, Mexican-style, kissing his thumb. Then he reached under the tarp and felt around in the cold pudding of the soldier's chest until he found his dog tags and pulled them out. Baxter. He wiped his hands on the soldier's sleeve and tucked the dead man's hand under the covering, then pocketed one of Baxter's tags and left the other for ID. He stood and poured a dollop of the brandy on the ground beside the soldier.

"Respect," he said. "Did what I could, brother."

—

The line of survivors was neither joyous nor grim. But their eyes. Irene had never imagined the look of true gratitude a person could display over watery black coffee. If they were happy about anything, they were happy to still be standing. They stared up at Irene, smiling vague thanks, and she stared back down at them. They seemed to enjoy it when their fingers touched hers. Their tears might have been from the smoke. The children were louder than their elders. Over and over again, they jumped up to try to touch Irene. She searched their faces, hoping the girl from last night would appear. Nina? Lila? She looked for the girl's mother. For her father. A hundred faces and not one of them familiar.

"The mayor?" she asked. "Have you seen the mayor?"

People just stared.

"Mayor. Of your town?" She could not remember the French word. She put her hand over her eye. "*L'oeil?* Blind?"

They shrugged and shook their heads. They reached for donuts.

Their only visible excitement surged when a gaggle of Resistance fighters ambled into town. They were magnificently insouciant: wet and muddy, a couple of them shirtless, several wearing berets. They wore rope belts with revolvers tucked into them and had old hunting rifles and stolen German machine guns hanging from their shoulders. They smoked without touching their cigarettes. They hugged the townswomen with one arm, kissed many of them, slapped the backs of old men. They guzzled their coffee with sugar and cream and wolfed down as many sinkers as they could grab. The bastards all winked at Dorothy. One of them handed Zoot a German dagger, which he stuck in his belt.

A woman stood among them, dark as a rainstorm. She had a machine gun slung low off her shoulder, dangling behind her. It swayed when she moved. She wore a red beret. Dorothy hopped down from the galley and walked directly to her. She handed the warrior queen a smoke. They took each other's measure, nodding once.

"Dorothy."

"Colette."

"I want to be you," Dorothy ventured.

"No, you do not," Colette said, in English.

"Come have coffee."

"I want brandy."

"Got that, too."

Colette smiled. She slapped Dorothy's shoulder. "*Bon,*" she said.

They walked back to the *Rapid* with the brandy bottle.

Colette looked the truck over and regarded Dorothy in her besmirched and charred outfit. "Good work," she said.

Dorothy blushed. They sat in silence for a while, passing the brandy back and forth. Dorothy tried to think of how exactly to ask what she wanted to know.

"What do you do?" she said, finally. "With them? I need to do something." Dorothy held up a donut. "This is not enough."

"What do I do with who?"

"Those Nazi pigs."

Colette didn't hesitate. "I go to dark alleys together with them. I tell them we need to talk."

"And then?"

"I kill them." She kissed Dorothy on each cheek and hurried to catch up with her brothers-in-arms.

—

American jeeps drove in.

In the leading vehicle, a photographer jumped out before the jeep had even stopped to snap shots of the victors lounging around. "*Stars and Stripes!*" he shouted. "*Stars and Stripes!*"

Soon, jeeps and trucks and American tanks swarmed into the outskirts of the town, filling the road. Troops appeared and fanned out into the fields. Pigeons billowed before them in panicked clouds. Machines rolled forward and parted the cadres in the road. They bounced over rubble and soon encircled the Clubmobile. Civilians backed away to watch the show.

An officer stepped up and Garcia saluted him.

"Son, was it you who liberated this town?" the officer said. "There's a medal in it for you if you were."

"No, sir," he replied. He handed the officer Baxter's dog tag. "It was him."

The officer studied the tag somberly. Garcia shuffled away. Some kind of colonel stood in his open staff car and declared the siege a major victory. Clean-uniformed desk jockeys with shiny bars and medals pinned to their chests handed small American flags to the tattered citizens as they drove through at a crawl. Ol' *Stars and Stripes* got his camera going.

"Oh, hell no," Dorothy said. "Close the shop, Gator."

They slammed the shutters and turned the handles to lock them down. Neither of them could abide the thought of eight more hours in the galley spent feeding ground pounders and officers and the boys from the rear. Irene ripped the needle off Piaf's record—it had played enough times anyway. A pair of American fighter planes passed overhead, and she waved, just in case.

Rusty Penney suddenly appeared and trotted toward the *Rapid City*. "Y'all okay?"

"Sure," Dorothy said. "We're squared away. Shipshape."

"Somebody shot our truck," Irene announced.

Dorothy looked him up and down. His uniform was immaculate. "Fought hard, did ya?" she said.

"We were in the rear," Rusty explained, clearly not appreciating her tone. "Helping coordinate."

"Coordinate what?"

"How did you ever survive?" Irene said.

Garcia wandered back to the women, a bottle of fruit brandy dangling from his hand. He took a big swig, emptying the bottle, and threw it into some rocks. He smiled at them like a moray eel. "I'm drunk as hell," he confided.

"Did you drink it all?" Rusty asked, incredulous.

Dorothy finished her smoke. She tossed the butt away, pulled a stick of gum out of her trouser pocket, and unwrapped it and put it in her mouth. She put another stick in Irene's mouth. Irene chewed with her mouth open like some bobby-soxer. Garcia opened his mouth and Dorothy gave him a stick, too.

"Do I know you?" Rusty asked.

Garcia blew a bubble. Just stared back at him.

"I don't understand the attitude," Rusty said. "Is something wrong?"

The three ragamuffins shrugged, almost in unison. Dorothy popped her gum between her molars.

"What could be wrong?" Irene said. She felt the autumn sun on her face. She thought it would comfort her but she disliked it immensely. It was far too bright. "This guy," she said, tipping her head toward Garcia, "saved us at the last minute."

"And he can really play piano," Dorothy said.

"But we fought the Germans single-handed," Irene said.

"All night long." Dorothy popped her gum again.

An officer with a cigarette stuck in a long holder stepped up to the shuttered Clubmobile and said, "Get me a cup of coffee, would ya, doll?"

"No sweat," Dorothy replied.

"I'll be over there. I take it black."

"I'm on it, sir."

They watched him stride away.

"Let's get on down the road," Dorothy said. "C'mon, Garcia, we'll give you a ride."

Garcia laughed. He was so drunk that he rode upon a world whose surface boogied and shimmied. "Bye, baby," he said, pointing a finger pistol at Rusty.

"Miss Dorothy," said Rusty, "our bivouac is right down the road, about ten kilometers." He waved his arm. "Down thataway."

He said the name of the town, but they didn't understand him. It was getting to be a thing, not knowing where they were.

"You can't miss it," he said. "You'll see the gun emplacements and the tanks."

"We got rooms?" she said.

"Yeah. You got rooms in L'Hotel Singe Bleu."

They strolled toward the *Rapid*.

Apropos of nothing, Dorothy called back, "Irene's wearing a girdle."

With that, they walked back to the truck. Irene climbed into the front seat. Dorothy opened the driver's door, but just stood there.

Garcia recognized that look. He walked around to Dorothy and put his hand on her shoulder.

"I am just...so...tired," she managed to say.

Garcia knew he could collapse later; Dorothy needed to collapse now. He shook his head hard to get his bearings. "I've got this," he said. "I'll drive us to the next checkpoint."

Dorothy let Garcia walk her around the truck and tuck her in next to Irene. She leaned her head on the window as the Clubmobile pulled onto the road.

PART THREE

The Autumn Road

23

THE SISTERS NEEDED to sleep for a year. But they were afraid of the dreams they might have. The army wisely sent them to a pretty little hotel in safely occupied territory to regroup and catch their breath. They would have a couple of days to rest, but then their orders were to establish a Donut Dugout in the lounge of the hotel. Same great service, but for many more GIs coming through. They could use the *Rapid City* as an extra kitchen.

Le Singe Bleu—the Blue Monkey—was a tidy little three-floor hotel on a traffic circle with a dry stone fountain in its center. Two stone lions stood sentry at the hotel, flanking the doors—one of them had lost his nose to gunfire. The hotel bore the indignity of a half dozen bullet holes in the road-facing wall. It had been built in the nineteenth century, which made it nearly new by French standards.

Six rooms per floor, three on each side of a narrow hallway that creaked like a pirate ship when they walked down it. The rooms were small and had oddly padded walls covered in patterned fabric. Irene's room was deep blue with white fleurs-de-lis every five inches, separated by pale orange vertical ribbons. Each of them got her own bed with five pillows and a fat bedspread, and each had a private bathroom with its own tub and an alarming bidet. At first Dorothy announced that she wasn't about to sit on that, though she later confessed that she had ridden it "like a pony."

Irene felt quite superior to her. Had no one ever read a book? *Très chic,* the facilities. The hotel made her imagine herself a heroine in a novel, doing European things her unsophisticated friend could never imagine. She filled journal pages with every detail except the awfulness of the last days. She decided she would not allow that experience into her thoughts. There had to be some way to make that all go away. She wrote, instead, of her delight to have laundry service at last. Of the astonishing joy of padded, perfumed hangers in the closet, and the luxury of sweet-smelling clothing and underthings. Of the perfect moments in her new nest. The bottles of wine.

Their rooms looked out over the dead fountain and the short road into town, which cut between them and a stand of poplars. They could look down on the good ol' *Rapid* lurking off to the side of the lions. Not long after they arrived, Irene had watched a fuel tanker with camo splotches painted on its flanks pull up to the *Rapid*. Two troops in coveralls had hopped out, unscrewed the fuel port on the Clubmobile, and run out the fuel line from their rig. They attached it to the truck and hit a switch and pumped loud gurgling gallons into it. After a few minutes, they reversed their movements, undid the line and twirled the gas caps, and jumped back in their cab and were gone.

Various army officers and a chaplain had the rooms below theirs. Their jeeps were parked near the *Rapid*. She wondered if the boys, too, had bidets.

—

Dorothy knocked on Irene's door the first morning. When Irene opened it, she was startled for Dorothy to hand her the heavy .45 automatic.

"We should have killed that Kraut ourselves," Dorothy said. "We let Zoot do our soldiering."

Irene's hand drooped from the weight of the pistol. "I don't really know how."

"That's ending today."

"But—"

"Let's go."

On their way downstairs, Irene—feeling helpless in the tide of Dorothiness—said, "Other girls in our group don't shoot anybody."

"We're not them."

The concierge's eyebrows rose as Irene walked through swinging the gun.

"Don't put your finger on the trigger unless you plan to shoot somebody," Drill Instructor Dorothy said.

Irene consoled herself by repeating, *This will be over in a minute.* She had been planning to do nothing this morning but eat croissants and take a bath. Perhaps savor an espresso.

They marched across the traffic circle and through the hedge of trees across the road. Dorothy yelled at soldiers on the main highway that they were going to have target practice. Fair warning. She walked Irene into the sun and pointed at an oak standing alone. She strode out there, pinned a handkerchief to its trunk, marched back, arms swinging. When she snapped her fingers and held out her hand, Irene extended the gun.

"No!" Dorothy snapped. "Don't point that thing at me. Butt first."

Irene, irritated, turned the gun around and handed it over as directed.

Dorothy went through some theatrical inspection, sliding this and clicking that. "Got it?" she said.

"Sure."

"Ready for me to shoot? All clear?"

"Actually, I'm rather opaque," Irene said. She snickered, quite pleased with herself.

Dorothy posed sideways to the oak tree, raised the pistol, and fired. A black hole appeared in the hankie. She handed the smoking monster to Irene.

Irene raised the gun, squinted, closed her eyes, and jerked the trigger. The recoil kicked the gun up and directly into her forehead. She fell over.

"You missed," Dorothy commented. She grabbed Irene's proffered wrist and yanked her to her feet. "Now," she said, "what did you do wrong?"

"Be born?"

"You tried to aim. You won't have time to aim. It's intuitive. And now you know the gun has a kick. So adjust to it." She positioned Irene so that she stood in profile. "Less of you to hit if they shoot back."

Dorothy stood behind her and gripped her gun hand, wrapping her fingers around Irene's. Together they raised the pistol.

"Keep your eyes open," Dorothy said.

"Yes, ma'am."

"Don't aim. Point. Just point. Like you're pointing at a house or a train or a bird."

"Got it."

"And think of him."

"Who?"

"That little bastard in New York."

"I never—"

"Put one into him. And don't jerk the trigger. Squeeze it slow. Shoot his ass."

Irene did as instructed. She hit the tree.

"Now you're talkin'," Dorothy said.

Irene handed her the gun, butt first. "Would you care to join me in a croissant?"

They marched back to the Blue Monkey.

Dorothy spoiled breakfast, though, by poring over the daily dispatch telling them which division was in combat and which towns had fallen. She didn't even put marmalade on her croissant.

Irene, just for a moment, simply didn't want to know about any of it.

—

A cobblestone thoroughfare came off the main highway and skirted the hotel and went around the bend and into town. It was broad, which was why the brass had chosen the town—room for trucks and tanks and their half-track, which seemed to have become some kind of mascot. Zoot Garcia and the troops called the vehicle the Kill Pig. Behind the town stretched fields, for tents, and a landing strip the Germans had helpfully left behind when they fled.

Later that morning, Dorothy strolled down the road, looking for Garcia. With the luxury of a few empty hours during which no one needed anything from her, Dorothy just wanted to see how he was doing. She kept her right hand tucked in her jacket pocket. Since the siege, she'd noticed a slight tremor. Perhaps, she thought, he was the one person she could ask about it. He wouldn't think she was weak.

She walked past tents in the square and a well-sandbagged radio-ops center near the churchyard. Two garages, a barn, and a soccer field now housed the motor pool and repair squad—tanks, jeeps, wounded Jimmies, busted trailers, a convertible staff car, and a couple of German vehicles including a weird motorcycle/army tank contraption that Garcia had already commandeered for himself. He had a 1936 Indian back home in Arizona, he told people. He even had a sidecar for that big bike. But nobody back there had ever seen anything like this thing. It would be nice as hell to get this monster back home for desert rides. Maybe blow up some sheds.

Garcia parked the contraption outside his quarters, an abandoned schoolhouse. The building had a shell hole in its roof. He didn't mind the pigeons that sought refuge with him. He and Dorothy smoked and spun yarns in there in the afternoon, like tenth graders playing hooky. Dorothy noticed the tremor in her hand had stopped. Maybe, she thought, this was all she needed.

Garcia was shocked that Dorothy, like his mom, enjoyed crocheting. He didn't feel foolish at all confessing to her that he'd like to learn to do it. And she didn't laugh at him.

"I can teach ya, don't worry."

"Cool, cool," he said. "When we get married, we can make baby clothes together."

"I'll make you special underpants. Nice and cool for the desert heat."

They toasted each other.

"You ain't gonna cheat on me, are ya?" he asked.

"Probably. Yeah. Sorry."

"Oh. Huh. Me, too."

And they drank another toast to each other.

"Wicked ways," Dorothy said.

—

"Never thought I'd cheat death like we did," Irene said. "I keep reliving it."

"You're a damned iron woman," Dorothy said through a cloud of cigarette smoke.

They were lying across Irene's bed.

"So are you," Irene said.

Dorothy thought about it. "I guess I am."

"I know we're always supposed to be so jolly. But I feel mopey."

"Jolly is our jobby."

Irene laughed.

Dorothy lectured: "Look at Bob Hope. What do you bet he's drunk as a skunk every night after those USO shows, wishing he could do something more than make troops laugh. But that man never stops. He keeps the sad crap to himself."

"But he's a hero. He keeps the boys uplifted."

"What do you think I'm sayin', Gator?"

Dorothy slammed her feet onto the floor and gave Irene a pat on the shoulder and motored on down the stairs and outside into the perfect sun and breathed in the gorgeous scent of trees and plants and listened to the crows and sparrows and chickens and idiot ducks in the ponds as she went ambulating along that delightful cobblestone road to see her misfit boys.

She enjoyed the motor pool. It reminded her of days at the farm with her brother. Shooting cans with Pop. Riding beside him on the tractor as they cut soil for corn. She liked the smells of the motor pool, the funk of it. Taking a wrench to an engine or a gas line made it feel like she was actually fighting the war. Even playing five-card stud for bullets or salt peanuts. Not like frying a damn donut.

Nobody knew how shy she really was, how it flushed her cheeks and clawed at her guts to stand in the corner trying to look like somebody else, or to pour a hundred cups of coffee like she was working in some diner in South Bend. She felt counterfeit. These knuckleheads knew what it was about. They were the working guys now ordered to go into combat.

Being around Irene day and night reminded her of all her worst nightmares of girlhood. No matter what she did, she was the giant, the tough bunny who knew how to drive a truck. Even the fact that she liked to drive the truck embarrassed her a little. She wouldn't have admitted it but she yearned to have one spoonful of Irene's class. Even if Irene would have explained to her that people with real class would never use a term like *class*. Damned Irene! Sometimes just thinking about that little snip made her laugh, but she didn't know what was so funny.

She felt restless now. After one weekend, she was already bored with the hotel. Everything froufrou, perfumed. She couldn't breathe. It had a cute sign out front with a blue monkey on it. And it specialized in "Provençal" cuisine, whatever that was. Quail eggs and snails.

Out back, there were piles of abandoned Nazi crap that she kicked around. Swastika flags. She pilfered those and cut them up at night to make patches out of the red parts. She was going to make herself a red silk evening gown out of those flags, the only way she'd be able to afford it. Maybe even make herself a wedding gown. She hated to admit it but she wanted one—more than she wanted a husband. She found a bayonet and took that, too. Ammo boxes and belts and coats. Those Nazi sons of bitches dressed sharp, Dorothy had to give them that much. Some of the stuff still had dried blood on it. Lugers and rifles. They must have run like rabbits.

Lately, she was grinding her teeth at night—she woke up with headaches and a sore jaw. She pined for the US of A. Not homesick, she wouldn't say *homesick*. But she would have appreciated a root beer and a hot dog, some cotton candy and an awkward country dance where nobody was watching her. The closest she could come to it was the motor pool.

The chow line was set up in the church hall in town, and it had real food: hash, scrambled eggs, burgers, beans. RC cola. Even shit on a shingle, which she used to hate and now sopped up fast, then begged for seconds. Compared with the hotel food, this was all a relief.

As for the motor-pool garage, it had cussin', smokin', and jokin'. She didn't have to explain herself or pass a single test once she changed the oil in a jeep while the boys gawked. The garage was her clubhouse. Lots of grunts came through and had a smoke or a secret beer, even those rangy haunted guys with dead eyes. She traded gibes with all of them. She was free.

She called the boys out all day: "Zoot, you're so dumb you could lose an argument with a lug nut." Next victim: "If brains were gas, you wouldn't have enough to drive a pissant's motor scooter around the inside of a donut." But on her third afternoon, she set the mockery aside and admitted: "I don't know, boys, I have an itch."

"I do too," said one grease money. "Wanna scratch it? I'll scratch yours."

They all laughed. Good ol' Stretch.

"No, I do not want anything to do with your filthy little willy, you ass."

Everybody laughed again, punched shoulders.

"What's so funny?" she said.

They stopped joshing and looked her over.

She stood with her arms hanging loose. She stared at the greasy floor, shaking her head slowly. "I just," she said, "I want to... I need to, I don't know, *make trouble*."

"Like how?" Zoot asked.

She took a breath as if seeing how it felt to breathe. "I'm... so... angry. My brother. All of this. Those Krauts—I want to..." Her voice trailed off.

The guys watched her uneasily and glanced at one another.

"I want to hurt them," she said. "That's what I really want."

This revelation appeared to be deeply awkward for the men—they had no wisdom, no humor, no flirting to come back with.

"Hey, Stretch," Garcia finally said. "If you're serious, we can help you with that."

—

The *Rapid City* had been out of service for only three days and they had fallen apart. Irene slept late every day. Dorothy was furious with her. When she was awake, she swanned around, leafing through old issues of Paris *Vogue,* bobby pins in her hair, French moisturizing cream on her face, her door locked. She sipped coffee all day and switched to white wine in the evening. Worst Clubmobile in the war.

Darling Dot seemed to be done with both her and the *Rapid City,* Irene noticed. She now referred to it as "that old bus." Irene was offended on behalf of the truck. It was as if Dot had become a GI. She wore the .45 slung low, like some Billy the Kid. She left her boots unlaced. Made it clear she wasn't taking a broom, bucket, mop, or sponge to the Clubmobile. Came wandering in late at night, smelling of oil and cigs and booze.

Irene could no longer afford to relinquish one jot of herself to this malaise. She combed out her hair until it shone in the light, like pure silk. She painted her lips, did her nails, spritzed herself with No. 5 so she'd smell like a human being. She wore a lovely peasant blouse she'd bought in London. It made her feel like a young woman in a Thomas Hardy novel, awaiting her shepherd to walk out of the far hills.

Irene knew one thing: she never wanted to go back into combat. She wrote letters to Handyman and her mother and Aunt Eva. She never confessed her dread to her elders, but she knew Handyman would understand her feelings. She expressed her terror to him alone—never knowing if the censors would cut those things out, naively believing he would intuit her message even if they did.

With no sign of Dorothy, Irene had set up the lobby of the hotel as the Donut Dugout. The staff had moved in a couple of tables and some chairs and there was a serving area and plenty of space for lingering. But for the *Rapid City* to function as a kitchen, it needed a thorough cleaning and Irene decided to undertake it alone.

She swept out the galley. She collected the rubbish and the spilled flour and sugar and the curds of hardened boot mud and the dead crushed sinkers and the leaves that had blown in and wads upon wads of crumpled waxed paper and newspaper and napkins, and she filled two barrels with all of it. The hotel's gardener took the barrels out behind the building and burned everything.

She scrubbed the counters and the fryer. Hand-washed the sullied plates and cups. Drained the foul coffee makers at each side of the service windows (who knew old coffee would grow clots of mold that floated like islands in the dregs?). She scrubbed the urns shiny. Alphabetized all the records. She even blew the accumulated dust off the record player's needle.

She pried the drain plug out of the cooker, poured the rancid vegetable oil into a ten-gallon bucket, and wrestled new oil into the machine's maw. She was appalled to discover hard-fried globs of darkened dough amid well-crisped flies at the bottom. She reminded herself not to eat the donuts ever again. She then swept the cigarette butts and candy wrappers out of the cab, along with fifty pounds of dirt. She had never been so domestic.

"In New York," she told the truck, "we had a maid."

She muttered curses and lodged grievances as if with God himself, just like some adolescent being punished with homework. It wasn't fair. Why did she have to do everything? Was she the only one with some sense of responsibility? There came no rousing answer from Jehovah.

Irene's faced burned with embarrassment when she remembered her tormentor, back in that apartment on East Twenty-Eighth Street. The night it all broke. She was weeping after yet another incident. He was sipping a scotch, rocks. Outwardly calm as a lizard. He had this way. He just knew what would dig into her. The scene went through her mind repeatedly: the clink of the ice in the glass, his slurp, his swallow—all sounds she had learned to detest. His bored voice: "Oh, Irene, stop being so goddamned precious."

She threw a sponge from the front of the *Rapid*. "I'm here, aren't I? Do I look precious to you now?"

Unbeknownst to Irene, Dorothy had come to the truck and stood nearby in the dark, listening.

Irene was exhausted. She climbed up on the fenders with a rag in hand and wiped the shellac of grime and dead bugs off the windshield. Everything was lit a mellow orange by the lamps in front of the hotel.

Dorothy moved forward, materializing out of the gloom, an apparition in unlaced boots, scuffling and crunching gravel. She leaned against the truck's fender across from Irene. "Getting the truck squared away?" she said.

Irene didn't reply.

"Were you cussing at me?" Dorothy asked.

Irene ignored her elaborately.

"Are you mad at me, Gator?"

Irene glanced at her. "I wasn't cursing at you," she said, went back to her task.

"I probably irritated you a million times."

"True."

Dorothy sighed. It was a half groan. Irene resumed failing to acknowledge her.

"Oh, Irene," Dorothy finally said to Irene's back. "Don't be mean."

"Mean? Really."

"We've had a rough couple of days. That's all." Dorothy rubbed her eyes with her thumb and forefinger.

Irene stayed silent.

"Hey?" Dorothy said. "You've got nothing?"

"I have been here all along, dear girl. Doing my duty." She gestured at the *Rapid,* grandly. "Day in, day out."

"Hiding," Dorothy said.

Irene turned her back, stung. "Like the motor pool?" she said. The ensuing silence told her that she'd made her cheap point. "And are *you* all right, Dorothy?" she finally said.

"I've got to do something."

"How do you mean?"

"Something about... this."

"About what, Dottie?"

"All this. I'm just so..." Dorothy said quietly. "I'm just so... you know. Aren't you?"

With her back still to her friend, Irene said, "I don't know what you're saying."

"I'm so... very... angry."

Irene turned to her with words at her lips, but Dorothy had already moved away in silence and was absorbed into the darkness of the hotel.

—

At seven in the morning of the following day, Group F Captain Martha Levin of the American Red Cross, along with a driver from the U.S. 8th Army, appeared before the hotel. Their jeep skidded to a halt amid a shower of gravel. The captain dispatched the driver to the lobby. There he dispatched the deskman to rouse the ladies. Upstairs, the deskman instructed the Sisters to report to their captain.

The pair eventually stumbled down into the lobby, in the most languid stampede, to find Captain Levin pacing, hands behind her back, doing her finest impatient Eisenhower imitation. The driver tossed off a salute, but they didn't know if they were supposed to salute him back or not.

"Martha's Irregulars," Captain Levin grumbled.

They were a motley duo, at best. Irene was well-dressed, although half-untucked and barefoot. At least she had painted her toenails. Visibly hungover, Dorothy was still wearing last night's besmirched coveralls, with oil stains on her knees. She had tied a rag around her semi-vertical hair.

"Where is your third?" Captain Levin asked.

"No third, Cap," Dorothy announced.

The driver jotted in a notebook.

"Well then. How are we today, ladies?"

"Squared away, Cap," Dorothy replied.

Irene smiled fetchingly.

"You don't look squared away," Captain Levin said.

"It has been a complicated week," Irene confessed.

"So I hear." Martha reached into the jeep. "This will help," she said, and produced a letter. "Direct from HQ. The top brass is aware of your heroic actions in recent combat."

They elbowed each other.

"Citations will be placed in your files and forwarded to Red Cross main HQ, Stateside. Good work. Holding up our standard in the Red Cross way." She shook each of their hands one after the other. "Ladies, listen up. You have earned R and R." Captain Levin noticed Irene's expression of incomprehension. "It's a military term," she explained. "*Rest and recuperation*. Group B will be joining us here, and elements from that group along with our own Good Ship *Cheyenne* will fill in for you for the next week."

"A week," Irene said, sighing.

"Cap?" Dorothy said. "Do you know where we're going?"

"I do. Be advised: a week at the Riviera. Cannes. On the beach. Be advised: liquor will be involved. Whatever happens next is your concern and not my own."

"Holy crap," Dorothy said.

"Indeed. A plane will be here for you tomorrow morning. Out at the airstrip. Oh six hundred. Be at the field ready to go."

They offered their first salute, then raced each other up the stairs.

24

THE FOLLOWING MORNING, as the Sisters walked toward the plane, they felt the war flake away like old paint, and some of it blew off in the breeze. It was as if the war were also taking a vacation. Irene had heard soldiers talk about this—how the war ate you alive, killed everyone around you, ruined your nerves and made you suffer, and then... it just paused. It pulled away like the tide. Dawn broke. And magical things seemed to overtake you. But it only worked if you didn't think about what might be happening ten miles away.

They had told her as they stood in the serving line before the *Rapid City*. A perfect morning would come. An empty house full of wine and food would appear. A friend you hadn't seen since Normandy who you were sure had died would saunter into your camp with his patrol. A local girl and a quiet place to lie with her would break your heart in the best way. The boys had a million examples.

Was it grace? Was that the word she was reaching for? She feared that word. She had a dread that it meant nothing more than a temporary lull, a respite. A drawing in of breath, as if the war had only paused to collect itself for a fresh assault. A last small blessing before your brains were blown out. Irene thought that a bullet already knew her name.

Often the shriek of "I want *Kaffee*!" woke her in the night, and she felt foul water falling on her in the dark. She could sense the child they'd denied standing beside the bed. She would jerk awake poisoned by guilt, ashamed that she could not remember the girl's name. Once the bad dreams dragged her out of sleep, her worries would not let her go back. When she closed her eyes, she thought she saw bright flashes of spotlights cutting through the curtains. But when she sat up staring, the night was black and trilling with crickets.

Perhaps most horrid was the awareness that surely the war had not yet done all it could to her. She had come to war with no idea what might happen, she realized. She remembered the one-legged soldier a hundred years ago on the train to DC. She wished now that she could tell him she understood a little of what he'd been trying to tell her.

Time for repair, Irene told herself. *Start with Dot*. "Are we all right, Dottie?" she asked.

"I guess this vacation changes things," Dorothy said as they neared the plane.

"It can't hurt."

"You'll have to take charge. I'm not used to this fancy stuff."

"I will be your general."

"Let's not go that far."

The plane ride to Cannes was a nightmare. They sat on benches along the walls of the C-47. Dorothy laughed at Irene's horror—she snapped pictures of her praying frantically—until she remembered they actually could be shot down. Then she sent up a good practical Presbyterian prayer of her own: "Dear Lord—whatever the general said."

The roar of the engines kept them from talking, and the fuselage groaned and creaked as they bounced through the sky. Irene imagined Handyman up in the clouds with her, keeping her safe. She had sent him a last-minute letter yesterday, after they received the news of their R & R from Captain Levin, to tell him where she was going. Ridiculous. She knew it would never even get to him in time. And if it did, he surely would not be able to drop everything and appear on the beach. But that was what wishes were for.

Once they finally landed and stumbled off the plane, she held her breath like a schoolgirl, hoping he'd be waiting, though she knew it was impossible. She hid her red face from Dorothy, feeling silly, when of course he wasn't there. She hadn't told Dorothy anything about this little romantic drama, though Dorothy had intuited exactly what was happening with her friend.

The two of them dragged their bags across the French airfield, and a taxi waited for them. It seemed like a decade since they'd seen a taxi. So much fancier than a jeep. They felt like walking banks—their pockets stuffed with francs from Captain Levin. "Spend it all in one place," she had told them, and winked.

"You need a beret," Irene told Dorothy.

"I want a beret."

"I shall get one for you!"

"A red one. Like Colette's."

"Who?"

"The partisan."

"What partisan?"

Dorothy could not believe Irene didn't remember the freedom fighters. Colette had apparently changed nothing for Irene, and Dorothy didn't want to explain that Colette had changed everything for her. "It was just something I saw in a movie," she lied. "I'll get you a black beret."

"*Très chic!*" Irene trilled.

Back in August, Operation *Dragoon* had landed on the beaches down the coast from Cannes and had come up through Provence, pouring Allies into the South of France and decimating the surprised German forces, driving them all the way back to the Vosges Mountains, several hundred miles to the north.

As they drove, their cabdriver often proclaimed, "I love America!" He scared them by taking his hands off the wheel and waving them around, the cab apparently driving itself as he cried, "America number one!"

Irene and Dorothy beheld the fruits of what their army had done. On the streets GIs were being stopped by children who handed them flowers and sweets.

"We celebrate now forever," the cabdriver said.

The Sisters waved at everybody.

"What a happy day," Irene enthused.

"Every day," the driver agreed.

"It's like we're in a parade," Dorothy said.

"Riviera!" he cried. "Antibes!"

He took them up the hills so they could look down upon the madness of that sea against the battlements and towers and bright colors. The green and the blue.

"Cactuses!" Irene said, realizing she had never seen cactuses as tall as trees. In fact she couldn't recall seeing any cactuses outside museums. These looked like those big Arizona ones in Western picture shows. *Garcia would feel at home here,* she thought.

"*Oui,* but of course," their driver said dismissively. "Famous."

Irene popped open her little notebook and wrote *famous cactus* beside a quavery sketch.

"Voilà," their chauffeur announced as they rounded a curve and beheld all below.

They were dazzled by the sun, the porcelain dome of sky, the elegant swoop of the coastline. It was astonishing—a trip to another planet. Hills velvet green. White walls, white gulls, white sails. Blue walls, stone walls, glass walls, flags, red brick, yellow stone, glittering ocean, and, in the distance, the gray security of warships. Warships like islands for miles.

Irene and Dorothy reached out without thinking and took each other's hands. The driver parked.

Dorothy hopped out. "Palm trees!" she shouted. She clapped her hands.

Irene had never seen her go giddy. She stepped out of the cab and was alarmed when Dorothy jumped up and down.

Their driver joined them and leaned on his cab and crossed his ankles. "Usually," he said, "*c'est blanc.* The docks. All white with boat. Yacht. Sail. Fishing. But soon again."

They piled back into the cab and Irene tapped the driver on his shoulder. "*Monsieur? Bérets, s'il vous plaît?*"

"Ah!" he said. "I know perfect hat shop!"

Based on the excitement of the shopwomen at the driver's appearance, Irene suspected the shop belonged to his sister or his mother. They found exactly what they were looking for and the shopkeepers presented Irene and Dorothy with beautifully wrapped packages.

After the quick shopping stop, they got back in the cab and started their serpentine descent to the hotel.

"I never thought I'd see places like this," Dorothy said. "After the war, all I want to do is travel."

"Good plan," their driver said. "Where you go?"

"Africa!" Dorothy said. "On safari. Lions. Elephants."

"To shoot?"

"Pictures. No guns."

He nodded sagely. "*D'accord*. Guns." He blew a puff of air. "*Stupide*."

Dorothy put on sunglasses and looked like Hepburn.

"How you holding up?" Irene asked her.

"Having some dreams."

"Me, too."

"Don't like 'em."

"Me neither."

"Cannes will help this," the cabbie said. Suddenly, he was outraged by a donkey pulling a cart and laid on his horn as if appalled that such an unsophisticated scene could demolish the trance he was creating for his new *amies américaines*. "Stay with us," he requested. "Here is the whole world, voilà."

—

The driver dropped them off in the empty street before the Carlton Hotel, with its famed domes supposedly designed to celebrate the breasts of a well-known courtesan. "They have a pool!" Dorothy enthused. Irene had never witnessed this sixteen-year-old version of ol' Stretch.

After they'd checked in and signed the ledger, they carried their purchases and let the bellboy bring their bags to their second-floor rooms. In her room, Irene took great care to set her beret at a fashionable angle atop her head. It sloped perfectly to the left, barely clearing her eyebrow. She believed she looked like a French cinema star.

When she stepped out of her room, she found Dorothy in the hall, already wearing her red beret. Irene had to stifle a laugh—Darling Dot had dragged the beret onto her head like a knit cap, pulling it all the way down to her ears so they stuck out like a monkey's. They hurried down the stairs, sniffed the bistro, and spied on the golden bodies around the aquamarine pool.

Eagerly, they stepped into the early afternoon and strolled down the streets, arm in arm. They sported loose slacks and white blouses and bought sheer, sherbet-colored scarves. Women wore bright white pleated skirts that danced around their legs as they walked. Black buttons, black belts. Comfortable and stylish flat shoes. Irene and Dorothy peered in shopwindows and smelled the bread. They used 20 percent of their army allowance to buy tiny bottles of perfume. Irene bought lavender bath salts.

"I'm beat," Dorothy complained.

"No wonder. We've walked for miles." Irene pointed at a white-and-blue bistro with geraniums painted in wreaths up its sides and white wrought-iron tables arrayed on the sidewalk under an orange-striped sunshade. "Let's," she said.

Exhausted, they collapsed at a table. Bistro Antibes.

"Got steam coming out of my shoes," Dorothy said.

They started with tea and coffee thick with foamed cream.

Édouard, their unimpressed waiter, sprinkled cinnamon and nutmeg on the foam and set down a small saucer stacked with sugar cubes and silver tongs. "*Américaines* good," he noted. "We like."

They watched his bottom as he sauntered away.

"Butt good," Dorothy noted.

"Shh!"

He had to be a ballet dancer, or a tango master, Dorothy thought. "He could crack a walnut with that keister."

"Dot!"

Édouard then brought them a glass jar full of water with a single yellow rose swooning over its lip. They enjoyed the front view of him as well. When he placed the rose on the table, he fluttered his eyelashes at them, made moochy lips, and raised his eyebrows fleetingly.

"Now, we eat?" he asked.

"We would enjoy a *jambon et fromage* platter," Irene said, slaughtering the French sounds. "Oh, and red wine. Um, *un vin rouge*?"

He tipped his head forward in the smallest nod.

"And bread!" she added.

"Oh yes. But of course. France and bread—is love in your mouth. Fresh baguette." He kissed his fingertips. Tourists loved that, he knew, though he never did it for the Germans.

"Perfect," Irene said.

"*Oui.*"

When he slouched away, Dorothy said, "I think he likes you."

"They all like me."

"I noticed."

"He's after *you,* darling."

"That'll be the day."

Édouard landed the baguette nestled in red cloth in a long straw basket. "Good with *fromage,*" he said with great solemnity. "Now I pour the wine." He went back inside for the bottle and the glasses.

"I like a man who narrates his day," Irene said, breaking off the heel of the loaf.

"This doesn't make sense, does it?" Dorothy said. "We were being murdered a week ago. Now this. It's—what?"

"*Surreal,*" Irene offered.

"What's that?"

"What you just described. Like a painting of melting clocks."

Dorothy's brows were knit as she thought about it.

"The strangeness of dreams," Irene said. "Made visible."

"That's what I said, huh?"

When Édouard came back, they tried out more of their barbaric French on him.

He opened the bottle and poured their wine, then took away their plates, wiped down their table, and lit a candle. "Is night very soon," he explained with a different and somehow wiser shrug than he had deployed earlier.

He disappeared inside and reappeared once more with a cheese bell on a cart, which neither of them had ever heard of or seen. A glass dome covered two glass shelves of cheeses.

"Free for you," he said. "The boys they send it out for you. *Américains.*

Libération. Merci, baby." Then he frowned slightly and pointed at a seething wad of something on one of the little glass shelves. "Not this one. *Américains* do not eat this one."

"What is that?" Irene asked.

"Tiny, eh, how you say it, worms in the *fromage.*"

"Ew!" they cried.

When he left them, Dorothy offered Irene fifty francs to eat the maggoty cheese. Irene firmly declined. They were not aware that cheeses had so many flavors. The pale soft cheese wrapped in the leaves from a chestnut tree made them crazy. Soon, they were into their second bottle of wine, and the marvelous vista was tipping slightly as it darkened. When they looked up, Édouard was hovering.

"We are tipsy," Irene confessed.

"It is a good way to be, no?" He offered them Gauloises cigarettes and lit them, then sat at the table and slouched stylishly. He winked at Dorothy. His feet touched hers under the table.

She was delighted to have stolen a man from Irene.

After several silent minutes of meditation on the sunset, he rose like some alley cat and ambled inside, only to return with "ze deezerrt." Crêpes Suzette for Dorothy, clafouti for Irene. And two small glasses of cognac.

Dorothy managed to say, "Could you call us an ambulance to take us back to the hotel?"

"Yes, yes!" he cried, laying their check on the table. He went inside and brought back a dahlia and a mint for each of them.

Once they'd paid, one of the chefs puttered around the corner in an exhausted Fiat. It was a requisitioned German staff car, he told them when they squeezed in. It had no brakes, he explained, but the tires tied around the nose of the car were there in case they ran into anything. He kept it in first gear and had a death grip on the emergency brake. They were delivered very slowly to the hotel four blocks up the hill.

"This French bit might improve my attitude," Dorothy said to Irene as they spilled out.

Inside the Carlton, they rose in a birdcage elevator to their rooms.

25

In the morning they were back at the café, wearing bathing suits under their trousers and sweaters. They ate *pain et beurre* with *confiture et café.*

Édouard dropped some franc bills on the table and wagged a finger at them while not really looking at them. "You pay too much last night," he scolded.

"It's a tip," Irene explained.

"What is this thing?" he said, and walked away.

They had both strawberry and orange marmalade. The butter came in a magnificent golden clot that had been scooped into a white-and-blue bowl. The breezy morning was redolent of the Mediterranean. Salt, food, African wind. In their minds they were now so very French.

Édouard reappeared. "Is warm," he said, sighing. He had red eyes and smelled vaguely of liquor. "Édouard," he proclaimed sadly, "is always here."

"We want to go to the beach," Irene said.

He pointed to the beach with his lips. "Simple, no?" he muttered philosophically.

They left their former tip to pay for their current breakfast, then took to the sand like conquerors, pausing on the way to assault a kiosk manned by some Gypsy-looking *jeunes hommes* in horizontal stripes. They rented two folding canvas-bottomed lounges and a bright yellow umbrella. They had borrowed blue towels from the hotel. Édouard had provided a bucket of cold Bière de Garde in bottles along with a cap opener.

"This is the life for me," Irene said.

"Yeah. I'm finally living like you do."

"Oh now."

"Tell me I'm lying."

Irene ran both hands through her hair and let the breeze sort it all out. "To freedom," she said, digging in their bucket.

They clanked bottles. They chugged down their brews and belched, which amused the hell out of them. All along the beach, on towels in the sand, lay the paper-white bodies of American officers, every one of them probably wondering how to get out of going back to combat. Occupied as they were in regarding the men, Irene and Dorothy didn't see Handyman and his buddy Smitty step off the street above them and onto the beach.

—

The boys wore black trunks and stupid straw hats, though they had at least thought to take off their socks before putting on sandals. They were craning around, on the lookout.

Irene sensed their male presence in her general radar way, and turned to admire the abdomen of the tall one. Then she realized who it was. "What!" she said.

"What?" Dorothy said.

"That. It can't be possible."

Dorothy glanced over. "Surreal," she said with a smirk.

Smitty, all five foot six of him, trotted to them and crawled into Dorothy's lap. "Hello, hot mama," he growled.

Dorothy didn't even bat an eye. She put her arms around him and held him against her chest. "What took you so long?" she said. "Grab a beer."

Irene was doing double and triple takes.

Handyman stepped up to her. "Miss Irene," he said.

He put out his hand. She took it. She looked back at Dorothy, blushing, laughing a little, but Dorothy ignored her. Handyman pulled her up. She fell against his chest.

"I'm happy to see you," he whispered.

"But how—?"

"I told you, I'm everywhere."

They stared at each other.

"Come," he said.

They walked down the beach, following the waterline, Irene's laughter blending with the crying of the gulls and the rush of small waves.

Once again, Dorothy found herself watching, mesmerized, as Irene and her Gary Cooper floated away into their movie-scene romance. The flash flood of Smitty's enthusiasm brought her back. He seemed to have grown a second set of hands, and he used all of them to wrangle her into kissing range. The chaise squealed as they wrestled.

She wasn't opposed to his shenanigans, but she was more interested in Irene and her walk down the beach. Dorothy turned away from Smitty and leaned over the starboard side of the chaise to watch the handsome couple in the distance. They looked like a painting in a museum. Thin, long blue shadows, white foam at their feet. They appeared to be laughing. Irene was leaning her head against her pilot's upper arm while he wrapped her in a loose half embrace.

Smitty busied himself with Dorothy's neck. She laughed and shoved him off a bit even as she leaned into his affections. When she came up for air a few minutes later, she put her left hand on Smitty's chest and pushed him away again to see what was happening with the other lovers. Farther down the beach now, Hans had Irene in his arms and dipped her backward. She extended her free leg dramatically, pointing her toes to the sky.

"You've got to be kidding," Dorothy muttered.

Hans cradled Irene's head in his hand and kissed her neck. Dorothy knew Irene was imagining it all on a movie screen, scoring it with her own private love theme. She was sure of it.

Smitty pried the cap off another beer and grunted at her. Dorothy turned back to him. She didn't want to hurt his feelings, but after a bit she stood up and searched again for Irene and Hans against the blue and green of the sea.

And there they were, far from her now. They were dancing. Handyman spun Irene once and pulled her close. Her feet left the sand and the lovers wheeled in their embrace.

"You ever dance without music?" Dorothy asked Smitty.

"I never danced at all," he confessed, draining his beer.

"Maybe I'll teach you," she said, turning her back on the lovers. "Let's get out of here."

"Gimme a hand?" Smitty said, reaching out to her.

She yanked him up brusquely and led him away from the beach.

Later, the two couples met in the lobby bar of the hotel. A quick round of drinks. Dorothy discovered daiquiris. As the couples parted, Irene pulled Dorothy aside and slipped her a handful of prophylactics, Army issue.

"You tramp!" Dorothy whispered.

Irene winked at her and tapped her head. "We stay smart," she said.

—

Irene stretched languidly.

She was lying naked across a large white bed, in a white room, with a warm sea wind lifting white curtains whose shadows made shapes like angels on the white walls, one corner of the silk bedsheet loose over her right thigh, almost hiding her lower body, the wind wickedly ruffling her pubic hair. She felt careless and brazen. It was delicious. The taste of champagne was still tart in her mouth.

Her equally naked lover was sprawled beside her, snoring softly, one leg over hers, every part of him showing in the tender copper slant of light. That splash of illumination flowed from his groin to his chest, and his flat stomach still glistened with sweat, and the light filled the shallows beneath his ribs. His arms were thrown open as carelessly as wings. The scents of their bodies mixed with the smell of the waves. The Mediterranean showed itself in a thin turquoise gap between the curtains through which the sounds of gulls and a boat's horn reached them. He had tasted salty.

Irene had to laugh. It was as though these moments on the Riviera could have been predicted. As though one of her favorite novels had allowed her to enter for a few pages. Fate's shadowy hand. To what else could she attribute this turn of events?

She reached across to Hans and took him in her grip. He stirred, even gasped a little, and she felt his awakening. She could see his heart bumping in his chest, feel his pulse in her hand. Her own heart was banging in her throat.

He opened his eyes, looked down at himself, then over at her. He ran a finger over her breast. His gaze traveled down the length of her body. She squeezed her thighs together, to try to hide herself.

"Don't," he said. "You're so pretty."

She lay back. He leaned down to taste her again.

"Can you again?" she asked. "So soon?"

"Oh, all right. If I have to."

Laughing, they turned into each other.

—

Afterward, he poured a little white wine on her stomach and kissed it off.

"I love your tongue," she said.

He made muffled noises against her skin. Sipped a few drops from her navel. Smelled her.

"What will you do after the war, Hans?"

He rolled over on his back, put his hands behind his head, crossed his ankles. *My Tom Sawyer*, she thought. *My Wild Bill.*

"I'd like to keep flyin'," he said. "I hear Continental is hiring pilots. Pay's good. Though I'd probably pay them to stay in the air." He looked over at her and grinned. "It's better when nobody's shootin' at you."

She idly played with the hair around his navel.

"You?" he asked.

She shrugged one shoulder. Her breasts bobbled and she didn't care. So intoxicating to be so free. "Oh, I don't know. Return to New York and be fashionable, I suppose."

They both laughed.

"I honestly don't know," she admitted.

"The key is to get out of this war in one piece," he said. "Everything after that is gravy."

"Is that a promise?"

"Would I lie to you?"

She lay back and stared at the ceiling. Their fan was lazily spinning. Of course it made her think of his airplane. "I don't even know you," she said. "Seriously. Would you lie to me?"

"Hope not."

"You don't owe me anything, Hans."

He lay there grinning again. "I owe you this right now, this deal right here. Because you know what? It's all we've got."

"Is it?"

"We could die tomorrow."

"I need tomorrow."

"One day this war will be over. I hope we're celebrating again then. Maybe get that *tomorrow* you're talking about." He just kept grinning.

"You don't have a care in the world, do you?"

"Irene! Why spoil the perfect moment?" he said, stretching.

She looked at him a long time. "You're so free."

"So are you, sugar. You have some duties, though. You have to decide if you want a bubble bath, for example. And if you do, if you want me in there with you. I been thinking about that since London."

"You're bad."

"You bet I am. And I'm smart. Stop thinking for a minute and just relax. We can worry when we leave here. That's just what I think, though—I'm not telling you what to do."

She moved over and put her head on his chest. Listened to the engine of his body running. "I'd like you in the bubble bath with me."

He smiled up at the ceiling. "This right here is the best day of my life," he said.

—

They lounged in the bubbles, facing each other. Her feet were on his chest. He took hold of her right foot and massaged it. He had foam in his hair. He tasted her toes.

"Maybe one day you'll step on my airliner and we'll be flying across the Pond to Paris," he said. "Could happen, right? We might see each other as we disembark. It might be raining. I might hold my umbrella over your head and we might run through the airport to a taxi and ride around all night looking at the lights shining on the streets. What do you think?"

"Come here," she said.

He caused a flood on the floor when he pulled himself to her.

She held his head to her chest and prayed that time could suspend itself—not stop, simply slow. A longer afternoon. A longer night. A small island of whatever this was that they had made. Just this small mercy.

"Are we in love?" she asked.

"It doesn't seem outside the realm of possibility."

Neither of them wanted to ever fall asleep.

26

It was a kind of trance. *Trance of romance in France,* she wrote in her journal. Then crossed it out, embarrassed. But she only drew a thin line through it because she knew she'd want to read it again when she was old and spent.

Champagne afternoons at the pool in their new swimsuits. Irene saw that Dorothy had a fine figure and remembered running into her that time coming out of the showers. Amazing what getting out of those overalls could do for her. Handyman was pale and muscular. Smitty was hairy as a monkey.

The boys surprised them one morning by appearing with the chef's brakeless Nazi staff car, the Fiat, which they had borrowed or leased—they wouldn't say. Hans, ever the pilot, took the controls, Smitty and Dorothy folded themselves into the rear, and Irene rode up front. They drove—carefully indeed—to Nice.

Irene was startled by Dorothy's appearance. Her friend wore a gorgeous sky-blue dress that flared just below her knees, with pleats that flowed around her legs like water. It was cinched around her waist with a black belt. She wore her hair free and sported new French sunglasses. Irene felt plain and gray beside this Valkyrie. Handyman didn't seem to think anything of the sort, though he did once whisper, "Look at the gams on Dot," and Irene smacked him.

They gambled in casinos. They drank sidecars and 1789s. Smitty had a sudden craving for eclairs, and they crept at seven miles an hour through the towns to avoid catastrophe until they found a bakery. Somehow they got back alive, though the brakeless wonder did carom off a light post or two and had a troubling encounter with an even slower truck.

That night Irene slept lying on his chest and when she woke up hoped he hadn't noticed her drool on him before she wiped it off.

—

The next day the foursome paired off. Irene and Hans found themselves walking along a rattling complex of picturesque docks away from the boulevards full of soldiers. They admired insouciant fishermen hauling bacalao and sharks out of their boats and into ice wagons. Bluefin tuna, swordfish. No haute couture here, though rich-looking seafood lovers haggled for bargains up and down the quays.

The boats were as louche as their crews, lounging casually in their slips with nets seemingly tossed on their booms like jackets thrown over a shoulder. Their few flags were bright in the sun, their hulls leaning left with the tide, masts swaying metronomically above them. The ocean beyond detonated with a hilarity of sparkles.

The whole view put Irene in mind of a Raoul Dufy poster. "When you come to New York," she told Hans, "I would like to take you to the museums."

"I'd like that. I hear you have a good zoo. I want to see a rhino."

She thought: *He's eleven years old.*

He steered her to an ice-filled cart inside of which nested fat, gorgeous oysters. They dragged tall three-legged stools to the serving shelf and ordered a dozen.

"Catch this morning," the cart man boasted. "So fresh, yes?"

"Maestro!" Handyman cried.

The oyster master smoked out of the corner of his mouth and shucked the oysters while eyeing Irene. He placed the dozen on icy trays and laid out citrus and sauces and ivory two-pronged forks, then beamed benevolently as they slurped the shellfish down. They were drunk on them, as though the taste of the sea were brandy.

As they ate, Irene looked over to Hans. "Are you ever afraid up there?"

"Of what?"

"To die?"

He took another oyster, then dabbed at his lips. "We don't think about that. If you do, you probably can't fly combat. You'd get to thinkin' about it more and more and freeze up. I've seen it happen. Guys dread getting in their plane. And you're going to think I'm crazy, but the plane knows."

She wiped her lips. "I don't think you're crazy."

"Does your truck think?"

"Oh yes. It thinks: *Let me force Irene to make more donuts.*"

The oyster maestro joined them in their laughter, though he spoke little English and probably didn't care for it all that much, either.

Handyman ordered another dozen oysters. Irene demurred, crying, "I just couldn't!" when all three of them knew full well that she could. The maestro didn't need English to understand the romantic charades of couples. This woman could eat very much if she didn't want to impress her man with her petite ways. The maestro smiled at them benignly and proffered two small glasses of brandy along with the oysters.

Salt and seaweed and smoke tinged the air. Gulls and pelicans on the uprights of the docks looked like philosophers.

"Can you smell Spain?" Handyman asked, playing the poet for his lady. "Can you smell Africa?"

She did a minor swoon in spite of herself.

—

Arm in arm, they went to every dock.

"Irene! If I go AWOL, will you come with me? We can hide out in some ruined castle by a lavender field in Provence. I hear it's almost as pretty as Oregon. You can read me poems, and I'll sing you some Lead Belly. We'll live on oysters and grapes. I'll fly a mail plane and deliver love letters all over France."

"Is that a proposal?"

Hans smiled, took her hand, and kissed her fingertips. "My Pearl of Great Price," he said, tucking her hand under his arm.

They strolled along. On the farthest dock, away from anyone but old sea dogs in rubber boots, they came across a stack of slatted crates. When Irene bent to look into one, a tentacle slithered forth and reached for her face. She jumped back. The octopus stretched its arm as far as it would go. It quivered in the air.

"Got a friend there," Hans said.

She put out her finger—the octopus's suckers stuck to it. "She wants to live." Once Irene had said it, the realization upset her. "Can't we save her?" she said.

The octopus gently held her finger prisoner. Handyman didn't waste a minute. He took out his wallet and haggled with the pertinent fisherman. Then, triumphant and broke, he strode back to Irene and picked up the crate. The fishermen were laughing and pointing. It was the stupidest thing they'd ever seen, but it was for love, and thus heroic.

"What did you do?" Irene said.

"Bought it."

"You bought my octopus?"

"Bought the whole box of them." Tentacles from the crate inspected his shirt collar. "C'mon, darlin'," he said.

They walked to a stone jetty covered in barnacles. Handyman grunted. Lugging thirty pounds of worried octopuses was an interesting way to get exercise. He set the crate down on the rocks and fished his folding knife from his back pocket and started to pry off the top off the crate. Irene held her hands up to her face because she didn't know how to respond. Would the octopuses burst out like confetti?

"Here goes," Hans warned and popped the lid off, flinching back.

Inside, an oily swirl of bodies, then the arms, began to rise.

"Free the octopuses!" he bellowed.

The octopus and her companions swarmed out and plopped onto the stones. They knew where they were going. They flowed like thick water down between the stones and under the seaweed and Handyman and Irene stood watch and waved the curious gulls away.

As they walked on, she hooked her arm through his and said, "That was strangely gallant."

"Thanks," he said. "But...I'm gonna have to borrow cab fare from you now."

—

That night, in her room, she asked him to sing her song again. He didn't feel right singing without his guitar, but he sang it anyway. His voice sounded like a boy's, quavering slightly. It made her cry.

Before they slept, he whispered, "I'm naming my plane *Good Night, Irene*."

She fell asleep to that, wondering the next day if she had dreamed it. Had she really murmured "What a lovely lie, darling" as she slipped away?

—

It was a dawn flight call for all of them. Handyman and Smitty pulled up to the front of the hotel in the brakeless staff car. The men were in their leather jackets and caps, prepped to return to the front after an all-too-brief R & R. In an attempt to lighten the mood, Irene and Dorothy wore their berets. The drive to the airfield was subdued, Irene with her head on Handyman's shoulder as he drove, Smitty and Dorothy holding hands in the back. The C-47 was already waiting. After they climbed out of the car, Dorothy took Smitty's arm and led him away.

Irene and Handyman held each other for a long moment. When they pulled apart, Hans started to speak. But Irene put her hands up to his face and cradled it between her palms. "Don't say goodbye to me. Never say goodbye to me."

He stared hard at her, as if trying to pour all of himself into the depths of her hazel eyes. "I can't ever say goodbye to you," he said. "Don't you know that?" He took his cap off and leaned into her for a kiss.

When the kiss finally ended, Irene's eyes were misty. She put her hand in her pocket and withdrew something small clenched in her fist. Flashing a mischievous grin, she reached up and tucked it into Handyman's jacket pocket before walking backward toward the plane.

When they finally broke eye contact so Irene could board the plane, Handyman reached into his pocket. He felt the silk she had left there and knew immediately what it was. He grinned and blushed a little.

Smitty wandered back to him after seeing Dorothy safely to the plane. "Handyman, you okay?"

Handyman rubbed the silk underwear hidden in his pocket and grinned again. "Yeah, it's gonna be okay."

—

The Sisters were mostly silent on their plane ride. They occasionally chuckled, nudged one another. Looked at each other and said, "What?" at various moments.

"I never met anyone like him," Irene said.

"I'm sure he says the same about you."

"Do you think so?"

"Sure."

"I watched his little ballsies roll around," Irene confided. "Did you know they did that?"

"Ballsies." Dorothy snorted.

"Did Smitty's do that?"

"Madam," Dorothy said in her best snooty accent, "a lady does not screw and tell."

"Stop."

She relented. "Poor Smitty. He got all weepy. I told him to grow up."

"Did you know he was going to come here?"

"Girl, I invited him."

Irene gawked at her.

"We write to each other," Dorothy said, as if it should have been obvious.

"I didn't know anything about it," Irene complained.

"Get over it, hon. Everyone has secrets."

In silence they watched the coast recede out the back window of the cab.

"I'm afraid," Irene confessed. "What if I lose him? What if this is all there is?"

"Dorothy says, *If you lose him, move on to the next*. Wasn't this enough? Move ahead, Irene. Move ahead. Keep rolling. Don't look back."

When they got back to the Blue Monkey Hotel, after another seemingly interminable ride on another bulky C-47, they discovered a prim woman in a crisp new uniform sitting in the *Rapid City*.

"I'm Holly," she said. "I guess I'm your new partner. I just moved over to Group F." Then she leaned forward and whispered, "Me and Rusty, we're gonna get married." She had his same Southern accent.

27

THE IMPENDING WEDDING was the major excitement at the Blue Monkey. The lovers were in a big hurry. Nobody knew if they'd be alive tomorrow. Any damned thing could happen at any damned minute. Handyman had been trying to tell her that very thing, Irene reflected.

When Rusty showed up at the Blue Monkey, Irene and Dorothy buttonholed him against the side of the *Rapid City*.

"Don't get us wrong," Irene said. "We're really glad to finally get our third girl. But what the hell, Russell? You're getting married?"

"And who is this girl, anyway?" Dorothy added.

Russell put his hands up defensively to block their frontal assault, sheepishly looking around to make sure nobody was witnessing this. "Whoa, whoa! Been sweet on Holly since I was fifteen," he said. "You don't know how much work it took for me to finally get her into the *Rapid City*."

It suddenly hit Irene and Dorothy that they had been shouldering the extra work all this time so that Russell could have his sweetheart close to him. And also that this was likely only a temporary fix.

"This doesn't make any sense," Irene said. "Why would you put this girl you love on our truck? You know where we're going. You're really gonna send your new wife up to the front with us? *You* haven't even been up there."

Rusty flinched. "Look, you ain't the only women who want to serve in this war," he shot back. "Holly wanted to be a part of this and I need her to be safe, so she's with you." The plan, though she didn't know it yet, was to send her home once they got married. She would go back the wife of an officer and he could know she would be okay, no matter what.

The desperation on his face melted both women.

He pulled out a pack of cigarettes and offered them each a smoke. "I feel like I'm running out of time," he said softly. "Can't you help me? Ain't I still your Rusty Penney?"

It was a plaintive cry that overwhelmed them both. This skinny, awkward redheaded jug-eared boy with freckles, Irene realized, was every GI she and Dorothy had sworn to serve and support. In the end, they were all scared lonely boys lost in a world they hadn't created, trying so hard to be men, often broken by horrors they'd never imagined. Sometimes their only succor was a kind smile, a cup of coffee, a donut.

"Oh, Rusty," Irene said, and stepped to him with a hard embrace. "Of course we will help you."

Dorothy resisted for a moment but then joined the group hug and kissed Rusty on top of his head. "But you still owe us one hell of a third girl," she whispered in his ear.

—

Holly and Rusty wanted to get married right there, at the hotel, before marching orders came down. Patton and Eisenhower were notoriously restless. The Western Front was calling: they were shoving Adolf back into his hole, and there was no time for romance. Brutal struggle awaited. So they engaged the chaplain, and he agreed to marry them. Why not? Sky pilots were in the field to offer comfort and spiritual support, after all.

Irene teamed up with the crews of two other Clubmobiles, including the *Cheyenne*, to form a handsome perimeter and reception kitchen around the traffic circle. The ladies were crazy for the thought of a sinker wedding cake, and spent hours planning this engineering marvel. The hotel cook had plans for a buttercream frosting.

Dorothy, though she might dream in her private reverie of a wedding gown, as usual didn't care for this henhouse stuff. She left her fellow

Dollies at the hotel and went in search of something that would make this field wedding a legend.

—

The blessings of VIII Corps, meanwhile, arrived in the form of a letter.

TO WHOM IT MAY CONCERN:
There are no military objections to the marriage of Russell Penney and Holly White.

C.C.B. WARDEN,
Colonel, A.G.D.,
Adjutant General

—

Irene was in the hotel lobby with her wedding squad. They had sketches and notes scattered around the room.

The concierge, who found it all amusing, provided them with pitchers of coffee. One consequence of the war was that it had made him abhor boredom. Yes, the Occupation had been an opera of awful stupidity, with bellowing and sneering villains in the wings, outrages and swan songs, sirens and explosions and shortages and well-hidden crates of wine. Executions and guerrilla fighters shooting and burying Nazi officers. Then these mad Americans had swarmed the land, and amid further explosions and screaming machines they had spread their *Pagliacci* clownish pathos and uproar in place of the recent Wagnerian doom. But while he had yearned for the peace of a cease-fire, it turned out that unless something was happening at every moment, he thought he was sinking. Amusement extended only so far, and now he was worse than bored. Everyone had gone insane, he thought.

It was he who first heard the engine. It grunted and shifted outside, coming up from town. The rhythmic *clank-clank* of the treads echoed through the air. He rushed behind the reservation desk and dropped behind the counter.

Irene looked up from her notes. It wasn't unusual to have tanks move up and down the road, she knew, but her terror of them after that last battle had become a thing in her bones, in her stomach, beyond reason. When she saw the concierge duck behind the counter, she sprang out of her seat with a shout.

The other women fell silent.

"What is it?" Holly cried.

"Tanks!" Irene whispered.

The tank paused outside, rumbling. Irene was two steps toward the window when the tank changed gears, lurched, and belched as it rolled, its treads squealing on the cobblestones. It came off the road and toward the hotel. Objects on the counters began to vibrate and dance.

Irene splayed herself across the window and stared. It was a Sherman, she told herself—their protector—not a Panzer. The other ladies jammed in behind her.

"It's American!" Irene called out.

The concierge stood tall and tried to reinstate his insouciance.

"What in the world?" Holly said.

"I don't know!" Irene said.

The tank passed behind the *Rapid* and went along the side of the hotel, out of sight. They could hear it snapping branches off the trees. The ground shook with its passing. They fled the front window and stampeded to the back windows.

The concierge joined them there. "*Mon Dieu*," he said.

They wrestled for space. Suddenly, the tank reappeared. It pivoted right, rumbled around that side of the hotel and rolled across the back of the property. Chickens scattered in panic. The one turkey the Germans hadn't eaten took umbrage and puffed up its chest, dragged the tips of its wings in the dirt, and challenged the tank to a fight. The tank ignored the fowl and rumbled by and spun to the right at the far end and headed back to the front of the hotel.

Joined by the concierge, the women trotted to the front porch and hid behind one another to watch the big machine round the far corner and lumber toward them again. It pulled up across from the steps. The engine suddenly shut down, its silence like a gut punch. Its turret suddenly swung around and faced them. The cannon lowered until it was aimed right at their faces. Holly ran back inside. The concierge crouched behind Irene.

Up top, the hatch popped open. Two hands appeared on the rim of the opening, and Dorothy slowly rose into view from below. Unable to contain the grin on her face, she hollered, "One of you dames call for a cab?"

—

The wedding day was cloudy, but nobody minded. Holly, diplomatically avoiding the ill will that would've resulted from choosing between her two new crew members, picked a gal from Group B to be her bridesmaid. Irene and Dorothy were flower girls. Rusty wore his dress uniform, and Holly wore her full Red Cross outfit, including the smart little cap that she didn't really like.

Garcia drove the Kill Pig half-track across the road, blocking it so no unwelcome vehicles could intrude. Its twin .50s in back swung left and right. A small contingent of musicians (primarily bugles and tubas) had assembled and managed to play martial versions of sentimental favorites. Only slightly sour. From somewhere, no one knew whence, a squad of Aussie blokes in uniforms and bush hats had appeared and immediately bought everyone beer.

Four army tanks, in a double row of two per side, stood before the hotel. Their turrets were turned toward each other, and their guns were raised and crossed at the top, forming a ceremonial arch, which the Sisters had decorated with bunting. The couple walked together under the gun barrels.

The gathered Clubmobilers wept—they couldn't help it. So did Rusty.

The chaplain hadn't had to travel far. He just walked down from his second-floor room, half-soused on sherry, no doubt a libation he'd never thought about back in Southie. His face was red and he smiled broadly at the gathered. When he declared Russell and Holly husband and wife, cheers and gunfire startled pigeons out of the eaves.

Orders came in that night. It was just as they suspected: destination Belgium, first thing in the morning. Along with the orders, a letter from Handyman arrived, already opened and read by the censors. Irene laughed when she saw their work.

XXXXXXXXX

XXXXXX, XXXXX

Dear Pearl,

I am XXXXXXXXXXXXXXXXXXXXX.

But don't worry, I hope to see you XXXXXXXXXXXX.

XXXXXXXXXXXXXXXXXXXXXXXXXXXXXXXX.

Won't that be fun?

Yours,

XXXXXXXXXXXXXXXXXXXXXXX

28

IN THE FRONT seat of the *Rapid City* that first morning, Holly was squeezed in between Irene and Dorothy. She was a bit uncomfortable, but it felt like an old home to her truckmates.

"Your problem, Irene, is you care what men think."

"I certainly do."

"Well, snap out of it."

Holly had been listening to Irene and Dorothy squabble for what seemed like hours. She sensed she had dropped into the middle of an argument that had been going on for months. She felt a sense of whiplash between the emotions of her wedding the day before and the boredom of this endless convoy heading to Bastogne.

What irritated them all was missing Paris. Irene especially longed for a Parisian idyll. But the convoy had bypassed the city and rolled on.

Winter was still a bit off but the hills and mountains were already icy, and Dorothy had to drive cautiously, double-shifting on the curves, always following the *Cheyenne* and a cinemobile.

All their meals were eaten outside—they balanced their mess kits on fenders and dined with guys from the 35th Special Service Company. Irene sent a letter home.

Dear Mother:

We are always traveling to our next assignment. The weather is cold and very rainy.

Our dinner times would amuse you because we eat outside. It is raining so hard that we have to eat very fast before the water fills our mess kits and ruins what rations we have.

It makes one long for our elegant Thanksgiving dinners in Richmond Village. I understand that you must be far too busy to respond but I wanted you to know that I remain

Forever yours, Irene

—

While they'd driven that autumn road, torrential rains had turned fields into swamps. It was the most miserable service they had ever known. Holly got caught in the black mud one day, buried to her knees. Dorothy had to wade out there and drag her free. Holly's boots vanished in the muck and they never found them again. An army quartermaster in the convoy had some small men's boots for her in the back of his truck, but she still had to wear three socks on each foot to keep them on.

A week later, they parked at one edge of a pestilential and frigid black swamp that had recently been a plowed field. A hundred yards across from them stood the *Cheyenne,* dragging its little supply trailer, which promptly half sank like some leaking dinghy just offshore. Men formed two serpentine lines at each end of the swamp, dropped planks and pallets on the mud, and waited miserably for coffee.

Since it was too muddy to wade across the field to each other, the two crews Handie-Talkied on their SCR-536 transceiver units, which they'd pilfered from the engineers.

"Don't tell me we're not heroes," Irene radioed Phyllis.

"Say *Over,* over."

"What?"

"Say *Over,* Irene, when you're on the radio and finished talking. That way we know you're finished talking. Over."

"I feel silly."

"*I feel silly, over,*" Phyllis corrected her.

"Well, we all think you're silly, too. But don't feel bad, Phyl. We forgive you. Over."

The Sisters laughed stupidly about that one for an hour.

Irene wrote to Handyman as often as she could. She knew he was flying secret missions, deadly missions. He would want to write to her, she told herself, but would not be able to. But she imagined the smile on his face whenever one of her letters arrived. She placed letters in every mailbag when it came along. Writing the letters kept her on the earth, she felt.

She'd gotten into the habit of keeping his most recent letter tucked in her brassiere next to her heart. The letters were never very long, just enough to let her know he was thinking of her.

> *Dear Pearl,*
> *I don't even know where this letter will find you. But then, you don't know where I am at either. I think we are everywhere. I look for you everywhere. I know you look up every time XXXXXXXXXXXX goes by.*
>
> *This is a big ol' war and I think it is going to get real interesting before it all ends. Even if we don't hear from each other for a bit we will find each other after it's over.*
>
> *XXXXXXXXXXXXXXXXXXXXXXXXXXXXXXXXXX and I will do the same.*
>
> *Good night, Irene.*
> *HMan*

Time was a slippery concept for the *Rapid City* crew. Mile 200 of the journey evolved into Mile 375 of the journey. One week rolled into the next and the next, and soon they were well into November. But it was all one endless day of little sleep, gobbled rations, a relentless drudgery of service. Their feet and backs hurt; their shoulders and hands were numb. By the end of a service session, they were mumbling like drunks, and it felt as if as soon as they fell asleep, they were roused to drive again.

Irene brushed her teeth in the cab of the truck, swished her mouth out from the canteen, and spit out the window.

"Guess you're not so fancy now, huh, Gator," Dorothy said.

Holly chose to ride in a nest of sleeping bags and sacks in the back of the truck. She claimed it was to get more room but Dorothy and Irene knew she was catching a nap.

At a service stop outside a field hospital, Holly and Irene manned the galley, as usual, with Dorothy outside wrangling the troops. Irene thought Holly was an excellent Third Girl. This morning, though, she was putting her hands over her gut and groaning, bent over slightly.

Irene asked if she was all right.

"Aunt Flo is paying me a visit."

Irene turned to her. "Me, too!"

"Crampy," Holly said.

Suddenly, Dorothy's face appeared in their window. "I heard that. Same here!"

"Well, damn," Holly said.

Dorothy hurried inside and they dropped the shutters and laughed like maniacs, ignoring the soldiers outside. When they were done, they gritted their teeth through the service and afterward rolled out again.

—

It was getting colder. The roadside streams were ice-edged, and snow fell most days. They had to chip ice off the *Rapid*'s windshield every morning and sometimes during the day. It grew an icicle beard under its grand front bumper, and the doors to the galley in the rear froze shut. They had to kick the doors to crack them loose. Irene was grateful that she now had several pairs of socks to wear, and the women opted for long johns under their uniforms. They tried to do the service with gloves, but it was nearly impossible. For once they were thankful for the heat inside their little kitchen.

The troops suffered the cold. They didn't stop. GIs rolled through everything. With the deepening cold and the rain turning to sleet and the exhaustion and stomach infections and rotting toes, hundreds of faces all became the same face. Every khaki saint stared at the women with million-year-old eyes.

One morning, they found a bullet hole in the *Rapid*'s side. They were all furious. This seemed like a clear violation of the Geneva Conventions.

Dorothy went monosyllabic for days, and a few nights later began to disappear after sunset. Scuttlebutt had it that she wandered into the countryside with a small knot of Rangers. Commando stuff, it was whispered. They called these men the Gray Ghosts. Nobody knew for sure if they existed, or if Dorothy was really with them. Other guys said Stretch was just playing poker and drinking with the ground pounders. Both things could have been true. Neither Holly nor Irene wanted to know. They didn't dare ask Dottie what she was up to. It scared them both. They simply maintained their patented banter and faux good cheer, hoping they were throwing out a lifeline that Dottie could follow back if she was in some trouble.

The frivolity of Cannes seemed a lifetime ago.

When Dorothy finally dropped from exhaustion one day and was unable to drive, Zoot had to step up and manhandle the Clubmobile. She lay in the back, on old sacks and sleeping bags, snoring wetly in the sleep of the anesthetized.

Zoot was more patient than Dorothy. He took care to reintroduce Irene to the gears. It felt like ten years since she had been trained to drive the truck. Mrs. Penney had zero interest in any of that. Her mind was already gone into her domestic future—a cabin on a Tennessee ridge, looking over the lakes. Calculating how many babies they could afford to have, and when.

"Your main problem," Zoot told Irene, "is trying to reach the pedals." He laughed his *skitch-skitch-skitch* laugh out of the corner of his mouth.

—

Bastogne was supposed to be a reprieve. A civilized service area known as a *minimal fire zone*. Lots of troops were gathered all along the Siegfried

Line, which ran along the Western Front of German territory, either buried in or skirting the great Ardennes Forest. The city was near the line, though it was generally thought to be a posting for inexperienced GIs, or for older more battle-scarred troops to catch a bit of a breather. Rear command was just a few miles to the west. The guys all believed the Germans were in retreat, and everyone needed mocha java and sinkers and some happy gab and maybe a Sinatra record.

When the women had a day off they could drive back to Brussels for some high life and culture. Or down to Luxembourg. Once there, they even drove over to shop in a liberated chunk of Germany. They were in the southernmost province of Belgium, and the highway led both to command headquarters and to the rest of the border between Belgium and Germany. The many roads that converged in the area made it a major target for the German army. The Clubmobiles on duty were not only the *Rapid City* but also their old pals the *Cheyenne*, the *Miami*, the *New Haven*, the *Albany*, the *Boise*, and the *Atlanta*. They barely saw each other, though, given that their range of service stretched from HQ to Luxembourg itself to scattered encampments and villages. They roamed as far as Brussels to the west, and hit outposts in towns such as Charleville-Mézières, across the border in the north of France, and Wiltz, Clervaux, and Ettelbruck in Luxembourg. From the 106th at St. Vith to the VIII Corps rest center in Arlon.

Martha Levin, their loyal Group F captain, tried to be everywhere at once. Her jeep was now known as *Mighty Martha*. It kept its top up since the weather had changed, though its flimsy canvas doors did nothing to slow the snow. Riding in the jeep was a miserable business. But she had a duty to perform.

She inspected the buses, poked around in the supply wagons. Like the Dollies, she wore long johns, along with a fleece-lined leather jacket and an ear-flapped knit cap, and still she shivered. She huddled next to the window of the *Rapid*'s galley, its service windows halfway down to force some of the warm kitchen air out to the freezing soldiers. Everybody gathered there had sweaty foreheads and icy toes.

Captain Levin stood with a soldier named Manuel, who said he was on his way to the Maginot Line, to their west. That was the famous barrier of blocks and walls and tank traps and reinforced concrete towers that allegedly kept the Germans at bay. It stretched for nearly three hundred miles, including seventy-five miles or more through and around the Ardennes Forest.

"We're on limited rations today," Captain Levin told Manuel. "One smile per customer."

He laughed. "Ho-kay," he said.

Captain Levin smacked the side of the galley and called, "Good work, *Rapid City*! Carry on, ladies." She drove off in search of the *Cheyenne* and the *Miami*.

December now, and the snow was falling a little harder. The tarp above the serving area began to sag. Dorothy had to periodically lift it with a broom handle to let the snow slide off. When she wasn't careful, it fell on blisterfoots standing in line. They jumped away, their clouds of breath heavy with curses.

One of the boys ducked under the tarp and shook the snow off the top of his head. He stopped when he saw Irene. "You sure are a sight for sore eyes!"

She laughed at his eagerness. "Why, aren't you a fast talker."

"I am a devil with a pretty lady," he said with a grin.

Irene picked up a pencil and flirted back with him. "Now don't make me report you with your fast talk."

The other soldiers gathered around the truck laughed.

"The name's Jerry," he said. "Jerry Bregstein. Go on and report me. That way, when I get the Medal of Honor, you'll remember me."

"Ah, Jerry," she said, handing him an extra donut, "I could never forget you. You'll always be my hero."

This was the sort of levity that was getting harder to come by. They could almost hear the freeze on its way, rolling down from the dark north, creeping west from Russia. It was a kind of roar that hid in the heart of the forest. The dark earth compressing, the water cracking into ice.

"Don't worry, boys!" Irene shouted. "We will keep you warm. You can count on that!" She held each steaming cup for an extra second to get warmth into her hands.

29

THE BOYS WANTED to be at the Clubmobiles all day every day. They lived under constant threat—the German army was out there to the east. The whole nation of Germany. The Siegfried Line. The dark woods. Monsters could be out there for all they knew. Because the trees were planted in straight lines, like some giant's cornfield, the forests were deathtraps. There was no cover. Shells could scream right down the rows.

Many of them were doing miserable duty out in those forests. Building breastworks out of sandbags frozen into fat misshapen bricks that clacked loudly when they fell on each other. Clearing saplings for line-of-fire corridors. Making latrines and trying to burn frozen blocks of feces. For that they had to resort to pitchforks. When Irene heard a soldier call it "forkin' turds," she laughed behind her hand.

A wide arc of foxholes was being expanded with pickaxes and oratorios of cursing. Shovels squealed against the rocks frozen into the ground. It was wise for the grunts to make frames to cover their holes and affix ponchos to the wood to keep the rain and hail and snow out. It was so cold that sometimes the wood frames cracked. The troops wrapped their feet in burlap to keep them from freezing. Some guys even wrapped old newspapers around their boots, then mummified them in layers of burlap. Nobody was going to run fast wearing that, but it was better than losing toes or whole feet to frostbite. They helpfully wrapped Irene's feet for her. She was afraid her toes were blue in their tombs.

The boys wore knit gloves. And then they wore socks over those gloves. Those with scarves wore them encircling their heads with only their eyes exposed. Soon they had icicles in their whiskers and frozen tears in their eyelashes. Those who could not get warm no matter what they did bartered for blankets when back in town, then cut them into broad strips to save their cheeks and noses and ears from being burned off by the frost. They put sections of blanket under their helmets, and when the ice fogs rolled in they looked like strange witches and Norsemen. Those fogs felt like needles. The helmets sprouted small icicles that had congealed from their breath. The ground crackled when they walked, the trees coated in glass. It was eerie the way the branches and twigs tinkled in the dark.

The boys felt abandoned, but they were not alone. Now and then, German soldiers shouted from the gray distance: "Are you cold?"

GIs called back, "No, your mama is keeping us warm!"

Then the occasional round zipped through their front line like an ice wasp. They had been warned not to take the bait. Not to shout insults back into the void. Not to shoot back, lest they reveal their exact locations. Not to waste ammo. But to hell with it—every once in a while a couple of teams let loose with everything they had. "Light 'em up!" After these eruptions, the forest was even quieter. Eerier. Because they had deafened themselves. The iced twigs they had cracked fell and pinged around them. But the barrels of their weapons were comfortingly hot.

Everyone was getting a little slaphappy. Especially the crews of the Clubmobiles. The whole bunch were astounded when Jill from the *Cheyenne* got a toothache and hitchhiked all the way to Paris, more than two hundred miles, to see a dentist. Dorothy was mad that Jill had outdone her in audacity.

—

Though combat was fleeting, almost underground, men still fell. A bullet could hiss home before they heard the rifle's report. A light artillery shell could carry away a soldier's arm.

The ground had become too hard to bury the dead. Blood formed small crimson skating rinks on the ground. Chaplains and corpsmen hauled the stiffening bodies to small groves and open spaces next to the road, where they laid their brothers down and stacked them, neatly, as if they were firewood, their bodies wrapped in ponchos, all feet facing the same direction. A last act of tenderness.

They constructed A-frames out of logs to protect their brothers' sleep. When they passed by these mausoleums, they averted their eyes, ashamed they had stacked their comrades and abandoned them to the elements. There was something ancient in this place. Something that counted these sacrifices. Something that hoarded them. Something that was so very much not...American. The GIs didn't believe in ghosts. Or they didn't admit that they believed in ghosts. But at 3:00 a.m., every one of them could be convinced that some malign spirit stalked him.

—

The Sisters of the *City* were billeted at the Auberge Bastogne, where the three of them shared a bare room. The military had taken over the hotel along with several buildings throughout the center of town. In eyeshot of the front door were old stone arches and a small park. Military vehicles and soldiers were often moving through the streets. The hotel's abandoned and stripped lobby housed the bags of sinker mix and sugar, stacks of milk cans. Tins of ground coffee formed a pyramid behind the sandbags covering the front windows. But the hotel had running water and working boilers. A flush toilet and a bath were all one could ask for.

"Our kingdom," Irene liked to call it.

The three women camped out on the second floor. The rooms up there and in the lobby had fireplaces, and the GIs were generous with wood and planks and broken-up furniture. The fires were comforting, joyous. Some of the guys—the smart ones, the ambitious ones—were building cabins for themselves out behind the foxhole lines. They saw no reason to suffer. They put up these little cabins and made rock beds to support tinder and burned small fires to keep their feet warm. Besides, the cabins were funny. People never failed to laugh when they found one. Those soldiers brought sawed logs to the hotel and stayed for coffee. They could be jolly bastards.

At night, Holly sometimes wept about Rusty, so worried for him.

"He's at HQ," Dorothy scoffed. "Sippin' hot coffee with brandy in it."

Both Irene and Dorothy were secretly terrified every time the old wood of the floor creaked or swayed. Holly, despite her concern for Rusty, seemed unshakable herself. She was too practical to imagine the building collapsing for no reason. But Holly hadn't been where they'd been. She hadn't spent the night trapped in a flooded basement in a collapsed house. Irene was afraid that she would always fear the floor falling out from under her. It was one of her jolts, a small flash of panic that could rip open her sleep a minute after it had been achieved.

Both she and Dorothy braced for the drop whenever there was a creak or a groan, or when a shell fell outside town. The ground shook and powder sifted down from the ceiling and they were outdoors before they could even notice that they'd run. But sooner or later, the warm yellow voice of the fireplace called them back.

Fire. That was the best thing. Even if it went mad sometimes, lost control and burned homes and towns and forests. Fire was older than people and owed no explanations, Irene believed. Dorothy and Holly would have told her she was too philosophical for her own good. But fire was everybody's best friend—they would all agree to that after a hot meal, a hot cup, a shot of booze, relief from the cold. Good old fire. Full of color in this white and gray place. Crackling and popping in this foggy silence, fire was filled with fleeting faces and shapes and ghosts and scents. Childhood was in it. Home was in it. Fire connected everybody through time. Their grandmothers had seen the same shapes, felt the same heat. The most ancient ancestor had known the same flame they knew in Bastogne. Irene thought it was all the same fire. It traveled somehow with people, and this one had come from Staten Island with her. Fire was the antithesis of this permanent winter.

The lobby had a large stone fireplace, and the grunts who came in baked themselves before its blaze. If there was anything to be had in Bastogne in those impossible days, it was wood. Every soldier thanked them for his donuts and coffee with it. The truck was parked outside the hotel with its galley and heaters running, while in the lobby Irene maintained trays of sinkers and a full urn. It was double duty—the *Rapid* and the Donut Dugout. Walk-up service outside and a lounge inside. Irene trotted out regularly to change records on the Victrola. Holly was in the truck, serving at the freezing window, imagining herself in her father's Nashville barbecue joint. She pined for her new husband all day. Dorothy, meanwhile, kept the motor running and the supplies moving and the soldiers motivated. They were now the ideal Clubmobile commando team.

—

The GIs would have given their teeth for a fireplace and a dry wooden floor. The widest foxhole wasn't spacious enough even to get in a good stretch. They had to climb out for that. They slept sitting up, curled around their weapons. A kick often awoke them, and they groaned en route to their guard-duty spot while their foxhole mate sank into the trance of sore back and bruised ass. Several grunts lost their earlobes to the cold.

Some big foxholes had small fires in them. Narrow ones might have Sterno fires in their little cans, giving off the strange alcohol scent. Not much heat, but they were comforting to have just for the light. Maybe thaw out some fingers, brew a tin cup of tea, warm some rum. They could cook slices of mystery meat from the rations. What passed for the finer things in life here.

Stones, hard frozen soil, sandbags, and tree trunks formed breastworks on the eastern-facing sides of the foxholes, in case a sniper spied their fire glows or the lighting of a cigarette. They knew that the invisible enemy could see their thin smoke tendrils wafting down the empty alleys between the bare trees. But relentless danger in unsparing cold grew boring. They knew those goddamn Krauts were miserable, too. If peace broke out, both sides would either still kill each other or share a bottle and trade girlfriend pictures and ask each other what the hell that was all about, anyway.

—

In spite of the threat in the dark wood, Irene loved running through the trees. After everything, she was still a child of the shady groves. Somehow, even that night in hell with Dorothy, in that French town whose name she could not remember, had not yet taught her that bad things could truly finish her. On Staten Island, after all, she had jumped from her second-floor bedroom window to escape an unwelcome midnight knock on her door. The silence of those oak trees had sheltered her. Both there and here, she had always been certain of the mercy of the trees. The harder the war got, the more she discovered friends in the world—birds, campfires, water, trees. They were better than all but Handyman and her Dorothy—the first best friend she had ever known.

She did not imagine that German snipers spied her from the walls of brush out beyond the perimeter. She wasn't their target—they were watching for an unfortunate American soldier to dawdle a minute too long in the open—but she became famous among them.

They tracked her through their binoculars and scopes. She fascinated them. They called her the Lady Deer, or the Deer-Girl. A fellow from Warnemünde wanted to shoot her, but his rifle was shoved down by his mates and he was scolded and forbidden to track her through his scope. She was too amusing to kill. She was their girlfriend. She was like some stanza of Goethe those professors had once drilled into them. Running from tree to tree with her excited, wide-eyed intrigue. The Deer-Girl. Besides, watching her was the closest thing to sex they'd enjoyed in months.

Irene was also in the forest to do her duty: she carried mail and candy and sinkers to the men stationed there. She soon recruited Holly, who had been on her high school girls' cross-country team. They hefted heavy bags on their backs and sprinted hard from tree to tree, from forward post to foxhole to sandbagged forward radio position. They listened for the high-pitched *zeee* sound that told them a sniper round had just missed them, and for the hard *pop* that told them a round had just broken the sound barrier on its way toward them.

They carried a top secret chart of the placement of each foxhole and forward entrenched observation position. That chart bore the names of the guys in each of the holes. The invisible Germans would have considered shooting Irene after all, if they'd known, just for the extra rations and liquor such a list would have brought them from their commanders.

Irene had sorted the mail as dictated by the strategic chart. She made packets bound by twine and stacked them in the bags with the nearest outpost on top. She and Holly divided the mail between them, careful to label fruitcakes or bundles of stale cookies sent from Mom or Wifey back home. Holly carried each of these packages under her arm like a football.

It wasn't uncommon for them to be invited into the malodorous holes to share a slice of cake or a few of the tired cookies. Fruitcake on the tip of a bayonet became a delicacy for them. They carried two canteens each full of hot coffee, but these were drained long before they got to the last foxhole.

The two Sisters trudged back to warmth and shelter utterly spent, with legs shaky and throats sore from gasping the frigid air. But exhilarated. Full of a love they could not define. They often appeared at the hotel with arms thrown over each other's shoulders. For some reason, this would irritate Dorothy. "Drunken sailors," she was known to say when they stumbled in the door.

The women posed for snapshots. Dozens of snapshots. It seemed as though every soldier had a Brownie camera in his ruck. They imagined their images in a hundred homes in a hundred cities, and those picture albums lying in a footlocker or a drawer for decades. They imagined that, long after the soldiers had become old, perhaps even after they'd died, someone would come to wonder about these women holding up rifles or tommy guns or donuts and laughing with their grandfather in front of the big dark truck.

30

WITH LITTLE MORE than a week till Christmas, Dorothy suggested that Irene run the Bastogne Dugout, inside the auberge, while she and Holly did a quick run up to Vielsalm. They wanted to rustle up some holiday treats for the boys. Cookies and chocolates. Fresh sausages. They also needed to buy presents for Hellcat of the *Cheyenne,* who was having a birthday, as well as some special ingredients for a Christmas meal in the hotel and decorations for the tree the GIs had cut down for them. And Holly wanted to get a Christmas gift for Rusty. They would be back in a few days, tops.

It was fine with Irene to stay behind. There was a well-provisioned trailer outside, and though she didn't have a cooker for sinkers, she had stacks of day-olds left over, along with enough coffee to float a warship. She would be grateful for some solo time.

The night before Dorothy and Holly went on their errand, the giddiest moment of the war came through the hotel like a wave. None of them was even sure what had set them off. Some jape. Some outrageous comment. But the Sisters were suddenly on the floor, all three of them, laughing so hard they were weeping. Falling on their backs, kicking their feet in the air. Crawling to one another, unable to breathe, begging, "Please make it stop!" in ragged, painful gasps because it seemed they would all die of laughter.

The day they left, Irene had lunch with the officers of VIII Corps. Rear HQ in Bastogne. What a relief—split pea soup, ham and yams and vegetables and salad. Where had they gotten salad? Rum pudding. Beer. The bread and butter seemed like the best thing ever invented.

The following day, after the *Cheyenne* also left town for some road duty, Irene cobbled together a one-woman service in her lobby. She accessed the old skills of Aunt Eva and sacrificed cans of evaporated milk and bags of sugar and some powdered egg mix from the grunts' rations, then found a bottle of vanilla in the truck. Over a low fire, stirring tirelessly, she managed to invent some custard. Or custard-like pudding. She melted and charred more sugar in a pan and drizzled it onto the pale yellow dessert.

The guys put the stuff in their tin cups and stuck it out in the snow until it hardened. They were delighted. They broke their chocolate bars into it. They dribbled rum and whiskey over it. They crumbled stale sinkers onto it. They lounged around feeling fat. Everybody in the lobby and the old dining room was cheerful and a little tipsy and balancing out the booze with coffee.

"Miss Irene, you're the best pal a guy ever had," one slightly weepy private insisted.

That was December 18. The next day, when the Germans surprised them by breaking through the line, Bastogne was under siege and the Battle of the Bulge was under way. Irene was alone, unwittingly abandoned by her Sisters.

—

Everyone in Bastogne was trapped. Irene knew vast events were churning all around them. In her own small section of the world it was flashes: the cold, sprinting, explosions, yelling and bleeding and endless fire coming in and going out. The sky was heavy and low, relief flights couldn't get to them. The air support couldn't bomb or strafe the Germans, either. Uncertain if the shells that were hitting their street would strike the trailer parked outside the hotel, Irene hauled what she could from the supply wagon into the lobby. Of course, the hotel itself might be hit, too, but there was nowhere else for her to go. She said her prayers and dragged her belongings into the basement, which she knew was her best choice, especially since this building, unlike the shaky little house in which she and Dorothy had almost been buried, was solid stone. The basement would be like a fort. She kept the fire going. With buildings on the street constantly being destroyed, there was an endless supply of wood.

She prayed often that her friends were safe away from the city. Blessings on the *Rapid*. Blessings on Wild Dot and Sweet Holly. Blessings on Handyman, always. Blessings on Patton and the United States and the soldiers out in the forest and the nurses and corpsmen manning the emergency medical facilities. *And, Lord, if you're not too busy, please spare me once again. I know, I know—you've been more than generous so far. But...just once more?*

The scream of an incoming shell climbed in pitch as it fell and Irene jammed herself into a corner of the heavy stone walls and waited for the shaking of the earth.

—

Without her Sisters, she was bereft. Unearthed, if there was such a word. She was losing track of what was really happening and what wasn't. She knew that last night's dream of Auntie and Mother putting a warm brick under her blankets by her feet was just that—a dream. Still, she felt it like a real memory, as though her aunt and mother had just stepped out this morning after a friendly night together with her. No. That was silly.

But what of the Belgian professor in the bowler hat and the long coat? Had they really stood together outside, in the snow fog? With the rockets and shells falling across the city. The guns popping wetly like spoiled fireworks in the distance. Their hands in their pockets, she wearing her heavy military jacket and he in his scholar's clothing, his dapper hat. He'd offered her a cigarette, and she'd taken it for the human interaction. He lit her with a wooden match—he'd held it too close to the end of her cigarette and the taste of sulfur had come through the tobacco and into her mouth. Had it not? And they could have died, easily died, for they could not see far down the street in either direction. For all they knew,

Germans were everywhere. Did a whistling sound really come and a flying brick shatter on the cobblestones before them, flown in from who knew where?

Irene felt drunk. Either from exhaustion or growing hunger or an overdose of fear.

The professor had spoken to her, in English, but for the life of her she couldn't hear what he was telling her. She kept saying, "Excuse me?" and smiling apologetically, while he kept talking. She leaned toward him. He seemed to be speaking of anything being possible, anything happening, in a world of chaos, where chaos was the norm and normalcy was the aberration.

And at that moment, had a bear really come out of the fog? Had it been harried out of its winter den in the Ardennes by the combat? Were there bears in Belgium? Oh yes, she remembered her professor saying, Germany has bears, right over there. She recalled how the bear didn't care about them. It trotted along, head down, silent in the fog, with smoke curling from its fur, and it cast off a wave of odor as it passed and then vanished into the fog farther down the road. She was certain that the professor had said, "You see, *madame,* anything at all is possible now. Nothing is good, nothing is bad. All is chaos." She was certain he had tapped his head before walking away and said, "All is here. Nothing is real."

—

How many days had the siege lasted so far? Five? She thought so.

On December 23, a day earlier, the sky had cleared and American planes were finally able to fly over and drop supplies. Fox Company of the 327th Glider Infantry Regiment appeared with support and reinforcements. The crew of every Clubmobile with Group F—the *Cheyenne,* the *Atlanta,* the *Miami,* the *New Haven,* the *Boise,* the *Albany,* and the *Rapid City*—was out in the field or far away from Bastogne. Irene alone manned the Good Ship *Basement,* as she had taken to thinking of it.

Was a GI hailing her now in the night from across the street? Had she heard him through the broken window of her Dugout? Had he seen the glow of her fireplace?

"Dolly!"

Was he calling her?

"Hey Dolly, are you there?"

This had to be real. "Soldier?" she called back.

"I need help."

"Come on over."

"I can't."

"Oh come on. Run across."

"I messed myself."

"You what?"

"I'm a coward. I was so scared. I—"

"You are no such thing. Everybody's scared." Was she really stepping out into the street? "Come in," she said. "It's too cold, soldier."

"I crapped myself. I can't."

"Oh now," she said. "Everybody has a little accident sometimes. Even ladies." She braced herself. "Especially ladies! I have had many a slip, dear boy!"

"No."

"I'll go get a bucket and fill it with warm water. You can go in the dining room. It's empty. Nobody will see you. C'mon over, it's just us. We'll wash your britches and dry them on the hearth and nobody will know the difference."

It was the last thing she wanted to do, of course, but while the soldier hid in the battered lobby's public toilets, Irene held her breath and scrubbed his trousers. She tossed him one of Dot's jumpsuits and laid his pants on the mantel of the fireplace to steam dry.

It was Christmas Eve, she realized.

Her night was not over. A bunch of soldiers double-timed it out of the forest with a small pine tree. Two others appeared with holly in their arms.

"We brought you Christmas!" they called. "We can't spend no Christmas in a foxhole!"

Mother Irene took them in and showed them to the basement. They set the tree up in a corner and decorated it with foil-paper tatters, battle ribbons, shell casings, colorful yarn. She ended up with nineteen guys plus the soiled GI in Dot's jumpsuit. They set out their bedrolls and mess kits. They hauled water and wood down the stairs for her and set a roaring fire in the fireplace. Then a small Christmas miracle happened—Captain Dick Withers and their favorite sergeant, Sarge Taylor, made a mad run from shelter to shelter, under fire, hauling hot food in wagons for their boys to have Christmas dinner.

"You're a legend, Cap," Irene said, when they made it to the hotel.

"Aw heck, you're the legend," he said.

"Gimme a smooch before I die," the sarge said.

This one time she kissed a soldier. Then the two officers were gone again as fast as they'd appeared.

The soiled kid, much more cheerful now than he'd been two hours ago, hollered, "Who was that masked man?!"

The other soldiers christened him *Kemosabe*, the name he would be known by for the duration of the war.

He was the first man to kiss Irene since she'd left Handyman behind. Unbidden, the taste of Hans, salt on her tongue.

—

Every time an artillery round came in, the hotel wept dust on their heads. The soldiers were melancholy. Those who had received Christmas packages shared them with their comrades. They carefully took the wrapping paper off their bundles and used it to further decorate the tree. A perfumed hankie made the rounds, going from hand to hand and nose to nose. Cookies and hard candies and rum-soaked fruitcakes circulated through the basement. The room was doom-dark, the only light provided by the writhing orange flames of the popping fire.

One guy broke out a guitar.

"Where've you been hiding that?" Irene teased him.

He strummed a few ballads and three Christmas songs. The out-of-tune ragged choir that accompanied him was the tenderest thing she'd ever heard. All these guys, dads and sons and grandsons, baseball players and farmers, high school dropouts and a high school teacher, stone-cold killers and softies, goofballs and hard cases, jailbirds and fancy college boys, all warbling like a choir of altar boys embarrassed to sing in front of one another, yet unable to remain silent. Everyone in the room, having recently escaped harm or death, had seen friends fall in the snow, and, unsure if they would be alive to see next year's holiday, they chose to sing. Whether badly or well, they sang together. Irene stayed in a shadowed back corner and wept, for them and for herself.

Finally the guys fell silent. The room was heavy with their sorrows. They sat hunched with the fire at their backs, their arms around their knees or a pal's shoulders, their heads down. The scattered sniffles in the dark suggested that some of them were also crying.

Irene stepped forward. She passed through them slowly. Her hands went out to either side, and she brushed them along the tops of their heads, mussing their hair like a night breeze. They smelled like draft horses after a hard day, though soaked with cologne. She could make out only their silhouettes and profiles. She turned to face them. No one made a sound. Irene cleared her throat. She lifted her head a little. In the deeper shadows at the back of the basement she felt the presence of her mother and Grannie Effie, those Christmases in Mattituck.

She interlaced her fingers before her stomach, closed her eyes, and began to sing: *O Holy Night, the stars are brightly shining*...

Just her voice. And the crackling wood.

When she finished, the boys implored her: "Again. Please."

In the morning, she and a couple of the soldiers used the sinker mix to create Christmas-morning pancakes. They made syrup from the leftover sugar from the previous night's pudding. It didn't matter that the pancakes were tiny and misshapen, flecked with ash from the fireplace where they were cooked in mess kits. Irene made sure everyone was served.

And when they helmeted up again and grabbed their weapons to go back out to it, she hugged each man as he stepped through the door.

—

Dawn. Three days later.

The Americans had at last broken the Germans' encirclement of Bastogne, and the *Rapid City* came roaring into town to rescue her. There were more stories than anyone could tell. Things unbelievable. Wrecks and rescues and executions on the road and the whole time Dorothy and Holly were trying to push back to Bastogne. Irene threw her things into the back of the truck and pressed in beside them. The Allies were beating the Germans back across the Siegfried Line. Atrocities were scattered throughout the Ardennes. But she was back with her Sisters. Heading east, following Patton and his warriors into the heart of Hitler's empire.

31

On a distant Tuesday, unwitnessed, unrecorded, a lone mirror plunges from the sun. Below, forests still burn. Wrecks of great machines like charred bits of wood lift tendrils of smoke over the white fields. Murdered trees are splayed as random as broken arrows dropped by accident in the snow. All of it spinning.

The mirror spirals as it drops, a corona of silver flashes. There are no clouds to hide it, just the ceramic dome of sky east of Bastogne. The sky is nearly purple close to the sun and fading to metal blue all the way to the whiteness of frozen earth. The wind howls around the falling mirror. The mirror answers the wind: it screams, its engine's twelve cylinders pushed to the limit. A shrieking Rolls-Royce wild mustang being ridden through the sky by Handyman.

Four Luftwaffe planes fly in formation below—gray Messerschmitt Bf 109s heading west toward the Allies on a long haul out of Munich, a loose rectangle with air space between them. Handyman grits his teeth, both thrilled by the ride and half-terrified by its madness. He plans to bag all four of them. It's the oldest trick in air war. The sun's glare hides the attacker, so that his targets are unaware of what's coming. He's a lightning strike smashing out of a clear sky.

Like all fighter pilots, he can see himself from outside the cockpit, as though he were starring in an action picture, a man in control, an agent of fury, an artist and a coldhearted warrior, a spirit of awe doing a ridiculously impossible thing. The hand of judgment. Behind his mask, his teeth are bared, as if his will alone is what holds the plane in the sky, keeps it from shaking apart.

He accelerates, augmenting gravity and surpassing his former speed, his teeth grinding now, his grin savage. His mirror dives for the opening between the four enemy planes. Inside the cockpit, Handyman's knees are banging against the tight walls, his ears popping and whistling, the edges of his vision darkening and sparking as he corkscrews. No time to wipe the stinging sweat out of his eyes or worry about the adrenaline and pressure pushing at his bladder. He rips off his mask and grabs the stick again. He is snarling, all his teeth gleaming in the sun as it seems to rotate around him. He is the center of the solar system. The sun appears and disappears a dozen times. Light like a flashbulb strobes in his face, hypnotizing him.

"Irene," he says. That is the sum total of his prayer. He is always talking to Irene, even when he doesn't know he is.

He licks the sweat off his lips. It already seems as though he has been falling for an hour, but he has been in his trajectory for only thirty-seven seconds. The white Nazi insignias on the German planes taunt him. His P-51 bucks and shudders, as angry as he is to see these birds heading out to kill his boys.

"Got another thing comin', Fritz."

He goes cool inside, loose and in a place unknowable to anyone else: everything slow now and lovely and terrible and his. He owns the entire sky, and he owns the last moments of their lives, and his fingers slide to the red triggers, the vibrating, kicking stick, jammed down hard and pulled to the side so the fighter spins, hurts in his grip. Roads sweep down below as though they themselves were propellers driving the earth up toward him.

He's still invisible in the sun, though the flares of sunlight on his wings continue to throw flashbulb blasts into his face. He squints. The stick is pegged to a nearly vertical dive, flaps hurtling him forward like a Roman candle. The bullets, when he unleashes them, will spiral down and spread.

"We're gonna bag two of 'em," he informs Irene, whose frilly underwear is tucked inside his jacket. "Drop between them bastards."

He plunges down through ten thousand feet. The cold burns his nostrils. He smells the musty stink of the cockpit, of the engine, of himself. His eyes still water, but he blinks them clear and squints at his targets. His leather jacket almost keeps him warm. And he's upon them.

He aims himself at the gap between the German planes and squeezes the trigger and his twin machine guns fire .50 caliber tracer streams from each wing, tearing the starboard wing off one of the fighters and stitching holes into the fuselage of its partner.

The German pilots have no idea what just happened, and he's already gone.

Without its wing, the first Messerschmitt flips out of control and falls in flame, trailing a fraying black column of smoke.

Handyman has no time to watch. He has gone far below, like some shark in the sea, and is curving back up, screaming into a vertical version of his primary attack. His body makes an unintentional growling whine as the g-forces slam him.

The other wounded plane above him staggers in the sky, spits gray plumes as it dives away trying to escape him. The two outliers speed forward. He is through them and climbing, an ecstasy of power. It's now a race of deadly intent.

He loops hard to get in behind the two remaining Germans, but they pull straight up, as though intending to reenter the gaping sun that spewed him out. He sees one parachute: the plane he shot through the fuselage drops almost in slow motion as its pilot seems to walk in the sky above it.

Handyman's rage tells him to shoot the falling man out of the sky, but he has no time to waste. No one in this dogfight has any illusions: it is all instinct and training. They move like machines. But they never lose their own sense of style. Their own dance moves. They speak the same aerial language.

He is chasing both remaining birds straight up. They can't go as high as they need to—they will pass out if they're not careful. He knows their bloodstreams are no different than his.

"Do it," he says. "Go to sleep, Wolfgang."

They go over the top of their climbs upside down. He follows. He's still behind them—they can't get a shot in on him. He thumbs his triggers and tears apart the back end of the plane closest to him. Its tail breaks into shrapnel and the plane is gone, dropping out of his line of sight like magic.

Handyman whoops, his fist banging the air. But it is only a moment of celebration. And he knows better. Because when he looks for it, the final Messerschmitt has vanished. He spits a curse. He suddenly needs to piss. He cranes in every direction but can't find the German fighter.

In a scream and a flash, they pass each other, the Messerschmitt already banking to sweep in behind him. Even at this speed, he catches the slightest glimpse of that Luftwaffe jockey looking at him and then he's gone.

What an elegant move, Handyman thinks, and knows he has failed.

He dives again, but the German cuts a dropping loop and locks in behind him. Handyman whips the Mustang into sideslips, rocking the plane wing to wing, like some raft in a violent set of rapids. Rounds burn past him. All is engine noise and wind noise and he might be shouting over it. It's so loud he can't hear anything—he can't even hear the guns behind him.

And just at that moment Handyman sees the way, imagines the surprise move that will shock the German: stall and drop under him like a submarine, let him fly over before he has time to respond, then power up and rise behind him and overtake him. But right as he pictures it, the worst happens. Some giant seems to kick the tail of his plane and the end of his left wing disappears.

He is baffled by the spray of blood that spatters across the inside of the cockpit. The clear canopy around him goes red. He doesn't know where he's hit. He must be hit. But he doesn't feel it. He is struggling so hard with the stick he can't check himself. He knows it's bad because he is stupidly fighting to stay aloft when he should be parachuting out.

"Come on," he tells himself. "You know what to do."

But part of him is confused by the violent bucking of his plane. It's a puzzle he can't quite solve.

He's a little dizzy. He's trembling now. Yes, it must be bad. Or bad enough.

"Come on, Irene," he says, groggy now. "Don't let me go to sleep."

His goggles are smeared red. Oh, he's going down, how odd.

He pulls the lever and the cowl slides away and the air is sucked from his lungs. He is spinning much closer to the ground. And he is flipping upside down. Enemy tracers sizzle around him. He punches the release on his seat belts. He's jammed back into the seat at the same time he feels as though he is being thrown into space.

Agony suddenly burns inside him. His legs won't work. It would be nice to lie on his back in that field, he thinks. He wipes his goggles into smears and watches the ground coming at him through them. He uses the last of his arm strength to drag himself out of his seat.

"Oh mercy," Hans says.

He falls forever.

PART FOUR

This Is How We Forget

32

IRENE STUFFED A letter to Handyman in the mailbag and opened a fan letter in a flimsy international airmail envelope.

Dear Irene—

You may not remember me, but I remember you. I flew on Major Ellis's crew. I'm sure you remember him. Did you know he was lost in action? What a great man.

I got rotated out of service after I fulfilled my mission count. It's not all that bad. I'm living the good life back in Albany. My folks and me. Back to teaching fifth grade and coaching baseball on the weekends. It's what we all fought for, right?

I swear, though—I think I went into combat just to get some of your donuts and coffee (and whiskey) when we landed. It's all about your eyes, honey. I was wondering tho—you still crazy about that fighter pilot? Because there are about 2,000 of us standing in line just in case you're not. Time to go—the bell's ringing. Just a small fan letter to say thank you. One day this war will be over, and I know you will live a beautiful life.

—Billy G.

—

With their trucks empty, the Clubmobile crews had to regroup and resupply before joining the push into Germany, and they retreated sixty miles west to billet for a night in the sere, gorgeous town of Fumay, on the River Meuse. It hadn't been shelled, and lay nestled between those tan bare hills, watched over by an ancient-looking stone church with a tall spire. Civilization, undamaged. But they were sent downhill, to the right of the church, into a house that was so filthy they didn't want to unroll their sleeping bags. There was no food, no water, no toilet. Holly joked that she could make a stew from one of the rats. They went back out to sleep in the *Rapid*.

The morning was better, if rough and unkempt. Perfume helped. Headscarves hid several sins the night had committed with their hair. They brushed their teeth with canteen water and spit it out like a bunch of sailors. They looked like three mother bears in their heavy coats.

"In spite of everything," Dorothy announced as they bounced and banged along another muddy road, "it's a red-letter day!"

"Another day above the ground," Irene concurred.

"Who doesn't love a car ride?" Holly added, too cold to really pitch in, but striving to do her part in the daily celebration, fantasizing about her Stateside honeymoon trip down Route 66, with Rusty at the wheel.

It's a good thing I like riding in cars, Irene thought, *because all we're doing, it seems, is driving up and down and back and forth, all over this stupid border. France, Belgium, France, Belgium.* Because they had lost communications with VIII Corps and no one was sure exactly where the corps was, the *Rapid City* was assigned to a new armored division that had been sent to the area. Strafed by German Stukas at night, they were still up before dawn to turn on the cookers, wait for the solid congealed grease to melt, mix the sinker recipe, brew coffee, open the service from the truck or a hastily constructed Donut Dugout, and welcome weary GIs. All this on little to no sleep, few meals, and miles on muddy roads full of military vehicles.

"Just remember, Holly," said Irene. "Keep smiling."

"Girl, you've got that right," Holly said.

Dorothy said nothing.

In early January, all of Group F convoyed to Charleville-Mézières, France, where the *Rapid City* finally reunited with VIII Corps. That night, sunset came down like mist, then a deluge of darkness. Dorothy led them through the war machines in the dark to a dug-in artillery position at the eastern end of the field where they were bivouacking. They had missed a chance to celebrate New Year's Eve, and tonight she carried a black-market bottle of champagne by the neck. Where Holly and Irene were timid, crouching at each *boom* of a weapon, Dorothy strode like Custer. She was blessed with some supernatural charm, an invincible aura.

The gunnery crew was wraithlike in the gloom, lit by small fires and flashlights. Their cannon was deafening. It was a Black Dragon—a 240 mm howitzer M1. Those who didn't wear earmuffs turned their backs and used their fingers. Even from across the field, the roar was bone-shaking. The flash of fire illuminated the men—bent double—in quick friezes.

When they got to the firing position, Dorothy popped the cork on her bottle and caught the erupting champagne in her mouth. The boys pulled the lanyard on the cannon once more—*boom!*—and grabbed the bottle. Dorothy shouted and waved the champagne at Irene, who shrugged and took it from her and had a swallow. The ground jumped when the big rounds roared toward the enemy lines, the noise a heavy gut punch. Irene handed off the bottle to Holly, who shouted a toast they couldn't hear.

Across the great meadows, balls of fire blew trees apart.

"What do you think?" a gunner shouted.

"Poor trees!" Irene yelled.

"Jerry is gonna fight like a bastard now. We're taking the Fatherland! Watch your ass!"

"Roger, wilco!" she hollered.

The soldiers fed another shell into the hot cannon and handed Dorothy the lanyard.

"Now you're talkin'," she said.

"When I signal," a gunner said, "yank that thing."

"Ready."

He raised his hand, made a fist. Irene and Holly plugged their ears. He chopped his hand down. Dorothy yanked the lanyard and fired the shell into the sky. They heard it scream as it arced toward the far ground and cheered when things blew up over there. The gunners grabbed the bottle and each took a swig, foam erupting from their mouths as if they were rabid animals, passing the bottle around until it was dry, at which point one of them threw it in the direction of their shelling.

The head gunner pointed at Irene.

"Your turn, Gator," Dorothy said.

Irene was feeling giddy. "It goes to your head," she said. "I feel it in my head." *Woozy gun,* she thought, putting her hand on its flank. She jerked her hand away. It was like touching a hot iron. "Whoa there," she said, shaking her hand and blowing on it. The gunners guffawed and she giggled drunkenly. "Isn't this fun!" she cried, wanting to kiss the soldiers.

"You bet," a guy replied. "Babes 'n' bombs."

The gunnery team cranked the gun's elevation higher and rotated it to the north.

A soldier carrying a field phone cranked it and spoke into the handpiece, then nodded as if the person on the other end could see him. "Roger," he said. He handed Irene the lanyard and went through the gestures.

She felt self-conscious, worried that she'd fail, somehow. But the Black Dragon was made to spit fire. It was not hard to pull. The boom rattled her ribs. "Again!" she shouted.

"What a fuggin' beast!" said the soldier who'd passed her the lanyard. He slapped her on the back.

She took a gulp from a different bottle.

"Ready," the man said.

"Let's dance!" she cried, and pulled the lanyard again.

"Fireworks!" Holly yelled.

Irene rained destruction on the far horizon. She thought she could see tiny buildings in the flashes. Her efforts were greeted with cheers and whoops all around.

One of the gunners punched her arm. "Lady," he said, "you musta taken out twenty of 'em!"

"What?" she said.

"Oh hell yeah," Dorothy said. "Irene smoked a whole bunch of Krauts over there."

Irene watched the flames. Smoke rose against the illuminated sky. Somehow it hadn't crossed her mind. She hadn't meant to kill anyone. She was unsteady on her feet, trying to manage the lopsided grin of incomprehension on her face. "What'd I do?" she said.

The shadows around her were jerky. She backed away. Holly stepped up for her turn. Everybody was laughing. Soldiers behind her were shooting into the sky. Cheering the new year, their year of triumph. They all felt it.

Irene covered her ears and ran for the truck.

33

It was astounding to be halfway through January without knowing how they'd gotten there. They were too tired and anxious and filthy to have kept track. So deeply sick of the cold. So tired of frostbite and wrapped feet, of ice in the coffee pots. Even the *Rapid City* seemed devoid of spirit. They focused on the troops. That was what mattered, they told themselves.

Irene tried to hide her despair when the *Rapid City* drove back into Bastogne and she saw that their original billet in the old hotel was completely pulverized. That most sacred place, where she had cared for that basement full of frightened GIs, was gone forever. Obliterated. She felt she was the only person alive who would remember that night.

Dorothy pulled the *Rapid* over for a moment so they could try to comprehend what they were seeing. Both she and Irene stepped down into the scattered rubble, which was all that remained of their part of Bastogne. When they drove on, they eventually found their way to the old bombed-out Belgium barracks where they had been assigned. With the destroyed streets so deep in icy mud that transportation was impossible, the three set up a Donut Dugout in the VIII Corps headquarters for whoever could make it there.

Ever since the troops had begun the hard push toward Germany, liberating and conquering, celebrating and killing at the same time, it felt lonely in the truck. Fraught, too—every bend in the road could be a step into a firefight, or a shelling, or a strafing, or a sniper ambush, or a charge by sappers carrying contact mines, or a wave of marauding tanks.

Every fallen tree trunk could be hiding machine-gun emplacements—and there were many fallen trees. Or the road could lead to another dirt field busy with exhausted, hangdog blisterfoots—their helmets in the dirt, their rifles scattered like fiddlesticks—and to hours of fresh duty, cooking up sweet smiles and brewing hot cups of joy. If they served until nightfall, they could finally drop.

The Gentlemen from Hell of the 101st Airborne were there. Tankers. Truckers. MPs. Drivers in the Red Ball Express convoy. But none of them had heard from Handyman in a while. Ambulances rolled along with them. The remnants of German vehicles lay slumped into the hills like the filthy ruins of ancient temples, and trudging groups of sullen, drag-ass German prisoners passed them several times a day headed in the opposite direction, staring at the dirt, some of them limping.

It was savage battle followed by speeding motion followed by stalled waiting and restless boredom. The unexpected was expected. Irene was still jittery from their hell night in that poor nameless French town and from the siege at Bastogne. She watched for Garcia, but that whole cadre of guys had vanished into the tide sweeping east.

Irene was so exhausted she hadn't struck a pose in days. But as battle fatigue rolled over them all, the troops had gotten grabbier. The Sisters spent too much service time deflecting sexual innuendos and romantic maneuvers, too much energy smiling at come-ons because it was incumbent upon them to be accommodating and supportive. Irene wrote in her journal: *The dirtier and uglier we get, the more haggard we are, the more they wolf-howl and come sniffing. Even the sincere ones, with their watery puppy dog eyes, are too much for us. There was no contingency for a kind shoulder we could rest our heads on.*

She knew all the tricks. Arms held close to her ribs to block a grope. A quick scoot of the buttocks when an unfamiliar brush landed. A fixed grin and a quick pace and a volley of repartee. Some nights, their trusted male allies pitched pup tents beside the truck and stood unofficial guard over them.

"I swear," Dorothy told them as she drove, "if one more yahoo grabs my ass, I'm gonna go all Pearl Harbor on him." Beset by Krauts and her own soldiers alike, she had retreated to love of her truck. Love of her Sisters.

She handed Irene the newest *Insider* newsletter she'd stuffed above the sun visor. Dateline: Saturday Midnight. There was so much reading material floating around that they knew they'd never run out of toilet paper. The Clubmobile's favorite, of course, was *The Sinker* and *The Sinker Junior*. Pure ARC news and gossip. Written by gals like themselves. *Overseas Woman* was a kind of *Ladies' Home Journal* for women in combat.

Dorothy wanted Irene to see the boxed notice above the headline of the *Insider:* ALL GERMANS ARE GUILTY OF TERRORISM, AGGRESSION AND WAR FOR TOLERATING THE NAZIS FOR 14 YEARS. DON'T FRATERNIZE.

"No mercy," she said.

—

The mailbags continued to find them. One rare typed note read:

> *Dere Stretch,*
> *I'm rememberin abot that bivwak outside of Brest where you sowed me how to dance. You din;t want nobody to know haha but I aint gonna forget something like that, honeypot. See you back in Indana! Right me when you can—*
>
> *Henry B. Niles, Sgt.*

—

In the towns and villages, they encountered many practical Germans who expected nothing but were prepared for anything and were riding it out, whatever this new assault was. They were the ones who waved and smiled. The truly celebratory citizens cheered the Americans and held flags, but Irene and Dorothy were unmoved. Their soldiers and each other were their only concern. The tight focus was oddly freeing. It kept them from thinking about going home.

The times they laughed were when they saw the *Cheyenne* or any other Clubmobile on this stretch of the road and flagged it down to have a chat. Or when a German professor told them, "Germany started the war to conquer a country where it doesn't rain all the time." Otherwise, drudgery. They might be doomed to serve around the clock all the way to Moscow.

One day, though, something unexpected broke the monotony.

Holly seldom got correspondence, other than the random missive sent by Rusty from wherever HQ happened to be, but that morning, when the mail run deposited a pile of envelopes inside their galley, she had an official letter on heavy paper with insignia in the upper-left corner. Her face turned red, then blanched, as she read it. She slammed it down and picked it up again. Irene and Dorothy side-eyed her.

"Well I'll be," Holly said.

Irene took the letter from her. It was from Red Cross headquarters. Apparently, having married an active army officer, she had forfeited her contract and would no longer receive her weekly stipend, since she was now considered to be under his financial care and maintenance. The Red Cross applauded her for her service and thanked her in advance for continuing gratis in the Clubmobile Corps. Sincerely, Big Betty So-and-So, Washington, DC; cc: Bob Big Man, etc.

"*No bueno,*" Gator said, exhausting her Spanish.

Dorothy grabbed the letter and squinted. "Dip me in chocolate and call me Eskimo Pie."

Nobody laughed.

"What are you going to do?" Irene asked.

"Screw this—I'm going home."

And she did. Just like that, Holly was gone.

—

"Again?" Irene complained.

"Third Girl number three. Vamoosed."

The *Rapid City* felt like a ghost town now.

"We should have been nicer," Irene said.

"Hogwash. We were nice enough to her. It wouldn't have a made a difference. This one's on the Red Cross."

"She was a good egg."

"She had her moments."

They were aiming for Weimar, where they were to set up a Donut Dugout. The roads were exquisite. Tanks on the Autobahn. Irene had always wanted to visit Weimar and the houses of its luminaries—Goethe was a favorite. It would be worth the trip to see his house. Dorothy was enamored of the smooth highway. Rumor was that Uncle Sam was winning the war now.

Meanwhile, everybody had the squirts again. That was enough to deal with. They didn't need combat in their days. The running battles and skirmishes and blown-up bridges and rubber-raft assaults on rivers melded into one weirdly explosive memory. It was a knot they might never be able to untangle.

"Every day is exactly the same," Irene complained.

Dorothy just grunted.

Flashes and booms and geysers of rocks and dirt and roaring horizons of machines and executions both whispered about and discovered. Busting through the woods was sheer terror: mazes with death and mayhem waiting around all corners. Sleep was roughing it in dugouts under the truck, with the Kill Pig often standing guard nearby. The soldiers in that beast were sometimes ordered to "lower the profile" of their vehicle, which meant digging a trench to drive it into. The guys called it "building a fort," along with much more colorful things, accompanied by their folding shovels and operatic cursing. And the ladies were there beside them, thankful that the *Rapid* never had to hunker down in a pit.

When the Catholic chaplain came along, Irene asked him to sprinkle the truck with holy water. The guys gathered around and took off their helmets and bowed their heads. Then it was sinker time again. It took gallantry to make the coffee and donuts with regular fire and incoming mortar rounds and cannon shells flying and falling around them. It also took gallantry for the soldiers to stand there in line. Some of them didn't even duck, though if a whistling shell was curving down toward them, everybody had enough sense to sprawl facedown. Even Irene and Dorothy inside the galley. They all had a scabbed-over nonchalance about it. The heroics of exhaustion.

Before long, they could no longer remember Holly's last name, or even what she looked like, though they didn't forget her Southern accent.

—

One day in February they got a brief respite from the cold, another of those red-letter days that Dorothy liked so much. She felt like a ship's captain sailing across calm water—scudding clouds beneath a buttery sun, no one shooting, fabulous war machines all around her. It was a small mercy.

"Irene, you should drive a few miles. Get in some practice while you can."

"Must I?"

"You must."

Dorothy grinned and pulled over. She left the engine idling and hopped down, stretched her spine, shook her legs, pried the coveralls seam out of her rear end. She hated how sweaty it got. Her hands were quivering again. She hid them.

Irene crawled down from her high door and walked around to Dorothy's side of the cab. "We have beaten this poor old thing to death," she said, petting the *Rapid*'s snout.

"I'm going to see if they'll sell it to me after we win this war," Dorothy said. "I can open a rolling donut shop. Drive all over the country. Make a few bucks here and there doin' odd jobs to buy gas and grub. I'd never stop."

"But you don't like coffee and you don't like to serve donuts."

"I was planning to hire you for that part."

"You love me."

"Tolerate, Irene. Tolerate." Dorothy reached up and popped open the door for her. "It's smooth going," she said. "Hitler has built you a great highway."

"How thoughtful."

"Nice and easy, girl. Just put her in gear and let her roll."

"I hate the clutch."

"The clutch hates you. So you're even."

Irene climbed up as though she were on a cliff face; Dorothy trotted around and hopped into her seat with ease. The springs squealed and fretted as she bounced in place.

"Are you wearing perfume?" Irene said.

"Might be."

Irene pushed the recalcitrant clutch pedal as far as she could, then wrestled one of the stick shifts, hoping it was the right one, until she found first. The truck grunted and complained.

"Hey, Gator. Easy."

"I got your *easy* right here, Toots."

Oh boy, now she's some George Raft gangster, Dorothy thought. "Just don't hit nothin'," she said.

"Nah, this is gravy," Irene boasted out of the corner of her mouth.

"Don't make the Jimmy buck around like a mule when you shift to second, either."

"What are you, my mother?"

Dorothy noted that Irene's knuckles were white as she strangled the wheel. She appreciated that Irene had learned to BS her way through her fear. *Act tough and you'll be tough when you need to be,* her daddy used to tell her.

Irene pulled the air-horn chain so she could bully her way into the convoy.

"That's how you do it!" Dorothy enthused. "Ballin' the jack."

"I have this under control. Though I have no idea what you just said."

Dorothy just snorted and stared out the window, riding Irene-style. She sat on her hands to keep them still. Her foot began tapping randomly. "Hell," she drawled, "it isn't bad over here on this side. I might do an Irene and write a damn poem."

Irene laughed at herself.

—

It could have been an hour, could have been ten minutes, could have been the next day: Irene's forearms ached from her choke hold on the wheel. She was so worried about all this heavy machinery around her that she clenched her teeth until her jaw hurt. The clutch was killing her left leg. She ground the gears.

"Sorry," she mumbled.

They were deep in Germany now. The enemy had blown up bridges. They were often stuck in traffic jams while the Corps of Engineers pieced together pontoons. Giant machines hauling sections of bridge shook the earth. The Kill Pig and other big vehicles aimed their weapons into the distance and they all waited for an attack. GIs used the *Rapid* as a kind of wheeled fort, leaning against it, peering around the fenders, hiding. Irene handed down donuts from her window.

"Kill 'em all," Dorothy said to a soldier below her.

"Let God sort 'em out," he said.

Any bridges not destroyed by German soldiers had to be examined for munitions. It wasn't rare to find explosives attached to them. Word ran up and down the line about massive piles of bodies. The master race had been leaving trenches dense with dead civilians.

"How'd someplace so gorgeous come up with something as ugly as they did?" Irene asked aloud, as they waited for yet another pontoon bridge to be constructed.

Nobody had an answer. Of course, there was no answer. She didn't expect one.

Irene and Dorothy were like an old married couple, their outbursts and rhetorical questions a form of connection. A nest of self where they felt safe. It was the same with the guys on patrol, who talked one another's ears off. The boys in the foxholes could boast and bitch for hours.

Irene thought the secret ingredient of war was hot air. She massaged her thighs, happy to be idling. She flexed her hands. Every part of her was sore. "I've gotten a cramp in my leg," she told Dorothy.

"Hop out, I'll take it."

"You sure?"

"Driving across a pontoon bridge is a job for me, anyway," Dorothy said.

"Oh, if you insist."

Dorothy startled her by saying, "Indubitably," in an arch English accent.

—

Neither of them was prepared for the beauty of the land. They had images of Nazi ugliness and destruction in their minds. Black-and-white newsreels of goose-stepping hordes marching by torchlight. Amid the sylvan dales and craggy peaks lay the remains of embattled towns ruined beyond habitation, yet active with furtive civilians. By now Irene and Dorothy knew of the devastation of Dresden. What American bombers had done there. None of that was wrong, they thought. Or hoped. But these forests and fields—these villages with white church spires rising from almost black trees—were an utter surprise.

Along the way there had been the usual occasional letters and a package of socks. A loaf of fossilized fruitcake for Irene from Mattituck. They softened it in coffee, though Dorothy would rather have gnawed on it than tasted coffee. She'd gotten a note on blue paper from Smitty—he'd sent it to Bastogne before the siege had begun and the army had forwarded it.

At the very bottom of the mail sack, stained and partially torn, lay a thick envelope for Irene from Handyman. When she opened it, she noted that his letter was undated and not heavily censored.

Dearest Irene,

I catch myself talking to you, but of course you are not here. I don't know where you are. You can't possibly know where I am. I don't like that. I am starting to want to know where you are all of the time. It was all so random, wasn't it? There are so many air bases and I could have gone to any of them. To be honest, I only flew to XXXXXXX for your talent show. But as soon as I saw you again, I knew that wasn't why I flew to XXXXXXX. As soon as I got out of my plane, there you were. And I've been thinking about you ever since. I hope that's not too much to tell you. I also want to tell you that I would like to find you after this madness is over and take you home.

I am not proposing anything but what it would mean to me to take you to the shore of Wallowa Lake. You wouldn't believe how pretty it is to look up into those mountains, to see the aspen trees, the smell of the wildflowers and wild grasses, the smoke from the chimneys of the cabins and ranch houses. I don't know if you fish or not, but honey you've got to have some rainbow trout panfried in bacon grease, cooked over a cottonwood campfire. We could ride a couple of Appaloosas over the moraine and on up into the mountains. Don't worry, I'm the XXXXXXXX—I won't let a bear get you! What do you say?

Meet me in the XXXXXXXXXXXXXX in London after we beat Hitler. I'll be the guy wearing a cowboy hat.

By the way, I think I finished your song. I can't wait to sing it to you, my Pearl of Great Price. Please take care of yourself. I need to see you again.

Everything always, Hans

As was her habit, Irene folded the letter as small as possible and tucked it into her brassiere. She pressed her hand to her chest, knowing she would read the letter over and over again, even after she had it memorized.

34

THE RANGER CARRIED a small metal clicker in his hand. It was a child's toy, made in the shape of a cricket and painted to look like one. You could buy them three for a penny at Woolworth's. It was a leftover from D-Day, when the night crawlers and paratroopers had used them during the invasion to signal one another in the darkness, a way to maintain radio silence and eliminate the sound of voices.

It was 11:45 p.m. now, civilian time, by his watch. Not much moonlight, and what moon there was remained hidden behind greasy-looking smears of cloud. Out here, The Ranger called all the shots—he was his own general. He moved silently. His sniper rifle was wrapped in camo cloth and hung across his back, barrel down and to his right.

He took a knee in the shadows between the dark rigs parked for the night. The sentries never saw him pass. He could hear snoring and muttering. Scattered about were pup tents and lumps of human darkness under trucks. He clicked his cricket three times, paused, and three times again.

Dorothy crawled out from under the *Rapid City*, dressed and booted and ready. She bent to him and he took burnt cork to her face—cheeks, forehead, chin—then handed her a black ski cap that she dragged down to cover her hair. He jerked his head toward the woods and rose and she followed him away from the field.

When they reached the edge, Garcia was lurking there along with the other Gray Ghosts. He had his hand cupped around the bright cherry of his cigarette end, smoke rising like fog.

Dorothy took a hit. She hadn't seen Garcia since back before Bastogne. "I thought you were gone," she said.

"I been 'round. How you been, Stretch?"

"War-dazzled."

"You talkin' like Irene now."

Dorothy had walked with the Gray Ghosts before, had even seen one of their combat operations. But until The Ranger approved of her participation, she could only be an observer. That in itself was an honor. But tonight, for the first time, she would become a full member.

"You the first lady doing this job," Zoot said. "I'm proud of you."

The other guys on the team nodded at her. The Ranger presented her with a long gun, scoped. Like the other rifles, it was wrapped. Every metal thing, everything that could clank or clack, was taped or wrapped as well. Belt buckles, dog tags. Even their watch faces were covered.

"Single file," The Ranger said. "Northwest. Ten kilometers. Zoot, walk point. Stretch in the middle with me. Brewer in the rear. Sergeant Brown, keep an eye on our guest."

"Sir," the sergeant said.

The Ranger spun his finger in the air and pointed ahead. Zoot field-stripped his cigarette and let the breeze carry off the tobacco. The team moved out as one, single file, long as a shadow snake.

"We are the men who ain't here," Zoot said.

"And me," Dorothy said.

"You're especially not here."

"Secret agent," said Brown, walking behind her.

"Did you hear anything?" Dorothy said. "Did somebody say something? I didn't hear nothin'."

"'Cause ain't nobody here, man," said Brewer from the rear.

"Cut the grab-ass," The Ranger whispered.

They zipped it, walking lightly in silence, their passage from that point on as soft as wind in the grass.

Dorothy felt alive. She always smelled like donuts and cooking oil and sweat, but everyone in the team had scrubbed themselves earlier so no sharp odor could give them away, and whatever remnant stink of the kitchen galley might remain drifted off her as she hiked. She breathed heavily as they cut up ridges and down into foggy depressions and between black trees that murmured with night birds. She worked at breathing silently. No gasps. No gulps.

The heavy rifle in her hands felt like a great sword. Or a lance. It could slay anything that dared threaten her. It summoned thunder. She wished she could carry it with her everywhere. She was no baker, no cook, no driver. She was here to pay the Nazis back, she reminded herself. Blood for blood. She was here to save America, and it wasn't even slightly ironic. She was here to pay the enemy back for the night she had spent in the underworld.

The Ranger was a schoolteacher from Urbana, Illinois. He'd done his Ranger training at Fort Chaffee, Arkansas, collecting ticks and chiggers on his ankles. Brewer was a Lakota long-range recon operator from the Pine Ridge Reservation, in South Dakota. He bore a circular cluster of scars on his left upper arm from flesh sacrifices and twin burls of scar tissue on his chest from being hung up on pegs during the Sun Dance. Brown was a radioman in his real army life, with Appalachian roots. His father had fought in World War I, and before that, his great-grandfather had fought for the Union in the Civil War in a Negro brigade. Zoot was the son of a revolutionary guerrilla fighter who'd ridden with Pancho Villa into New Mexico. They had all been humping since the landing at Normandy, now an eternity ago.

Ain't we a bunch, Dorothy thought. *Ain't we America.*

—

Zoot's cricket clicked twice.

They dropped, rolled away from the path, and held their breath. The Ranger patted Dorothy's arm and pointed behind her. She rolled deeper into the bushes, a sound slight enough to have been a rabbit going to its burrow. The entire team had become invisible. They heard male laughter. Then the quiet crackling of a small fire. Non-American vocal tones coming from two speakers.

Brewer tapped Dorothy's boot to let her know he was coming up behind her. He spider-crawled—fingers and toes—keeping his body off the ground. "Krauts," he whispered as he shadowed past her.

Unseen by her, he and Zoot drew their Ka-Bars from sheaths on their thighs and slunk toward the campfire. It was over quickly. One muffled cry of alarm and some awful grunts and choking sounds. Then just the dying sounds of the campfire, whose smell made the woods feel homey.

Three cricket clicks, and they moved forward.

Dorothy was surprised that the dead soldiers didn't shock her. But then again, they weren't the first dead men she'd seen on this little vacation. She didn't look closely, though. She kept her eyes on the silhouette of The Ranger.

When she stumbled, Brown gripped her arm and kept her vertical. "One step at a time," he whispered.

And then they were on the bluff above the German radio-and-command complex, a scattering of sandbag dugouts with tarps over them, plus five tents and two vehicles. The moon had cleared the clouds, and though not full, it cast a ghostly purple-gray light. Their eyes were now so attuned to darkness that everything below them glowed. Dorothy's body was tight, her muscles clenched, her skin rising in goose bumps. They lay on their stomachs, weapons before them and aiming at the compound.

"The target's tall, like you," Brewer whispered.

"Got it," Dorothy said.

"He'll be in the main tent. That big square one in the middle. Radio center."

"Roger."

"Take your time to get your man."

"Can do."

"Brewer is on the target with you," The Ranger said. "Don't sweat it. Zoot and me are taking the other tents." He snapped his fingers.

Brown pulled the pin on a grenade and pitched it high. When it dropped between the tents it unleashed chaos. It looked like an ant farm down there.

Dorothy had been briefed earlier about her target, a German colonel who had allegedly overseen the flaying of two American pilots. It was apparently one of the Third Reich's million dark secrets—lynching American flyboys. The colonel had left them hanging upside down in trees for American patrols to discover. He was using this bunker to call in air strikes and artillery coordinates.

Keep cool, she thought. *Keep it cool.*

The Germans were shooting in every direction—they didn't know where the attack was coming from. Dorothy felt safe. They couldn't see her up here on the bluff. The rifle butt was snug against her shoulder. Her finger was on the trigger. The good smell of gun oil. She roved the scrambling soldiers below with her scope, catching several in the cross-hairs. It was just like nailing a wild turkey, she told herself. Her hand shook anyway.

Cool, now. Cool. Cool.

There he was. Yeah, tall. Not in his underwear like some of them. Not shirtless. But in full uniform, with his black formal cap. He was scanning the woods.

They all five opened fire then, knocking down troops and hitting their vehicles. The officer looked up at them and raised his pistol.

"Goodbye," Dorothy said.

She and Brewer fired at almost the same moment. She would never know which of them got him. The Colonel folded like a dropped shirt and crumpled to the ground.

It was time to run. Brown threw three more frag grenades into the pandemonium as they vanished again into darkness.

—

Irene rolled out from her bed under the *Rapid City*. It made for a cozy cave. She had no fear of Stukas tonight, and she needed a little fresh air. The combined aroma of sinkers, oil, and mud could get to be a little rich. She liked to drop by GI campsites and spread some cheer. Or to pick up a little for herself in the form of laughs or random snorts from flasks. She wondered which campfire Dorothy was visiting. They were all more lonesome in the dark out here in enemy territory.

She spied a campfire across the great meadow and headed in the direction of the laughter. They might have a tipple for her, she hoped. The smell of smoke reached her as she got close enough to see the men hunched over or sprawled on the grass. And there was Dorothy, her face streaked with black. She stood above them with a bottle in her hand, gesturing wildly as they laughed. The flame had turned her red and orange. Her shadow was inky and long and jerked wildly on the ground behind her. Her hair caught the light and looked like it might be on fire.

Something about the scene frightened Irene. She backed away, then trotted to her truck, where she climbed into the safety of the galley and closed the door quietly behind her.

35

It was March and every day seemed exactly the same, unless they happened to be assigned a billet with hot water and time for a bath. The *Rapid City* was reassigned every few days and bounced all over Germany between different divisions, small towns, and Donut Dugouts before landing in Idstein, near Frankfurt, just before Easter Sunday.

They challenged the GIs in the barracks to greet the day in their finest Easter bonnets. Kitchen sieves, wicker trash cans, and every scrap of ribbon they could find were put to service in the cause. Irene and Dorothy donned their French berets, elaborately festooned with spring flowers they picked in town. Dorothy found a raggedy pigeon feather she happily poked behind her ear.

When they saw how elegant and lovely the GIs looked in their spring chapeaus, Irene and Dorothy decided that a very special donut service was in order. Since they were wearing berets, they felt French accents were called for, even though neither one of them actually spoke French.

"*Messieurs!*" Irene bellowed. "We have 'ere for you ze *beignets et le café*!"

"*Oui, oui!*" Dorothy added, holding up a can of milk. "Alzo le moo-moo!"

Irene turned to Dorothy, "Ooh la la, *très bien*!"

A soldier in a bonnet made of an upside-down letter box and some cocktail picks rested his elbows up on the counter and said, "*Mademoiselles*! Gimme one of them café au laits, see voo plaze!"

The hilarity continued for some time, including an impromptu cancan dance line with the GIs. Irene was happy to see Dorothy come out of her strange dark mood, even if it was only for a day.

—

Ever since her night with the Gray Ghosts, Dorothy had wrangled with herself in silence. What had she done? She'd wanted blood for blood, payback for all she'd seen in this war. She'd wanted to wound the German army. But was it the right thing to do? Had she only managed to wound herself? She'd thought that she would feel liberated. That she would feel relief. That she would feel she had helped win some small part of the war. But she was shaken. She was folding up inside herself. Her stomach, her heart, somehow creased. And here she'd thought Irene—with her poetry and easy tears—was the sensitive one. Had she sinned? She drove and tried to see the world and she drove and breathed as deeply as she could and she drove. She wanted to confess to Irene.

As the early days of April passed, the forests turned luminous, bright green with fresh leaves as if these were the first leaves in the world. Trees formed tunnels, and their shadows formed a floor, and the openings down the road were lit like bright lamps that shone their glow toward the truck. When the sun set, the backlit hills were pitch-black, their summit trees like candles, and the clouds from the east, rolling over and toward them, were eerie and jagged. Contrails from American bombers marked glowing *X*s above the horizon. The names of the towns were strange to them: Edersleben, Voigtstedt, Eisenach, Bad Berka. On Dorothy's map, they found such mythological-sounding places as Thuringia. They imagined horned helmets and vast battle-axes.

Dorothy had always longed to travel. She should be paying attention, she realized, because here she was. But she was busy trying to evict the strange thoughts from her head. *Act as if,* she thought. "Everything's all right," she said.

"Yes, Dottie. Of course. Everything is fine."

In a small city with a name they couldn't pronounce, Schwangen-schwan-wan-shyster or something, they beheld men in lederhosen. A small parade for no apparent reason—tubas and drums and horses pulling a wagon full of women in Heidi dresses—exited the town and marched away toward the fields. Purple mountains in the distance. Everybody was waving. They waved back. The Sisters insisted on taking it ironically, though there was no evidence the marchers were in any way ironic.

"I need some leather shorts," Dorothy announced.

Approaching Weimar, the road climbed into hills. A handsome valley spread out below them on the left. A rail line shadowed the road on the right, cutting through the woods and climbing higher up Ettersberg Mountain and out of sight. They joined the vehicles turning downhill into the city. A rail spur also went down in that direction. Clothes and trash were strewn along the rails, which was rare for what they'd seen in Germany, even in all these running battles. The reached an intersection with a pair of signs, one pointing down to Weimar and the other uphill to someplace called Buchenwald. There were bullet holes in the wood.

The line of liberators was moving very slowly. Military Harleys with sidecars. Weary green trucks crammed with weary green soldiers. Down below, big diesel rigs looked like toys. A German cop car came up the hill going *wee-haw-wee-haw* and passed them. It burned around the corner at the road signs and headed uphill.

"That was interesting," Dorothy said. "I didn't know they still had cops."

The line stopped. They heard engines shutting down and Dorothy turned the Jimmy off as well. When Irene hopped down to stretch her legs, Dorothy joined her. Guys were lighting up, staring off. One truck driver got out of his rig and simply walked away.

Dorothy cursed him softly. "That's not going to help, pal."

One of the biker boys pulled up and lifted his goggles to the top of his head. "I had your donuts back in France. Thanks."

"Our pleasure," Irene said.

"What's the dope on the town?" Dorothy said.

"You'll be all right," he said. "'Bout fifty thousand citizens. They're under Colonel Costello now, after the Bürgermeister signed a surrender treaty with him. Apparently they have mixed feelings about us. A bunch of grunts on patrol found a crapload of Nazis hiding in the suburbs. Had a dustup."

"Oh?"

"Our boys weren't in any mood for that. They called in tanks and airborne and pancaked about seven blocks. You'll see it when you drive in. There's German officers hiding all over town, so watch yourselves. That professor in a rumpled suit could be a friggin' Gestapo man." The soldier pulled his goggles back down and kicked the beast to life, revving the engine. "Later." He roared away, leaned into a wide right-hand U-turn, and charged downhill.

Dorothy put her hands on the small of her back and stretched, feeling the sun on her face. *I can never go home*, she thought.

Crows were scudding up the mountain. Irene shielded her eyes to inspect them. She knew full well that crows were jolly brigands—she had fed crows in Mattituck many times—but they looked so ominous against the purple clouds. There was something brooding about these big hills. The whole scene was operatic—gravid with drama.

"But it's beautiful," Irene said.

"What is?" Dorothy said.

"Oh, I suppose I'm talking to myself again."

Dorothy leaned on the fender with her hands in her pockets. "You're right, Gator. This place is like some kind of painting."

"You take good care of me, Dottie."

"Do I?"

Irene wandered off the road, down into the railroad gap. A grasshopper ratcheted away through the yellow weeds and rough gravel. There were ants everywhere, also just like in Mattituck. She saw a dented metal cup, a soiled and torn wool suit coat, a broken shoe in the distance. The coat reeked, even out here in the open air. When the engines up and down the line began grumbling to life she wandered back to the *Rapid*.

"Here we go," she said brightly.

"You okay, girl?" Dorothy said.

"There is an atmosphere I can't define."

"Probably me. I could use a bath."

"I think Germany has made me profoundly angry. Even when I'm charmed, or delighted, I think: *You bastards*."

Dorothy nodded and downshifted. "You could use a bath, too," she said.

"You look out at this beautiful land and wonder where the evil came from."

Dorothy thought: *She is still talking*.

"What dark god came out of these mountains and woods."

"This morning," Dorothy said, "I burped up a chunk of breakfast. Where did that evil god in my gut come from?"

Irene crossed her arms. "Fine," she said. "Forget I ever said anything."

"I'm trying to forget, but you keep talking about it."

A gold bird the size of a paper airplane floated by.

A sign announced: AUSFAHRT. Dorothy thought this was funny. Irene stewed in her icy silence.

Suddenly: Weimar. A black-and-white beer hall. Colors and hotels and statues.

"Oh boy!" Dorothy enthused. It was the only way she could approach apologizing. She didn't have it in her to admit she hadn't been herself lately.

The demolished blocks of the outskirts revealed dogs and hunched people digging in the ruins. Buildings all around the firefight remains were scarred with burns and plate-sized bullet impacts and rips down their facades.

"Same old same old," Dorothy said.

They were both astounded to see Phyl from the *Cheyenne* walking down the street in her Red Cross outfit.

"Hey lady!" Irene shouted out the window.

Phyllis waved both arms at them. "We are staying in the Hotel Elephant!" she called. "Got orders to set up a Donut Dugout in town! See you at the hotel later!"

"I want schnitzel!" Dorothy shouted.

"This is the right place."

They waved and drove on.

"Good old Phyl," Dorothy said, pushing her luck with Irene.

"Yes."

Irene said nothing else, but it was an opening, at least. *Damn*, Dorothy thought, *but we do keep on dancing*. "Sure is quiet in here," she muttered.

"Maybe Phyllis will talk to you."

—

Thuringia, Irene jotted in her notebook. Everything here sounded Wagnerian. *Weimar. Goethe, Bach, Martin Luther, Bauhaus*, she wrote. *Why so much genius here? And here, in this old and gorgeous hotel, Haus Elephant, Hitler had a suite. One floor beneath us. He stood on the balcony shrieking his wickedness. I am breathing the air he breathed. Yet, not far from us, the statue of Bach stands at the mouth of a cobbled alley. How can this be? How can this be?* She threw in a sketch of a fountain. Two cats.

The Sisters were happy to get away from each other. Dorothy went off on foot to find the Donut Dugout, which she had taken to calling the Donut Dungeon. She wore their .45 on her hip.

Irene, of course, ran a hot bath and put all the bath salts she could find into the water, turning it blue. Her dirty laundry was collected in a rolling bin by the staff of the Elephant, and she donned her last and best clean Red Cross blouse, her last slacks, and her hat. They'd been warned that their caps looked like German-officer hats to snipers in the dark, but the day was bright. She felt invincible.

She descended to discover an VIII Corps Officers' Club Headquarters card waiting for her at the front desk. It was stamped OFFICIAL.

WEIMAR, GERMANY

NAME: IRENE WOODWARD

RANK: ARC

Apparently she was the Red Cross embodied. She tucked the card into her back pocket and walked into the street. She put on her Riviera sunglasses and basked in a romantic shiver. The city seemed to welcome her—its arches felt like open embraces. Around many corners the seventeenth century awaited her. But vigilant American soldiers manned the streets, their M1s at the ready. MPs rolled through in jeeps with burp guns and radios. She was almost always in someone's sight.

She wandered down alleys, running her hands over the stone walls painted yellow. She touched Bach on his pedestal, and when she found Luther she dared to give him a sinful little pinch.

The Albergo Giancarlo had a charming sidewalk café set up with Italian waiters shouting and fretting. She was both delighted and suspicious—Axis bastards. But they wielded their white dishcloths like bullfighters with small capes, whistled down the echoing *Strasse,* and called out to friends and colleagues in other buildings. Ugly squat German delivery trucks dropped off huge stinky wheels of cheeses and drooping logs of sausage.

Irene took a table and the waiters managed to be attentive while utterly ignoring her. It was oddly appealing, these divos starring in their own command production. They brought her cheese and fruit, small cups of deadly coffee, a glass of red wine, and a platter of schnitzel about as wide as the state of New Jersey.

"Oh, I couldn't," Irene demurred, then ate it all.

When they delivered cannoli, she ate those, too.

—

The Red Cross Donut Dugout was on the edge of the Theaterplatz, set up in a large, abandoned former bakery and café. The Clubmobiles were parked around the corner and could be used as mobile kitchens, if necessary. From the windows of the Dugout, they could see the Art Nouveau buildings that had once been the Bauhaus. Suddenly, the service was like every day they had spent on the road, only inside a clean, bright place that had tables with tablecloths. Their friends from the other trucks came in for duty, too. Each Clubmobile crew was relieved to have a cadre of other women to rely on. The talking never ceased, and the laughter was deafening. Men were moved to oratorios of boasting, fretting, bellowing, and flirting. The Clubmobiles brewed oceans of American coffee—the boys didn't want tiny sludgy cups of weird European coffee—and heaps of Uncle Sam's donuts.

"Sound off, boys," Dorothy demanded. "Who am I serving?"

"Lieutenant Blume."

"Hiya, handsome."

"Ma'am."

"George Vincent Warren!"

"Are you sure you're not a prince with a name like that?"

"He's a king!" Blume shouted.

"Aw shucks," Warren said.

Everybody laughed, everybody forgot the war was outside the door, just for a minute.

The plaza was crawling with Americans. The Weimar public appeared to be in shock over this. The locals didn't seem to know what to do with these invaders. The Thousand-Year Reich was crumbling, and the true believers, who had to know everything was broken but no doubt secretly hoped and believed that salvation would come, chose to act as though the Americans were invisible. They went about their duties and interests and businesses as if it were still 1939.

By their second day in service, the bonhomie among the Americans was all changing. The soldiers had grown sullen—spooked and untalkative. There were rumors of something on the mountain . . . something terrible. Allegedly, no one had seen whatever it was. OSS men refused to speak about it. People were claiming that the former Nazi vice chancellor Franz von Papen had been discovered hiding in a house and was being interrogated. General McBride, who had prevailed in the Battle of the Bulge, was supposedly in the OSS offices with Patton. *There is a sense akin to the pause before a thunderstorm,* Irene jotted in her notebook.

Soldiers were muttering about Buchenwald, the "Beech Forest," five or six miles up the road. Irene thought it was a lovely name. She had read that Goethe had regularly visited a beloved tree there where he wrote, seated like the melancholic poet he was, in its shade. As if in partnership.

—

The following day, the mood was subdued at the Dugout. Word spread that President Roosevelt had died the day before. Some of the women were crying and GIs lining up at the door were somber.

Suddenly MPs drove into the Theaterplatz and sealed off one end of the square. Fresh soldiers in pressed uniforms appeared in the plaza with shiny-clean rifles held at port arms.

"I think I'm going crazy," Dorothy said. "What is happening now?"

Irene, craning to see out a window, didn't hear her.

A staff car flanked by motorcycles wheeled in off a side street, sounding its jarring Klaxon, and sped toward their door. The Germans in the square froze—the last time such ostentatious vehicles had raced through their city it was Hitler or Göring in the back seat. This big car had its top down, with flags on stanchions mounted to the front fenders. Two helmets were visible in back, one of them silver.

The Sisters crowded the windows of the Donut Dugout. Dorothy crossed her arms over her stomach and looked at the floor. She found herself wondering if Adolf had ever come in here. His filthy shadow seemed to skulk in the corners like a demon.

The staff car halted outside their door. Armed guards appeared and the driver jumped out. Everything was still. The driver opened the back door of the car and General Patton himself rose and looked the crowd over.

He turned to the other officer. "General?" they heard him say.

They recognized the man he'd addressed as McBride. "No, George," he said. "I could use a little bit of sun. You go ahead."

Patton nodded once and stepped down from the car.

"He's packing those ivory-handled pistols," Irene whispered. Then, "Wait! Dot!" she shouted. "He's coming in here!"

They pulled back from the windows and Dorothy straightened up and put on her game face. "Too late to get this joint squared away," she said. "Look sharp, boys."

"Atten-HUT!" the head MP shouted through the door.

Those already at attention stood even straighter. Patton carried his riding crop and flicked it off his brow in a no-nonsense salute. Old Blood and Guts paused at the threshold and quickly glanced right and left, then stepped into the Dugout. The women were frozen in place. The men audibly leaped into formation. One soldier dropped his gun. Utter silence thereafter.

"At ease," Patton said. He took off his helmet and eagle-eyed them all. He appeared to recognize Irene and Dorothy and tried to grin at them, but it looked like a grimace.

They fervently hoped they weren't in some undisclosed trouble—probably the same thought that was floating through every soldier's head, too.

"Hello, ladies," he said. "Good to see you again."

"General," they said in unison.

There was an uncomfortable moment and Irene blurted out, "Sir, I am sorry about FDR, sir."

Patton looked at her stoically. "Yes," he said, "a terrible loss for all of us." He turned to the men behind him. "But we prevail, right?"

"Sir, yes, sir!" the GIs answered as one.

The soldiers in the room stood stiff as statues.

"Boys," Patton said, "could you give us some privacy?"

It was not a request. The men stampeded out the door, saluting in fast motion as they fled.

Patton eye-scorched each soldier as he passed. He seemed to relax a bit when they were gone. He laid his helmet and riding crop on the counter. "I hear a fellow can get a cup of coffee in here," he said.

Jill and Phyllis rushed to the urn.

"Black is fine," he said.

"Donut, sir?" offered Dorothy.

He shook his head. "Have you heard any gossip from these fine men?" he asked.

"No, sir," Irene said.

He put the cup down. "Fibber." He stared out the window, posed like a Greek monument. When he turned back to them, he said, "You will need to help me with something in the coming days. Something that will be hard to believe."

"Sir?" Dorothy said.

"I thought I'd seen it all," he said, and took a small sip. "I need you to do some damn hard duty."

"Whatever you say, sir," Dorothy replied. She made herself not salute.

He nodded almost imperceptibly. "We discovered something yesterday. Something bad. Up the hill, at the Buchenwald forest. It's a"—he paused—"prison camp, I suppose you could say. But, ah, this is something…different."

Irene and Dorothy glanced at each other.

"I've asked for the *Cheyenne* and the *Rapid City* to come up with us first thing in the morning," he said. "I don't think my men know how to adjust to what we've found. They have seen what they are fighting against. I need you to help remind them what they are fighting for. I can't order you, but I am ordering you."

"Yes, sir!" the Clubmobile crews answered in unison.

He picked up his helmet. "You'll depart at oh six hundred. Get some sleep." He stopped at the door and half turned. "No donuts. It's not the place for that. We will all need coffee, though. I apologize in advance—I know you're busy enough as it is. Oh, and full uniforms."

With that, he went out, remounted his car, and sat back with McBride. He raised one hand to them before he was swept away.

36

PREDAWN AT THE hotel the next morning, and they stood outside Irene's room, fortifying each other.

"How bad can it be?" Dorothy said.

"I'm scared," Irene admitted.

They grabbed their jackets, and Irene borrowed Dorothy's camera, and they went downstairs and out the back doors of Haus Elephant, where a soldier already sat in the driver's seat of the *Rapid City* with the engine running, a development that Dorothy appreciated not one bit. They climbed in beside him, Irene in the middle. The *Cheyenne* was also visible behind the hotel in the twilight, its engine idling. For once, Dorothy stayed quiet. The soldier put the truck in gear and they rolled out.

"Old Blood and Guts assigned me to be your guide," the driver said. He never so much as glanced over at them as they maneuvered through town.

"What is it we're supposed to do up there?" Irene asked.

"Sister, it beats the crap out of me."

Dorothy and Irene exchanged a look.

The driver banged through the gears as they cleared the edge of town and turned a hard left at the road sign. "You need to know there's still Krauts in the woods," he said. "You should be careful. Those cowards ran away when they heard we were coming. They're hiding all over the mountain. We have security set up around the camp, but be aware." His jaw rippled. He had sweat in his bristly hair, though the air was cool.

Dorothy saw all the square-jawed Indiana sons of guns in his face. She didn't dare ask him what position he played on the football team. There had to have been a football team. She knew she was scared now—her thoughts were babbling. She reached over and grabbed Irene's hand.

—

It was five and a half miles up to the camp. They could see Weimar to their left, far below, through birch trees and pines. An ambulance and two trucks full of soldiers were ahead of them. Birds were rioting in the trees as the purple glow of predawn came on. In the silence inside the truck, Irene clutched Dorothy's arm like a life ring. Dorothy was stiff in her seat.

At the top of the long hill, they maneuvered a tight right turn into a broad open space in the gorgeous woods. American GIs nodded to them. Machine-gun emplacements were aimed into the forest, with jeeps and trucks crammed into the open space and other vehicles lined up along the service road on the left near several rows of two-storied buildings painted in sherbet tones. Roses bloomed everywhere.

The soldier parked the Clubmobile. "SS barracks," he said as they got out. "Classy pieces of shit. 'Scuse me."

Lovely country houses were evident among the trees.

The soldier nodded toward the fanciest house, one with wood carvings on its facade. "That's the commandant's." He waved his arm to the right. "There's playgrounds for their kids over there." He spit on the ground, as if to demonstrate his revulsion at the thought. "You like bears?" he said. "You like petting deer? They built a zoo."

The breeze shifted and Irene recoiled at the strange scent.

"Yeah," he said and kept walking. "That first smell, that's the zoo. Ain't so bad. But when the wind changes, that weird smell? That's the camp. Some of the grunts say it reminds them of dogs. But it ain't any smell I ever knew before, I'll tell you that much."

Irene and Dorothy kept close behind him.

"Your nose kinda goes numb. But you'll really smell it hard at first."

They passed Patton's staff car standing empty. GIs sat on the running boards of trucks and slouched against fenders, most of them smoking, nobody talking.

"Hey, it's Dollies," a young man said, then stepped forward and embraced Dorothy.

She stood there taking it, then put her arm around him and gave him a pat. He went back to his fender and studied his rifle.

"The camp's down that way," the soldier said, pointing. "I'm going to take your truck down there, you just follow that path."

They trudged through the SS quarters, both growing more reluctant by the step. There was a pressure in the woods around them, as though an invisible barrier forbade them to enter. They came upon a rail spur and a crude concrete train station. Bullet shells littered the ground. A locomotive stood dead on the tracks, and empty wagons behind it reeked of feces. Platforms with rough steps led down toward paths that descended into the camp. Though Irene carried Dorothy's camera, she had yet to take a photograph. The women held on to each other. They knew they were standing on the precipice of something very deep, black, shadowy.

The *Cheyenne* had pulled up, and some GIs were directing it to the service road that would take them down to the vehicle gates, a distance from the main entrance that was coming into view as they walked. It was an ugly wide building, with a bridge formed by a second layer of what they took to be offices. The crunching of their boots was very loud.

A square tunnel ran through the center of the building, and whitewashed single-story wings stretched out to either side. The wire fences and their stark concrete stanchions marched off in either direction. Gun towers loomed black against the sky. To their far right a dead chimney rose over yet another ugly squat building with what appeared to be some sort of warehouse or office block behind. Countless shacks filled the camp. On a vast parade ground within, a sea of human shapes, both soldiers and liberated prisoners, stood about and shuffled along. There were ambulances parked willy-nilly. A U.S. Army bulldozer moved around behind a large structure to the right.

Irene stopped. Dorothy grabbed her and tried to pull her along, but Irene resisted. She understood instinctively that to pass through this gate would be to cross some invisible border into a place from which there might be no return.

Dorothy put her arm around Irene's shoulders. "You all right, Gator?"

"I'm not."

Nearby, a GI meandered over to stand in a sad little clutch of trees under which three ghosts congregated. He was handing cigarettes to two of the ghosts. The third was a boy. They wore filthy and tattered striped pajamas. One had bare feet. They were skeletal. The little boy wore a cap. Their faces were gray and their eyeholes were black and they turned their heads toward the Sisters and stared. The child lifted his cap to them. The men lit up.

"I can't, Dottie. I simply can't."

"You can, Irene. You will. *No choice, no problem,* as my daddy used to say."

They stepped toward the gateway. To enter the camp they had to pass through the main building. The low wings spreading on either side had barred and shuttered windows, pegged open. The doorways into either wing were housed on the inner flanks of the square arch. Their heavy metal doors yawned open.

The air grew heavier as they approached the gate. Welded to its iron bars across the top were the words:

JEDEM DAS SEINE

An armed sentry slouched against the wall moved to push the gate open for them. Irene asked if he knew what the words meant.

"An inmate told me it means *You Get What You Deserve,*" he said.

Irene and Dorothy stepped through. Inmates milled around, staring at them. They looked like bundles of sticks wrapped in rags. Most of them appeared dazed. Still, a few smiled, even tipped their caps if they wore them. Brown stains ran down the backs of some of their striped rags.

A specter stepped up to them and said, "Thank you," in English.

Not a specter, Irene corrected herself—a man. She was ashamed. For simply being there. Well-fed. Clean. She knew already that she was not allowed to weep or to shrink back or hesitate. She shook offered hands firmly. She realized she was still clutching Dorothy's camera and stared at it there in her hand.

"Yes," a man said. "Take, take. Picture." He signaled for a few of his comrades to come close. "Take."

Though reluctant, Irene obliged them, snapping a picture. "Are there ladies here?" she asked.

"Ladies," the man who'd invited the pictures repeated. The men murmured to each other. "Ah, women. No women."

They posed, grim-faced, and Irene clicked again.

Dorothy was offended by Irene taking pictures. She could not articulate it. Yet anger burned in her center. No, not mere anger, rage. Screw this. She backed away and peeled off on her own.

—

It was a brilliant, radiant morning, with the new sun. But everything within the fences was gray. All color had been scorched out of this vast square of cinders and gallows and ash. Emaciated men were everywhere, leaning or hanging on fences, unmindful of the barbed wire. Others sat on the wooden steps of their cell blocks, bony arms on knees, hands loose and still. Others lay on the ground, or walked aimlessly, or talked to soldiers and chaplains and nurses. Medics went from prone body to prone body.

Another prisoner came near Irene and gestured around him. "Thousands," he said. He touched his chest. "Thousands us. But more before." He wept. "All gone."

"Yes, sir," Irene said, dazed. "Thank you, sir." She had no idea what she was thanking him for. And where was Dot? She needed Dot.

The man nodded very slowly and walked away, studying his feet, placing each foot on the ground with great care.

Irene's most vivid impression, one that would give her terrible dreams, was that military bulldozer, dull green, its smokestack burping out black clouds while the huge blade in front moved white birch trunks toward a huge pit.

"Why bury all that wood?" she said aloud.

She raised the camera, then lowered it. Those weren't tree trunks. No, not at all.

"Oh God," she whispered.

The bodies were toppling into a large grave.

Medics and soldiers nodded to Irene, even patted her on the back. Everybody but her seemed to have something very important, very human, to accomplish. She was so useless.

"Where do I go?" she asked a nurse. "Where do I start?"

"What are you good at?"

When Irene shook her head, unable to muster a response, the nurse moved on. She didn't have time for Irene.

An inmate—a lawyer from Kraków, he said—joined Irene on the parade ground. He smelled tangy. She hated herself for noticing it. She had thought to bring two packs of cigarettes, imagining GIs needing to fire up a smoke.

"Cigarette?" she asked the man, offering up a pack.

"Yes. Thank."

She lit him up. "What happened here?"

"Right here? We stand here. They make us stand for hours. All night, all day. Especially in snow. Men die. Boys die. Dogs kill men here." He paused and smoked philosophically. "Guards laugh." He took a long drag and blew the smoke away from her. "Excuse," he said. "Day, night, anytime. They make us stand. If you sleep, beat. If you fall, shoot. We watch them hang on those wood. We watch them whip. Kick. They laugh a lot."

"How many?" she heard herself say.

"Hundreds. Of hundreds." He blew air out between his lips. "Hundreds more of hundreds. We're all dead. You cannot count the sand on the shore." He put a finger to his ear and gestured at the surrounding wall of forest with his eyebrows. "Listen. Birds. Beautiful, no? We listen to that as they kill."

Irene hung her head and tears dropped to the ground. She looked away and swiped at her eyes so the man would not see her weep. She was practiced in hearing terrible stories from GIs and knew to be the comforter. She could not be the comforted.

The man continued to smoke his cigarette and regard her passively. "But no birds in here." He looked at the now-slumping and useless fences, the meaningless strands of barbs. "Birds know, stay away." He pointed at the rest of the camp. "Obey. Not obey. Either way we die, my dear." The lawyer gave her a slight shove, not unkindly. "Go. See," he encouraged her. "In there. Maybe pray. I cannot. No more." He held up his cigarette, smiled and nodded his thanks, and gestured for her to go.

Irene walked past the infectious-disease barracks. Dead men were stacked outside it, half-covered in muslin tarps. She thought typhus might be invading her lungs. She battled within herself, then decided and raised her camera for a picture. Her face burned. She looked around to see if anyone was watching, cursing her. Nobody seemed to care what she did at all.

She tried not to look to the right or left as she stumbled through the camp, hoping to find Dorothy. Dead bodies were everywhere. She was simply moving. A tourist in Gehenna.

An 8th Army translator named Freedman, believing Irene was lost, asked if she knew where to check in.

"Check in for what?"

"Ain't you a nurse?"

"I make donuts."

"No kiddin'," Freedman said. "Huh. Well then." He gestured out beyond the fence. "There's the zoo." It was only feet from the fences. "The inmates told us those bastards fed the animals every day right in front of 'em as they were starvin'."

Irene snapped pictures of the zoo because she did not know what else to do. Then she put the camera away and turned back to the GI. "Have you seen a tall woman, dressed like me?" she asked.

"No, but she might be inside there," he said, pointing to the building next to the zoo. "There's a door on the other side."

There were wagons on either side of the large building's doorway, stacked with bodies. Irene had an overwhelming sense of dread. Why was she going inside? But she was. She stepped through a portal between worlds, and walked into a big room with a drain in the floor. Six large ovens stood with their doors hanging open. Each one was stuffed with human cordage, bones, and ash. Beside the furnaces were empty high-sided wagons.

Damn you, Dot. Damn you for leaving me alone. Damn this camera. May God damn the ones who thought this up, who did this.

She was done. She couldn't breathe and stumbled out into the light. But there was no breath of fresh air outside. She was breathing ghosts.

There was a gap in the barbed wire and Irene just wanted to be outside the fence. She climbed through the gap and sat for a moment on the wall of the empty bear enclosure. Suddenly, she heard a wail. Outright sobbing from the other side of the enclosure. She walked around the pit and was astonished to see Garcia. What was he doing here? And why was he crying? He was huddled with his face pressed to the wall, weeping as though his heart were falling out.

"Zoot," she said, rushing to him. "Hey now."

He turned and buried his face against her shoulder. "I-I-Irene."

"Now now, Zoot, it's all right."

"I killed him. I killed him!" He was wailing into her chest.

She combed his hair with her fingers. "Who? Who did you kill?"

He crushed her with a frantic hug.

"Tell me," she said very quietly.

"Valentin. I killed Valentin."

She sat in the dirt beside him and pulled his head into her lap. "Tell me," she said. "I'm listening."

They had entered a barrack and found the harsh stacks of wooden boxes the prisoners slept in without blankets or mattresses, one above the other, and some of them still occupied by the dead. He had been shocked by the new smell—the smell of sickness. And he didn't understand the crackling under his feet until he realized it was lice, fleeing the cooling bodies.

An inmate had weakly reached out. His stick arm rose and he spoke in a frail whisper. Garcia went to the bunk and opened his canteen and gave the man a sip.

"Careful, Zoot," one of his buddies warned. "You don't wanna drown the poor guy."

Garcia had taken the inmate in his arms and carried him out. He felt as light as some kindling, and as dry. He laid him out in the sun and that's when Valentin spoke his name. His bird-claw hand held Garcia's and he wept dusty tears to be in sunlight again. Garcia wanted to comfort him. To do something, anything. His buddies were saying, "He's a goner, Zoot." But Garcia was remembering his own grandfather dying of cancer in the desert rancho outside Gila Bend. And he committed his sin.

He knew better. How could he be so stupid? The nurses had told the soldiers not to feed any of the inmates. *Their bodies won't be able to process food,* the nurses had warned. But Garcia wanted to help. He wanted to show the man some kind of love. He dug a chocolate bar out of his top pocket and unwrapped it and broke off a piece and slipped it between Valentin's peeling lips. And the man soon turned blue and choked and the thin thread of life slipped away.

Now Garcia could not stop sobbing.

Irene sat with him for a while, patting his back and head until he fell asleep, snuffling like a little boy. This stone-cold killer. Her rescuer. *Pachuco y que?* as he would say. Just the two of them, trying to save what was still alive in them.

When Zoot finally stopped crying, Irene promised never to tell anyone. She hugged him again, kissed the top of his head, and went off to find the *Rapid City*.

—

Dorothy had left Irene because she did not need to gawk at the dead any longer. It was obscene to do so. She needed to find a calm place to hide for a moment and gather herself. She eventually found her way to the big building behind the crematorium. The depot—clothes and personal belongings.

Inside, she was confronted with stacks of suitcases. A room piled high with eyeglasses. The toys and crutches and leg braces and wooden legs were almost too much. But what finished her was something she could not explain. Some sorrow that she knew she would dream about for the rest of her life. The big room stacked with shoes. No, not stacked, piled. A pyramid of shoes. Within the shoes were stamped the visible imprints of feet, the sweat stains and the discoloration of the leather. She hung her head in that shadowy space—there where no one would see her—and her sobs beat her like body blows.

Then she squared herself away and said, "Let's go."

When she made her way back to where the *Rapid City* and *Cheyenne* were parked, Jill, Phyl, and Helen already had coffee brewing. Dorothy was filling the electric urns when Irene appeared and the two worked in silent tandem. Exhausted GIs, grateful for the smell of coffee, were drawn to the trucks.

It was their first silent service of the war. No joking, no flirting or chatter. Not even much eye contact. The men silently put their tin cups on the counter and accepted the coffee. Irene had to ask if they wanted milk or sugar. The men would nod or shake their heads, take their cups, and walk away to drink alone.

Dorothy reached under the counter for a small carafe. "For the general," she said.

Irene grabbed a large mug and the two headed toward the small fenced yard where Patton was raging beside a pair of long tables being loaded with gruesome objects from the commandant's offices. Patton whipped the air with his riding crop. His helmet lay on the table, and his white hair seemed to burn in the sun. Curses churned the air around his head. *Sons of bitches* and *Kraut bastards* and *shitbirds* flew out of his mouth.

He whirled and saw the donut Sisters standing there. "Am I right?" he yelled.

"Damn right," Dorothy said. "Sir."

"Roger, sir," Irene added.

He nodded and spun back to smack the tabletop with his quirt. He pulled his staff together and scattered them with various instructions. Then he snapped his fingers at the Sisters and ordered them over with his index finger. "Look at this," he said. "These lampshades." He stood alongside them. "I'm going to beat these bastards into the mud, so help me God." He started away and sat heavily in a chair at the far end of the table.

Dorothy and Irene brought over the carafe and poured him a mug of coffee.

Patton smiled gratefully and took the mug, thanking them. "I need to tell you I made a mistake," he said, "and I want to apologize to you. I thought bringing you here might be some comfort to my boys, who need a bit of that right now." He gestured to the camp around him. "But that was naive. I was foolish to put you in an impossible situation. I am releasing you from this duty. There is movement toward Munich and plenty of work to be done. I want your trucks to join the boys in the morning."

"Yes, sir," they answered.

He stood up and shook each of their hands. As they walked away, Irene looked back at Patton, coffee mug in hand, staring at the table of atrocities.

—

Neither one of them could eat anything that evening. When sleep came, it was an ocean of pale faces and reaching hands.

At five o'clock in the morning, Dorothy stepped into the bathroom of her hotel room and, using a knife she had pocketed at dinner, hacked off all her hair. Irene said nothing when she saw what her friend had done. They were in the *Rapid City* and following the short convoy by 6:30 a.m. The trucks and jeeps rolled up the long road out of Weimar and when they reached the crossroads, they turned and sped south toward Munich.

37

THEY HAD BEEN driving mostly in silence for a couple of hours. That wasn't unusual, but today it felt different to Irene. She stole glances at Dorothy, who drove with grim intensity.

Finally, she had to say something. "So, are we going to talk about your hair?"

Dorothy ran the fingers of one hand through her new cut, making her hair stand in wild tufts all over her head. "What about it. Don't you approve." Dorothy's voice was flat and her tone stung Irene.

"I just don't understand, Dottie. That's all."

Dorothy's jaw clenched. "It was better than putting my head through the goddamn wall, don't you think, Gator?" Dorothy said. "I had to do something. I *have* to do something. We were useless back there and I am sick of it. People actually died at our feet and we did *nothing* except make some goddamn coffee."

Irene reeled. "Dottie, we did what we could. We're here to support and comfort and be the place where these boys can catch their breath. What else *can* we do?"

Dorothy snorted harshly. "Ah, a port in a storm," she said. "That's not enough for me, Gator. That's never been enough for me. And you know that. You know *exactly* what I'm doing and you pretend you don't and you let me do it for both of us."

Irene felt as if she'd been slapped. She looked away from Dorothy and concentrated on the passing scenery out her window. "That's not fair, Dot," she said, after a moment. "But if you think I'm that hateful to you, maybe you should pull over and let me out of this truck right now."

Dorothy scoffed. "That's the best ya got? Stop being a precious little princess. Look around you. We are back at the front. We are part of this."

Dorothy suddenly downshifted and Irene looked up to see an MP step into the road and flag down the Clubmobile. He motioned to Dorothy to open the window and pointed to a muddy road through the trees.

"Red Cross!" he said. "We've got a field hospital set up down there and you need to get to it. We're seeing a lot of action and they need a lot of help."

Instead of explaining that they were coffee-and-donut specialists and not nurses, Dorothy pulled the truck off the road and headed toward the field hospital. "Okay, Irene," she said. "I don't think we're making any coffee today. Let's see how we do."

As they approached the field hospital, orderlies and nurses waved them in. Dorothy parked the *Rapid* in the mud and hopped out. Irene was right behind her. They ran into the tent and were immediately wrapped in surgical gowns and given masks.

"We're not nurses," Irene tried to explain to one of them.

"I do not care what you are," the exhausted woman said. "We need your help and you can do this. Just do what we tell you."

Wounded men were stacked up. It was a surgical assembly line—some men wept or screamed, while others never awakened. There was not time to think or to feel. They gripped soldiers' hands, helped hold down flailing legs, turned their eyes away from incisions and wounds. Irene helped with a soldier who had taken an impossible number of rounds from a German machine gun. Dorothy held a soldier's unwounded hand while the surgeons extracted ragged shrapnel from his other arm. When the emergency crush was over, they emptied the *Rapid* of all its chewing gum and cigarettes and candy and distributed it among the wounded GIs.

The Sisters headed back to the *Rapid* carrying a bottle of Bordeaux the grateful nurses had pressed on them. Neither was ready to get back in the truck just yet and they sat on the back step, leaning against the galley doors. Irene pried the cork out of the bottle and took a big swig.

Dorothy held her right hand flat toward Irene. The tremor was unmistakable. "Still shaking," she said.

Irene reached out and took her friend's hand, stilling it with her own. "I know, Dottie," she said. "I know."

—

It wasn't long before the *Rapid City* had caught up with the convoy. Light lingered long and tender above them at dusk. In spite of the battles, birds flew overhead, nested in what trees stood along the rivers. Incredibly, irrationally, flowers poured out of the ground all around them. It was as though another world forgotten was reasserting itself on the wreckage of the current failed one.

When Irene pointed out to Dorothy that they'd been riding around in the Clubmobile for nearly a year, Dorothy could only shake her head.

"Feels like we have always been in this truck, don't it, Gator?" she said. "I don't even remember what it was like before."

The *Rapid City* was festooned fore and aft with graffiti, insignia from the many outfits the Sisters had served, drawings, names. That old hulk had been well loved. Its many scrapes and dings were noble in everyone's eyes. Its bullet wounds—one on the hood, one on the side—were a big hit with every service. Soldiers had been calling it "the only rig with a Purple Heart."

And though the workload was almost impossible for two women—the Red Cross had a reason for three crew members, they'd learned the hard way—they did everything they could to stall the replacement process. They'd complained at the extra work, yes. But they had their own system for maneuvering the confines of the galley—*behind you, to your left, on the right*—and didn't believe anyone else could step into their square dance.

The Allies were focused on the final push through Germany. Hitler was missing and rumors swirled he was hiding in the mountains near Munich. For the exhausted crew of the *Rapid City*, it was service, service, service with little time to think. It was clear the war was accelerating toward its climax and everyone was a bit jittery.

Irene was not allowing herself to worry about Handyman and his lengthy silence. Mail was even more sporadic than usual, and she hadn't had time lately to write any letters herself, so it wasn't difficult to imagine a fighter pilot would have even less opportunity. Instead of worrying, she comforted herself with the promises they had made to meet in London after the war. She daydreamed about the first glimpse of his face, about wandering Paris together, about that lake in Oregon.

What she was worried about, however, was Dorothy. On the outside, her partner was as reliable as ever, happy to put on the charm for the boys and quick with the coffee and one-liners. But Irene knew that for the first time since back before Cannes, Dorothy was having bad dreams again. Irene had been startled awake on several nights when Dorothy started to whimper or cry out, when she kicked her feet. Until now her friend had usually just snored but otherwise lay at peace.

The nightmares were terrifying for Dorothy. And they were every night now. Great machines and fire. Running feet right behind her. Nude white bodies on the darkened ground. She was defenseless. Dorothy was afraid she was going mad but she had resolved never to tell anyone. Not even Irene.

—

They were halfway down the highway to Füssen when they pulled over for the night's service. It had taken the convoy almost a week to traverse those 150 miles. The fighting was fierce and no one wanted to make any mistakes.

It was that hour when dusk falls into night. The line of light still above the far horizon was purpling. Dozens of soldiers had passed through. The resupply truck had dropped off supplies. The water tanker had reloaded their tanks. Even the filthy old fuel truck had hooked them up and pumped more life into the *Rapid*. They'd stopped cooking sinkers because everything smelled and tasted like fuel whenever that hose was gurgling into their tank.

Irene was cleaning up, and Dorothy was leaning on the back counter by the sink, resting her hips against the cabinets. Soldiers outside were saying the same stuff they always said. Dorothy was a pro at shooting the breeze: *Me? I'm from Indiana, how about you? Hey nice, I've always wanted to go there—I hear the girls are pretty and the beer is cold. Aw, thank you, I don't feel pretty in this getup. Well, I'm a football gal myself, though Irene follows baseball. You saw me where? Oh yeah, I remember you. Nope, never married, but give me a holler when this is all over. Sure, I'll take a picture with ya.* They looked like Boy Scouts out there, all filthy and grizzled, their upturned faces lit orange by the galley's lights. It could have been a fairground, a traveling circus midway ablaze with old Christmas lights on drooping strings. Irene provided the music on her trusty Victrola. All they needed was a pitching game and hot dogs.

It was into this winding-down that Swede appeared. They all knew him by that name. Nobody had ever heard another. Most GIs steered clear of him. He was some kind of gangster, they whispered behind his back. He dealt in stolen booze and pilfered cigarettes. Rumor was he'd figured a way to smuggle gold out of Europe. He was a brawler who showed little mercy. Some of those ratlike losers who huddled at the edge of things counted on his protection and did his will. The only soldier Irene and Dorothy had ever seen stand up to him was Garcia, the day Swede had hurled that slur at him.

Swede came ahead slowly, helmetless, chomping on a cigar stub, his head high and tilted, with a look on his face that could have been from indigestion. But around that busted cigar he wore a rancid grin. He used his chest and gut to move through the gathered soldiers.

"Swede! Hey, Swede!" some called out.

He stopped at the edge of the galley's lights and crossed his arms, glaring at the rig. "A perfectly fine deuce-and-a-half," he boomed. "Best truck in the world. And they gotta screw it up sticking a friggin' kitchen on it."

Some guys guffawed.

"Fulla bitches," Swede added.

Dorothy pushed herself up off the cabinets and leaned on the counter, peering out to glare at this buffoon. "You again," she said. "What are you doing here?"

"Just checking out the Ladies Auxiliary, I guess." He turned to the guys, right and left, big grin. "They letting you stay in the girls' club with a haircut like that?"

"You got a problem, big man?" Dorothy called.

Irene peeked out from behind her.

"What a peckerhead," Dorothy said.

"Ignore him, Dottie. He's just a bully."

Swede stepped closer. "Your coffee's piss and your donuts are dog squat," he said. "I don't mean to be rude. But somebody had to say it."

"Oh wait," Dorothy said, snapping her fingers. "Yeah, you have a point. I peed in your cup. Sorry, I had to go. Thought you'd like it, though."

The soldiers laughed hard. Swede's face darkened.

Irene put her hand over her mouth and moved back out of sight. "Dorothy! Seriously!"

Swede stepped closer to the truck. "You should watch your mouth, tits," he said.

Dorothy barked out a laugh. "Is that supposed to crush my spirit?" She rested her chin on her fist and batted her eyelashes. "Did your momma not nurse you enough, ball sack?"

He rushed the window and tried to take a swipe at her. Irene hurried to her side, fists raised.

"Oh Jesus," he said. "Now fatty wants to fight, too."

"What did you call her?" Dorothy said.

Before Irene could grasp what was happening, Dorothy was gone. It was an explosion, a blur accompanied by a cacophony of things clanging as Dorothy dived out the serving window. A storm of coffee cups and sinkers blew out the side of the *Rapid City* all around her. Sugar and flour filled the air. The last thing Irene saw of Dorothy was the soles of her boots. Beyond the window, the soldiers bellowed.

Irene caterwauled, "Dottie! Dottie! Dottie!" She jumped out the back of the galley and ran around the truck to burst through the circle of shouting, jostling men surrounding Dorothy, who sat atop Swede, banging his fat head into the ground, his boots in the air, his fists flailing against her ribs.

"Dottie!" shouted Irene. "For God's sake, Dottie!"

"Bitch," he was grunting. "Bitch."

Irene shoved soldiers at them. "Help her!" she shouted.

"Her?" a soldier said. "Lady, she's kicking his ass."

It was true, Irene realized. Dorothy had a bloody nose and would have a black eye by morning, and she was favoring her ribs on the right side. But Swede had apparently swallowed his cigar stub. Blood and brown drool spilled out of his mouth. His nose looked broken. Dorothy was hammering both fists into his ears. He immediately stopped hitting her sides and covered his ears.

"Five bucks on Stretch," one of the GIs said.

Dorothy was weeping now. Irene stepped into the circle and put her hand on her friend's shoulder. She trembled like a wild horse.

"It's all right, sweetie," Irene said. "Come on now, let him up."

"I'll kill you!" Dorothy spit into Swede's battered face. "If you even *look* at us again!"

He grunted, his eyes wild and terrified.

"I. Am. So. Sick. Of. Stupid. Men!" She smacked him one last time.

"Crazy bitch," he gurgled.

"You have no idea how crazy this bitch is."

"Come on, now, Dottie," whispered Irene. "It's over." She pulled Dorothy off Swede.

Dorothy stood there, staring down at him. "It's never over," she said. She walked away and climbed into the galley and slammed the back door.

They all watched the serving shutters come down and heard their latches click.

Swede groaned to his knees, then struggled up, his joints audibly cracking. None of the GIs offered him a hand. He leaned and rested his hands on his thighs and spit blood. He looked at Irene and said, "She can't get away with that."

"Hey, mac," one of the boys said, "she already got away with it."

Swede didn't make eye contact with anybody. Before he faded into the darkness that had fallen hard on the camp, he said, "Tell your bitch friend I ain't done with her."

"She's done with you, though," Irene called after him.

He clanked away like a broken machine.

After he was gone, Irene said to the boys, "Am I really fat?"

They slapped her back and nudged her with their elbows and offered her cigarettes as if it were she who had trounced the thug. Truth be told, they were a little afraid of Dorothy now. So was Irene.

In the morning, when they opened up to let some sun in, they found that the guys had put flowers all around the truck, along with gifts: wine bottles, chocolates, bundles of cookies from home. Somebody had even left a bag of jelly beans.

Dorothy was so sore she let Irene drive.

38

"I COULDN'T LET him talk to you like that," Dorothy said.

Irene had gotten to the point where she almost enjoyed driving the beast—it kept her away from the darkness in her skull. "It was something to behold," she said. "What a fight! You were like a lioness."

Dorothy held a wet rag to her eye.

"I wish I could do that," Irene continued.

"I have my first shiner since fourth grade," Dorothy said.

"Did you beat up a boy then, too?"

"My brother threw a football too hard."

"My cousin Arthur knocked out my front tooth," Irene said.

"Goddarned men," Dorothy said.

Irene shifted. The road was empty and bright. "Are you okay, Dot?" she said.

Dorothy stared out the window at the landscape fluttering past. "I'm never going to be all right again," she said, shaking.

"I feel the same."

"Maybe we can go hide out at your farm."

Irene half-grinned. "Or at yours."

Dorothy fell silent and Irene was deciding to leave her in peace when they heard the sirens.

Two jeeps sped up to them. The occupants' white helmets told the women they were MPs.

"Snowtops," Irene said.

Dorothy craned around.

The jeeps wailed past on the left and slowed down in front of them, two men per vehicle. One of them waved back at them and pointed to the shoulder of the road.

"What the hell," Irene muttered, wrestling the *Rapid* over to the right shoulder. She always thought of the great wheel, so hard to control, as the helm of a pirate ship.

They both knew this was probably some bad business from the night before, with Swede.

The jeeps positioned themselves as if to block the truck should Irene decide to make a run for it. The snowtops piled out. One of them held a burp gun loosely. All four had pistols on their belts.

"Coppers will never take me alive," Dorothy said quietly, a joke that had no laughter in it.

The head MP signaled to Irene to cut the engine. She did. He directed them to dismount, which they also did.

"Identify yourselves, ladies. Driver?"

"Irene Woodward."

"Passenger?"

"Dorothy Dunford."

"You look like you had a rough night, Miss Dunford."

"You should see the other guy."

"We did," he said, with no change in expression. He pointed at Irene. "Miss Woodward, you can get back in the truck. Do not turn on the engine."

"Yes, sir."

"You outrank me, ma'am."

She smiled a little. This was perhaps the weirdest scene she'd ever experienced. "Was I speeding?"

"No, ma'am. We need to have words with Miss Dunford."

"Are you okay, Dot?"

"Don't worry, Gator."

"Please don't talk to each other," said the head MP.

Irene climbed into her seat. She left her window open so she could listen.

The coppers formed a semicircle before Dorothy.

The head MP handed her a sheaf of papers. "You want to tell us about Swede Olsson?" he said.

"He opened his dirty mouth and I stuffed my fist in it."

They started to laugh, then lit up a smoke for Dorothy, too.

"There will be an investigation. Sorry."

Dorothy stood silent, looking at the papers. "The Red Cross won't be thrilled," she finally said.

"No, ma'am, I suspect they won't."

"Will I be arrested?"

"Not right now."

"I see. There will be a trial?"

"It's complicated. We don't get complaints like this every day. Not of a dame whupping ass on a GI."

She looked at him sharply.

He put his hands up as if to stave off an assault. "Sorry I said *dame*."

"Funny," she said, taking a puff.

"I guess they might choose to send you home. Somebody will come around to investigate. They will at the very least compile a dossier. That Swede, he's a talker."

She flicked away her cigarette and seemed to shrink just a little.

"You haven't been up to any other crimes, have you?" the MP asked.

She simply stared at him. The MPs glanced at one another.

"Right," the boss said, and took a deep breath. "Get your ducks in a row. I don't know what you've gotten yourself into. But chances are, they'll find out."

"You don't want to know."

"No, I do not. This jackpot was what I was ordered to pursue, and I pursued it." He dusted off his hands. "Okay then. Mind your p's and q's, Miss Dunford. We don't want to come after you again. If you need counsel, the army will provide you with one. Or the Red Cross. But whatever happens, my advice is either head home voluntarily or face the investigation. But do not go AWOL."

"I'm not a soldier," she said. "Can they really lay that on me?"

"Let's not find out."

They walked back to their jeeps and burned U-turns and sped back the way they'd come.

Dorothy climbed back in and slumped in her seat.

"It will be all right," Irene said.

"I don't think it will."

They sat for a long while, just watching clouds move across the sky.

—

On the second night after the legendary brawl, they'd finished service and were setting up their pup tents beside the truck—fresh air for a change—when Rusty Penney walked up to them.

"Russell!" Irene cried.

He wasn't interested in hugs. "Miss Irene," he said. Then he gazed at Dorothy with baleful wonder. "Got your foot in it, Miss Dorothy."

"I guess I did."

"Not optimal."

"No."

"I told Cap Levin I'd swing by. Give you a little talkin'-to. No need for more drama."

"I'm squared away, Russell."

"I don't think the Red Cross is goin' to appreciate your boxing career."

"Surely Washington will understand," Irene said.

"Can't wait for this war to be over," Rusty said. "I look forward to fishing with the missus. Got a good little lake in the hills I go to."

"Does Holly fish?"

"What Southern girl don't? She can just lay around and look pretty if she wants to, though. I'll bring her the fish."

"You Tarzan," Dorothy said. "She cook."

He crossed his arms. "Do I need to babysit you? Or can you two keep out of trouble for a whole day?"

"We can," Dorothy said.

"I'll try to figure out what steps we can take to pull your bacon out of the fire, Miss Dorothy." He put his hands in his pockets. "I guess you gave that boy the whuppin' of his life."

"I guess I did."

He nodded and it seemed he was going to say more, but he didn't. He just sighed and walked off into the darkness.

Later, after they were bedded down, Irene awoke and realized Dorothy was gone.

—

When Dorothy appeared in the morning, she seemed manic. Her spiky hair was full of duff and straw. She was accompanied by two soldiers, Garcia and a tall silent companion. They had a bundle wrapped in black cloth, which they shielded from Irene's view. Dorothy carried a duffel bag that seemed to be full of both clothing and some kind of clanging metal. She stowed the bag inside the *Rapid*.

"Let's roll," she said to Irene. "C'mon. We've got to get some motoring done."

The two soldiers joined the duffel in the galley, carrying their bundle. Dorothy locked them in.

"What's this?" Irene asked. "Zoot?"

"Security."

"Dot?"

"Let's go. We have to get into the Alps by dark." She jumped into the driver's seat and kicked the *Rapid* to life. "Irene, get in."

Irene was simply staring at the closed galley, unsure of what was about to befall her. But she climbed in.

"We'll drop the boys off as soon as we're out of this area."

"Okay, Dottie. Whatever you say."

The truck kicked up rocks as it sped onto the main road. Dorothy was double-clutching, leaning into the wheel. She tossed Irene her famous driving map.

"Stow that for me, wouldja?" she said.

She was as one lit from within. Irene had the impression of extra heat pouring from her friend. She took the folded map and stuffed it into the satchel by her feet.

"Tell me what is going on," Irene said.

Dorothy drove on, with no reply.

Irene thought she hadn't heard her. "Dottie, tell me—"

"I heard you the first time." She turned and gave Irene a look devoid of any obvious emotion. "Swede," she said. "He knows."

"Knows what?"

"You know what."

"I do *not* know what."

"He's been talking to everybody, Gator. He's onto me."

"What are you going on about?"

"The Gray Ghosts. Come on. You know. He found out I went on patrol. And did things." She banged it into another gear. "The boys are guarding us. We're going to Füssen."

"But what are we doing in Füssen?"

"I have to get up in the mountains. The fellas arranged a contact for me."

"To do what?"

Dorothy grinned. "I'm going to run. I'm going to take the baby and run. I figure I'll just blend in with the other war refugees."

"What baby?!" shouted Irene, suddenly weeping—from fear, from confusion, from anger. "*Refugees?* Dorothy, what in God's name are you saying?"

Dorothy pulled the truck into a glade off the road. She gestured for Irene to disembark, then got out and went to the back of the galley and unlatched the door. The soldiers were sitting on the floor, braced against the heavy duffel, their bedrolls spread out beneath them, their weapons on the floor. They each had sinkers in their hands. And the black bundle Irene had observed before wiggled in the arms of Garcia, making the smallest keening wail.

"She's hungry," he said.

"This is not possible," Irene protested.

"Miss Irene," Garcia said. "That's Brewer."

"Your buddy is a great warrior," Brewer said.

"He's an Indian," Garcia said. "They talk like that sometimes."

"Stop this!" Irene cried. "What is happening?"

Garcia had used a can of evaporated milk and a little water to improvise some baby formula. He'd added a pinch of sugar. Dorothy dug in the duffel and brought out a bottle. She'd made a nipple out of the finger of a rubber glove.

"There's lots of babies in my family," Garcia reported. "I know how to do this." He got the tiny child to latch onto the nipple and begin gulping.

"Are you insane?" Irene said, unsure whom she was asking.

The soldiers crawled out of the galley, handed Dorothy the baby, and went to the woods to urinate. They came back, collected their belongings, and slung their guns over their shoulders.

"We're clear of that Swede," Brewer said. "Just remember what we told you: Füssen. The eastern road into the hills. Go ten kilometers. You'll see the signal fire on the port side of the road. They'll take you to Salzburg. You can find transport there."

"They've got a network," Garcia offered. "You'll be fine. You just gotta get to Salzburg. But there's bombing up there, so watch yourself. There's still Krauts in those hills. If you're not to Füssen by dark, you'll have to tape down your headlights—there's a blackout rule."

"We were never here," Brewer added. He had given Dorothy a leather bomber's jacket, much too big for her. "That baby will fit inside with you," he told her. "Carry her safe."

They each shook Dorothy's hand then, nodded to Irene, and started walking.

Dorothy dandled the burping child.

"This is insanity," Irene said.

Dorothy rocked the baby, made soft cooing sounds, kissed the wrinkled forehead with its feathery crown of black hair.

"How old is she?" Irene asked.

"Dunno."

"You rescued her."

"Yes, ma'am, I did."

Irene gazed upon the child.

"The way people starve in this war," Dorothy said, "she could be newborn, she could be a year old. Who can tell?"

Dorothy was breaking Irene's heart just a little.

"Irene," she said, "she's the Third Girl in the Truck. We have to help her."

—

Irene drove now and the going was slow.

Dorothy held the baby in her arms. The child was very quiet. Irene had to admit that much. She was a mild little creature, with a slightly angry monkey face. Dorothy unzipped the bomber jacket and tucked the child inside, the tiny face against her chest, then zipped the jacket back almost all the way. She looked pregnant.

"I had to get her out of there," Dorothy said. "Hear me out. I'll tell you the whole story. I've been going on patrol with those guys."

"Yes. I knew that."

"I suspected you might. But it was better that you weren't sure. In case there was blowback. And see what happened?"

"What happened?"

Dorothy took a deep breath and finally let it out. "This war. This destruction...death...the faces of these boys. The people who've lost everything. I'm just so sick of it. I'm angry. Aren't you?" she challenged Irene. "I mean, it's changing who I am. I feel hopeless, powerless, when what I need is to feel a sense of justice. I wanted to kill the enemy. I wanted to take the lives of a million bad guys. I wanted payback. And the Gray Ghosts—I wasn't sure exactly what they were doing, but I knew they were doing something, and they let me join them."

"And?"

"I stepped over the line. I killed a German officer." Dorothy put her hand over the bump of the baby's head. "I went out on long-range night patrols. And we took down a German communications unit."

"Good Lord, Dorothy. I'm speechless."

"Then just listen. After we went up to that death camp, I think I broke. I was already feeling bad. So bad. So much. And then to be there and know there was nothing I could do—that I could not help a single person. But then, last night, we found the baby. Everybody else in the abandoned boxcar was dead. But we heard her fussing. Do you get it, Irene? It can't be about killing. It has to be about living. Saving even one life. I was so useless at that terrible camp. I was just a tourist. But this one, I can help her. And I can't risk anyone taking her away from me now. She is my payback, don't you see?"

Irene glanced at her. "So instead of a death for a death, a life for a death?"

Dorothy hugged the child to her chest and smiled at Irene gratefully while Irene wrestled with the wheel. The baby fussed and Dorothy rocked her inside the jacket.

"Funny how we never forget how to do this," she said. "I used to take care of the babies at our church. I loved taking care of babies."

An uncomfortable silence followed. Irene felt trapped in a huge wrong. Caught as if in one of Dorothy's fevered nightmares. She was driving them both into some terrifying fate. She did not understand any of it, yet she drove for the love of Dottie even while frantically trying to find the argument that would make her friend come to her senses, turn around, and face whatever trouble she believed she was in.

"Do you want to know the whole story, or don't you?" Dorothy said.

"I do."

39

Many guys in camp knew about her connection to the Gray Ghosts, Dorothy explained. It had been whispered for months. But anyone who knew covered for them by spinning yarns about Dorothy loving poker and sitting in on as many games as she could. Nobody much cared. After all, the flow of scuttlebutt was robust and far-reaching. Rumors, tall tales, and full-on lies circulated through every camp, every battalion, every squad. Ghost stories, monster sightings, tales of swashbuckling daring, encounters with Nazi evil, brilliant smuggling, sexual exploits. Bullsh was rampant. But once the dustup occurred, somebody—Swede—suddenly cared very much.

The Gray Ghosts had come to her last night on their way to a town a few miles south. They wanted to see if she was all right, and to learn whether the MPs had mentioned them in their recent confrontation with her.

No, she said, and gave them the all clear.

They knelt a safe distance from Irene and the others snoring in their half clusters of shelters. They were on their way, they told her, to help women being held against their will by a collaborator mayor. They weren't to execute him. But he needed to be delivered to headquarters by dawn. Uncle Sam had a good idea that the war was about to collapse on itself—American victory felt assured. And the American forces were moving in clandestine fashion to apprehend as many of these traitors as possible before they discovered they were targets. This mayor was thought to have valuable information on others worse than he.

Dorothy volunteered immediately.

The Ranger shook his head. There was too much heat, he said. But the rest of the Ghosts spoke in favor of Dorothy and he relented.

—

The mayor was snoring, quite drunk. His wife ran naked from the bedroom. They tackled her and gagged her. Half of the squad fast-walked the mayor out of his house and into the woods, where they would rendezvous with a truck several miles away. Dorothy went with Brewer and Garcia to the train yard. The guards had already fled. Everyone knew what was coming. They were suddenly civilians again, rushing to Poland or Austria, or fading into the crowds in Hamburg and Munich, where they would deny having been soldiers for the rest of their days.

The women in the locked cars cried out, coughed, banged on the doors. The soldiers began to throw the door levers and slide them open. Lifeless bodies fell out. But some within were alive and frantic to escape and jumped down to run into the dark.

The woman with the baby was in the third car. When they opened the doors, a tide of stench flowed out. Urine and vomit and worse. The car was horribly still. Garcia used his flashlight to scan the inside—it looked like piles of old laundry. Dorothy and Brewer climbed up, reeling from the cold fluids they knelt in. There was a sound, the only sound, from the corner where the woman lay. Her face was pressed against the rough wood.

Dorothy went to the woman but she was dead, too.

"I heard something, though," Brewer said.

Garcia, whose back was to the open door, swept his rifle back and forth before him in the dark. "Let's get rollin'," he said.

"Wait," Brewer said. He turned the woman's body back toward them.

The baby was wrapped in a shawl. They had heard her congested attempts to breathe.

"Hello, little one," Brewer said. He scooped the child up and tried to hand it to Dorothy.

"I cannot," she said, shaking her head. "Not me, honey."

"You gotta do it."

The dead mother's head was shaved. Dorothy covered her face with the soiled shawl that had been swaddling the baby.

"Come on now, Stretch," said Brewer. "We save her or we leave her. Choose."

He covered all but a sliver of his flashlight lens with his hand and switched it on, so that only a narrow gleam hit the child. Her hands were so tiny. Her little ears looked like small pink seashells. And she had so much hair for an infant. A name was stitched there in the shawl.

Dorothy swung a little, rocking the baby back and forth, looking into the pale little face, those pale eyes staring up at her as if astounded. Brewer helped her down from the car.

Garcia turned to her. "What you got there?" he said.

She showed him as Brewer jumped down to join them.

"Mira no mas," Garcia said. "You a mama now, loca."

"What do I do?"

"We beat feet," Garcia said. "We gotta get out of here. If I was you, I'd zip that little one inside your coat. We got to make tracks in case those Kraut guards come back."

The three were strangely relaxed on their way back to the camp, sharing family stories about the babies in their own lives.

When the baby began to fuss in Dorothy's jacket, Brewer took her up in his giant hands. "Call me Uncle Duane," he murmured and his deep rumble put her back to sleep.

40

THEY HAD DRIVEN all day on winding roads, more than two hundred miles from their camp, skirting Nuremberg and Augsburg and arriving at last in the Alpine foothills. With darkness nearing and their gas running low, Irene pulled over. They left the baby swaddled on the floor of the truck and stepped out to pour fuel into the tank from the front-mounted gas cans. The truck drank three of them.

"Just like your baby," Irene said.

Dorothy knew she was trying to be a good sport, and she loved her for it. "She wants to live, Irene."

When they finished with the gas, Dorothy began taping down the headlights, so that only a sliver of light would be able to escape.

"I'll be blind as I drive," Irene complained.

"You heard Garcia," said Dorothy. "Better than being shot by a sniper."

They climbed back aboard and Dorothy took the child and zipped her into her bomber jacket again.

"I have to do this," Dorothy said. "You know I do."

"I don't think you do."

"I can't go to prison. I just can't."

"Why would you go to prison?"

"I can't. If I do, what happens to this darling girl?"

"Dot, look, someone will take care of her. And I'm sorry to say it, but honestly she's half dead. It might be better to get her to a hospital."

"Go to hell, Irene."

The road up the mountain was rough. Terrified, Irene leaned over the wheel as far as she could, squinting into the slim bar of light cast before them.

"I can't see anything," she said.

"There will be a small fire on the left side," Dorothy said. "Be careful when you pull over. They warned me it's right at the lip of the slope."

"What are you planning on doing?"

"Do you really want to know?"

"Yes."

"What if they catch you? Isn't it better for you not to know?"

Irene, focused on the dark road, didn't respond. The *Rapid City* shuddered, hitting ruts in the hard-packed dirt. Pines loomed around them like huge black creatures.

"All right," Dorothy said. "There is a guide. From the Underground. He feeds the Gray Ghosts their prime targets. He's a fixer, I guess. But he also gets people to safety. Until now, from the Germans. He'll get us out. Me and the baby."

"Just like that."

"Best I can do."

"Dot, this is crazy."

"I'm not stupid. I know it won't be easy. But this little nugget and I can get free. I'll find my way back home. I'll look you up. This is not goodbye. Long Island, right? That little farm."

"That is the most ridiculous—"

It was the last thing she said.

A violent bang bounced the truck three times on its left tires. Irene had hit a bomb crater in the dark. She struggled with the wheel. Dorothy shouted once. Their last bounce catapulted the truck into the air again—when it came down, the left berm of the road gave way and they pitched over the side.

The *Rapid City* slammed into an ancient pine. Dorothy curled herself and wrapped her arms tight to make a fortress of her body for the baby. Something cracked against her head and she heard no more. The galley detonated and sent cascades of ruin flying down the slope. The truck rolled in the air. Irene flew out the door. The truck hit the ground again and exploded. Lindens and oaks became torches. Tornadoes of oily smoke writhed as the tires burned.

41

Irene awoke to screaming.

How odd, she was on her hands and knees. In mud. Was she in Mattituck? Who was screaming? She was suddenly in terrible pain and realized it was her own voice. She was in a cold pool of her own blood.

She could not get herself to snap out of it. To stop this screaming. But she knew enough to look above, to the road, where flashlight beams cut back and forth and downslope. How long she had been unconscious she did not know. She heard the voices of men up there starting down, heard their equipment clattering. And still she could not stop screaming. She was drawing her assassins right to her, yet her body refused to be silent. When the soldiers were close enough to blind her with their lights, she was able to clench her teeth.

"Jesus," a man said, "it's a goyl."

She collapsed. *New York*. New York had come for her.

The men didn't know what to do or how to help her. They all crowded around to get a look.

"Jeepers," one kid said. "She's all tore up."

"Lady, ya gotta relax. A'right? We're here. We got ya now. Don' worry, doll. We won't let ya down."

"Medic!" another shouted. "We need a medic here!"

"Ain't no bad guys gonna touch ya now, lady."

The men stooped to her and took hold of her tenderly and pried her out of the mud.

She shouted about Dot. Dot. Dot.

They didn't know who Dot was. But everyone could see the burning pyre of the *Rapid City* a couple of hundred yards below, setting off the surrounding trees like firebombs. Its heat reached them even here. They looked at one another and shook their heads. Even if they could reach her, Dot was already a goner for sure. They set up a perimeter around Irene in case any hostiles had been attracted by all this noise.

"Medic!"

"Got it!" the medic called as he slid down the slope.

He inadvertently kicked pebbles all over Irene, who was lying on her back shivering in shock now, her eyes rolling wild, dark red from stomach to feet. The medic whistled softly, then cut apart what was left of her trousers. The other soldiers mostly looked away. Her skin was terribly white beside the deep red of what was beneath it.

By flashlight the medic poured sulfa powder into the rips in her legs and the red grimace that cut into her abdomen. "There now, there now," he whispered.

"Oh no, Loot, is that a bone?" said one of the men.

"Quiet now," he replied. He looked around the circle. "Pray, boys. Pray."

He wrapped her and wrapped her with all the bandages he had. He called for a shirt, which he cut apart to wrap around the wrapping he had affixed to her legs. Then he pressed a pad against her torn gut. Everything turned pink, then deep red in the middle. She was crying, rolling her head in the mud, calling out to Dot.

"Don't bleed out, ma'am," the medic ordered. He tied a tourniquet on the worst thigh, up near her groin. He pulled his only morphine setup out of his pack and plunged the needle into her. "Try to rest."

In a few minutes, the drug put her into a snoring sleep.

"Now what do we do?" said one of the GIs, staring up the steep slope.

They didn't have any kind of stretcher. They were on foot patrol. There was no vehicle waiting up top to transport this woman to the rear. Krauts surely lurked.

The medic stood and started to unbutton his battle blouse. "Gimme the rest of your shirts," he said. "We're making a sling."

He began to tie their shirts together, knotting their sleeves and tails, and the other soldiers joined in. When they had finished, they lifted Irene gently onto it, and the medic laid an extra shirt over her like a blanket. The final shirt he wrapped around her legs, tightly, in case she kicked or they dropped her. But every man there knew he would not drop her.

"Time to hump," the medic said.

Two men took her upon their backs, with two more behind them, clutching the makeshift sling in their fists, each being as tender with her as he could. Oh Jesus in heaven, but that slope was steep. And they were carrying their weapons as well as her dead weight. They rasped and panted as if she weighed two hundred pounds.

"This is what boot camp was for, boys," one of them encouraged the group.

The medic spelled a guy who was ready to puke from the climb. It took twenty minutes, but they topped out on the damaged road and laid Irene down for a minute of gasping, their hands on their knees as they stared down into her ivory white face.

"Boys," said somebody. "We've got a six-mile hike ahead of us."

"At least it's downhill," said another.

They rotated sling carriers and picked Irene back up, bending to the weight of her, then set off walking.

—

The field hospital was a fresh nightmare. She never awoke, so it was simple for the sawbones to flush out the wounds as the little flags of her flesh waved in the saline. They pushed tissue back into the openings, wired her bones together, stitched her flesh, injected her, and ran an IV into her arm. Nurses sponged the filth off the rest of her.

She dreamed. Dorothy, Handyman, Garcia, Patton, Ellie, Holly, Grannie Effie, Mother, Aunt Eva. They passed her like falling stars as her bed drifted down through the sky.

42

Irene lay in the recovery tent for the rest of April. The nurses and the orderlies and the doctors peered grimly at her chart. It was a miracle she was alive, they told her. She never found out who the heroes were who had climbed down there to save her. That was the real miracle, she thought. As for being alive—was that a mercy? The thoughts in her head told her no. She made a vow to never, not once, think of that baby. She could not ever think of that baby. And Dot. Darling Dot. There would never be any forgiveness for what she had done.

She could smell her wounds, which reeked of expired meat in a country butcher's abattoir. And she stank of sweat and grime. There were no words for the pain that twisted her on the bed. After the surgeons had ruined her legs further with more brutal stitches and protruding steel pins near her knees and a shunt drooling pus out of her thigh, she could not even stand, much less walk. She often refused to eat. She was a ghost. But she was also the only female patient, and was disgusted that some of the men flirted and actually made passes at her even in her awful state.

She'd been put in the tent closest to the surgical suite, so that orderlies and nurses could check on her constantly. She was their mascot, though she didn't talk. For a few days, they thought she had brain damage. Tears rolled out of her eyes, fat and slow. She didn't respond to either happy chat or serious questions for the first week she was awake. The day she finally spoke made the orderlies rejoice.

The one named Darrell asked her what her name was.

"Water, please," she croaked.

"Funny name."

She did not smile.

—

Though the surgical tent was walled off by sandbags, from her bed Irene could still hear the screams and the bone saws and the hideous wetness. The medics put a record player in the tent, but it didn't cover the sounds. In fact it made her cringe, as the records could have been playing in the *Rapid City*. *Buck up, Gator,* she told herself, *you hardly got a scratch.*

She was separated from her wounded neighbors in the tent by a curtain hung on noisy metal rings attached to a steel frame. They called her Miss America and Greer Garson, certain that she was a fashion model or starlet, though they had never laid eyes on her. She still hadn't told them her name, but they heard her voice and her sobbing and that was enough.

"Cheer up, doll!" gruff voices called. "We'll go dancin' when we get out of here!"

Pain, she learned, was all-consuming, as if the earth and the sky were made of it, as if the wind itself were nothing but moving agony. It taught you something new every day. It was a wisdom she would do anything to escape.

A swiftly passing orderly made enough of a breeze that the pins rising from her inflamed flesh sang with shocks. The sheets on her wounds were too heavy for her to bear. When a nurse tried to cleanse her with a sponge and hot water, everything howled as if it had a voice. But there was always Dot. Dot and the child. An agony far worse than the torment of her bones. Even the thought of reuniting with Handyman would never be able to touch this. She begged for morphine whenever a corpsman or nurse checked on her.

Once, she yelled at the nurse who denied her: "I had one friend in the world, and I killed her! I can't...let me sleep!"

Some of the corpsmen feared her. When her hair stood on end, she looked to them like a witch.

Darrell brought her another dose and, when she started to snore, tucked her in.

But whenever she surfaced, it was into the same old pestilence. The lovely morphine dreams proved to be lies. There was no walking on the shore with Dorothy. There was no drive to the Grand Canyon in the *Rapid City*. No horse ride into the mountains with her cowboy. No cocktail party at Ellie's Chicago apartment on the Lake Michigan shore. Russell and Holly did not make her fried chicken.

She'd awaken again to the odors of bedclothes turning sour. The groans and snoring and incessant bullshit of her tentmates. Her legs were elevated at the knees with pillows. The surgical pins that held her together were bright red where they entered her skin, and her thighs were dusted with sulfa powder. She tried never to look. Never to move.

"This is not a life," she said.

"Lady," the grunt on the other side of her privacy curtain said, "it's what we got."

Red Cross nurses stopped by her bed three times a day with bedpans. It was humiliating. She could not believe the levels of shame this place had bestowed upon her. She knew the men could hear what she was doing. The nurses tossed on a record to cover for her. It was helpful. They called her Cousin.

"Morphine?" she'd ask.

"If you don't watch out," her nurse said, "you're going to have a problem."

It was the first time Irene had laughed. A hideous, rasping snarl—her mouth opening as if in a scream.

—

The medics had rigged a half tent above her lower body—a sheet raised over her on a frame. She was naked below the waist under it, with a modesty cloth across her privates. The orderlies moved her up and down when she needed to change positions. A young Belgian nun appeared one morning with a pan of warm water and shaved her legs for her, avoiding the ruinous wounds. It made Irene weep with gratitude. Above her, they had constructed a shiny metal frame that she could reach with her hands and use to heave herself up from the bed a little, though the pain made her cry out.

Days on days.

The tent held twelve wounded soldiers. She was the thirteenth occupant. The spot for a fourteenth cot was taken up by a night-watch desk, though there weren't enough staff to man it every night. A wood-burning stove squatted halfway down the room. But the nights were getting warmer anyway—rain instead of snow. The tent was raised out of the mud on wooden pallets. Irene could smell the latrines now, though worse was when the grunts burned the waste with gasoline.

She had nothing to read or look at except the drooping gray-white canvas above her—even its stains had no interesting pattern that she could imagine into a story or landscape. The only thing she had to amuse herself was a Gideon Bible that a visiting sky pilot had dropped off. Each GI got one, even the ones who were dying or in a coma.

She let the Bible fall open at random. A message from above. *Do your bit, Lord,* she thought, then peeked at it. From Psalm 35: *When my prayers returned to me unanswered, I went forth mourning.* She closed the Good Book. "Thanks a lot, God." It was nearly funny.

She couldn't reach her satchel on the floor under her bed. It was frankly a mystery to her how it had gotten there in the first place. Surely one of the GIs who rescued her had found it? She didn't know. It felt like its own miracle. She knew Dot's map lay within, folded up, though she could not look at it. Or at her own notebooks. She didn't care to see what she had written, and she was afraid of what she might write now.

Dorothy would be alive in her notebooks, warts and all, and that proximity would be too much to endure. The Sisters of the *City* were so close, such friends, that they could hate each other occasionally. They could fight. Insult each other. Mock each other. But now Irene could not bear to find anything critical of Dottie. She wanted nothing to do with the wretched, spoiled creature who had written those words.

At night she listened to moans and snoring in the dark. The man on the other side of her curtain touched himself. She could hear his harsh breathing, the squeaking of the cot. She imagined her mother's outrage, her aunt's utter shock. To Irene, it was interesting, though odd. Sex. That was gone now. She could not imagine feeling those things ever again. She hated the thought of sex. Not sex, really. More so, the horror she felt for her body now. How would Hans receive her? Oh God—he would be kind. But what lover wants kindness? What lover thinks kindness is in any way as precious as a swoon, as shaking passion, or fever? She would see the look of pity in his eyes. She'd see him wince. She never wanted to look at herself in a mirror, much less reveal herself to him. She put her fingers in her ears.

—

She was finally allowed food and they took her off fluids: she mostly insisted on beef-and-barley soup. She found every other thing nauseating. The Red Cross girls, though, got her to accept pieces of chocolate. "It's a miracle drug," they told her.

She indulged in endless half-awake dreams of Hans coming into the tent, still looking like Gary Cooper, and covering her face in kisses, lifting her tenderly and carrying her out into the sun. She would be wrapped in gauze sheets, modest and hidden, with only the gift of her hazel eyes and her lips visible.... It was ridiculous, adolescent, yet she blushed, she shivered. He would sing the "Irene" song to her. He would take her away in his aeroplane. To the ranch where they would ride horses.

Most days, though, the morphine made her sleep in fever dreams. Swollen colors and rushing wind. If she didn't have the drug in her veins, she dreamed of fire. She dreamed of the wreckage on the mountain setting the trees ablaze. She saw broken records burning. When she was awake, she often wasn't sure if she was dreaming.

43

Once the doctors and nurses finally got her name out of her, they called her Silent Irene. She turned her head when army officers patted her shoulder awkwardly and posed for news pictures with captions like "In This Man's War, the Gals Were Heroes Too!"

Even when Martha Levin came to deliver a Red Cross service pin and a fresh Group F Clubmobile patch to her, Irene just clutched her hand and wept, holding the captain's knuckles to her forehead. She had managed to say one trivial thing—"Are you still driving *Mighty Martha*?"—before melting down.

Captain Levin sat on the edge of her bed and let her cry. "You had a rough break," she said, then bent closer to her. "You'll be Stateside soon, Woodward. It's all over. You did a good job. We won."

Hoarse from the sobbing, her breath bitter, Irene managed to croak, "I'm sorry about the truck. I am so sorry."

"It's behind you now. Think about home. That's all you have to do. Come see me if there's another war. You could be a group captain." Captain Levin stood and gave her a salute. "I'm going home, too," she said. "Look me up."

And then she was gone.

—

Irene had no idea what time it was. Late. So very late, she knew that much. Outside of time. The eternity of 3:00 a.m. The entire camp was silent. She could hear the meadow breeze outside, the fussing of some night bird. Her tent was thick with snoring, the muttered complaints of the dreamers. They were each as alone as she was, surrounded by people who could give no comfort. Had she been dreaming of Mother? Mother and her heated brick for the foot of the bed, her sweet bourbon toddy. She remembered asking, "Mother, could you just put your hand on my brow?" But it had all collapsed in echoes and frightened her awake. She was certain that she was awake now, because of the pain. Didn't pain fade away in dreams? She felt tears on her face. One doesn't feel tears in a dream, surely. One doesn't lie yearning for morphine.

She was aware of herself lying upon a dark sphere of rock spinning in eternal blackness. Hans had said to her, late at night in that Cannes hotel, "What if the whole solar system is just an electron? An atom? What if the earth is just a particle in God's little toe?" She had actually smiled a little in the dark then. Handyman with his wide-eyed ideas. "I'll always be around," he'd whispered when she wept. And how could she not weep? He was going to fling himself into the sky again in days. He could disappear in smoke and she might never know. "Not me, Miss Irene. We don't ever die. You'll see. And if I do, I'll wait around for you. We don't need no planes where we're going. I can teach you how to fly." And then he pulled away the sheets and they showed each other, again.

She might have nodded off. She didn't know. Her eyes opened once more upon darkness. Maybe she had died. She looked into the night for Dorothy. She imagined Dear Dottie would appear in a glow and forgive her.

Then she heard a guitar strumming outside. His voice floated into the tent: *Good night, Irene, good night, Irene, I'll see you in my dreams.*

"Hans?" she whispered. "Hans?" She cried it out now. She didn't care who she awakened. "Here! I'm in here!"

And then he was there. She didn't trust her perceptions—time was slipping. But he had to be there. He was pressed against her. She could smell his cologne.

"Shh now, darling. I've got you." His arms took her up.

"I have missed you so," she whispered.

"I only have a few minutes, Irene. I just came to tell you to sleep. How you gonna get better if you don't sleep?"

"No. No, you're here, I can't..."

He eased her hair off her face. "Sure you can. You have to. I'll be here." He pulled back her sheets and bent to her wounds.

"No," she said. "It's awful."

He kissed her where the skin was reddest and swollen, then came back up to her and embraced her from the side, his body stretched along the length of hers and hanging off the end of her cot. They laughed and he whispered, "I'll be back."

Her eyes were heavy. *No,* she told herself. *No. We are not falling asleep now, Gator!*

"I'll be with you," he said. "Don't worry. Handyman will help you through."

Her eyes kept closing. *Damn this morphine.*

He snapped his fingers and made a rhyme: "It's what he do. Boop-boop-ba-doo."

Irene, you mustn't fall asleep.

As she drifted into sleep, she reached out her hand one last time to touch him, but felt only the cool breeze of his passing.

44

THEY STROLLED AROUND the raspberry patch, carrying baskets filled with berries. Irene wore a straw hat her aunt had given her. Grannie Effie wore a huge sun hat that cast her face in deep shadow. Both of them wore canvas gloves. The bushes were alive with bees. The unripe berries looked like wax, while the ripe ones burned with color. An inordinate number of butterflies drifted down like great flakes of multicolored snow.

"So many hummingbirds this year," Grannie Effie said.

Irene's hands shook. They paused to watch the butterflies explore the bushes.

"Don't go out on the main road," Grannie Effie warned. "There's a Panzer parked beyond the trees."

"I have to learn to walk again," Irene said.

They ate as many raspberries as they put in the baskets.

"Just float, dearie," Grannie Effie said.

"I feel like I'm dying."

"We are all dead until we awaken, child."

Irene jumped. Her eyes were open. Shouting and laughter had erupted outside the tent. She strained until she had sat up.

"War's over!" somebody shouted.

"Is it a dream?" she said, to no one, to everyone.

Lots of running. Lots of hooting. The guys around her were struggling to get out of bed. But she was oddly unmoved. Her war had already ended. Now it was going to be better, though. Handyman would come back for her. She would fly to the great American West and soar over the mountains with her man.

When Dorothy entered her mind, she jerked away from the thought.

The shouting and the car horns and the music outside made her realize suddenly that her tent was in a large complex. She had imagined they were standing alone in some forlorn pasture, flanked, perhaps, by the surgical tent. She'd imagined a few battered ambulances abandoned in the barley. But she was actually in a village of wounds. A canvas town spread out in some German field. Somebody was blowing a trumpet.

Her favorite orderly, Darrell, came along. He had recently revealed to her that he was not only a Cajun but also a serious poet, which had made her quite fond of him.

"Miss Irene," he said. "*Ça va* today? It's a good day."

"He came for me yesterday!" she said. "Where is he?"

"Who?"

"Handyman."

"What handyman?"

"My sweetheart. A fighter pilot."

Damn that dope, he thought. "That's good, then," he said.

"Darrell." Her voice was rough. "Have you any—"

"Morphine? *Cher,* you get that in another hour. You know how we do. You don't want that handyman to find you in a state, do you?" He pulled her chart off the end of the cot, added his initials to a column. "But there is somebody here says he knows you. Maybe it's him."

For a moment, her heart burst inside her. "A pilot?"

"I don' know, me," he said, giving her his best Cajun accent because it created rare smiles on her face. "How you can tell?"

"Is he a patient here?"

"I don't think so, no. He's a scruffy fellow. Just pulled in."

He's back! No, it couldn't be. Oh Lord, it's him.

She was embarrassed about her appearance. He couldn't find her like this. Oh no—she didn't want him in the tent by daylight. So squalid. She could smell her own armpits. But before she could say more, Darrell was gone again.

She listened to the ruckus outside but couldn't hear Handyman's voice in all the tumult. Once the jubilation had subsided, it was a typical morning at the tent hospital. Trucks were moving past. Men raising hell. Life went on. It was hard to process all this sound. She wished for a window. She didn't deserve a window, though. But what if...? It wasn't him. But maybe.

The tent flap at her end opened. Light and cool fresh noise entered. She heard boots stomping off mud, a heavy footfall on the boards and a wooden creak and Darrell's laugh. The other guy coughed. They appeared through her curtain.

Darrell winked and left.

The soldier had his arm in a sling. A patch on his eye. Otherwise, he looked the same. It was Garcia.

"Oh," she said. "It's Zoot."

"Well, hell, I'm happy to see you, too."

"You look well, Zoot," she said. Her face burned with disappointment.

"All reet, complete, and sugar sweet!" he proclaimed, pulling off his cap. "Just wanted to check on you. 'Fore they ship me out."

"Thank you for thinking of me."

"You know it. Claro que si, weesa. Ya sabes."

"Have you seen Rusty Penney?"

"Nel," he said, which in his lingo meant *no*.

"I never did know what you were saying, Zoot."

"I ain't saying shit."

They studied each other, each trying to hide the shock they felt.

She was gray, Zoot noticed. Her eye sockets were almost black. She looked like one of them sugar skulls down in Nogales. "Hey," he said, breaking the silence. "You can see the mountains out there. They still got snow."

"I haven't been outside." She looked down at her legs, made a little regretful face, and squinted up at him. "What happened to your eye?"

He sat down at the end of her cot, after asking for permission with his eyebrows. "Shrapnel," he said. "Just a splinter. The big pieces got my arm. I ain't be pretty no more, but I can still play the piano when I heal up."

"You're still pretty," she said.

"Yeah, you're right. Even with half a face I'm two times the man of any one of these guys."

They sat in companionable silence.

"Listen," he finally said. "When I heard what happened, I joined in on the search. Up at the crash site. You know, lookin' for Stretch. We would never have just left her there."

She would not meet his gaze.

"We found nothin'. Everything was burned so bad, Irene. There was nothing but ashes. We couldn't tell one thing from another. I don't know how you got out, but you're lucky. No way anybody survived that fire."

Her only acknowledgment was a nod. He started to apologize but she reached out and put a finger on his lips. "I'll tell you one thing," she said. "My legs definitely won't be as pretty as your face."

"I don't know about that." He patted his shirt pocket, looking for cigarettes and coming up empty. "Heard you were here," he said. "As soon as they finished bandaging me up, I got a ride out here to see you."

A full minute might have passed before she said, "Here I am."

He stared at the floor, the old bloody boot prints on the planks, dried brown, and wondered if it was her blood. "No prob," he said. "Man. This whole thing's been a bitch, ain't it?"

"I would say so, yes."

"I'm glad it's over."

Again only a nod from her.

"Irene, you got me through that, uh, thing. Back at the bad place—"

"Shhhh." She put her hand on his arm.

Neither of them could say *Buchenwald* out loud yet.

After they were quiet again for a minute, she said, "I'm sorry."

"'Bout what?"

They gave each other melancholy grins.

"Yeah, it's the shits, ain't it?" he said. "This whole mess we been in."

"Why, yes, it has been. The. Absolute. Shits."

Her cursing made him grin. His hand went to his breast pocket again.

"Zoot. There are cigarettes in my drawer."

He dug into the little nightstand. Stale Luckies. He pulled his Zippo out of his pocket, snicked it open, fired up the end of the coffin nail.

Irene could hear the tobacco burn. When he offered her a drag she shook her head. "Thanks ever so, though."

He let luxurious ribbons of smoke curl up from his nostrils. It suddenly smelled delicious, overwhelming the stink of bandages and urine.

"Actually," she said, "I will have a puff."

He handed the cig over and looked at her leg tent. "Sorry that happened to you."

She handed the Lucky back. "So much to be sorry about," she said.

"You don't need to tell me," he said, and took a puff.

She held up her fingers. He tucked the cigarette between them again and nodded at her to finish it. Tears burned her eyes. Kindness, Jesus. The smoke fled from her lips as she tried to keep her composure. She turned her face away. *Don't be dramatic,* she scolded herself.

Garcia reached out and touched her wrist, then snagged a fresh cigarette from her pack and clamped it between his teeth. "It's okay, princess," he said around the butt. "We'll be Stateside soon. You'll be a movie star. I'm gonna be a wrestler. Mexican Gorgeous George. Catch you in Hollywood."

Irene pulled the sheet up to her face. She wrung the edges in her fists and covered her mouth. She began to shake.

Alarmed, Garcia went to the tent flap and tossed his butt out into the mud. He whistled for Darrell and waved him back, then returned to her side, snuck the pack of Luckies into his pocket, and laid hands on her. She was rigid as a plank. "Hey," he said. "Hey. It's gonna be all right."

Irene felt the cot coming unmoored and beginning to drift in the current. It bobbed beneath her. She moved her hands over her eyes. Zoot's voice was echoing now. He was talking. He was always talking.

"Miss Dorothy, right? Hey look, she's in a better place, I'm sure..." He paused and stared at the floor a minute. "I gotta find that Smitty and tell him. Remember Smitty? He was sweet on Stretch."

"You know Smitty?"

"I know just about everybody," Garcia said. "This is gonna really mess poor Smitty up after what happened to his friend. You heard about that, right?"

Irene, growing weary, wasn't really listening. "What friend?" she said.

"You know. That cowboy. The one that won your talent show back at Glatton. You know that guy?"

Irene couldn't speak. She just stared at Garcia with wide eyes. "What are you saying? What?"

Garcia was confused by her expression. "Yeah, that poor guy's missing in action," he said. "But it's been a while now. They say he got shot down sometime after the Bulge. Smitty told us when they found what was left of his plane there was no trace of him. Just his crusher cap in the wreckage. Smitty's pretty broken up about it."

Garcia immediately regretted having said anything when he saw the look of utter horror on Irene's face. He wasn't sure what he'd said, but something was going very wrong.

"What!" she shouted. It was not a question. "He was in my bed last night! Right *here*!" Noise filled her ears now. She put her fists to her temples.

Garcia looked around. Nobody was coming to his rescue. She'd gone Section Eight. She was in the clouds, man. "Oh jeez," he said. "I'm sorry, Irene. Was he your boy? Cowboy's a survivor.... I'm sure folks were wrong, he probably parachuted.... Them stalags are opening up now. We'll find him in one. He musta made it. Sure, he's gonna come back. For real."

Her panicked scream drove Garcia out of the tent. His hands shook and he made a sound like a whinny and backed away between the tents with his hands over his ears.

45

DARRELL SAT AT the foot of her bed. "I understand, *cher.*"

"Do you?"

"I think I do, yes. And I apologize."

"But you couldn't know."

"I could. I should know."

"The baby. I think that's the worst part."

"*Mon Dieu.* Thanks for telling me all of that, Irene." He stared at the dirty floor.

"I think I'm going to be sad," Irene said. She put her hand over her eyes and lay there, still as a statue.

Darrell crept away.

—

For supper that night, Irene requested Uncle Will's favorite breakfast. "Army eggs." Two pieces of white toast with circles cut through their middles, a single egg fried in each. With bacon. They stared at her. She got a metal plate full of hash.

She fell asleep and dreamed that General Patton was kneading her poor legs through the blanket. When she came to, all the horror she had thought she could tamp down or muscle away would no longer be denied. The dam finally and completely ruptured, and she started shouting, "Hans! Hans! Hans!"

Darrell and the nurses rushed in. Nobody knew what to do. Darrell kept shouting, "What's the matter with your hands?"

She kicked and kicked and felt the abused flesh of her thighs tearing. One of the nurses slapped her. They dared not pour any more sedatives into her. A surgeon came in and loomed over her.

"Hans!" she cried.

The other patients in the tent grew sick of it in short order. They whistled, catcalled, cursed. Darrell went over to get the men quieted down.

"Goddamned monkey house!" the surgeon snorted, throwing his hands up and stomping away.

All these foreign faces terrified her. She wanted to shout: *Don't be angry with me!* She desperately needed to be home.

Darrell sat on the edge of her bed, not saying anything, just being with her, until she finally fell back, exhausted. That healed her just a little.

When she awoke, her mind was clear. She was ashamed of having lost control. It was humiliating to have been bawling like some abandoned calf, hitching and sobbing. She didn't see Darrell again and regretted that his last sight of her was so terrible. Worse, she hadn't thanked him for his kindness.

—

Suddenly, though she could not yet get out of bed, much less walk, the army was shipping her away. Flying her to France.

The surgeon from the night before came in to tell her she was going home. "Try to get this war out of your mind," he said. "Frankly, you've got shell shock, what we call *battle fatigue* with the fellas. Give yourself a few months to get squared away."

She wanted to protest: *There is nothing wrong with me a little relaxation and aspirin won't fix. Perhaps a stiff drink or two. I am a Woodward, dear boy. Who might you be?* But she said nothing.

He lit a pipe and walked out of her tent.

All she could think of was going away to a therapeutic clinic that would get her steady on her legs again so that she could ship home. And yet she had no desire to return home. She knew she had no words that could explain any of this to anyone. If they hadn't been here, they wouldn't understand a word of it. Besides, none of them deserved the story anyway. She could imagine them thinking, *Isn't she something*. Thinking, *So dramatic*. Thinking, *Oh, come now—typical Irene*.

Except there was no Irene left now. There was just some ghostly creature who had somehow destroyed everything she held dear. She couldn't bear the thought—being expected to offer thrilling tales, witty aperçus, travel highlights. She still had her notebooks and Dot's driving map. They remained untouched in the satchel, covered in dirt and pine needles.

Dorothy never appeared in her dreams anymore. Irene wanted her to come back and walk with her on the shore again, ride with her again in the *Rapid City* through some wide-open vista on an endless ribbon of highway under a dome of sky. But her friend had taken herself away even from Irene's dreams.

She was ready to go. The nurses had cautiously pulled a skirt over her legs. Someone had scrounged up a fluffy pale blue sweater. They brushed her hair and she tied a scarf over it. That would have to do. The Belgian nun, of all people, brought her a small hand mirror and some lipstick and powder. They laughed over it, the nun blushing. Irene saw her face for the first time since that night. She was thin. Her cheeks were hollow. Her eye sockets shadowed and gray. The powder was Chanel. My, the nun had good taste. Irene patted it on her face until she looked a little less like a vampire. *That's not too gruesome,* she thought. Dear Dottie would have mocked her. She applied lipstick—it was coral pink. *My God, Gator, you almost look alive*.

She was embarrassed that something as trivial as makeup made her feel cheerful.

There was an air transport coming. The staff was going to transfer her to a stretcher. She suddenly wanted her satchel clutched to her chest. She wondered where her footlocker was. She realized everything inside her trunk was sacred. Dried flowers from Holly and Rusty's wedding. Her sketches. Photographs. The berets—Dorothy had wanted her to keep them both together. So many things that she couldn't remember what was stuffed in there. All of them treasures that she dearly wanted. They were the only things that would let her know that she had really been in the war. The only things not scars.

Although she was worried about going home, she found herself delirious to return. First France, then New York. She felt a stirring of excitement, or hope, for the first time since that night. When they came for her with her stretcher, though, they told her she had one last duty to perform.

46

"BITE THE BULLET, Irene," Irene said out loud, and drew a deep breath.

They had two soldiers in another tent. These men, well, they had been burned, the nurse said. A horrific mishap with flamethrowers. And they were dying, you see. They were not going to live. That much was understood. And the nurses were busy, they said. They were shorthanded and out of time, and they needed someone to comfort these men. That would have to be her. Red Cross, after all. She was trained to make these boys feel better.

"But—" she started to protest.

"They are going to die," the nurse said. "There's nothing we can do. So you can't hurt them, you see? Just be there, make them feel not alone."

They carried Irene into the tent against her wishes and set her down on the empty bed between the burned men. The floor of the tent was wood like hers. It was ghastly with fluids and ointments that had turned brown, and bandages with peels of flesh on them. The men lay on thick pads on the beds. Tubes were needled into their elevated arms. Sullied bandages mummified them, except in the spots where charred and overcooked skin showed. The men wheezed as they struggled to get air into their lungs. The tent was empty except for serum bottles on stands and machines and these two.

Irene closed her eyes. "I'm so sorry," she said to the men. "I am so ashamed.... I can't." She thought: *I make donuts and coffee and small talk—for the love of God, get me out of here.*

One of them was silent, unmoving. He might have already died. There was a clear mask of some sort over his face. Oxygen?

The other man leaned up on his bent arm and looked through a gap in the bandages, ointment greasing his eyes all around, and he reached out that other charred hand and patted her softly, so softly, on her own pale hand and said, "It's all right, lady. It's not so bad. You're going to be all right. I promise."

He died twenty minutes later.

She thought: *This is my last action of the war.*

The orderlies came to load her onto her transport plane to France. This was not the way she had expected to be leaving the war. She had come to the war alone and now she was leaving alone and she could not grasp what had changed or what had failed to change.

The only thing Irene knew for sure was that she was no longer the young dreamer who had boarded that train in New York City hoping to change her life. How would she explain to her mother and her grandmother who she was now when she couldn't even find the words to unburden herself? Would carrying all of these sorrows and torments inside her condemn her to a life sentence of silence? She could never apologize enough or give thanks enough for being the survivor.

When she saw France again, it was a quilt of fireflies and colored stars below her, and she held tight to her blankets as the plane tilted into its gradual descent.

PART FIVE

Last of the Line

47

THEN THE OLD woman stood on the far side of the decades, in a bright field long untended, telling herself that the war was now simply a distant memory, safely packed away. Nothing special. A common dream shared by millions. Mostly forgotten, forgotten more each day. The Clubmobilers, at the very least, had apparently been erased from memory. She found no mention anywhere of the service she and her fellow Dollies had performed.

"I might be the last," she said to nobody.

As the sun began to dip toward the horizon, her eyes squinted in the late summer light. She was well aware that her eyes squinted most of the time now, yet how was it that memories could remain sharp when a pile of clothes across the room looked just like the cat? Old age, this was the real war. A truck went by in the distance, and for the briefest moment she caught herself thinking the *Rapid City* had come with fresh supplies from the rear—a habit of slipping out of time that had begun to happen with worrying frequency. She checked herself and beheld the land spread out before her. *The war is long gone,* she reminded herself. Ages ago, that truck consumed by fire had settled into the soil unknown, even if she still had repeated nightmares of her partner's bones lying in the wreckage.

"Stop it," she said. She was here now, she told herself. It was a lovely day and she was alive in it. *Pay attention.*

She often narrated her days to herself, afraid of the moment when she would lose it all and forget what she was doing. She fretted about finding her reading glasses in the icebox and wondering who'd put them there.

"Not ready for the glue factory yet," she told the wind.

Back here again for the first time in fifty years. It was difficult to read the small headstones in the family graveyard, which needed mowing. A weedy little patch of black-eyed Susans had grown behind the markers. It seemed tender to her. But lately, everything did. *One thing you have more of in old age is tears,* she thought.

In spite of the sun, the wind through this meadow as evening came on was relentless, and she was just a touch cold. Part of her, it seemed, would always remain in the long winter of Bastogne. She was still plagued by her ancient wounds. Her headaches made her favor a knit cap, as if that warmth could ease the throbbing, and her leg—well, she'd be damned if she was going to use a cane.

This last year, though joyous, had been hard on her. Hard because of change. She did not appreciate it. She had done as much as possible to create a stable, gloriously dull life for herself and her loved ones. Now she was far from the safety of her house, out in the wind and bedeviled by memories she hadn't invited. Bats, these thoughts, swarming out of a ruined belfry.

This trip was a bit of travel for her granddaughter, a high school graduation gift, before they dropped her off at college. A journey around America to see what of value was left. She and her daughter were the child's Corps of Discovery.

"Why be grim?" she admonished herself. "There were so many wonderful times." She often spoke even when there was no one near to hear her, though she believed the ghosts were always near.

Her granddaughter, nineteen, was behind her, no longer puzzled by Grannie's weird spells. "You've still got it, Grannie!" the kid said and sped away across the yellow grass as if she were a child of seven.

Grannie—God forbid. A moniker to which she had never grown accustomed in all these years. She squinted into the distance. There was no sign left of their old house, the shaky barn, or the old well her great-grandparents had dug. Not far away, the county road skirted a ditch teeming with giant sunflowers, and she liked to think those were the descendants of her own grandmother's garden. Otherwise, this end of the cemetery was nothing special. It sprawled behind a wire fence that protected the back lot of a Target service-center loading dock.

Her ancestors were gathered here in peace, looking over the flat roof of the Target at all the colors and scents, the sounds and the birds of her girlhood, the very same clouds from sixty years ago gathered as if they had been awaiting her. The two-lane highway was shiny-new, the lines in the road still bright white and yellow. Trucks and foreign cars cut around the one slow and muddy tractor hauling a load of—corn? Damn her eyes.

"Pretty soon, I suppose, we'll all be flying around in spaceships."

A rangy old oak shaded the family's plot. A squirrel scolded her from above. A truck exited the Target lot and went forth on its mission.

"I am not lonely," she said aloud.

Her daughter, Andrea, the young girl's mother, had joined her, sitting down nearby on a low cement bench next to the fence. "Of course you aren't, Ma." She lit a cigarette and blew the smoke away from her mother. "You have us."

The old woman turned to her daughter. "And blessed I am."

When Andrea looked at her mother standing there, she saw a woman who had tried to keep the past locked inside herself for fifty years. She let the ghosts out only when she drank a Manhattan. Always a double, rocks. She called it *joy juice*. Fifty years. The number could still startle Andrea sometimes because she didn't feel like she was fifty years old. That meant Mother was—what?—seventy-five now? Seventy-seven? She was embarrassed to say that she had lost track.

Her daughter, that young colt, wandered through the meadow. Miss Dolly. Nineteen and thinking she was some wise faerie child. She loved history and had somehow been admitted to Harvard, which had thrown them all for a loop. A possible archaeologist. Currently reading Sappho, Le Guin, and Wonder Woman comics, scribbling stories of her own in a notebook she kept to herself. The kid was apparently communing with the tall grasses, her hands outstretched to butterflies; she was no doubt talking to the bluebirds and blowing dandelion tufts into the air. Andrea shook her head. She was outflanked by two willful women.

Dolly had once asked her grandmother what the point was, the donuts-and-coffee thing? Like, driving into the war? Nazis trying to kill you? And you were feeding snacks to soldiers? And the old woman had replied, "Women are called upon to piece the broken world back together. The boys blow everything up. Including themselves. And then the rest of us. And we bind it all back together—the boys, the world, ourselves."

After a long silence, Dolly had finally sighed and said, "Men. We'd be better off without them." She was wearing a T-shirt with somebody named PJ Harvey on it. Andrea smiled at the memory.

It was because of Dolly that they were here at the boneyard, staring at the headstones. Mother had never wanted to visit this forlorn spot. But the child wished to pay respects to her ancestors, to her family history. Hence the idea for this meander around America in a rented motor home: a fat aluminum box with panoramic windows and a CB radio that broke out in unexpected male voices drawling road conditions and wit. The vehicle was called a Chieftain or some such.

They had rented the rig in Chicago. *The heartland,* Mother had insisted on calling it as their plane landed. From there they could go anywhere in the country. They chose to drive south, to the Dollywood theme park—because they thought it was hilarious—then wandered around the Midwest searching out battlefields and dinosaur parks. Dolly was perfectly happy to sleep on the bed they'd made on the folding breakfast table in the main galley.

Mother seemed to enjoy the truck, but Andrea knew she was in a reverie. The more they drove, the more Mother seemed to relax, the more she stared and sometimes chuckled, remembering some secret scene that her two companions wished they could see. Then she'd cover her eyes for a minute and possibly weep. It was over as soon as it started. Dolly had caught Grannie surreptitiously patting the rig's dashboard.

"This truck," the old woman announced one sunflower morning, "needs a donut machine."

"Thought you hated donuts," Andrea said.

"I eat them. I just hate to cook them. You and Dolly can cook them."

They hardly noticed when Dorothy began to call the Chieftain a *Clubmobile.*

Andrea could not begin to imagine what a long haul in a truck might mean to the old woman. She'd bought a few cassettes at one of those immense truck stops: *Best Love Songs of the 40s* and *Sinatra Forever* and *Jitterbug Boogie: The Hottest Hits of WWII!* These seemed to please Mother. Along with the jug of Baileys that Dolly had suggested. They kept a thermos ready at all times. The expedition's mood lifter.

Andrea did the driving while Mother marked up the Rand McNally road atlas, tracing their route with a highlighter. Dolly rode in the back and rolled her eyes when Grannie called her "the Third Girl in the Truck."

—

Dorothy turned to Andrea now and motioned her over. "Time for Mother to sit down," she said.

Andrea jumped up, put out a steadying hand. Her mother took hold and let her assist. Ma only looked frail, she was an army tank. Her grip was firm, if bony. She could squeeze a hand like a longshoreman. Still, the ground was treacherous and Andrea could not abide the thought of her mother falling here, in front of these ghosts. She was always shocked at how cold Mother's hand was, how clawlike. As if she had become some kind of bird. They sat together on the cracked bench, breathing in drafts of the long clean wind. The golden heads of tall grasses weaved patterns all around.

"I'm glad we let that little snip of yours talk us into this trip," Dorothy said.

"I thought it was your idea."

"Oh, well. That's possible, I suppose."

"It's quite a drive," Andrea apologized. "Let me know if you get tired."

Dorothy poked her in the ribs with one finger. "We drove in a truck all over the war, you know." She stared into the distance, then closed her eyes and sat, unmoving, resembling, as she often did, a wooden carving.

"Grandma is time-traveling again," Dolly said, walking up to them.

"You sneaky child," Dorothy said without opening her eyes.

"Are you meditating, Grannie?"

"Resting the backs of my eyelids." She opened her eyes and stared up at her granddaughter. "I am apparently too tough to die," she announced.

"Ja, mor," Andrea agreed.

"Andrea, your baby girl is going to Harvard."

"Yes."

"Brilliant child."

"Ma, are you up for this trip? The next part? Cambridge is far."

"Of course. Don't be silly."

"But we stop first," Dolly said, "on Long Island."

"Yes," Dorothy said. "To lay flowers on another grave."

"What was it she called you?" Andrea said.

"That dear girl used to call me *Darling Dot*."

After a moment, Dolly said, "I know she was your best friend. I know I'm named after her. I've heard the stories my whole life. But for real, what was she like?"

It seemed as though Dorothy hadn't heard her. She just stared off into the distance again. But then she turned and looked deeply into their eyes. "She was like the springtime," Dorothy said.

Then she and Andrea and the Third Girl in the Truck took in the orange light of the sunset and said nothing more.

48

IN IRENE'S PARLOR, it was always 1945.

Music from the war years played on her phonograph through the majority of her days. She didn't just listen to the music, she breathed it. LPs stacked on the spindle. Betty Hutton, Ol' Blue Eyes, Harry James, Benny Goodman, Kay Kyser, and the sad and fabulous Billie. Models of warplanes hung on nearly invisible nylon strings—a green B-17, a silver P-51 Mustang. An unpainted C-47 Gooney Bird. A memorabilia collector had procured for her a recording of the engine of a P-51 Mustang revving in all its twelve-cylinder Rolls-Royce ferocity. Unfortunately, there was no recording of a Clubmobile engine, or the clatter in the galley. But that was just as well—she didn't think she could bear that sound.

She had arranged her world into a long forgetting. But try as she might, she could not escape. What mattered to her she kept here in Effie and Eva's old house. Hers now. Her haunted museum. It seemed ironic to her that she had always been searching for some fulfilling future, when all that mattered now was in the past. Lately, she had been thinking of that day so long ago when this adventure began. The train ride south out of New York. The one-legged soldier. The way he stared at her when she said she didn't understand what he meant about surviving the war. How right he'd been. Being the survivor had meant a lifetime of trying to understand. A lifetime of... *I killed my best friend.*

She was the last of her line, and had inherited the land and house outright when her mother died. It had been Woodward land as long as anyone could remember. Now Irene lived mostly in her music and her books and still wrestled with the iron pump the family had always used to bring up cold, hard water.

When Irene had come home from the war, broken in body and spirit, she chose to return to Mattituck, rather than her mother's home on Staten Island. Aunt Eva and Grannie Effie tended to her wounds, comforted her during her nightmares, and listened to her cry. Mother, still stung by the way Irene had left, visited every week or so. Irene never asked why she hadn't answered her letters, and Mother never asked about the war.

As she healed, Irene tried to return to her old life. But she had no witty repartee, no desire to wear lipstick, no friendship to offer anyone. She didn't trust a world that she had seen to be so cruel. The one safe place was here, on the land of her ancestors. The stone walls of the farm had sheltered generations of Woodward women. Now it was her turn.

When Mother grew exasperated and demanded that Irene return to Staten Island and get a job, Irene suggested that she needed a bit more time to get over the war.

Mother laughed in her face. "That is ridiculous," she said. "You weren't even a soldier. You were making cookies. What could you possibly have to get over?"

Irene, knowing it was hopeless for her mother to ever understand, didn't bother to correct her.

That first Christmas, Mother forwarded a card from Holly and Rusty. Irene could not bear to open it. It made her wonder what had happened to Garcia. She imagined he might be the only person who missed Dorothy as much as she did. But this was a dark pit she did not want to fall into and she threw the card into the trash. Any reminder of those who had survived was a plunge into the agony of memory for those who had not. There would never be a card from the ones who really mattered.

To have a future, Irene knew she would have to build a barrier between herself and her past, something as sturdy as the stone walls around the farm. So she had stayed in Mattituck, growing stronger. She fed the chickens and baffled her aunt and grandmother by demanding they not kill any more of them for food. Eventually, she was able to venture into town, where she maintained a friendly distance from her neighbors.

She regularly visited the library and the grocery store and might, of an afternoon, enjoy a cup of coffee and a scone at the local bakery. These excursions always left her exhausted and melancholy.

As first her grandmother and then her aunt grew frail, Irene tended to them and eventually buried them in the family plot at the Presbyterian church. When Mother died and Irene inherited the farm, she sold fifty acres of the family holdings and kept close tabs on the nest egg. And, like every Woodward before her, she clung to that family name. The last of the matriarchy.

And now she was the old woman. As far as whatever awfulness awaited outside the front door, she had escaped it. She amused herself with what was left of the gardens, and with her small projects. Until she stopped going altogether, her occasional visits to the VFW Hall for Bingo Night had been quite pleasant, though tiresome. People saying "I don't got no" this or that. Goodness. She had trained herself not to correct their grammar, even when they said *ain't*.

Her regular ten-cent purchase of books from the library sale kept her happily reading. She loved Travis McGee and Spenser. She often bought a *Yankee* magazine and a *New Yorker* when she ventured forth to get groceries. One had to have ice cream and coffee. Though she didn't drive, a few of her friends were always available to come for her.

Atop her bookshelves rested a model Jeep and a plastic Sherman tank. Across the room, a model of a 2½-ton six-by truck. She had not figured out how to build a galley on the bed of the truck. Nothing German in the room.

On the wall nearest the kitchen, beside the old door, above the breakfast table always set with whatever fresh flowers she could harvest and arrange in her Friendly Village soup tureen, hung a large photographic portrait in a heavy frame. The woman in it wore the uniform, a cap pinned at an angle in her blond hair, chin up, eyes looking into the sky, as if watching the bombers come home to Glatton. *Love you, Friend! Dot,* scrawled across the bottom.

Before the couch, on an ancestral oval rug, sat her army footlocker. Its green had faded to a near gray. It was covered by a tablecloth she had embroidered with memories of places she'd been. Somehow, the trunk had found her here, dropped off by an army truck in 1946. She could not make herself open it. She knew her old dirty boots were inside it. Most of her uniform. And two things she wanted to save but could not bear to retrieve, to touch or smell—the red and the black berets she and Dot had bought for themselves on the Riviera. She knew they were wrapped in white satin and newspaper and were tucked under her soldier jacket, that battered green jacket the boys had decorated with insignia: the 457th, 8th Army, Big Red One, Army Air Force.

Better the trunk stay closed.

She suspected her journals and sketchbooks were also in there. Unfinished and abandoned. And the photographs, loose and alive. These frightened her. She did not know what they might unleash in her house. So many grinning GIs. Phyl, Jill, and Hellcat in front of the *Cheyenne*. Those pictures from Cannes—she and Handyman, both in black bathing suits, both of them still feeling the ache of lovemaking as Dorothy snapped their portraits. Bright young bodies in the bright light, now just ghosts. And the dead stares of Buchenwald. The stacks, the piles, of cold bodies. That strange smell that still filled her. And the long-gone *Rapid City*, glamorous in the portraits she took, the old truck an obsession—at first sparkling and new, and later filthy and bullet-pocked and covered in graffiti. She was sure if she ever opened this box, the spirits trapped there would swarm out and fill the house.

Mounted on the wall above the record player was a well-marked map, tattered about the edges, crisscrossed with spidery ink and pencil marks, that showed her all the roads they'd traveled—through France, Belgium, into Germany. Even the quick spins to friendly towns for chocolate or stockings. Its coffee stains and chocolate smears looked like the shadows of clouds. Dot had pressed this map into her hands that last night and Irene had tucked it into her battered satchel, the only thing to have come off the mountain with her. Someone had laid the satchel under her cot in the MASH unit, unaware the crumpled sheet of paper within would be her most precious talisman. Each inky scratch revealed a movement of her dear friend's hand.

Her last notebook had also been in the satchel. Still less than half-filled, it had sat on the shelf with the GMC truck model for decades. When the air was warm or the fire pleasant on a chill day, or when—even better—the first snow slanted through the light of the lampposts out on the road like glowing moths inside perfect cones, she'd make herself a hot toddy with rum and butter and cream and cinnamon and sugar. Then she'd pry open the old book and smell the thousand scents of her past. The silly poems she had written. The oak leaves from Staten Island. Pressed European flowers. A single filigree of dried fern. The journal was no memoir. She didn't care to reenter her history, she told herself while looking away from her walls and cabinets. And she no longer tried to record her daily observances, since they were repetitions of the same day, the equal fear of and yearning for death. Besides, what was there left to say? *Fed the cat? Had a nightmare? Slept too long, looks like rain. Handyman once said...*

Instead, she startled herself by jotting poems in her book. Well, attempts at poems. She knew no one would ever read them. They were her own, her songs to what had fallen. She meant to write a list of directions for her funeral, and the first item would be: *Place the unopened journal of my days in my coffin with me.*

"Come now, Gator," she told herself. "You're being morbid."

—

Upstairs were three tidy bedrooms, each one small, as befitted a nineteenth-century farmhouse. The place was somewhat shabby but rendered joyful by the up-island sun bursting through the lace curtains. The hallway between the bedrooms was narrow, the floor tidal in its unevenness, groaning and squeaking as it rose and sank beneath her step. The entire second story smelled faintly of lavender. At the south end of the house, the loo (as she still called it) held a toilet with an overhead tank and a pull chain. An iron tub on weary lion's feet. One high window allowed her to spy on the far edges of town.

Like all old houses this one had secrets, and the most precious of these were hidden in its doors. Her bedroom door, and the downstairs front door, were portals to another time, another place. Mother had taught Irene the riddle of these spaces when she was a child. Because she dealt in antiques, Mother knew that these brass doorknobs had been made in the 1860s, and they were hollow. The small void within each knob was sealed by a round brass shield held in place by six narrow flanges. These could be pried off easily, then pressed back into place. When they visited from New York, Mother often hid a hard candy inside Irene's doorknob for her to discover on Sunday mornings before church.

Irene had shown her terrible cousins the secret sometime in the 1920s. They'd pried open all the knobs in the house and created a series of secure caches for concealed treasures and folded messages. Mouse skulls, small shells, an arrowhead, coins, marbles, jawbreakers, a .22 bullet. But now, only her bedroom door and the front door held her hidden heart and no one would ever know to look. A hundred visitors could turn the knobs and have no idea there was a sacred space cupped within.

—

Far from her war memorabilia, Irene kept a small picture in a golden frame. Happy Jack Dashiell. The mad driver of Mattituck's beloved hot rod, *The Platform.* That bare frame of a Model-T Ford with two overstuffed chairs and a broken couch tied down on its back. Uncle Will had said there was more rope than metal in that car. One day after high school graduation, Jack had appeared without his entourage and asked her to take a ride on *The Platform.* They went to a place she'd never seen, and could not find on a map—Goat's Neck Beach. He had a flat bottle of hooch. They lay there drunk on youth and the sips and the wind and watched ospreys fly to their huge nests in the pines. The stones of the beach were egg-shaped and oddly comforting.

"You don't want nothin' to do with me now, lady," he said. "But one day I'm gonna marry you."

She was feisty in those days. Boys. Really. She'd simply turned to him and said, "Quack quack quack."

After the war, Jack had returned from the South Pacific with a bit of a gut, blurred tattoos, and a U.S. Navy pension. He checked in on Irene regularly during her convalescence. He sometimes took her on a country drive along the coast. His presence was a comfort for her and in all those years he never married. After the old women passed, he was her favorite distraction. Their wedding reception was held in the VFW.

—

Happy Jack acquired a cream-and-brown two-tone Buick Roadmaster, and he was her chauffeur. After the war, Irene refused to drive. When Jack suggested, often, that he could teach her to drive again, she'd blurt, "Horrors!" and pour herself a snort of sherry. Then he'd walk her to the big car with her arm cradled in his own, and he'd hold the door open for her and toss his cigar stub so as not to fill the car with its stink. She was always amused by his little waddling trot around to his side, rubbing his hands in excitement. VFW Bingo Night was his great joy, aside from bowling with the boys at Mastic. The steering wheel had a contraption called a *brodie knob* that allowed him to steer with one hand as if he were a skipper taking his tugboat out to harbor.

At the Bingo Night gatherings, he traded badinage with other old soldiers: "*Marine*. By God, son, you know what *Marine* stands for? *My Ass Rides In Navy Equipment!*"

Jack's most romantic gesture besides the chauffeur routine was telling her, "Gator, you're a good pal." But they had great fun together, and if Jack suspected that her heart belonged to another, he never let on.

They got fourteen years. She was grateful for them. The night his heart gave out he had kicked back in the recliner to watch TV and drink his Rolling Rock while she lay abed upstairs and reread Fitzgerald. She thought she heard a brief cry.

"Jackie?" she called. "You okay?"

The quiet told her everything. She crept down the stairs as if a cat burglar were in the house. For some reason, she held her breath. He seemed merely to be asleep, one slipper on the floor, the other hanging from the toes of his other foot. His mouth was open, the beer spilled in his lap.

Irene could not stop shaking. She didn't know what to do, so she called the VFW Hall and Mrs. Livingston from down the road. She then sat out on the front porch to await the new life she already knew would be one of silence and solitude.

—

Gradually, she withdrew. She stopped her visits to Bingo Night, even when Mrs. Livingston offered to drive. For several years she continued to ride in the Veterans Day Parade, sitting in the back of a Willys jeep, waving at well-wishers and war fans and patriots. She waved like a starlet at bored kids and soda-swilling parents and grandparents holding up little flags. Everybody lined the route in lawn chairs. When she realized that those bored children were now the beer-drinking parents of new children, and the grandparents were gone, she quit. She would dearly miss the vintage airplanes doing their overflights, sounding like Handyman circling Glatton. But she could stand out in Effie's ancient raspberry patch beside the parlor and listen to them, sometimes even see them.

Neighbors checked on her, of course. Occasionally they gave her rides to the supermarket. But she also took her folding cart out and hiked down the road, telling herself she needed the exercise. It was only half a mile, though when she was tired and hauling the cart home laden with soup and potatoes, bacon and sherry, it seemed ten. And the cars that rushed past her felt like insults.

49

It had been a successful trip already for the Chieftain. All three of the women wore their favorite souvenirs from the visit to Dollywood: hot-pink baseball caps emblazoned with DOLLY! across the front. The rig gulped fuel like an elephant hitting a watering hole. During their adventure, Dolly had revealed her superhuman affection for something called Bugles, stocking up on bags at every truck stop. She often put the corn cones over the ends of her fingers as if she had claws. There followed appalling crunches.

For her part, Andrea enjoyed coffee. Gallons of it. The on-board toilet liberated them from stopping, so they could burn down the highways uninterrupted, like John Steinbeck and his dog Charley. At Dollywood, Dorothy had rediscovered MoonPies and kept a couple of boxes in the little fridge in the rig, a gift from the highway gods. Dorothy still referred to it as *the icebox,* which her daughter and granddaughter thought was cute. Dorothy, aware of this, used the term precisely to prove she would not change her ways for the likes of them.

As the sun dipped away, she examined Indiana from her passenger-seat throne, the landscape still replete with hand-painted fence post signs: HELL IS REAL, JESUS IS COMING, FIREWORKS, JESUS OR HELL. She felt like she was back on that Greyhound in 1943, heading for the war and that darned Gator. She was torn about seeing Gator's grave. For her, it was easier to tell herself that she simply hadn't seen Irene in a while. That maybe Irene had found Handyman and lived on some idyllic Oregon ranch. Flying cargo planes together. Crop-dusting. He would have taught her how to ride a horse, taken her up those snowy trails to some high country teeming with elk and wolves. Imagining that was how Dorothy often got to sleep on the worst nights. Imagining poor Irene trying to trot up a verdant trail, bouncing and slipping, losing her ridiculous cowboy hat, insulting the horse—"You recalcitrant beast!" It was enough to make Dorothy fall asleep with a chuckle. Though on some nights, Irene, unbidden, turned in her saddle and simply stared at her. That made sleep impossible.

Dorothy knew that actually seeing Irene's grave would put a heart-breaking stop to that foolish fantasy. However, even that would be far better than the image burned in her memory of Irene frantically trying to steer the *Rapid City* over the treetops before the truck exploded. It had taken fifty years, but Dorothy thought she finally had the strength to say goodbye.

—

Dorothy liked to stretch out her bum leg whenever she could. At a truck stop with what seemed to be a few thousand gas pumps, she walked around the rig in the last light of the day, watching magpies battle over McDonald's fries. She pressed her hands into the small of her back and stretched. Andrea squeezed a few more cents' worth out of the nozzle and slotted it and screwed down the gas cap. She looked over at Dorothy and gave her a grin and a thumbs-up.

When Andrea's fisherman husband had been lost at sea, she relied on her mother's insistence that women will always find a way. Dolly was still an infant when they moved in with Dorothy, and Andrea took the unexpected insurance windfall and invested it in a bakery she would run with her mother. Dorothy could not think of a better way to spend her retirement money from teaching English as a second language.

Andrea had learned to bake as a child. She would often awake to find Dorothy in a half-sleep stage, robotically baking pies or biscuits or bread for hours. Andrea would take up a mixing bowl and work alongside Dorothy, who sometimes cried silent tears while she baked. One early morning, as the sun rose and the bread cooled, Andrea put her arms around her mother and asked, "Does all this help with the nightmares?" Dorothy's eyes filled with tears. All she could do was nod and cut her daughter a slice from the loaf.

They set up their bakery in Christianshavn, alongside a canal that ran past the city center of Copenhagen. The shop was called Rapid City American Bakery. Tourists and expats loved it. Locals loved or loathed it depending on who was the American president. The youngsters seemed to enjoy it because Dorothy allowed them to lounge all day as long as they refilled their cups and dropped coins into the jar. They also knew that all would be well so long as they slipped her a cigarette about once an hour. The bakery was a success, and when the owner of the shop next door died, they expanded into it, adding old couches and potted plants for the beatniks, which was what all the wandering hostel backpackers were to Dorothy, never mind that it was the '70s.

Baby Irene had grown up in the shop. Dorothy had started calling her *Dolly* when she was just a toddler, as an inside joke, but the silly nickname had stuck. They all laughed out loud when she yelled back, "Don't call me *Dolly*!"

The three women formed a tight unit at the shop. Dolly did her homework at a back table, played pinball with her little Viking girlfriends, and ended up serving as their unpaid barista, relief baker, record-player technician. She was a kid magnet, especially for those awkward English-speaking tight-jeaned boys. She had made the sign that said: SORRY—NO DONUTS!

Dorothy opened her eyes and found herself back in the fuel lot on the interstate with that old scent of the American Midwest coming on. It hit her: *Europe had never smelled like home*. She ran her hand down the side of the truck. What would Irene do if she were here? She'd hop up into the passenger's seat and smile at Dorothy, expecting to be chauffeured.

A sunburned biker on a chopped hog rolled in. He wore a dirty bandanna and a vest with a rocker patch that said SUNDOWNERS. Tattoos of eagles and a flag decorated his forearms. He slouched over the bike, filling his tank.

Dorothy complimented him on the motorcycle and he thanked her.

"Veteran?" she said, nodding at his tattoos.

"Yep."

"Red Cross," she said. "I was with Patton."

"No shit." He nodded appreciatively.

"Can I catch a ride?"

He laughed and asked where she was going.

"Nineteen forty-five," she said, then waved and walked back to the Chieftain. She opened the driver's door to find Andrea at the wheel. "I'll take it," she told her daughter.

"I've got it, Ma."

"You don't think I can do it?"

"Just looking out for you."

Dolly peered across from the passenger's seat, which she had claimed. "You don't even have a license, Grannie."

Dorothy suddenly wanted a cigarette. She leaned over and spit. What the hell ever happened to Zoot and Rusty? "I forgot more about driving a big rig than you'll ever know, Toots."

Dolly scooted back into the gloom of her den.

"Daughter of mine," Dorothy said, glaring up at Andrea, "I say again, un-ass that seat."

Andrea gripped the wheel and seethed. But she didn't dare resist her mother, crazy or not. She struggled over to the seat that Dolly had vacated.

"This is going to be interesting," Dolly said, from her converted dinette.

"Zip it, Dolly."

"Don't call me *Dolly*."

All three women laughed at that. The biker roared past them, one hand raised, and Dorothy honked at him.

—

Dorothy settled in as the rig, smoother than the *Rapid,* trundled toward the greater dark in the east. The driver's seat bounced along on spongy coils. And this beast was almost silent—nobody had to shout. The power steering meant she could maneuver the motor home with a finger, while the automatic transmission relieved any worry about working a clutch with her bad leg. A cardboard cutout of a pine tree hanging from the rearview made the rig smell like cologne rather than oil, exhaust, and sweat.

"I could get used to this," Dorothy muttered, trying to figure out the knobs and various lights.

Andrea inhaled butter rum Life Savers. Dolly was back there, plugged into some device called a Walkerman or something like that, listening to music. All Dorothy could hear from her little headphones was a rhythmic *tsst-tsst-tsst*.

The radio clicked and spit. A highwaynaut broke in on them in a haze of static and baffled the other two in the motor home by saying: "Got your ears on, good buddy? Scooter Bob ballin' the jack out of Xenia. What's your twenty? Come back. Over."

Dorothy knew he could be twenty or thirty miles away, but to her own amazement, she reached right for the microphone and pushed the talk button without thinking. "Reading you, Scooter, this is ARC *Rapid City* with a full crew heading northeast. Bustin' butt to keep up with the Eighth. That Patton has a lead foot, though. Over."

Scooter said, "Uh. Out."

Dorothy chuckled and hung up the mic with great satisfaction. She was having a ball.

After a while, she glanced back at Dolly, who had nodded off. Andrea, too, had been rocked into a road nap. Try as she might to avoid being left with her own thoughts, the feel of this rig beneath her was slipping Dorothy back to that terrible night—though the steady purr of the engine was nothing at all like the whine of the *Rapid City* as they tried to outrun the MPs; the imagined Swede and his henchmen; the Germans. She could still picture Irene wrestling with the wheel. *What were you thinking, Dorothy? What were you thinking? I wasn't thinking. I was crazy. Don't you see?* Somewhere out there in the shadows, beyond the reach of the headlights, Irene stared at her, saying nothing.

It was getting late and Dorothy knew she should have stopped for the night already, but she was helplessly caught in her memories. She drove the Chieftain into the dark highway before her, the woods and trees somehow blending with the memories she had worked so hard to stifle for the last fifty years. This time, though, she was driving. *This time,* Dorothy thought, *I can stop the nightmare from happening.*

And yet she could not.

—

The *Rapid City* falls, a dark avalanche breaking off the mountain.

The startling bang and jolt as the truck lurches into the air, the horrible crunch as it hits the lip of the road and topples over, the sickening rush of the instant plunge. The sounds of everything in back—the cups and saucers shattering as they fly around the galley. Her idiotic thought: *Save the cups.*

Falling, falling, and Dorothy crosses her arms over the baby, curling her torso around her, bracing her feet against the dash. Irene wrestling with the wheel, somehow trying to save everything, shouting her name. The most terrible cry of all.

Trying not to break the baby with the desperate ferocity of her embrace, Dorothy clenches her mouth so hard she might be cracking her teeth. The truck strikes earth or a boulder or a tree or all three, Dorothy's door bursts open, and she is in the air—the baby still zipped tight inside her jacket. In slow motion forever, split seconds fossilized into eternity, she flies backward out the door, spinning away from the truck as the truck spins away from her.

And for one infinite sliver of a second, Dorothy can see into the cab of the truck. The white flash of Irene's face turned toward her, her friend's mouth and eyes wide. Is Irene calling her name? Dorothy doesn't have time to respond before the truck explodes above her and she flies out of the burning sky to collide with the earth.

She has been falling for fifty years.

—

The smell of her hair burning when the ball of fire bloomed above her seemed to fill the Chieftain now, and Dorothy pulled into a highway rest stop, haphazardly parking the motor home across three slots.

The sudden stop woke Andrea and Dolly. Dorothy stared straight ahead, clutching the steering wheel, tears dripping from her chin. She imagined she could smell the sinkers stacked in their racks, the grease in the cookers. Taste the sugar haze that used to fill the *Rapid City*. Those were the only memories that gave her comfort from this nightmare. Those were the memories that sent her to the kitchen at 3:00 a.m.

Andrea had seen Dorothy after her nightmares, during those all-night baking sessions. But she had never seen her mother like this. "Ma?" she said gently, as if to wake a child from a night terror.

Dolly crept into the space between the seats, knelt, and leaned her head against her grandmother's hip. *Mom?* she mouthed to Andrea.

"Ma?" Andrea said to Dorothy again. "Are you okay? What's going on?"

Dorothy's head was bent to the steering wheel. All Andrea could see was her silhouette, backlit by the sodium lights of the parking lot.

"It was terrible, so terrible," Dorothy said, not looking up. "I never told you, sweetheart. It's so terrible."

She was speaking so softly that Andrea and Dolly had to lean in to hear her. Neither was sure what she was talking about.

"Grannie, you're scaring me," Dolly said.

But this unburdening was the reckoning Dorothy had denied herself for all this time. She had to face this moment and she wanted her girls there with her. And so she kept talking, in an uninterrupted stream, as if she hadn't heard Dolly, knowing that if she stopped she might never again say what needed to be said.

"There was no refugee camp," she began. "That wasn't where I found you. I was on a raid with a group of GIs. I wasn't supposed to be there and Irene didn't know. We found a group of women prisoners locked in a boxcar. They were all dead, but one of the guys heard something.

It was you, Andrea. You were crying. You were still in your mother's arms, wrapped in a dirty shawl with the name *Andrea* stitched into the hem. I couldn't just leave you. I saw your face and knew I could never leave you.

"I smuggled you into our Clubmobile and told Irene I needed her help to get to the border. I couldn't risk anyone taking you from me. I was hoping I could save you. Maybe what I needed was you to save me. You can't understand this, but I was so lost. And suddenly, it was as if you were my compass. Now I had a path, a plan. I made my own decision. I chose you.

"Irene was furious but I made her drive the truck because I didn't trust her to hold you. I was always the driver. That skill was the only thing I brought. Irene? Irene brought the joy. But now she drove us into the mountains. She begged me to change my mind the whole time, but I didn't hear her. I just kept urging her to go faster. She was so scared, she wasn't a good driver. The roads were dangerous and it was getting dark. We came around a curve and...I don't know what happened. Somehow we fell off the mountain. But I wasn't going to let you go. We flew out. The truck exploded. Irene was gone. But you were still there and you were mine.

"I opened my eyes, my ears were ringing. Blood all over my face. And there were some women there. I thought they were ghosts at first and I thought Irene must be one of them and I called for her. But the women wiped my face and made me look at the huge fire that had been the *Rapid*. There was no way to save her. You must have been crying now. One of the women pulled you from my coat and gave you her breast. I think I was saying *Bless you, bless you.* They knelt around me. My hearing returned, and they were speaking different languages. They were all escaping from the war, just like you and me. They brought me water from a stream in the valley. They pressed wet rags to my head. They put water on my lips.

"It was easy just to stay with them. No one asked why I had a baby. They only saw I was a momma. They bandaged my injuries and let me ride in their wagons until I was strong enough to walk. There were so many refugees. I started my new life then. I closed the door on everything that came before. I didn't let myself think about Irene or anyone I knew before. All that mattered was you and finding us a home.

"Europe was in tatters after the war. It took months, but eventually we made our way to Denmark. It made me laugh when the Red Cross refugee camp put us on a boat for Copenhagen. I refused to speak English and I guess they saw my blond hair and assumed. The rest of the story you know. But you should also know that for fifty years I have tried to bury this. I keep seeing Irene's face, in the truck, just before it exploded. I had promised her we would get home together. Instead, I sacrificed her and it haunts me to this day."

Finally, exhausted, Dorothy stopped speaking. She took her hands off the wheel. In the silence, Andrea reached for her mother's hand. Dolly's hands found them both and the three women sat for countless moments.

"When we get there," Dorothy finally said, "I will lay flowers on Irene Woodward's grave. Hold me up, because I cannot bear it."

50

IRENE WAS TOSSING and turning through one of her bad dreams. Flashlights cut apart the night outside. There was the sound of running feet and engines loud as dinosaurs tearing through her hedges and garden, of men yelling and the brittle reports of their guns like rocks hitting the outer walls. The women's screams awakened her and she cried out and kicked, knocking her old cat onto the floor.

She rose from bed exhausted and shuffled toward her closet like a drunkard, slowly returning to her body from that lightless night in the collapsing house. If it wasn't this dream of the house, it was the worse dream of her leg wounds and her abdominal scars breaking open and parts of her body falling through her grip and sliding across the floor. But every once in a while, on the best nights, she dreamed of a beautiful man with his guitar, singing that song to her.

She pulled off her nightgown and changed into decent clothes, a modest dress. She slipped her feet into very old shoes, then made the bed. The cat fussed from the bedroom door. Her legs and hip ached and burned and sent electric shocks from her knees to her navel. She had known not a day without pain since the war.

She went down the stairs, watching her step, minding her balance. The cat had learned to follow a step behind her. She crossed the room, leaned on the rocker, and pushed the Play button on the record player, which offered Louis Armstrong singing about what a wonderful world it was. She shuffled to the kitchen and turned on the electric coffee machine. It amused her to eat a plain donut each morning with her first bitter cup.

She could almost smell the mud and exhaust and the stink of a hundred unwashed boys outside the serving flaps. She loved the early-morning light in Europe. But was that only because the shooting had often not started for the day yet? Everything felt sacred and numinous when the sound was trees and quiet men.

Coffee ready, she took her donut and the cup in a saucer over to Dorothy's portrait and had her morning chat with the dear girl. "Looks like a red-letter day," she said.

Outside the window, the world was rushing toward the end of summer, though yellow flowers were still alive with bees, and along the far fence that helped block off the road the leaves on the trees remained bright green. There must be a Cape wind today—gulls above slid sideways in the sky.

When she was finished, the cup and saucer went into the kitchen sink, and she made her way to the front door, a butter knife in hand. She braced herself on the back of the nearby easy chair and lowered herself to eye level with the doorknob, her knee creaking, then jimmied the knife blade under the edge of the little round shield in the knob. When she pried, it popped out and bounced around on the carpet.

She peered inside. He was there. He was forever there. In black and white, the picture cut into a rough-edged circle. He wore his black swimming trunks and squinted under the Riviera sun, one arm thrown over her shoulder, his hand hovering over her heart. Protecting her. Guarding the door, she felt, so that no one could harm her in her sleep. Fifty years later and he was still smiling, still young.

"Good morning, darling," she said. "Yes, bad dreams."

How she longed to hear his song again, to hear him strum his guitar again. She reached one finger in and smoothed his hair, touched his cheek.

Back upstairs, she knelt again, this time at her bedroom door, groaning but making it down in front of the knob. Dot, feisty as ever, must have been in a mood, for when Irene took the blunt knife edge to the knob, her friend flew out and fluttered to the floor.

Irene picked her up and instantly remembered her smell, even when it was merely sweat. She touched that grinning face once and tucked her back inside the knob. She pressed the brass badge back into place and rested the flat of her hand against the wood of the door before getting back to her feet.

—

Irene had the afternoon habit of falling asleep in the rocker while watching *The Young and the Restless*. She pulled her knee blanket up and the cat hopped aboard and she was snoring softly before the show was half over.

When the cat leaped off her lap, Irene jerked awake. Some afternoon game show was on, all bright colors and idiotic hopping around. The cat ran upstairs, spooked by whatever Irene hadn't heard. She rubbed her eyes and a car door slammed outside, followed by raised voices. She turned off the television with the remote and listened closer.

"What in the world?" She sidled to the window beside the front door and splayed herself along the wall like a paranoiac, then pulled back the curtain to peek outside.

A motor home had pulled onto her property. It squatted in the middle of the gravel driveway, blocking everything.

Irene bristled. "The nerve," she said. Did they not see the NO TRESPASSING sign? The NO SOLICITORS sign?

A young girl stood beside the motor home talking to someone above her, lurking within the cab. Irene shaded her eyes. There seemed to be two other people in there. Jehovah's Witnesses? Democrats? The girl turned toward the house and shaded her eyes and then began to trot up to the front door.

51

How many miles had Dorothy driven during the war trying to tune out Irene waxing poetic over this little town? How many times had she heard about her uncle's hidden whiskey bottles in the barn? Her aunt's raspberry patch? The street that led to the crossroads with the Presbyterian church? So many times that she found herself able to navigate for Andrea as if it were her own neighborhood.

It was a bright day, but this far north, even at the end of summer the first hint of fall was beginning to appear on the highest branches of the trees. There were actually gulls in the air. After her haunted drive in the dark the other night, Dorothy had gladly moved over from the captain's seat in favor of Andrea. They had decided it would be better to start with a visit to the Woodward farm and Dorothy was glad of it. She had no desire to see Irene's headstone first thing in the day. She knew that after she laid flowers on Irene's grave, she would be wrecked for some time. *First things first,* as her mother had always told her, and Dorothy looked forward to finally seeing the place Irene had spun into reality for her.

When she spied the bucolic church at a crossroads, she knew they were close. She could almost hear Irene's singsong directions: *A left at the church, across the train tracks, another quarter mile down the road, you see the giant raspberry patch, and there it is!*

But after a couple of miles down the road, Dorothy realized there were no more houses and none of the mailboxes said *Woodward.*

"You'll have to turn around," she told Andrea.

"Are you sure it's here?" Andrea said.

From the back, Dolly piped up: "It's here. Grannie's never wrong."

With a bit of difficulty, Andrea maneuvered the Chieftain and they doubled back.

In her head, Dorothy repeated Irene's directions. "I know a lot can change in fifty years," she said, "but the Woodward farm should be right there. Isn't that a huge raspberry patch?"

Andrea pulled into the gravel driveway, and Dolly peered at the rusting mailbox on the side of the road.

"I don't know, Grannie. This says *Dash*-something." Dolly said she would just go ask at the house, and before they could suggest otherwise, the restless girl popped out of the motor home and headed for the porch.

—

Irene waited at the door with her hand against the wood, half-dreading the knock that was sure to come. Why people came to her door, she never understood. *No doubt Jehovah's Witnesses,* she decided. Time seemed to stretch out. How long was the little wench walking? Had she wandered out into the field in spite of the sign forbidding it?

Finally, the knock.

Irene fumbled with the latch and cracked open the door, keeping the gap as narrow as possible. She and the girl stared at each other for a moment. The girl pasted a false smile on her face.

"Yes, dear," Irene said. "Can I help you?"

"I'm sorry to bother you, ma'am," the girl said in a hard-to-place accent, "but I'm trying to find the old Woodward home." She glanced back over her shoulder.

Irene leaned a bit out of the doorway to see if anyone was hiding in the hedges. She kept one hand on the knob, in case she needed to slam the door quickly. She looked back into the girl's face without answering her query.

"Are your handlers waiting for you?" Irene asked.

The girl giggled nervously. "It's not like that, ma'am."

"I'm not buying anything," Irene said. "But thanks ever so for stopping by. Brightened my day." She started to close the door.

"Wait."

Irene stared at her. "And you are interested in the Woodwards because...?"

"We're on a trip and we wanted to see this place and pay our respects," the girl explained. "My grandmother knew somebody who lived around here." She was aware that she was starting to babble. "I'm heading to college, and I wanted to stop here first, on our way there, because of my grandmother's stories."

"Well, good luck with your search. Now, goodbye, dear."

Dolly glanced at the motor home again—its doors were opening—then back at Irene. She was making a fool of herself. Everyone watching her. "Just one question, ma'am."

Irene had already grown weary of this little creature and her peculiar accent. "I can't help you," she said. "Perhaps the town librarian can show you some newspaper pieces about the Woodwards."

Her plan was to shut the door firmly, but not slam it. Reflexively, Dolly put her hand on the door to keep it from closing. And then, absurdly, they were almost tussling with it.

"Wait, please!" the girl said. "I just need a...please..." She pressed a bit harder and the door creaked wider and she could see into the house. She stopped talking then and stood with her mouth open, staring just over Irene's shoulder.

Irene turned toward the room to see what could have startled the girl. Nothing was in her sight line but Dorothy's portrait, staring at the sky as if awaiting the squadron's return. Irene turned again to Dolly, perplexed. "What is it, young lady?"

"I don't understand," the girl said. "That's my grandmother. Why do you have her picture?"

Irene was already shaking her head. "Oh no, dear." She smiled condescendingly. "That woman was long gone before you came into this world."

"No, but that *is* my grandmother. Dorothy."

"Excuse me?"

"Dorothy Dunford."

Suddenly, the floor felt unsteady beneath Irene's feet. She could not comprehend what this girl was saying. Two women had disembarked from the rig out in the sun.

Irene's hands were shaking. "This isn't funny," she said.

Dolly looked back at the motor home. "That's her—my grandmother. She said her best friend in the war called her *Darling Dot*. That's the woman we're here to pay respects to. My name's Irene—I'm named after her—but they call me *Dolly*. My grandmother says I'm the Third Girl in the Truck."

Irene could hardly breathe.

"How—?" the girl said.

"They called me *Gator*," Irene whispered.

A light flared in the girl's eyes. "Are you...?"

Irene felt as woozy as if she were on that ship crossing the Atlantic fifty years ago, as confused as when the buzz bomb had fallen, so unsteady she could not stand. She leaned heavily against the doorframe. Tried to take a calming breath.

One of those ghosts out in the drive raised her arm and waved. "Everything okay, Dolly?" she called.

Every regret, every sorrow, every hope, all of this guilt, all of this fear, all of this loneliness—all there at once in her throat. Irene grabbed at the edge of the door. The world before her doubled, knocked out of focus.

"I'm sorry," she said.

It was as if a telescope that couldn't focus on the farthest star had suddenly sharpened its image and blinded the onlookers. That old one, the one wearing slacks—she was all Irene could see. She was all Irene had ever wanted to see.

"I'm sorry," she said. "Just give me..." But she stopped short, backing into her home and closing the front door. Dolly walked back to her mother.

"What's going on, Dolly?" Andrea asked, worry in her voice.

"I don't know," Dolly said. "But I think that's Miss Irene."

"Oh, honey, I'm sure you're misunderstanding," Andrea said. "That's not possible."

"It's her, Mom."

Suddenly, as one, they rushed to Dorothy, who wobbled, barely breathing, never taking her eyes off the front porch of the house. "I think I've just seen a ghost," she said.

All three of them stared at the front door.

"Come on, Gator," said Dorothy. "Open that door again." Her voice was so low it was barely audible. "You can do it," she said. "Don't let it end this way. Be tough enough to come back to me. It just takes a step."

"Are you all right, Mother?" said Andrea.

Dorothy seemed to grow taller, her bent back stretching completely upright for the first time in years. "I'm all right."

"How long are we going to wait out here?" Dolly asked, rubbing her palms at the tears she hadn't noticed until this moment. "Let's just go back and talk to her."

Somewhere above them the gulls squawked and the crows cawed. On the country road a car passed by.

"I'll wait as long as it takes," Dorothy said.

"Mother," said Andrea. "I don't understand any of this. How is this possible?"

Dorothy dug in the dirt with the toe of her shoe. Could it really be this easy? After half a century you drive a few miles and find that all you have ever wanted was just... right here all along? That you have spent most of a lifetime being catastrophically mistaken? She saw Irene's curtain pull aside, then jerk closed, and she grinned. "Girls," she said, "it's time for you to go back to the truck. This one is just for us."

Her daughter and granddaughter were clearly reluctant.

"You can watch from the Chieftain, ladies. But you need to scoot." Alone in that stark sun, Dorothy squared her shoulders and smiled at the house. "Come on out," she said.

—

Inside the house, after creeping up to the window again and pulling back the drape to peer at the lone figure out there in the sun, Irene sat down on her rocker and trembled. Her hands felt palsied, jittering and quivering. She could hardly breathe. None of this made a lick of sense. Was a prayer answered this simply? The world, wrong for fifty years, rights itself with a stranger at your door? Or was she dying and Dot had come for her?

Irene pressed her hands to her face. She smelled the burning of the truck, heard her own screams. *I drove off that mountain,* she remembered. *And I left her there. She was alive and I left her. Oh my God, I left her there.* She stared at the portrait, tears filling her eyes.

She was finally beginning to understand. To survive meant a lifetime of forgiving. Since that night on the mountain, she had spent her days in a haunted penance she could escape only now by deciding to forgive herself. Whatever lay on the other side of her door, she knew that today she would find reconciliation.

"Darling Dot," she said aloud to the room, "I am not going to leave you again." She stood slowly and stepped to the door. She clutched the knob in her hand, drawing strength from it one last time. "Handyman," she said, "hold my hand. I need you." The brass warmed in her grasp.

Irene took a deep breath, closed her eyes, and opened the door. She stood revealed to the day and it seemed to take a very long time to find the strength to open her eyes again. When she did, she saw Dorothy at the foot of the porch with her own eyes closed, hands clasped in front of her heart, almost as if in prayer. Irene stepped forward and down the stairs, the boards creaking beneath her feet.

She had spent the last fifty years trying to make sense of what happened, to be able to reconcile her sorrows and traumas with the world around her. The war had been an exploding darkness, an inexplicable chaos. But here, now, was grace. Here, now, was forgiveness. When Dorothy finally opened her eyes, Irene let out a small cry and reached for her friend. Here, now, was joy.

Irene held Dorothy's face in her hands as Dorothy cupped her own. They could not look away from each other's eyes. Everything else disappeared—the faint shush of distant waves, the echoing cries of the gulls, the hissing of the wind in the trees. Riveted by the scene before them, Andrea and Dolly climbed out of the motor home and came closer, but the two old friends did not notice. It was as if no time, and yet all of time, passed in those moments.

They stood together under that wild sky, and their blood, their living blood, roared inside them. They were already imagining their next years, the adventures to come, the unburdening, the liberation, the whiskey, the waves of warm beaches, the nights that were no longer for nightmare and regret but for laughter until the morning light. Time had been returned to them. They would talk without ceasing now. Whatever the story that had brought them here, they had years to unravel it.

Finally, Dorothy cracked a small grin and leaned a bit closer. "Good morning, Irene," she whispered, with one eyebrow raised, and began to giggle.

"Darling Dot, are you really a grandmother?" Irene said incredulously.

"I am. And guess what?" Dorothy jerked her head toward Andrea and Dolly. "Her mother? That's the baby we saved. That's *our* baby."

Stunned, Irene just stared at Andrea. Here, then, was the real miracle.

Andrea and Dolly stood in the driveway and Irene smiled at them and offered a timid wave. Playing along, the women waved back.

"Look what you did, Dottie," said Irene. "Look what you did."

"Maybe we should go inside?" Dorothy suggested. "I'll tell you all about it."

"I can probably put together some sinkers and coffee," Irene said with a grin.

Dorothy snorted. "I'd prefer some whiskey!"

Irene put her arm around her dearest friend and helped her to the steps. "You'll never guess what I've got in my footlocker, Dottie. Our berets!"

The thought of it set Dorothy to chuckling. Soon both women were laughing so hard they were holding each other up. And Irene, who had believed for so long that the world was constructed of darkness, suddenly knew she would reside in light until the end of her days. Together with Dorothy she walked up the porch steps, arm in arm as if they were back in the streets of Cannes, and the Sisters held open the door for the women coming along behind them.

AUTHOR'S NOTE AND ACKNOWLEDGMENTS

The photograph that opens this book is of the ARC *Cheyenne* in Europe, during combat service. The three women standing before the wagon are (from left to right) my mother, Jill, and Helen. I like to imagine the ghostly male face in the service window is Handyman.

This book is a novel, a fiction. I think now it is also me finding my mother again. Sometimes a fable is the surest way to see the truth of the past. In writing this story, I found the wild and heroic woman she was before I came into this world. The woman who struggled to resurface after the war but who was lost in dreadful nightmares and inexplicable isolation. And I hoped to share her with you. Along with her forgotten sisters-in-arms.

Although the primary details are based on historical fact, the process of writing this book was an act of the imagination composed under the absolute necessity of adhering to those facts.

My original plan was to write a nonfiction account of my mother and the ARC Clubmobiles. However, this is a story unimportant to the historical record. Early in the research, we were told a fire in a Red Cross storage facility back in the 1970s had destroyed the WWII Clubmobile records. So there is no official map of the journeys of these women, no personnel records. I was unable to find any records of my mother's devastating accident or what field hospital cared for her. There is little to no information in any archives, only personal artifacts the women themselves saved. The only reason these stories exist is because the women of the ARC told them to their loved ones. My treasure trove was the letters written home, the self-published accounts, the few newspaper recollections, and museum recorded interviews. There is an ARC Clubmobile Archive at Harvard that has a wonderful collection of these letters. Though I have to stress that I relied on my mother's and Jill's letters and scrapbooks as my primary sources.

When we first started researching this book almost twenty years ago, we tracked down everything—including a beat-up copy of the "bible": *The Clubmobile—The ARC in the Storm* by Marjorie Lee Morgan, which was apparently self-published in 1982. Ms. Morgan met and interviewed the Clubmobilers—including my mother—during reunions and put together the only history available. She did not cite her sources, though, and I could find no further record of Ms. Morgan. However, I do not think this makes the stories these women tell of themselves and one another any less valid or valuable to the historical record of World War II. I thank Ms. Morgan for her devotion to acknowledging these women and their work and her perseverance in having this book published. I cherish my copy and the photos of my mother I had not seen and the story she told Ms. Morgan that I had never heard.

On my website, I have a more complete listing of the books and publications that informed me.

—

My mother, Phyllis Irene, had roots in Manhattan and the Bronx and Staten Island's Richmond Village; her mother owned an antiques shop on Broadway; and she spent many early and last years in Mattituck. All places foreign to me. Like the locations and experiences of the war, these places were only fractured memories and half-told stories, furtive peeks inside her WWII footlocker, idle inspections of her photo albums. Though I could not bear to read her diaries, Cindy did and helped me through the painful parts. The fictional journey of the invented ARC Clubmobile *Rapid City* generally follows the itinerary of my mother's actual truck, the *Cheyenne*. She and her crew were indeed members of Group F.

Mom died in April of 1990. She had a Bible and a Julia Child cookbook beside her in her bed.

Today, I know when I looked at her, I saw only Ma; but she saw herself as a Manhattan movie star with a fizzy cocktail in one hand and a fashionable cigarette in a holder in the other, and she was amusing a gathering of sophisticates as Bobby Short's piano jazz played and everyone called each other "dahling." She was not trapped in a barrio apartment or a San Diego suburb that felt like a desert to her. And she forever saw herself as that vibrant woman in cataclysms of laughter. I hope that, wherever her cocktail party convenes in eternity, wherever she is now reunited with her crew, she approves of my effort to tell it true.

—

Jill Pitts Knappenberger was of course an inspiration for the character of Dorothy, though Dorothy was created out of whole cloth. Jill's can-do spirit, wit, and patriotism certainly went into the character; she was also the only living witness both of my mother and of the Clubmobile experience. Jill drove the *Cheyenne*. My mother always referred to her as "Darling Jill."

But there was no mention of Jill in postwar years, and I had assumed she was dead. The implication was that the terrible crash that ended my mother's service had included another "girl" who was never found on the mountain—and that woman, in the fog of reticent explanations, was most probably Jill. I thought.

But while digging through my mother's letters for the umpteenth time, Cindy found an address label for Mrs. Jill Pitts Knappenberger and realized Jill must have survived the war. With a quick internet search, Cindy found an address for Jill just ninety miles from our home. Even more stunning, she found a local television interview with Jill that was only a few years old. Our Miss Jill. Darling Jill. Alive and telling her story. Nervously, Cindy wrote to Jill and told her what we were doing. Miss Jill called us the next day.

She called me "Louis." She was ninety-four years old. She told me we must come to see her right away. "Louis," she said. "Don't try to wait till I turn ninety-five. If you catch my drift." We sped to her apartment in Champaign the next day. When Miss Jill opened the door, the first thing I saw was a large portrait of my mother on her living room wall.

We visited her regularly, spent good long days with her, happy years, took her out to eat (and drink Manhattans—double—which she did indeed call "joy juice," something I stole for the book). She stitched many coasters for us with our initials on them. We shared all our war pictures with each other, we measured out the interiors of the Clubmobile on her living room carpet, she showed us the actual map she draped over the wheel of the truck as they drove, and we laughed and laughed. She even revealed Mom's beau on the beach in Cannes, who inspired Handyman in the book. His name was Jake. Cindy recorded an archive of hours of our chats.

Jill brought my shadowy imaginings into bright, real-world contrast. I hope you will notice her and Phyl driving around in certain scenes of the book. They kept me honest. (With that in mind, a reminder: this is a novel. At no time did Jill go out on night patrol. That was my own invention; that was Dorothy Dunford.)

Jill left us at the age of one hundred and two. Her personal archives went to the University of Illinois, where they reside now. One of her dearest friends and neighbors, a staunch guardian as well, was Nancy Johnson of U of I. She often sat with us all as we chatted, and she and her husband went with us to many meals at the country club. Nancy watched television with Jill every afternoon. After Jill passed, Nancy kindly allowed us a full day with her papers and letters and photos before they went into the library special collections department. The book could not have become what it needed to be without her help.

—

Ah, Handyman. The genesis of Hans the Handyman was inspired by two things in real life: Jill's scrapbooks and my mother's bedroom doorknob. A third thing made him a major character in the novel.

Jill was showing us her most precious scrapbook—she was very organized, and this private collection of images was mounted artfully in a smaller album with black pages. And each picture had some bit of notation beneath it in white ink. As she got older, she wanted to give it to us, but we thought it belonged with her family. As I sat with the book, and she chatted about some of the pictures, I turned to the Cannes portion. And there was Phyllis, on the beach, looking cute. I turned the page, and there she was with a tall grinning guy leaning into her, one arm casually over her shoulders.

"Who is this guy?" I demanded.

Jill leaned in and smiled.

"Oh," she said. "That's Jake."

"Jake!" I cried. "Who is Jake?"

The character of Dot was born in this moment. Jill looked at me slyly. She said, "Louis. It was a war. We all had men."

The doorknobs at the end of the book came from more immediate experience. After my mother died in her sleep, I discovered a picture of a dark-haired man tucked inside her hollow doorknob. I never knew who he was, but I knew she had put him in there to protect her as she slept. When I saw Jake, whoever he was, I knew he had to go in Irene's doorknob. Later still, looking through Jill's letters, we came across a mention of Phyl's hotshot lieutenant colonel fighter ace boyfriend. So that's how a character comes to life.

Though, as I mentioned, there is a third element to the character's genesis.

The sacred Wallowas looming above Joseph, Oregon. We have spent years leading workshops at Fishtrap, the great writing festival on the shores of the lake, begun by such geniuses as Le Guin and William Stafford. I often take part in fundraising events for the workshops, and one year I decided to raffle off naming rights for characters in the book. A gentleman named Mike Andrews bid a very generous amount and later told me a personal story that moved me deeply. He didn't know that Hans Enricus would become the love interest in the novel.

Note for literary detectives: there are several other characters named after real folks. Some were charity bids, some were written requests, some were pals, many come from the history books or assembled letters. Garcia comes full circle from my very first novel. I have been waiting since 1994 to tell his backstory. I've appreciated the stories I've heard from people over the years sharing war memories or a relative's anecdotes over a cup of coffee or a good Mexican meal. The harrowing scene of the torpedo strike and drowning sailors early in the book was inspired by long conversations with Bill "Paw-Paw" Somers (RIP).

—

Everyone who knows me knows that I could not have written the book without my bride, La Cinderella. From endless computer problem-solving to research, from floor-covering charts to thousands of miles of travel, from interviews to revisions that go on for epochs. So much of this novel was debated with our heads on our pillows late in the night.

As my first editor, Cindy helped me out on such potentially awkward developments as the romance with Handyman. Cindy had explored female trauma in her journalism career and always believed my mother suffered from PTSD and that it explained her many struggles. Together, we researched women's war-related PTSD, and this opened windows on the secrets of Irene's inner shadows as well as my mother's.

We traveled all over the United States, to every war museum and plane museum; to the UK, France, Belgium, Austria, Bavaria, Denmark, Sweden, and our epic train and autobahn exploration of Germany. We work hard together, as a team. This book owes its existence to her tireless energy. Viva Cinderella!

And the daughter who trudged along on thousands of the miles of this research, including the walking trails where young Phyllis escaped on Staten Island, Munich, London and Paris, Buchenwald, the Yank air bases in England, even Handyman's Wallowas. Finally, she came all the way to Miss Jill's house, where they became great friends. Thanks, Chayo. I am grateful that she has gotten to know and walk in the steps of the grandmother she never met, a grandmother who could never imagine a child would follow her journey so intrepidly.

—

All gratitude and love to the best literary agent on earth, the fabulous Julie Barer. Julie patiently waded through years of generations and regenerations of this novel.

Thanks to Ben George, editor extraordinaire. He edited so carefully, he actually knew what time the sun rose in Germany in the spring of 1945. Ben understood where I wanted to go and, more important, guided me to explore further. Thanks to my bosses at Little, Brown, Bruce Nichols and Craig Young, for believing in me. And to Michael Pietsch, as always.

I am so grateful to Little, Brown in general for their unstinting faith and support, as well as their various departments that have been so helpful. And to my delightful copyeditor/tormentor Allan Fallow, that loquacious fiend, that king of line edits: it was the first time I laughed and celebrated this duet/duel. Let's do it again. Betsy Uhrig, Katherine Akey, Sabrina Callahan, Lauren Hesse, Elizabeth Garriga, and Tom Mis have all cared for me and my book in a thousand different ways, and I am so grateful. And thanks, as ever, to Michael Cendejas at the Pleshette Agency—tireless agent who read draft after draft of this book with unflagging faith. Trinity Ray and the Tuesday Agency have always had my back. I would not do this without the amazing Michael Taeckens, the GOAT of marketing/publicity/media contacts/promotion. You hold me to high standard.

—

My dear friend Lyn Niles (RIP) did genealogy research on my mom and her family; my only regret is that she didn't live long enough to read the book. Fano Suarez, Spain's only Clubmobile expert, sent me data about the Clubmobile corps and invaluable schematic drawings of the interior of the galley. I am so grateful for the support of the Guggenheim

Foundation and the unexpected blessing of the Borchard Foundation. They provided an unexpected lifeline and validation when I needed them most. I am forever grateful.

One of the delights of researching this book was stumbling on the website and Facebook page for the 457th Bomb Group, which was based in Glatton. The families of the men once stationed there are tending to an amazing legacy, and poring over the stories and photographs gave such depth to my understanding of the early days for my Clubmobile crew. Through the FB page and its administrator, Erwin de Mooij, we were introduced to the caretakers and historians of the memorial at the Glatton base, Tim and Angela Newell. Because of COVID, the reunion we planned to attend in 2020 never happened, but Tim and Angie welcomed us two years later. We had sent my mother's photos from her time there, and they took us around to the places she once knew, an experience I will never forget. Tim grew up in Conington, right near the air base, and took us out to the old field. We helped clean the memorial and walked the old landing strips, now a regional airport. The farmer's field in the middle of the base is still there. Geoff, the manager of the regional airport, was a kind and generous host. We all drank a fireball toast to the lads and their planes, then we walked down the runway. Geoff pried up a piece of the original tarmac and gave it to me, saying, "Your mum might have stood on that." It sat on my desk as I wrote. All hail the eternal Leadbelly and his beautiful song. I hope I did it justice and I thank him for the inspiration.

Finally, thank you to all you ghosts who allowed us to pry our way into these shadows.

ABOUT THE AUTHOR

A finalist for the Pulitzer Prize for his landmark work of nonfiction *The Devil's Highway,* now in its thirty-fourth printing, **Luis Alberto Urrea** is the author of numerous other works of nonfiction, poetry, and fiction, including the national bestsellers *The Hummingbird's Daughter* and *The House of Broken Angels,* which was a National Book Critics Circle Award finalist. A recipient of an American Academy of Arts and Letters Award, among many other honors, he lives outside Chicago and teaches at the University of Illinois Chicago.

From the desk of

LUIS ALBERTO URREA

Dear literary companion,

I have spent most of my life preparing to write this book. Although some readers may know me for literature related to the US-Mexico border, I am also the son of an overlooked American war hero. My mother, Phyllis, was from New York City and never learned a lick of Spanish. In 1943, as a young woman, she fled Staten Island, in an escape from a difficult romance and family complications, to volunteer with the Red Cross. She signed up not as a nurse but as part of a new program called the Clubmobile Corps.

After two months of training, she was sent to Europe, where she would be assigned, along with two other women, to a converted two-and-a-half-ton truck equipped with a coffeemaker and donut machine. Their task, as they followed troops into battle, was to provide comfort to the GIs—with coffee and donuts, a friendly face, and "a woman's touch." The army imagined the women would remind the GIs of all they were fighting for. In fact, the women provided much, much more.

When my mother died, in 1990, she left me her journals and scrapbooks. She had been plagued by nightmares every night of her adult life, but it wasn't until I started reading and researching her story that I realized she had battled (undiagnosed) PTSD. She had been at the front—she and her truck mates were recognized as the foremost women in battle in World War II and were among the fewer than 250 elite Clubmobile women who accompanied the push through France, Belgium, and Germany after D-Day. Assigned to Patton's Third Army, she was trapped behind enemy lines in the Battle of the Bulge and was one of the first to help liberate Buchenwald. She could not speak to me of what she had endured. Few of that generation did, especially the women.

Because the official records of the Clubmobile Corps were lost in a fire in the 1970s, there is not a lot of information available. The history exists in a handful of self-published memoirs, letters home that have been saved, and a few scraps in war museums. For example, I did not know the Clubmobile uniform was a beautiful blue tweed, made by a leading London haberdasher, until a docent at the National World War II Museum in New Orleans opened a storage drawer and showed me.

But there was a miracle of sorts. My mother's best war buddy and the driver of their truck was always known in my home as "Darling Jill." I was under the impression she had died in the war. In digging through some of my mother's letters after her death, though, my wife found a note from Jill dated post-war. We learned that not only was she alive, but she lived less than two hours from our home. She called immediately on receiving our letter and invited us to visit. She had just turned ninety-four. When we walked into her apartment, there was a large photograph of my mother on her wall.

Thanks to Miss Jill, who was generous with her time and patient with our endless questions, I was able to get to know my mother at her best. Jill shared her scrapbooks and letters, and we spent a memorable afternoon using her living room rug as a floor plan to visualize the inside of their truck, called the *Cheyenne*. Miss Jill passed away in December 2020, just after turning 102. This book would not exist without her, and I am sorry she did not get to read it.

To write the book truly, I also needed to see what my mom had seen. We visited the thatched-roof cottage she lived in at Glatton, near the airbase in England, and walked those landing strips, even taking home a chunk of asphalt that our guide said "your mum might have stepped on." We drove all over Belgium and Germany, spending time at Buchenwald and Weimar.

This book is not a biography of my mother or Jill. Although both of them, along with their truck mate, Helen, and the *Cheyenne,* make cameos, there was not a Clubmobile known as the *Rapid City,* nor women

named Irene and Dorothy. I used the scaffolding of my mom and Jill's experiences to build this book, but it is a novel. Which means I was able to spin tales. Hans—Handyman—is a fictional character. Or so I thought. Well after I had imagined a war romance for Irene, Miss Jill confirmed that such a thing did happen for my mom, surprising us with photographs of Phyllis and her boyfriend Jake at Cannes. I can't tell you how happy that made me.

I am so looking forward to sharing this story with you.

Happy reading,

GOOD NIGHT, IRENE

A READING GROUP GUIDE FOR THE BARNES & NOBLE EXCLUSIVE EDITION

1. Why does Irene decide to go to war? Why does going to a literal war zone seem to present a better way for her to leave her fiancé than staying in New York?

2. "She was so filled with rage," the novel says of Dorothy. "She was no secretary. She wanted combat." How does Dorothy's rage manifest? How does her apparent zest for life contrast with her secret hope to be killed during the war?

3. What is the culminating factor in Ellie's decision to leave Red Cross service? What is different about her situation that makes returning home feasible for her, as opposed to Dorothy and Irene, for whom returning home would be far more difficult?

4. The relationships that Dorothy and Irene form with the soldiers initially seem to be superficial and shallow, amounting merely to good customer service. A key part of their role as Donut Dollies is performance: calling every man "honey," "brother," or "babe." Yet it soon becomes clear that their jobs are in fact crucial. What do Dorothy and Irene provide for these men, and why is it so important?

5. In addition to the close bond between Irene and Dorothy, the novel details many fleeting relationships and a revolving door of people who might never be seen again. Why do people gravitate toward one another amid such hardship? Are these relationships any less significant because they're brief?

6. Why, when faced with the threat of imminent death during the attack in France, do Dorothy and Irene rediscover their desire to live?

7. What is the significance of Irene's relationship with Hans? Why is she able to confide in him in a way that she can't with anyone else, not even Dorothy?

8. Throughout the novel, we get to read the letters that the soldiers send to Dorothy and Irene. What do we gain from their inclusion?

9. Why are many of the soldiers so eager to "confess" their sins to Dorothy and Irene?

10. Irene and Dorothy participate in the liberation of Buchenwald. The existence and nature of the Nazi death camps was unknown to the American military until they were liberated. What do you imagine the shock of discovering the depravity and horror of the camps for the first time would have been like for both the soldiers and the Red Cross volunteers?

11. The title of the novel hints at the centrality of Irene's dreams. What purpose do her dreams serve in the novel? What insight do we gain about Irene?

12. Many of the soldiers in the novel experience PTSD, what was then called "shell shock" or "battle fatigue." The experience of the women was not afforded the same nomenclature, but do you think Irene and Dorothy and their Red Cross peers also suffered PTSD?

13. What does the novel communicate about the power of friendship forged under extreme shared duress?

AMERICAN RED CROSS
CLUBMOBILE